AFTER THE RISING &
BEFORE THE FALL
CENTENARY EDITION

A TWO-BOOK OMNIBUS

ORNA ROSS

FontPublications

REVIEWS

AFTER THE RISING

VOLUME I

PART I
SPILL

1995

He thick double door beneath the sign – Parle's Bar & Grocery – is shut. A For Sale board juts from the side wall, with a Sale Agreed banner across it. The blinds are down, as if the house, too, has closed its eyes and died.

That's all I have time to notice as my taxi whips past. I can't tell the driver to slow down, as I have already given him instructions to hurry. I look back as we pass. Nothing about it has changed, I don't think, yet it looks different. Lesser.

Then the road swerves and it is gone, disappeared by the bend.

We fly past the post office, and Lambert's farm, and the two-roomed schoolhouse where I learned to read. "That's it!" I have to say, before we pass it. "That's the church there."

The car screeches to a stop, bidding goodbye to my hopes of a discreet arrival. Heads huddled around the door turn to look. I should have known the crowd would be spilling out of the church. My mother was the proprietor of Parle's, the village shop and pub. The village hub. It was always going to be a big funeral. The years peel away and I'm instantly laid bare.

But the driver is out of the car, taking my suitcase from the trunk, opening my door saying, "Here we are, so," in his strong Wexford accent.

I will do this well. The vow that seemed so potent yesterday in my apartment in San Francisco, feels puny now. Doing it well doesn't necessarily mean going into that church, does it? I'm so late. Wouldn't it be more discreet to shrink back into the seat and wait it out, catch Maeve later, on her way home? Or, even better, go back into Wexford town, lie low for today, return tomorrow, when all the fuss is over?

Catch yourself on! I admonish myself in the local lingo. You're not an over-sensitive child now, you're a 38-year-old woman. A magazine writer. An apartment-owner. A car-driver. Get in there! As I psyche myself, I'm putting on my sunglasses to protect me from the staring eyes. I'm taking out the clasp to let my hair fall forward, a veil of sorts. I'm taking a breath so deep it hurts.

And yes, I'm stepping out of the car onto Mucknamore soil for the first time in twenty years.

The heat is unseasonably sultry. Surely Ireland is never this hot? The air feels thick, hardly like air at all, and the nausea that's been plaguing me all the way down here growls again. I walk through the open gates of the little church yard. Here I am, folks, the entertainment of the day, the happening that you'll pass, one to the other, whenever Mrs D.'s funeral is recalled.

As I fix my stare beyond their curious eyes, it collides with the door of the black hearse, open like a mouth. It draws me towards it, inexorable.

I draw nearer. People begin to recognise that it's me. One voice says, "Hello Jo. Welcome home." Another, "Sorry for your trouble." Then there is a general murmur of greeting and sympathy. I nod acknowledgement.

"Yes, Jo, welcome home," says another man, turning the greeting to a snigger. I know his face, one of the Kennedys, who always used to mock me from his high stool at our bar counter.

At the door, they part to let me through and I walk towards

words I haven't heard for a long, long time: "Giving thanks to you, His Almighty Father, He broke the bread…"

The priest is a bald as a Buddhist, a big man, a performer, wallowing in emphases and pauses. "…gave it to His disciples and said…"

Two other clerics in purple robes stand behind him and the congregation is on its knees, heads bowed. It is the Consecration, the holiest part of the Mass. The quietest part of the Mass. Which makes the click of my heels on the tiles sound louder than it should.

People turn and nudge each other, loosening the holy silence. As whispers begin to swirl in my wake, Father Performer senses the loss of his audience and looks up. Seeing me, his eyes narrow, two specks of stone. Again I'm gripped by the urge to flee, but the pull of my mother's coffin sitting there on the trolley between us, all polished wood and burnished trimmings, is stronger. It is covered in glossy flowers. Funeral flowers, grown to be cut, already dying

I walk on.

The priest stops the ceremony and stands with his hands together in the prayer position, a column of forbearance. The other two clerics behind him imitate the pose, censuring me with that loaded, condescending silence they must get taught at religious school.

I am almost at the top pew, where my family is sitting. I can see Maeve now, looking thin, too thin, almost gaunt. She follows the eyes of the priest, turns to see what's causing the disruption and when she finds it is me, pure exasperation breaks across her face. Now, Jo? it says, before she turns her head on its long, elegant neck away from me, back towards the altar. Now?

I don't blame her. It must look so careless, so uncaring, to crash in like this, turning our mother's funeral into the latest act in the long-running Parle drama. And my sister will be grieving Mrs D.'s death sorely. I don't want to add to that.

At the same time I do blame her. I blame them all – Maeve,

Mrs D., Daddy, even Granny Peg. These scenes I bring upon the family are never just my doing, though I get the starring role. They all play their part, though they live and die pretending the stage is not even there.

That girl standing between Maeve and her husband Donal must be Ria, my eight-year-old niece. She stares at me with Maeve's eyes from behind a veil of red hair not unlike my own. Her expression tells me she has heard all about her Auntie Jo.

She and Donal push down to make a place for me but Maeve, in one of her childish gestures, kneels firm. I squeeze into the pew.

The priest begins again: "Heavenly Father, you gave your only son..."

The wood is hard against my kneecaps. The smell of incense sends another wave of nausea undulating but I kneel and stand and sit through the half-forgotten rites waiting, as I have waited out so many a day in Mucknamore, for it to be over.

WHY AM I HERE? All the way back – through the black night flight from San Francisco, in the taxi from Dublin Airport to Connolly Railway Station, through every chug of the rickety three-hour trip down south, and in the final cab ride from Wexford town out here to Mucknamore – I've been nursing the same question: why?

Why, when I spent twenty years not making this journey, when I had left it so late that I was unlikely to arrive on time anyway, had I nonetheless organised a last-minute ticket? Why did I feel I had to come?

And it wasn't just me. Why had Maeve, who so long ago gave up trying to get me back to Mucknamore while our mother lived, made such frantic efforts to contact me once it was clear she was dying?

Why does death demand such attentions?

What would Maeve say if she knew I had heard the first

words of her first frantic message last Friday? That I was halfway out my apartment door when stopped by my telephone's ringing and that I stood in the open doorway, letting the answer-machine pick up the call? That as soon as I'd heard her first words, "Hello, Jo, it's me. It's about Mammy...", I had answered aloud. "No Maeve, sorry. Not tonight," and slammed the door on the rest.

If I had waited for her next words ("It's bad news. I think you should come home..."), or if I had called her back later that evening, or even the following morning, I might have got back to Ireland on Saturday or Sunday morning. I might have been in time.

But in time for what, I ask? To visit the hospital and be confronted with a new Mrs D.: twenty years older, weak and wretched, dying? To snatch a few words from her, say something myself, then watch her go? What difference would that have made?

I know how Maeve imagines the scene: our mother looking up to see one of her girls ushering in the other, meaningful looks passing between us all, a clasping of hands and forgiveness all round. Then the two daughters together, watching her die, smiles and tears ushering her out of the world.

No, Maeve, too much was left to curdle for too long. No words, not even deathbed words, would have been strong enough to hold it all.

No. It was better the way it happened. Believe me.

The organ springs into sound for the last time and an elderly voice begins a quavering 'Ave Maria'. I look up to the balcony: it is Mrs Redmond, my mother's friend, chins a-wobble. While she struggles with the top notes, an undertaker steps up to release the brake and glides the coffin down the aisle. Maeve is crying, curling her sobs into her husband.

Outside, the heat crawls over us. Maeve is immediately engulfed by sympathizers, a wall of backs around her. Seeing me alone, Donal steps across and bends to bestow a kiss on my cheek. "So," he says in that cod-sardonic tone he affects. "The prodigal returns."

I have met Donal only a handful of times in the many years he has been married to my sister. When they were first engaged, Maeve brought him to meet me in London and that first encounter has always stayed with me: how he enfolded her as the two of them sat opposite me in the restaurant, her hand heavy with his ring.

"How is Maeve doing?" I ask, ignoring the jibe.

"Wearing herself to a frazzle. Your mother had very definite ideas about this funeral and Maeve, being Maeve, is carrying them out to the nth degree." This time the scorn's unmistakable. Maeve always claimed that Donal and Mrs D. were fond of each other, but when it comes to family relationships, my sister is prone to whitewash.

"Is she annoyed with me?"

"Your mother wanted to see you and Maeve promised her she'd track you down. When she wasn't able to…Well…"

I can't give him the response that leaps into my mind and find I can't think of anything to say instead. Maeve is the single thing we have in common; communication is strained when she is not with us. Just as the silence is stretching towards awkwardness, we are rescued by a loud shriek.

"Ahhh," says Donal, turning. "Our keening friends again."

At the church door are four young women in costume, made up to look old, with black wrinkles painted across their foreheads and around their eyes and shawls drawn up over grey wigs. I resist the impulse to cover my ears. "Keeners? What the…?"

"Professional mourners, one of your mother's many special requests. She left pages of instructions, practically a guidebook. How To Have A Good Old Irish Send-Off. We had a wake last night, complete with those four weeping and wailing and flinging themselves on the floor."

I look across at my sister, explaining to everybody what the sideshow is about and wonder how she can bear it. While planning all this, Mrs D. would have been imagining her celestial self scrutinizing proceedings from above, watching and weighing who did what so she'd know how to treat them when they eventually caught up with her. She wouldn't have been thinking about Maeve at all.

I feel a hand on my back and turn to see Eileen standing there with her husband, Séamus.

"Jo," she says. "Jo, I'm so sorry."

Eileen worked in our shop while we were growing up and lived with us until she married. I let her hold me. Her hug seems to give the others permission to approach and now people I haven't seen for years are coming across to grab my hand.

Faces I remember, names I've forgotten. Names I remember, faces I've forgotten.

My mother was a great character, they tell me. She was gone to a better place. God would give me comfort.

Only one old woman tells me anything that sounds like the truth and she gets herself dragged away by the arm for it. "Who are you?" she says. "I never heard Máirín mention you at all."

Then, out of the mass of well-wishers comes a particular hand and a particular voice, one I do know.

"Jo," he says, and my heart skips in recognition as I take the proffered hand. A second one comes to encircle mine in warmth and then he is there in front of me. Rory. Rory O'Donovan. All of him, looking down on me, our hands conjoined.

I had thought about Rory on the journey back, of course I had, and had planned my opening lines and the airy way I would deliver them, but in my imaginings, we met on the beach. Or on the village street. Not here, at my mother's funeral, the last place I would expect to find him, or any O'Donovan. Not here, in front of everybody. Not here.

"How are you, Dev?"

Dev. His old name for me. Extra weight has loosened his jawline. He is still the picture I have held in my head but blurred at the edges, like a photograph out of focus. His hair is gone, his long, black, beautiful hair. It used to flow down his back, soft and shiny as night-water. I used to sink my face in it, loop it through my fingers, knot it around my naked neck. All gone. Shorn and thinning and greying now: any man's hair. And he wears a suit, any man's clothes.

I look for what I used to know.

"I'm sorry for your trouble, Jo," he says, the conventional phrase again but in his voice, low and concerned, it sounds different. "But oh, it's good to see you."

The keeners choose that moment to raise their wailing to a higher pitch and he waggles his eyes at them. It is a look to share: confident of my amusement. Just like the old days, us against our families.

A deep flush begins at the base of my neck and tracks slowly up my face. I panic, point across at the undertaker slamming the hearse door shut.

"I have to go!" I say and that's what I do, almost running from him, decamping back to Donal who stands with Ria near the hearse. It's the shock, I tell myself as I flee. The suddenness of this new Rory sprung upon me when my mind was on Mrs D. and Maeve and everything else.

But I know that's not it. I know it's Mucknamore. Not even back an hour and already I am regressing, the work of twenty years coming undone.

Donal explains that we are to stand behind the hearse and lead the cortège down to the old cemetery. Only when he says this do I look across and realise: my father's grave lies flat and undisturbed.

"Let me guess: another special request?"

"Yep. She's to be buried with her own family."

Not with Daddy. I'm surprised she braved the scandal of that, dead or alive.

"And according to the grand plan, we all have to walk there."

To the old cemetery? That's down almost as far as

Rathmeelin, the next village up the coast. In this heat? I doubt I'll be able to make it. But now Maeve's bustling across, aggravated-big-sister expression in place.

"Am I supposed to say, better late than never?" she asks me, her kiss failing to connect with my skin.

"I'm sorry, Maeve," I say. "Really, I am. I didn't get your messages until last night and..."

"Honestly, Jo, you're impossible. Why do you have an answering machine if you don't bother taking your messages?"

I say nothing. Usually, I do pick up my messages as soon as I come in the door of my apartment, but these past days have not been usual.

"And couldn't you have let us know you were coming? Where were you when I rang, anyway?"

"Out."

"Out?"

What do I mean, out? She had rung at all hours of the day and night, left four or five messages on my machine.

Her red-rimmed eyes are ringed with black, circles gouged deep by distress, so I let her scold me, always one of her favourite occupations, without argument or interruption. It's a relief when the undertaker slides across and whispers in her ear and she moves away again to line us up in the order Mrs D. dictated. Father Doyle and two of the keeners are to go in front of the hearse, the other two priests and the other two keeners immediately behind, then us. Was I expected when Mrs D. made her plans, I wonder?

"Ria!" Maeve calls, with that voice that mothers use to address their children when they have an audience. "Just there, love, beside Daddy."

The black car slips into gear and rolls out the gates. The keeners lift the pitch of their noise another notch, and start to hold their notes for longer. The only words I recognise are the lamentation of the refrain: Ochón agus ochón ó. They are a troupe of actors, Maeve explains in whispers as we begin our march. Mrs D. must have been planning the event for months. Years, maybe.

We trudge down the village main street, making slow progress past the two-roomed national school; past Lamberts' little farm, still the same stench of dung mingled with sea salt; past the post office, green An Post stickers plastered all over its window. Rounding the curve in the road, I see our house. Mrs D.'s house. Bar and grocery in front, bedrooms above, living rooms and kitchen behind. When we reach it, the undertaker stops the hearse outside the front door, turning off the engine for two minutes' silence. The keeners drop quiet and now we can hear the sea.

Mrs D.'s house. Just a front-room bar and shop, but in her world it made her someone. A home that was bigger than most others around and a business that was central to the life of the village. So central, in her mind, that when she talked about the shop, she gave it the name of the village itself.

"Mammy's talking about selling Mucknamore," Maeve had said on the phone a while back. "This time I think she really means it."

And this time she really did. The 'For Sale' sign went up on the dwelling that had defined her for 76 years and quickly attracted an offer but before she had time to finalise the deal, she died.

Dead, Mrs D. that is what you are. But how can that be?

How can it be over?

After one hundred and twenty blessed seconds of silence, the keeners recommence their lament and we move off again, up the gently rising hill towards Rathmeelin. It's fresher up here, with a small breeze blowing off the sea, and we can see the curve of the sandy causeway that joins Coolanagh Island to the mainland.

As a child, I used to see the island as a giant head. The Causeway was its neck, the jutting bit to the west its nose, the small inlet beneath its mouth, and the marram grass of the dunes its spiky hair. Around it, on the three sides visible from here, are treacherous, waterlogged sands, that have inspired a lot of folklore and legend. Quicksand. It gleams at us now, flat and apparently innocent, in the almost-midday sun.

We pass the old police barracks, once a burnt-out husk, now a holiday-apartment block with landscaped gardens and balconies facing the sea. We pass a higgledy-piggledy line of bungalows, each built without any awareness of its neighbour, like a row of crooked teeth. Then the buildings stop, the road narrows and we are in a country lane that hugs the coast.

The sun bleaches the hedgerows to grey and seeks out white skin to burn. My nausea now is a squirming mass, thick and threatening. I no longer respond to Maeve's whispers. I must concentrate on my breathing and focus only on the way ahead. Slowly, slowly, on we tramp until, at last, we can see the cemetery, a patchwork of crosses and slabs of stone staring over a low wall at the sea, closed now to anybody who does not already have a plot inside.

Mrs D.'s open grave is there, waiting for us, and beside it a pile of earth, surface cracking as it dries in the sun. Three Celtic high crosses stand sentry over the hole in the ground. The smallest, newest one belongs to Auntie Norah: 'Norah Anne Teresa O'Donovan. 1900 to 1987. Ar Dheis Dé Go Raibh A Anam.' May Her Soul Be With God.

Granny Peg would have chosen this inscription for the woman who was not really our aunt at all but her closest friend. And Norah must have chosen to be buried here with Gran instead of with her own people, the O'Donovans.

The middle-sized gravestone, with the open hole gaping beneath, commemorates the Parle family – Granny Peg, Granddad, Gran's parents. Soon, Mrs D.'s dates and details will be carved beneath theirs.

And the third, most ornate stone is dedicated to the man that made the Parles what we are. Uncle Barney, Gran's brother. Uncle Barney who made what Gran used to call "the ultimate sacrifice", meaning he died for Ireland. This tall Celtic cross was erected by his old IRA comrades, its inscription in the old Gaelic alphabet, illegible to me and anyone except a handful of scholars.

A terrible thought strikes me. I whisper to Maeve. "Mrs D. hasn't asked for any IRA palaver for the burial, has she?"

Granny Peg, I knew, had had a full Irish Republican burial when she died: tricolour flag draped across the coffin, volleys from old IRA guns fired into the air as they lowered her down, report in the local paper…

"Oh no, nobody does that any more," Maeve whispers back, eyes to the crowd. "Not since things got so bad in the north."

The priest and the keeners have joined us by the graves and now the keening starts up again. We must stand straight and wait while the long string of people trudges in and gathers round. Father Doyle's face makes his feelings clear: he has no choice but to indulge these eccentric requests – the deceased was one of his keenest patrons – but he does not have to approve. The noise strikes at my temples in time with my blood. Shut up, beats the pulse. Shut up. Shut up.

Finally, at the height of the lamentation, they do, stopping abruptly and stepping back into the crowd.

Silence reverberates. A lone pair of hands starts to applaud, the claps faltering as it becomes obvious that nobody else is going to join in. As Father Doyle begins to pray in the name of the Father, the Son and the Holy Spirit, I spot Rory close by and, behind him, the entire O'Donovan clan. All of them: Paddy and Brendan and Martin and Joan and Mary and Kathleen and Benny and their assorted spouses and children. I'm so surprised to seem them all here, at a Parle funeral, that it takes me a moment to register the woman who must be his wife – a tall and elegant blonde – holding two little hands that belong to the boy and girl who must be his son and daughter.

I feel sick. It's physical, nothing to do with seeing this perfect family portrait. I've had twenty years to accept that while Rory O'Donovan may have been the love of my life, the one who spoiled me for everyone else, I did not mean the same to him.

He long ago moved on, to marriage, fatherhood and children: my sister had told me all about that when it happened.

And good for him. Why not? Whatever I wanted to do with my life – and I will admit that at 38-years-old, I'm a little tardy with the answer to that question – I do know, I've always known, what I don't want. It's a list that seems to include lots that's desirable to others: cars, careers, big houses in the suburbs, weekly trips to the mall, televisions, face-lifts…And tip-top, first and foremost, outright number one on the list of Things That Jo Devereux Does NOT Want is marriage and two kids in Mucknamore. With Rory O'Donovan, or anyone else.

Nausea twists again. And again. I try to beat it down, but this time pressure is swelling up into my nose and ears and I know it's going to come. My middle constricts; my head fills with the sound of somebody wailing. Father Doyle looks up from his missal, annoyance all over his face now. This is not what was agreed, this is supposed to be his time. He should have recognised that this sound is different, rawer than the ritual cries of professional keeners. Me.

I try to stumble away, floundering in the only direction free of people, and find I'm walking towards Mrs D.'s open grave. I can see the questioning faces of the crowd but it is as if they are behind a gauze. The cool earth-hole beckons and as I pitch towards it, a male voice calls out my name, "Jo!" and two strong arms shoot out. My body recognises him, sways towards him, but as it does my stomach erupts and I find I'm spurting vomit over his shoes. I try to apologise but the next wave is surging up. "You're all right, Jo," he says. "You're all right."

Oh, but I'm not. Again and again it comes, sick pooling on the grass around our feet. He holds me throughout – what must his wife be making of that? – and when the heaving stops he places a handkerchief into my shaking hands. I wipe my mouth and try to speak but my lips won't move and when I step away from him in an effort to stand on my own, the world comes rushing in through my ears, spinning me into a vortex of blackness.

Rory O'Donovan takes hold of me again and I sag, letting unconsciousness carry me off.

IT FEELS like days later when I waken, in a bed with heavy blankets pressing down on me like hands. It's been a long time since I slept under blankets. Above me, on the ceiling, strips of timber make a design of squares. I'm in my old bedroom. The old smell of sea air and lavender comes swimming into my nostrils, seeped with memories. I listen for it and there it is: pound, swoosh... pause... pound, swoosh...The backing track to my childhood.

Mrs D. didn't like the sea or the beach. It was the sand, the feeling of it between her fingers or toes, but also she blamed it for how it clung to the carpets, to our shoes, to the end of the bath after we let out the water. She didn't like the salt wind either, for the way it spattered the windows with stains and scoured paint off doors and window frames.

The sea didn't care. On it went, forwards and back, raising its volume whenever we opened a window or door. Smashing itself against the shore like an angry god in winter; in summer, sending glitter-blue invitations to us to come and play.

Granny Peg and Auntie Norah liked to swim all year round, "It does Norah good," Gran used to say. "Nothing better for a body." And it was true that Auntie Norah always seemed more cheerful, less impaired, out of the house, out of her clothes, in swimming costume and hat.

So did Gran. Sitting on the grassy bank, or paddling about in the shallows, I used to watch the two disembodied heads bobbing on the waves and wonder.

"Does Auntie Norah talk to you when you're on your own together, Gran?"

"Sometimes she does, pet. But not that often."

"Why doesn't she talk more?"

"Because she can't."

"Mammy says she's well able to talk if she wanted to."

"No, no, that's not right. If she could, she would."

A door opens downstairs, releasing a buzz of talk. The funeral. No doubt the drink is flowing by now, the craic flying, the sentiment oozing. I am grateful for the queasiness that allows me to lie here and avoid it. Twenty years on, and nothing looks much different.

We've been hearing reports in San Francisco about a new Ireland and everything I saw and heard on my way down here from Dublin — the advertising hoardings in the airport, the Irish newspapers I read on the train, the taxi driver who delivered me to the church — sang this hymn of change. Ireland now has cappuccino coffee-houses and designer boutiques, super-pubs and five-star hotels, high-tech multinationals and suburban estates, private schools and soaraway prices. They've had to bring in builders from England to cope with the construction boom, the taxi-man said, reversing the labour flow of hundreds of years.

To me, it all looks like a touch-up, not a transformation. Beside the little motorways and the out-of-town shopping malls are the thick bungalows and farmhouses and cottages, with their squinting, calculating windows. Grasping, grudging, judging, still.

Everything that drove me away is still here, in this village, in this house, I can feel it watching and waiting. I turn onto my side, roll myself inside the blankets into a tight coil and let the rhythm of the waves carry me back to sleep.

"Jo. Jo! Can you hear me, Jo?" I want to abscond back to my dream but the voice won't let me. "Jo? Are you awake?"

It is Maeve, standing at the end of the bed holding a tray. Tea and toast.

"I am now," I say.

"I'm sorry. I didn't know whether to wake you or not, but you haven't eaten a thing."

I try to sit up but my head, feeling like it's packed with gravel, pins me to the pillow. She sets the tray on the bedside locker.

"I'm sorry," she says again. "Should I have let you sleep on? I didn't like to go to bed without checking you."

"Bed? Is it bedtime?"

"It's early yet. But I'm going as soon as I can. I'm just shattered."

"I can imagine. You should go now."

"I wish..." And she launches into a long spiel about everything that went wrong as she tried to serve drinks and lunch and snacks and now teas and how she could never have managed without Eileen. Is this a muffled complaint against me, useless as ever in that department? I say nothing as the domestic litany of the day drones on until eventually she sighs herself to a stop and sits down on the bed beside me, her head bent so that her neck bones protrude like knuckles. "Seriously Jo, how are you feeling now?"

"I don't know, a bit woozy."

"Has this happened before? Were you sick before you left San Francisco?"

"No," I say and it is true. Not sick, not as such, not like today.

"I rang Doctor Woods, asked him to drop by."

"No need for that."

"He wanted me to drive you down to the surgery but I persuaded him to make a house call. Tonight or first thing tomorrow, he said."

"You don't look too hot yourself," I say.

"Thanks."

"You know what I mean...It's been a tough few days for you."

"Awful. The worst." Her eyes well up. "Jesus, I can't stop

crying! I think I'm all cried out but the bloody tears are only gathering for the next flow."

Which is better, I wonder, to cry too much when your mother dies or not to cry at all?

"I can't bear to think of her, in the kitchen, on her own... struggling to get to the phone..."

That's where Mrs D.'s heart attack had struck, early on Friday morning.

After Maeve has blown her nose and dried her eyes, I say, as some sort of consolation: "You were very good to her."

She was. Our mother was 76 when she died, severely arthritic and chronically cranky, but Maeve had converted the garage of her Dublin home into a granny-flat so Mrs D. could spend protracted visits. Every year, she and Donal brought her away on their winter holiday and, at least one weekend out of every four, Maeve and Ria drove the hundred miles from Dublin to Mucknamore to visit her.

Which is worse? To see too much of a disagreeable parent or not to see her at all?

"When Daddy died," Maeve says, "I had a lot of regrets. Whatever else, I didn't want that to happen this—" Her hand flies to her mouth. "Oh, God, Jo, I'm so sorry. I didn't mean..."

"It's all right," I say. "I know you didn't."

She looks so embarrassed. Does she really think a little gaffe like that makes any difference?

"Right," she says. "I have a favour to ask you." She wants ("needs, actually") me to stay on in Mucknamore to sort our mother's affairs. Things are complicated. Mrs D. auctioned the house and business a few weeks ago but it failed to meet its reserve price. She'd since agreed a sale with a German couple – who have given up their jobs in Düsseldorf to move across – but contracts hadn't been finalised. All this, on top of the usual issues that arise after a death.

"I can't stay," says Maeve. "I just can't. Ria needs to get back to school and Donal is up to his eyes in work."

"Whereas the spinster sister has no life worth speaking of?"

"Oh, come on, Jo," she says.

Come on: this is the first family duty you've been asked to cover in twenty years; come on: don't be so selfish; come on: it's the least you can do for Mammy and me and all the family, and might, in some small part, make up for all that trouble you inflicted on us for all those years with your unforgiving attitude. Quite a load for two little words to carry, but such is the verbal shorthand of families.

"If you can't do it, I don't know how we'll manage," she says. "But before you decide, there's something you should know. Mammy's affairs are being handled by Rory O'Donovan."

I guffaw.

"Really. He's been acting as her solicitor for months, apparently, ever since she started to seriously consider selling." She is looking out the window, not at me. "He has the will," she goes on. "She's arranged for him to come here and read it to us both tomorrow."

"But...But —"

"I know. I was as surprised as you."

Mrs D.? Telling her business to an O'Donovan? Talking to an O'Donovan, for God's sake. Especially to Rory O'Donovan. To Rory!

"I don't believe it," I say. "I just don't believe it."

"He's downstairs now," she says. "He's been there since he... since you...all afternoon. He wants to know, can he come up and see you before he goes?"

"No!" I almost shout. "No way. Tell him I'm not well enough to see anybody."

This reminds Maeve that she should be looking after me. "Aren't you going to eat something?" she says.

I put my hand on the blanket over my queasy stomach and shake my head.

"At least have some tea. You have to have something."

She pours me a cup of tea and I wrap my fingers around the

warmth of the cup and find it tastes unexpectedly comforting. I try some toast. Again, surprisingly good. Maeve sits on the bed again, closer this time. So close I can feel the tension humming in her, and – like everything else today – it brings me right back: I remember her circling Mrs D.'s moods, senses on full alert, seeking a gap through which she might enter to say the right thing. Usually she picked her moment with uncanny tact but not always. Not always.

I wonder how she remembers it all now. We gave up talking about the past years ago; we saw it all too differently. I take a second slice of toast and she pours me another cup of tea.

She says, "There will be money, you know, once the place is sold."

I chew my toast, the noise loud in my ears.

"You should think about what you'll do with a lump sum like that, Jo. You could lose a lot taking it back to the States, with the exchange rate the way it is. You might want to buy something here in Ireland?"

"Thanks for the concern, Sis. I know you think I am doomed to a miserable old age because I haven't got a pension but — even if Mrs D. should leave me some money, and we both know that's a big if -"

"Of course it isn't."

"It doesn't matter to me, Maeve. Things like that aren't…"

"Mammy just wouldn't do that. Surely you know that much about her? Surely you can admit that, today of all days."

I give up, go back to chewing toast, and she sits staring, twisting her marriage ring round and round its finger. My silence is getting to her. It always does, though this time I am not trying to.

"Jesus, Jo, would you answer me?" she blurts after a while. "Is an answer too much to ask?"

I make my face blank, a sheet of glass that bounces her gaze right back. I have to, I have to…If I fire off the answer that's searing my tongue, in seconds we'll be quivering into a fight, our faces wrenching into hateful shapes, our memories leaping back across the years to snatch up the old insults and injuries that lie in waiting all around this house, so we can fling them hard and deep into each other's weaknesses. I can't let that happen, not today.

Help me, Gran. And you too, Richard. Help me keep the vow I made to you both yesterday afternoon – was it really only yesterday? – in San Francisco: I will do this well. I knew it wouldn't be easy but I've got off to such a bad start. Help me.

After a long time my sister says, "You've something missing in you, Jo, do you know that?"

She picks up the tray and makes to leave. As she reaches the door, I call gently to her. There's one more thing I need to say – "Maeve?"

She turns, two hands on the tray, one foot in the door keeping it open.

"This business of reading Mrs D.'s will tomorrow..."

"Yes?"

"I won't be there."

I want to oblige her, and where I can I will, but even the thought of this sick little scheme of Mrs D.'s makes me boil: Maeve and I sitting at Mrs D.'s dining-room table while Rory O'Donovan sits across from us, reading us her requests and bequests.

No. Sorry. No can do.

"But, Jo, you have to...If you're not there —"

"You can tell me all about it afterwards."

"I really think —"

"Maeve, I'm not going."

We are looking at each other across an impasse when the tentative sound of steps comes down the corridor, followed by a male voice calling, "Hello? Anybody there?"

And then with great satisfaction, knowing it's the last thing I want, Maeve is throwing the door open and ushering Rory O'Donovan into the room.

"So, Dev," he says, after my sister has made her excuses and left us alone together. "What's going on? Why are you receiving us in bed, like a courtesan? You don't look sick to me."

As he's talking, he's pulling out the chair from the corner and bringing it over, close to the bed. "Don't think I don't know what you're up to. Lying low, avoiding the mob. Avoiding me too, you brat."

Brat-sh. The soft Irish T. He sounds so Wexford to my ears now, such a strong streak of Mucknamore in his accent: the nasal vowels, the singing rise and fall to his sentences. But of course it's my speech that has changed, not his. I am struck again by the newness of him, the short hair that makes him look unfinished.

"It's all a bit Mucknamore for me."

"I knew it."

"I hear you're a full-fledged resident now." I speak as if I only heard today, as if Maeve and Dee, my Wexford friend who also lives in San Francisco, hadn't passed on everything they knew about him since I left. "Was it the progressive liberalism that drew you here? Or the cultural stimulation?"

"No need to sneer, city girl. It's a good place to live."

I raise my brows into a question. The Rory I knew could not have been happy here.

"I like that it takes me only thirty traffic-free minutes to get to work. That my nice house cost half-nothing compared to a similar place in the city. That, after work, I can go walking in clean air or swimming in a clean sea. That I drink in a pub where everybody knows me."

"Stop, you're scaring me."

He laughs, then waves towards the window. "Look at it. Look at how lovely it is."

The window frames Mucknamore in full seductive act. Over to our right, the setting sun throws streaks of orange and pink and red along the sky and the sea borrows and flaunts the colours like they're its own. Waves shimmer around the curve of The Causeway and, between Coolanagh island and the sea, flat sands glisten with foam. Above it all, seabirds circle and swoop, silver-and-gold underwings flashing in the dazzling, dying light.

"When did you ever care about scenery?" I ask.

"I think I always did, Jo. I know I brought that sight away with me everywhere I travelled and never saw anywhere that looked better. And when the time came to..." He hesitates. "... To... figure out where home was," he says instead of what he was going to say: when the time came to get married. "Well... Here I am."

Here he is, turning around the chair to sit into it, backwards, his thighs straining against his trousers, his bulk too close. "And you? You've wound up in San Francisco."

"Yeah. I left London in '82."

"And that's home for you? You like it?"

"Sure. I like that I'm surrounded by millions of people. That my two-roomed apartment is worth a ludicrous amount of money that keeps on rising. That I can choose from a hundred bars where nobody knows me."

He tosses his head back into a laugh, the way he always did. It's all the same: the crinkles round his eyes, the missing tooth that shows only when his lips are stretched into his widest smile. "God, Jo," he says. "You haven't changed a bit."

"Of course I have."

"You look so much the same. I was surprised by that."

"I'm twenty years different. Just like you."

"Twenty years." He lets out a long whistle. "Is that what it is?"

Yes, Rory, I think but do not say. That is what it is.

When I was a girl, I had one person who was all mine. A secret person, into whom I poured everything. A boy.

He lived up the road from me and was my own age, but I was not supposed to speak to him. He didn't go to our local school. Each morning, his sister brought him into Wexford town in her blue Mini on her way to work. He never came into our shop, just like I had never walked up the side road that led to his family's farm. And if he, or any of his family, met me or any of mine, our eyes automatically went towards the ground or the sky.

I knew he was never given instructions in how to do this. Like me, he was born to it.

Outside school hours, I saw him often. Obedient until our teens, we never gave each other even a hello. But we did look. Whenever I would sneak a veiled glance towards him, across the road, or the church, or the beach, I often found him looking back. We could get locked in these stares, but never for long. We were afraid of being noticed and we were shy. Those few seconds could be so intense they hurt.

At night, in bed, I would summon up in my mind our most recent encounter and run it through my head like a movie, milking it for detail. I had no time for other Mucknamore boys, with their bruised legs and dirty hands and slow minds. Boys who always had to be in a group, jostling or jeering or running about, yelling and waving their arms. Pretending to murder each other with sticks, from behind trees, or yelling about doing it for real: "I'll kill you, I'll fucken kill you." For all their shouting, those boys could never do what he did: walk down a road alone. He was different.

Like me.

He became an altar boy and every Sunday he was on show at Mass, performing holy chores. Holy communion became the high point of my week, those few seconds at the altar when I let out my tongue for the host and his hand was beneath my chin holding the paten, close enough to touch. What ferocity I brought to watching him as he bowed low, or rang the little bell, so much that, even now as his adult self sits before me, I can see eleven-year-old Rory, good shoes and grey socks jutting from beneath his surplice, a sliver of shin revealed as he reclined on the altar steps, and remember how the thoughts of approaching the altar could make my hands shake so bad I had to sit on them.

What was all that? First, I thought it was pure love.

Afterwards, that it was crazed adolescent hormones. Now, I wonder what on earth I was projecting onto him. And how did Mrs D. or Gran or, especially, Maeve not notice, standing and kneeling so close to me? How could such fervour have been contained by my skin?

It led me to break the unspoken rule and ask at home about the O'Donovans, about why the two families were estranged.

Granny Peg said, "Ah now, pet, don't go digging up all of that. You'll only upset your mammy. And Auntie Norah."

Auntie Norah was the key. That much I'd figured out. Miss Norah O'Donovan: his aunt really, not mine. His aunt, but living with us. And — like us — never, ever talking to them.

Now his adult eyes are bouncing all over me, like they can't get enough of what they are seeing. "How on earth," I ask him, "did you end up with my mother as a client?"

"You were surprised?"

"Stupefied."

"I knew you would be."

"But how did it happen?"

"It began nine years ago, when I moved back to Mucknamore. If I was going to be living here, I decided I couldn't carry on avoiding Parle's pub. Most of the lads I hang around with drink here and anyway; the whole quarrel had come to seem so pointless. So I gathered up my courage and, one early evening after work, when I thought the place wouldn't be too busy, I took myself in."

"Wow!"

"After taking the big step, she wasn't even there herself. It was Eileen Power behind the counter. I asked her for a pint and she looked at me boggle-eyed. 'Excuse me one sec,' she said, and scuttled off, leaving me standing there like a right eejit. Three or four others were in, delighted with the goings-on, on the edge of their stools to see what was going to happen next."

I throw my eyes up to the ceiling.

"I know. Only they were all watching, I think I'd have run

out. I was so nervous. After what seemed like a day and a half, out she came, with Eileen running behind her. 'Can I help you?' she said in her best frosty voice, and I knew straight away it was going to be all right because I could see that underneath the frost she was flustered herself. 'A pint of Guinness, please, Mrs Devereux,' I said. She stood there a minute. Everybody was watching. When she picked up a glass and pulled the tap, it was like the whole place let out its breath."

"And that was it?"

"That was it. I've been a regular ever since. I even get – got – a Christmas drink. I even," he says, face wrinkled with apology, "became fond of her."

I groan.

"Ah, Dev, her bark was worse than her bite."

"Don't you start." I never try to make anyone else see Mrs D. my way. Why do they all feel the need to defend her to me?

"What about your own folks?" I ask. "They can't have been too delighted to see you tippling in the enemy camp?"

"I didn't tell them at first. I knew it wouldn't take long for it to get out. My father was given the job of tackling me. 'I hear you've been seen in Devereux's,' was what he said to me, as if it was a brothel or something. I just laughed, said the old feud had nothing to do with me, that what was past was past."

"That simple, eh?"

"What could he say, if you think about it?"

A familiar feeling coils inside me, deep and cold. "So…A happy ending all round. How moving."

He knows what I mean. That it could be that easy, after all they put us through. That he could just say, what's past is past and, miraculously…it was.

He leans forward in the chair. "I often wondered how things turned out for you, Dev, but I never got the nerve to ask your mother. Our association – hers and mine – was very much on her terms."

"That sounds like Mrs D. all right."

"So I never asked. But I often wondered," he repeats. He leans in close to me, picks up a strand of my hair. "You never changed it," he says. "When you made your grand entrance into the church yesterday, that was the first thing I thought: she never changed the hair."

He tugs the curl straight, then winds it around his finger. I let him, but only for a second, before jerking my head away, folding my hair over the opposite shoulder.

"You live alone?" I ask, knowing the answer.

"No." He tries not to hesitate. "No. I got married nine years ago."

I had a follow-up line prepared for this inevitable moment but, having invited it, my brain has now decided to evacuate. Silence lengthens and loads. It is he who breaks it. "We have two children," he says.

"Two? That's lovely." That's lovely? Oh God, is that the best I can do?

"Boys?" I manage after a while, though we both know I saw them this morning. "Or...em...girls?"

"Ella, the girl, is five. Dara is four."' His face is expanding with that look parents take on when they talk about their children.

"And your wife, is she from round here? Would I know her?"

"No. She's from Cork."

"So you've done it all," I say. "Wife, kids, law practice in town, big house in the country."

"I've been lucky, I suppose."

Does he not remember that we never wanted all that? Maybe he is right, maybe I haven't changed as much as he has. Certainly he's coming over as all grown up whereas I, since arriving in Mucknamore, am reliving the gauchest horrors of adolescence.

I am not normally like this! I want to scream at him. I am a syndicated magazine writer! I have a des. res. in Lower Haight! Sometimes people ask for my autograph!

"What about you?" he wants to know. "Are you married?"

"Oh no. No. You know monogamy was never my thing."

"Never say never," he smiles, which makes me want to slap him.

"Hey," he says, seeing my face. "I didn't mean that whatever way you're taking it. I just meant…"

"I'm single because that's how I like it."

"Sure. I get that."

It's true. There is a great deal about being single that I like. Or that I will like again, once I find my way back to myself. Back to the kinds of days I used to have when I first went to San Francisco — when I had lovers, not pick-ups, when I had joys, not dubious pleasures. When I had Richard.

Well Richard is gone, forever, and I have spent too long wishing he wasn't. I have to learn how to create myself – by myself, for myself – the colour and excitement he used to bring to my life. That much I've worked out.

"Look, I won't stay long, Jo. I dropped up here because I need to talk to you about your mother's will."

"Rory, I've already told Maeve. I don't give a fiddler's about—"

He holds up his hand. "I know that, Dev. We all know that. But can you just listen for a minute? Last January, your mother said to me, 'I'm not long for this world. I won't last the year.' I laughed it off, the way you do, but she started making plans and she hired me to carry them out. So this is business. And this," he says, reaching across to place the white envelope he has been holding onto the bedspread, "is for you."

An A4 envelope with my name written on the outside in blue ink: Siobhán. Mrs D.'s handwriting, still small and neat and tight as print. At the centre, between the folds of paper: something hard.

"Siobhán," I say. "Nobody ever calls me that. Nobody ever did, except Mrs D."

"Don't open the letter yet," he says, getting up. "There's something else you have to be given first. Wait here."

He goes out of the room and returns with a battered blue suitcase. I recognise it immediately. Six times a year, I used to fill it with blankets and sheets and uniform, and be driven with it from Mucknamore to my convent boarding school, or back.

He heaves it onto the bed where it lands at my feet with a bounce. "Jesus, it's heavy," he says, puffing. "I'm always surprised by the weight of paper."

"Paper?"

"It's full of documents. Family papers, photographs, newspaper cuttings, that sort of thing. The key is in that sealed envelope you've got there. You are the only one who is to have access."

"Why?"

"I don't know. I'm just following instructions. I was to make sure to give this to you myself and I was to tell you that the contents are for your eyes only, nobody else's. She was very clear about that."

I take out the key, pull the case towards me. The locks must have recently been oiled because one twist of the key and – click, click – they snap open. It is crammed with all kinds of documents. Packets of letters tied with faded ribbon. A stack of shop ledger diaries (author: Granny Peg). Sheaves of paper, close covered in black ink, tied with string (author: Auntie Norah). And a smell of yesterday as strong as bottled scent.

Half of me wants to recoil, but the other half wins, and I find myself picking through the photographs: heavy daguerreotypes, stiff sepias from the early part of the century, black-and-whites from the 40s and 50s and from around the time when I was born, colorful prints that bring us all the way up to now, to these pictures on top which were presumably taken by Donal, of Mrs D. – smaller and more wrinkled than I remember – clasped in Maeve's arms while together they watch Ria blow out the candles on a birthday cake.

Beneath the pictures are pamphlets and booklets, song-sheets with the words of old ballads, and pink files full of notes about what seem to be IRA matters, dispatches to and from various officers of Mucknamore IRA, written by somebody called Máire Parle.

Wasn't that the name of Gran's mother?

My great-grandmother.

Damn you, Mrs D., I think as I rummage through, reluctantly first, then greedily, until I become aware again of Rory looking at me looking, which is all too much for me. I replace the papers, close the lid of the case, snap the clasps on tight. "What was she up to?" I ask him.

"I honestly don't know. Apart from the fact that it meant meeting up with you" – that grin again – "I treated it as if she was just another client. I've had stranger requests."

"How was she so certain I'd come back?"

"If you didn't, I was to get your address and bring the suitcase and the letter across to you in the States. Make sure to put it into your hand myself."

I imagine myself in my San Francisco apartment, answering my buzzer one ordinary day and hearing Rory O'Donovan's voice coming through the speaker at me. At the behest of Mrs D. What the hell was she playing at? And him too, with his hair touching and his "never say never", and "you haven't changed a bit". I was crazy to have come here, to have delivered myself up to this.

"You can take it back," I say. "I don't want it."

"Ah, Dev…"

"Family papers. Can't you just imagine? Uncle Barney, the IRA hero. Fianna Fáil the fabulous. Spare me, please. Take it back to wherever it came from."

6th February 1995
Dear Siobhán,

A letter from beyond the grave, what do you think of that? I got one from your Granny Peg when she passed on so I can imagine some of your feelings as you read this. By now you'll have had the suitcase and seen what's in it. Most of these letters and records were kept by your Granny Peg – I don't think that woman ever threw away a piece of paper.

It was always in my mind that we should sort out those papers some day, destroy the rubbish and the private stuff, and give the rest to somebody who could put together a family history. When your gran died, she suggested, among other things, that the person should be you.

As you know, Siobhán, you come from a family that played no small part in Ireland's fight for freedom. I believe the stories of those who died for their country should be preserved and passed on to the younger generations who, I have to say, seem to take so much for granted these days. Some time ago, I sat down to tackle the task, but I found it impossible. Everything was all mixed up together and one thing seemed to hang on another. I couldn't work out what to leave in and what to take out.

After days of shuffling bits of paper in and out of different piles, I came round to agreeing with your gran. You are used to writing and would be much better up to the task.

So that is what I want you to do, Siobhán – the Parle family history. Focus on the part our family played in the Easter Rising of 1916, there is where you'll find our glory.

Contrary to what you'd think if you were to listen only to Dubliners, the glorious uprising that won Ireland its freedom took place in other parts of the country besides the capital. That Enniscorthy here in Co. Wexford was one such is down to your maternal ancestors. That is something of which you can be proud, I think, don't you?

There is so much ignorance today about the sacrifices endured by that great generation. Sacrifices made so that those who came after them (yourself included, I might add) could grow up in a free country.

Those men and women who worked and died for Ireland are half-forgotten now. The 75-year commemoration of the Rising in '91 was an unholy disgrace. It nearly killed your gran, how they failed to honour

our origins. It's time someone reminded the young people that not too long ago, there were Irish men and women who had interests beyond the raking in of money, who had principles and ideals they were prepared to die for.

You come from such a family.

There's a danger in me doing this, Siobhán, I won't pretend I don't know it. I'm afraid of what you might write, what you might choose to highlight. But your gran thought you and Maeve should know all, now that the knowing can do no harm, and I've come round to thinking maybe she was right. So I've destroyed nothing, not even Auntie Norah's ramblings and inventions, most of which no sane person could read anyhow, her handwriting so bad and her thoughts all over the place.

I'm putting three generations of Parles into your hands, Siobhan, trusting you not to make public anything we would prefer to remain private.

I'm also hoping when you read these papers you'll understand better why it was so terrible for me that time when you got yourself mixed up with an O'Donovan. I've played that last evening in our kitchen so many times in my mind and I greatly regret the pity of how we both overreacted. At the beginning, I was afraid that if we did make up and you came back home, you'd take up with him again. Your grandmother feared that too, I know. It might be hard to understand now but, at the time, the fear was very real.

Yet I was always expecting something to happen that would bring you back to us. Always, until Mammy died. When you didn't come back for your Granny Peg's funeral, I knew I'd go to my own grave without seeing you again. That's a hard thing to do to a parent, Siobhán, but I forgive you, as I hope my will makes clear. Everything I have, I leave equally to you and Maeve. I'm sure you agree it's a tidy sum. Invested wisely, you'll be free from money worries and able to do whatever you want. You could afford to take time off from writing in those magazines or, better still, give up that kind of thing entirely.

So there you are: the only thing I've ever asked you to do. Make us a family history that makes us all proud, something that can be passed

on to little Ria and her children and your own, if you're so blessed.
Don't write anything that would make me regret I didn't destroy the
lot and take their secrets to the grave.

Think of it as a way of making amends, of putting things right
between us. I regret that I won't be here to guide you but I'll be looking
down from Heaven. (Keep that in your mind as you write and you
won't go too far wrong.) I'll be praying for you as I always have.

Always, Siobhan. I want you to know that.

That through it all I was always

Your loving

Mammy

MY MIND HAS CRACKED around that letter. For months now, I've
been back in the place I thought I had conquered, where
thoughts hold me staring open-eyed into the dark, where self-
pity has me spinning scenarios about what would happen if I
ended it all. How, if I did, it could be days before anybody
would know. Not until I failed to return enough phone calls, or
missed my next deadline, would somebody – Dee, or Gary, or
Lauren, my editor – grow anxious enough to want to check.

How they wouldn't be able to get in. Since Richard died,
mine has been a one-key-to-the-apartment kind of life. So the
building super would have to be called. In the hallway, their
eyes would fasten immediately on my shut bedroom door.
Wordlessly, they would move across to open it and...

It's been bad in San Francisco, this imagining the worst. Now
this evening, in Mrs D.'s house, with her letter, and its
unanswerable questions and unspeakable schemes, burning in
my hand, it's unbearable. Outside, daylight is stretching itself
into a long dusk. I'd forgotten how, at this time of year, an Irish
evening doesn't fade until well after ten.

Barely have I thought the thought but I'm up, out of bed and
opening my suitcase, not the big blue one that still lies, looming,

on the bed where Rory lobbed it, but my own, all-the-way-from-San Francisco suitcase that Maeve must have brought up here for me while I slept.

I pull on my jeans and walking shoes and sneak down the back stairs. From the front room, the sound of the party continues, muted now. Only the stragglers – those who cared most for Mrs D. and those who cared least, turned out only for the free drink — are left. I get out the back door without being seen. The cool, summer evening is like a gentle splash of water on my face. Once I'm down the path and across the long lawn, far enough away from the house, I stop to gulp in lungfuls of fresh air.

I'm outside the cowshed we used to call the byre, the place where I used to hide out from my family as a child. Grass has grown across the bottom receiver of its big sliding door. I pluck it away and push hard against the stiff, rusty wheels to get the door open. Inside, all is dust and neglect. Two broken bar stools sit on top of a rusted bottling machine. A punctured sofa spews yellow sponge filling. Still, it has the sweet smell of earthy straw that I remember and the same soft, pale light. For a moment, I am eight years old again, climbing the ladder that used to be in here, hiding my treasures up on the ledge under its tin roof.

Here was where I used to read, and write, and draw, and daydream. Here was where I kept my shells and stones and other treasures that would have drawn my family's jeers on me. I had almost forgotten I ever did that, forgotten there was anything to forget.

I still feel it, whatever it was here that used to soothe me, and I linger, breathing in the silken, sodden air, its smell of soft times past. Resolving to come back, I pull the big iron door shut again. Right now, what I need after days of sitting in planes and trains and cars, is to walk. To get as much sea air as I can before dark.

I press on, down to the edge of the sandy, marly cliffside, down to the beach and on down to the water. I am here and Mrs D. is gone.

"She is dead," I shout it to the empty sea. "Dead."

The word skims across the water like a flat stone. It is over.

Over. Yes. But now there's this command of hers to write about it and to live it all again. If I was to do it — and I'm not going to — I wouldn't write the kind of book Mrs D. wants. The bits I'd be most interested in would be the last thing she'd want aired. And I wouldn't start with our family's glorious fight for freedom but here, at the end, with me and Rory and how we ended up. I'd probably start with that awful night in San Francisco, just before I heard she was dying. The night my own freedom ran out, chased by me.

And how could I write about how I felt walking along the solid city sidewalk that evening, through air thickening with the smell of spicy food, to meet up with Dee? How we sat at our usual table outside Benton's, heads leaning into each other over bowls of pasta, while the sky faded from blue to purple, and lights sprang on across the city, their pretend promise making me ache, so that the night stretched into a second bottle of wine, which for me was the wrong, but at the same time, the only possible thing to do.

I don't want to remember us, polishing it off, then going to that nightclub to gyrate around a dance-floor, pretending to have eyes only for each other and our own good time, pretending we were not on show, that we hadn't already staked out our quarry: two guys we knew for a while, Steve and Paul, friends of friends of friends.

Paul. I so definitely do not want to remember him, asking me to dance and whether I was enjoying myself and what I worked at, and all in that bland and hopeless way that made me simultaneously pity and deplore him, so that on question three I had to pull out of the ritual and deliver, with a deadpan, straight face, the reply: "I'm in the sex business."

It's a line I've used before on men like him and I knew how he'd react: the simultaneous, contrary pulls of attraction and repulsion. "Really?"

"Yep. Really."

His brain fizzed with options: Prostitute? Stripper? Lap-dancer? Telephone-sex operator? 'Glamour' model? Porn actress? Like me, he had had too much to drink. Unlike me, his thoughts slid across his face, clear to read.

"You don't look like someone in the sex business," he slurs.

"Why? Is there a look?"

He grins. "I thought so."

"What? Big breasts, blonde hair, plastic face?"

"Something like that, yeah."

"That's just a stereotype."

"I guess it is. Still…"

"Still…I don't look sexy enough?"

"Honey, not that…Definitely not that."

"What, then?"

"It's just…Oh hell…" We laughed at his tangle. "So go on then, what exactly is your business?"

"Can't you guess?"

"Uh-uh," he laughed again. "I'm not guessing. No way."

I relented. My corner of the sex market, I told him, was advice. I am Sue Denim. Sue Denim Solves your Sex Problems. Read by millions of glossy-magazine readers all over the States and in Canada, Britain, South Africa and Australia too. Sue Denim: the Sexpert with Sizzle.

Dear Sue, Nobody has ever loved me…

Dear Sue, My genitals are so ugly I could never let any man see them…

Dear Sue, My boyfriend raped me last night…

Dear Sue, My penis is too small to satisfy a woman…

Dear Sue, I like to be whipped until my skin breaks…

Dear Sue, I'm crying as I write this letter…

I don't flatter myself that I solve these people's troubles. My value is simply in prodding them to sit down and write out their dilemma. In order to write, they have to put some order on their chaos, define it to themselves.

And when I question whether that small benefit justifies the easy and ample living I make from their distress, I console myself by asking, who does heal the troubles of the world? Psychologists? Psychiatrists? New-age therapists? At least I do not fool myself. I am a stranger, not an aunt; a hack, not a healer. I take pain and shape it into reading matter.

Sue Denim: Fraud.

He starts to kiss me during the third track when I lean back my head in invitation. There was a time when I used to prefer the preliminaries, the chit-chat and hold-off, the let's-get-to-know-each-other-first, but somewhere along the line of my life, cutting direct to the physical came to seem more honest.

I try to settle into the soft small movements of lips learning about each other, the smell and taste of new mouth, leaning in so the kiss deepens, to the bone under the flesh, to the muscle of tongue. When the slow set fades, the lights come up and the thump of dance music resumes, we pull apart, our breath thick with the taste of each other.

I say, "Shall we get out of here?"

His eyes, heavy from our embrace, spring in surprise. It has been two, maybe three, minutes since we started kissing.

A sliver of hesitation, then he smiles.

"Yeah, OK," he says. "Why not?"

No. I don't want it, this memory. I shake my head to clear it, to return to where I am. I've arrived down at The Causeway, the high, compacted strip of sand dunes that joins Mucknamore beach to Coolanagh. A pathway, worn in its centre by feet, gets narrower and less defined the further out you go. Out here, the going gets tough, up and down the uneven surface of the dunes, and most turn back. I press on, allowing the physical effort to wipe my mind of thought.

The barbed-wire fencing and warning signs that mark off Coolanagh sands begin here: WARNING! they shout. DANGER! The Sands on this side of The Causeway are Unstable and Unsafe. Do not Diverge from the Path.

The past opens out at my feet. I realise I am retracing the steps I took on my last night in Mucknamore, twenty years ago.

Disobeying the signs, I squeeze under the barbed fence, walk down to the edge of the dip in the sands they call Lovers' Hollow and lie down for a time. I'm quite safe. I know Coolanagh of old and I know just where the dangers start, a little further out than here.

It was a mistake to stop. As soon as I lie down, I'm back in San Francisco, trapped in thought again. Seeing Dee wrapped around Steve in a slow lurch, as if the music hadn't upped its tempo; giving me a thumbs-up behind his back, happy to be abandoned. Hearing him, Paul, asking me "Are you always so... decisive?" as we wait for a cab.

I knew then, if not before, just how it was going to go, that I really should quit and go home, but also that I couldn't, just couldn't, face my too-empty apartment and my too-full head. I climbed into the cab.

His apartment was a mess, strewn with clothes and dishes, so I refused his perfunctory offer of coffee and we moved straight to the bedroom. I let him take the lead and found myself jerked from arms around each other to bra-opening in seconds. Protest rose in me and I opened my eyes, expecting to see arrogance, a 'we'll-see-who's-in charge-now' expression on his face — but instead he floored me with a grin. Eager and excited, expectant, and in no doubt that I was equally enthusiastic. I smiled back, despite myself, let him slide me out of my clothes.

Sue Denim would not have approved. I shouldn't be here unless it was what I wanted, she would say, and I should know why I wanted it. If, knowing that, I chose to remain, then proper physical attention was my due. Only I could guarantee my own pleasurable outcome. If he didn't know how to give me what I wanted, then I should show him.

And Sue was right. I was wrong earlier when I called her a fraud. It's the Jo who goes about her daily business who hides and evades. Sue is the better part of me who always rises with the right answer, the proper thing to do. She was right. What was I doing spreading myself naked on this stranger's bed, pretending he was doing fine when he wasn't? Why was I careful to lie on his pillow with one knee bent upwards, a position I know to be the most flattering to my ageing body, flattening the wad of fat that rings my abdomen?

Oh, we women deserve everything we (don't) get.

In moments he was leaning over me, expecting entry, and again I was gripped by the urge to call a halt, to start again, but where? Back at the nightclub? When I refused coffee? When we started kissing in earnest? Instead, I opened to him.

Propping himself up on his elbows so that we touched only at the hips, he began. It wasn't lovemaking, or even what I hoped for when we got together in the nightclub, sexual intercourse. No, he was the fucker and I was the fuckee. Slow at first, then faster and faster, ever more oblivious to the human being under him, until he came with a smothered groan and slumped down on top of me. As soon as consciousness returned, he rolled off.

Who would want to remember this? Or the next bit, even worse, when I met his eyes and found that look: distaste for his own need, now it was spent. A distaste that pointed in the same direction as mine: at me.

He lifted the duvet, half-heartedly inviting me into the hollow where he slept each night. Agreeing to that felt even more intimate than taking him into my body. He didn't really want me there, but leaving would have meant engaging him in conversation, getting up and dressed, and arriving back at my empty apartment across the city in the middle of the night, opening the door on its hundred thousand questions.

I stayed. I slipped between his sheets, pulled his covers around me and, careful not to touch him, pretended to fall asleep until, eventually, I did.

He's here with me still, in this sandy hollow six thousand miles away, making me groan aloud into the empty air. I get up and go further out, where the neck of The Causeway meets the chin of the island, then further on round to the far side where there are rocks and cliffs, where the sea birds swoop in and out of exploding spray each time a wave breaks.

On the west side of the island, there's another sheltered cove where it's safe to swim. I go down there, strip down to my underwear and run into the water, refusing to cower when the cold licks at my calves, my thighs, my groin. I push on until it's waist height, then I throw myself forward into it. Ice thumps me in the heart and I gasp out loud.

I stretch my arms wide into a breaststroke and feel the salt water begin to warm to me, feel it buoy me up. After a while, I turn to float on my back and stare into the blue eyes of the sky. Small waves crest under me, rocking me gently, a comfort that confuses me, so I pull my knees into my chest, wrap my arms around them and will myself down to the bottom where I hold myself on my hunkers, breath trapped and swelling behind my nose. All of me clasped close and shut tight, except my ears, open to the muffled sounds of the sea.

I stay down until the last moment, until my lungs are fissured with pressure, until my heart is hammering. Up I rise, brain about to burst inside its skull, breaking the skin of the water, memory choked off by my body's gulping need for air.

1966

Nine-year-old me lies underwater, holding my breath in the big old bath that is almost deep enough to swim in. Breaking the skin of the water, I surface, and feel for the stopwatch and the button to press. I wipe my eyes. Three minutes, twenty-two seconds this time. Fourteen seconds longer than the last try but forty-five seconds short of my personal best.

Now I have to get dressed and go downstairs. Drying off, I feel lighter as I always do after this underwater ritual, relieved of something. I have limits, but I can stretch myself.

Down at the kitchen table, I take my place across from my big sister, Maeve, in front of the bowl of soup that's been poured for me. Mammy's silence is packed full of the sounds of her work at the stove: sizzling meat, bubbling potatoes, clattering plates. Steam billows angry ghosts around Daddy's vacant chair.

Maeve is bathed and scrubbed and in her Sunday best too, though it's Monday. Easter Monday. And, even more special, the day Gran has been describing in capital letters, for months now, as The Golden Jubilee. Maeve tries to land a kick on my shin, her favourite mealtime occupation these days. I pull my legs to one side, afraid of the mark her shoe might leave on my white tights. That would give Mammy the out her anger is seeking.

This afternoon, our entire family, even Auntie Norah, is going to Enniscorthy, a town thirty miles away, to commemorate the jubilee. Fifty years ago today, Irishmen took part in a rising against British rule, starting the war that won Ireland her freedom. Gran was involved back then and, today, she is on the organising committee and has to get up on a stage in front of everyone to give the speech she's been practising around the house for weeks.

The kitchen door opens and in she comes. I perk up. Maeve won't have a free run at me now.

"Something smells good," Gran says, her voice all happy. Then she sees Mammy's face, which makes her look at the space where Daddy should be. "Ah no,: she says, "don't tell me, not today…"

She moves across to the cooker. Mammy says nothing, just slaps six plates in a row along the counter. I send a mental message: Come over here, Gran, over here, but no. She lowers her voice, though not quiet enough: "Have you heard anything from him?"

"Not a thing." Mammy divides the food among the plates. "I'm going to go in and collect him once we've eaten."

"Yerra, let him rot there."

"Don't you think I want to? But how can I? If he isn't with us today, we'll be the talk of the place."

I listen to this exchange, waiting for a pause. When it comes, I call across: "Hello, Gran!" and then notice, too late, the quiet lunge of my sister's leg. A leather toe cracks against my shin.

"Yeow!" I screech out loud. The two adults turn.

"What's the matter, pet?" Gran asks.

Maeve's eyes burn a warning into the side of my face. "Nothing."

Gran comes over anyway.

"I hope you two aren't fighting. What do I always tell you? Fighting…?"

"…solves nothing," Maeve and I both answer in a sing-song voice together.

"That's right," says Granny Peg. "So," she settles herself in between us, "how is little Miss Tickles today?" She curls her fingers at me in mock threat.

"Fine," I say. And I am, now. My heart hums with love of her.

"And Little Miss Manners?"

Maeve wrinkles her nose at her, pretending to object to this name.

"Listen, girls, come here till I tell ye," Granny Peg says, in that confidential voice of hers that we love. "Auntie Norah will be down in a minute and she's after going to great trouble to get ready. Wouldn't it be nice if we all told her how well she's looking?"

Auntie Norah's appearance is a great worry to Gran, who always has to coax her to wash her hair or have a bath or change her dirty clothes.

"So she's definitely going?" Mammy calls over.

"Now Máirín, I told you, she has to go. There's no question of her not going."

"Even though you'll be on the platform? Even though I'll have the children to mind as well?"

"I'm sorry, a ghrá, but it can't be helped. It would be all wrong to leave her at home on this day. You must see that."

Mammy brings food over to us all, then takes her place at the table. We feel the temper swelling against her skin.

"I don't know how I'll manage," she says. "You know what she's like when she's excited. She's been like a hen on a hot griddle for weeks."

Gran leaves the space where she should answer lie open.

Mammy tries again. "How will I ever manage the three of them, and probably on my own?"

"She has to be there, Máirín." Gran's quiet insistence is not like her. Usually she calms our mother, strokes her down from the heights of her anger with soft words and the right kind deeds. "Norah did her bit for Ireland as much as any of them who'll be there today, more than most. You can't expect her to sit home alone on the day that's in it."

Maeve sees a chance to step in: "We'll be good, Mammy."

Mammy momentarily parts the folds of her anger and lets out a smile. "I know you will, love. It's not you I'm worried about."

She turns back to her food and the unfairness of everything sweeps over her again, eats into her. Her eyes travel around the table looking for a target and land on a bowl of unfinished soup. My bowl.

"Who owns this?" She lifts the spoon so the soup slops back into the bowl from a height, looking straight at me. Anxiety curdles my stomach. Maeve perks up.

"Do I have to ask again?"

"It's mine."

"How many times do you have to be told? Only take the amount you're going to eat. Don't I always tell you? If you don't want it, don't take it."

"OK."

"God above, isn't that reasonable? Isn't that fair enough? I can't stand good food going to waste. You'd better eat up that fry, every bit. You'd better clear that plate, young lady, do you hear me?"

She takes the bowl away. My sausages swell on my plate. Gran sees my face, cuts them up small for me.

"And what about herself above?" She is picking on Gran now. "Is she ever coming down at all this morning? How am I supposed to keep the food hot?"

"She won't be long," Gran picks up Auntie Norah's plate. "Here, I'll stick it under the grill for her. You have your own."

Mammy settles into silence at the foot of the table, nursing her teacup, staring out at the grey sea. It's all right for her not to eat, but I know it won't be for me. My sausages show pink where Gran has cut them; a pink that twists my stomach shut. What am I going to do? Mammy's anxiety is inside all of us now but at no relief to her.

The door opens and Auntie Norah comes in. She doesn't look like herself today: her hair is swelling out from her face in fat grey curls and a peacock brooch glitters on a new blouse. A tidemark of make-up wobbles along the fold of her double chins, spoiling the dressed-up effect, and her red lipstick has wandered outside the borders of her mouth.

The lipstick makes the non-stop motion of her mouth more conspicuous. Though Auntie Norah rarely speaks out loud, she talks a soundless stream of patter to herself all day, every thought that rises in her head getting turned over by her lips. Gran smiles to see her, says: "Norah, you look lovely."

Auntie Norah shoves her big hips between the arms of the chair as Gran gets up to fetch her food. "There you are now. And I'm just going to tie this tea towel round you so you don't get any mess on your nice blouse. Did you sleep all right with those curlers in? They've done a lovely job. Isn't Auntie Norah's hair lovely, children?"

Auntie Norah puts a soft hand up to its surface, as if to make sure it's still there. Maeve sniggers.

"Auntie Norah is lovely," I say, to please Gran, making Maeve snigger again.

Mammy cuts across us all, saying Maeve is to help Gran clean up and I am to come with her in the car. "We're going to town to fetch your father."

This is even worse than being punished for not eating, but to say no to Mammy in this mood isn't an option. She clicks open the front door of the Renault, her car not Daddy's, and I step into the back, feeling misplaced inside its glass and pastel-blue steel, the colour of summer and babies and the wrapper on my favourite sweets. It takes us 35 silent minutes to drive in.

"Right," she says, pulling the hand-break into a stop on the hill outside Larkin's. "Go in and tell your father I want him."

"What if he won't come?"

"Make him come. Tell him we're not leaving until I speak to him."

The handle of the pub door is high up. Unlike my sister, I am small for my age and I have to stand on tiptoe to reach it. The door puffs open into a smell like that of our own pub, but also different. Daddy is on the wrong side, the serving side, of the counter. Has he got mixed up, I wonder, about which pub he's in? He has a pint of Guinness in one hand and is leaning over a newspaper, pointing something out to another man. "Iron Jack," he says. "Fifteen to two."

Mrs Larkin is standing behind the counter too, and it is she who notices me first. She nudges Daddy and points at me through her tea towel, making everybody turn. Daddy puts on the pretend face he always wears when he turns to see what everybody is staring at, and finds it's me. "What are you doing here?"

"Mammy wants you."

"Tell her I'll be home later."

I move around his side of the counter, so he doesn't have to speak so loud.

"Mammy wants you."

He shakes his head.

"She said we won't go unless you come out and talk to her."

"Is that a fact? She'll get to know the inside of that car right well, so." He doesn't keep his voice down. He is looking at Mrs Larkin while he speaks, like he's talking to her, not me.

I can feel the other men looking and it feels like they are laughing, though they're not. One of them says to me, "Would you like a lemonade, love?"

What I would like is to sit down at the little table in the corner and have a Coca-Cola and a packet of crisps and a comic the way I did once before, but I can't. That time Mammy walloped me across the head, said that having a Coke like that was one of the worst things I had ever done to her. So instead I say, "No, thank you," to the man and try to get closer to Daddy. I whisper to him. "Please, Daddy. Please. She'll go mad."

He makes his show-offy voice even louder. "Tell your mammy to go ahead, I'll follow on home when I'm ready."

And he goes back to the talk about horses. "Did yours come in, Francie?"

"Not at all, a dead loss, he's running still. But Nick had ten bob on Deuteronomy."

"Did you hear that, Maisie? The drinks are on Nick."

I go back out to the car. The door is open, waiting.

"He won't come," I say.

"Were you listening to me at all?" she screams. "Go back in there now and get him to come out or you'll get what's good for you."

I go back in. Daddy looks up at me immediately this time, expecting me while pretending he isn't. "Jesus, did you not hear what I told you?" he says. "Is it Easter weekend or is it not? Am I to have no peace?"

"Ah now, Christy, go easy," says the man who offered me the lemonade. "It's not her fault."

Mrs Larkin speaks up. "Maybe you should go on ahead, Christy."

"D'you think so, Maisie?"

"I do."

"Are you sure?"

"I am."

He nods his head, slowly. "Maybe I will, so."

The men are like children in school, laughter forbidden but just under their skin. Daddy picks up his Guinness from the counter. It's more than half full but he lowers it down in one big swallow, then bangs his glass down.

"And what are you grinning at, Nick O'Leary?"

"Nothin', Christy." The man has two teeth only, and both of them black. "Nothin' at all."

"I'm glad to hear it."

Daddy takes a long time putting on his coat. The froth from his drink slides down the inside of the glass, settling into a slop at the bottom. The clock on the top shelf whirrs then chimes: one o'clock, dee-dah-dee-dah. He makes a great show of taking his ease, not letting anybody rush him. Then he puts on his hat, tucks his Irish Press under his arm. "Goodbye, men. See you, Maisie."

"See you, Christy."

Out to the car we go. Mammy has what she wanted but she's not happy. Daddy makes himself very small, pressed against the passenger's door, trying to seal himself off, but she's not having that.

"That place must be the dirtiest hole in Wexford town."

Silence.

"If you must stay away from your family, you think you'd go somewhere with a bit of class, but oh no, you'd rather be with the dregs."

Silence.

"Acting the big fella with a crowd of no-good townies. Have you no shame?"

Silence.

"For the love of God, answer me. Is there no shame in you for what you do to us?"

"I'd be ashamed to behave as you are behaving now."

"And how am I supposed to behave? Am I to say, 'Welcome home, Christy'? 'Thanks for coming home to your wife and family, Christy. Thanks for doing what every other man does every day of his life without thinking about it'?"

"What man would want to come home to the likes of this?"

Mammy starts to cry. "Oh, the disgrace of it…That dirty townie tart—"

"That's enough now." He says it twice. "That's enough."

"Near young enough to be your own daughter..."

"Christ, Máirín, would you mind your mouth in front of the child?"

"Oh, the child, is it? It's little you care about the child or the other one either when you decide to take yourself off. On this day, of all days, to be away from us. You know what this day means to our family."

Daddy refuses to talk any more, no matter what she says now he won't answer her. On she goes anyway: how could he, that filthy place, no respect, the talk of the village, the talk of the town...I know why Daddy isn't talking: it's because he only has bad things to say. Gran told me about it, how important it is to keep the bad words to ourselves. Our thoughts come from the same place we came from ourselves, Gran says, from the Good Lord above. We can't help what we think; it'd frighten the heart out of you some of the things that pop into your head, but as long as they stay in your head, no harm done. Spoken words are a different thing entirely. The wrong ones let out don't fade. They stay in the air, smoking it up. Bad deeds are even worse.

I sit in the back of the car, holding my own breath, fingers discreetly plugged in my ears, trying to stop any bad words from getting inside me.

As soon as we get home we have to leave again, because Daddy has made us late. We squash the others in: Auntie Norah and Gran in the back beside the windows, Maeve in the middle, me on Gran's knee. Daddy is driving now and it's Mammy's turn to be quiet and stare out the window with ruptured eyes.

At the old cemetery, we all pile out again and walk up the little hill towards The Grave, where Granny Peg's mother and father and husband are buried and her brother, Uncle Barney, with his high cross all to himself, taller than the other cross that's for three people not one. Taller than Daddy, even.

Once we're arranged in a circle around The Grave, Gran makes a speech, the words coming heavy out of her mouth: "We offer this rosary for the repose of the souls of all our family and friends but especially for the soul of Barney Parle, who fell nearby in a glorious fight for Irish freedom on the 10th January 1923, who sacrificed his life for comrades and country. Dílis do Dhia agus dÉirinn."

We leave Uncle Barney's grave and plaque behind and set off again. In Wexford, the traffic is heavy along the quay, making Daddy swear and wipe the windscreen with his handkerchief, as if he could wipe the other cars away. Gran is listing off dates and battles as we go. The numbers melt in my ears but I like the words she fires. Rising. Resistance. Freedom. Rebellion.

By the time we get to Enniscorthy, we are cramped and glad to get out. The rain has stopped but the paths are still wet. Big drops fall from the trees and telegraph wires. Flags flutter everywhere: rectangles of green, white and orange hanging from poles and trees and windows and strings of little triangles in all colours stretched across the streets. In the distance, we can hear the boom-boom of pipe-and-drum music.

People I don't know nod at us as we pass, or tip their caps, or come up to say hello. Men and women admire us: "Aren't they lovely girls!" "Isn't the little one the spit of her mammy?" I wonder how that can be as five minutes before somebody said I was the image of my daddy. Hands pat my head, smiles shine down at me, coins are pressed into my hand. Gran accepts and returns the smiles and chat on behalf of us all. Mammy and Daddy are stiff as two trees but they won't fight here in front of everybody, so we're all right.

Auntie Norah's lips are whirring talk to herself. Too many people, that's the problem: Auntie Norah hardly ever goes out or sees anyone but us. Seeing her distress, Gran takes her by the arm and talks to distract her, as if she's talking to us all, telling us about President de Valera, and how if he didn't have to be at the big celebration in Dublin he would be here with us in Enniscorthy, because Enniscorthy was one of the few places outside Dublin that rose in 1916. President de Valera always had a soft spot for Enniscorthy, Gran says.

Gran has a soft spot for President de Valera. Once, a long time ago, he slept in our house and afterwards she had the bed moved into her room. Dev's bed, she calls it, and she sleeps in it still. He wasn't President then – this happened the very first time Fianna Fáil went for an election.

"In the olden days, Gran?" I ask, making her laugh.

"Yes, modern millie. All the way back in 1932. Like yesterday for some of us."

Mr de Valera was in our part of the country to canvass for votes and he stayed in our house to acknowledge that our family had made the Ultimate Sacrifice. When we won that election, he was ushered into Enniscorthy by fifty white horses. Gran will never forget it.

We are at the square now where she is to get up on the stage and make her speech. A band is playing 'A Nation Once Again.' Other old people are up on the platform already. Gran hands Auntie Norah over to Mammy and we squeeze through to the seats that have been reserved for us up near the front.

We sit and wait. The music changes to 'God Save Ireland' then stops.

A man comes out. "Testing," he shouts into the microphone at the front of the stage. It lets off a loud squeal. "Testing one… two…squeeeak…Testing one…squeeak…three…"

Once he gets it working, another man walks on and everybody claps. He talks for a long time about Easter 1916 and the Rising, about Ireland and England, about brave men and fine soldiers. He's boring.

Another man gets up and goes on with more of the same but at the end he turns around to point out Gran and the other three old women behind him. "Without the brave girls of Cumann na mBan," he says, "Many a flying column would have collapsed. When almost everybody deserted the soldiers, those girls stood by them and the more dangerous the work, the more willing they were to do it."

I stare at the old women, sitting in a row in their black coats and hats, like blackbirds on a wire, wonder if he's made a mistake.

Then, at last, it is Gran's turn. Maeve and I stand up to join in the clapping for her. We listen with great pride to the speech we all know inside-out by now, about how Ireland can never call herself free while her six northern counties remain part of the United Kingdom and how we need a new movement for freedom in our country. She's just getting herself to the part where she gets all worked up when Auntie Norah shifts in her seat and stands up, holding her hand above her head like we do in school when we want to talk to the teacher.

Gran puts her hand over the microphone and leans past it. "What is it, Norah?" Her voice sounds low without the microphone, as if she is whispering, though really she's almost shouting.

Auntie Norah's fat cheeks are jumping and twitching like two small animals are having a fight inside her mouth. Words whirr through her lips, louder than usual, but indistinct. Mammy catches hold of her coat, tries to pull her back down into her seat. I can see that Gran, up on the stage in front of everyone, doesn't know what to do. She looks across at the man who did the talking earlier and he shrugs back. She looks again at Auntie Norah, who still holds her hand above her head but seems unable to do any more.

Gran decides she has to ignore her, turns back to the microphone but just as she is about to resume, Auntie Norah finds her voice. Her out-loud speaking voice that I've hardly ever heard. "What about Dan?" she asks.

Now the silence crackles all around us. Gran's face and body collapse, like gravity just got twice as strong. Daddy's lips fold around a nervous smirk. Mammy pulls harder at the coat and hisses, "Sit, Norah. Dear God, what are you trying to do to us?"

Behind us, a buzz of talk breaks out, people passing around what she said like a parcel.

"Sit, would you? For the love of God, sit yourself down."

Auntie Norah tugs her coat out of Mammy's grip and turns around to face the audience behind us. She says it again, addressing us all. And then again. "What about Dan?" she says. "What about Dan?"

1995

"Can I do it?" Rory asks. "I've always fancied pulling my own pint."

I hand him a glass. "Let the first one run off. What's in the pipes will be stale."

"I can't get used to this place being closed," he says, tilting the glass as the creamy black liquid pours in, then letting it settle. He and I are together, alone, in the pub, the business that sustained our family for generations, now closed. Maeve and Donal and Ria left for Dublin this morning, after the reading of the will, and it's been a long day here alone with the ghosts and memories.

So I was glad, I admit it, when I answered the doorbell and found Rory standing on the step, tie loosened, excuse for calling on his way home from work in place. The German buyers have been on, could he come in and let me know what the Germans said. I brought him through to the kitchen but it felt too awkward to sit him there and the sitting room would have been worse, so I said, "Would you like a drink?" and, without waiting for an answer, walked him through to the pub instead.

So here we are, with the shutters closed so the punters know not to try to get in, and all the lights on. He seats himself on the high stool behind the bar. Mrs D.'s stool. I uncap a bottle of fizzy orange for myself, take it round to the customer side to pour, putting the counter between us. The place smells of musty smoke and alcohol and feels abandoned, like it's shocked to have been stopped so suddenly in its daily doings.

"Everybody misses it. And it looks like it'll be gone for quite a while."

"Is that what the Germans said?"

"They don't intend to open again until they've done major renovations."

"When are they arriving?"

"Next Tuesday."

"Oh."

"Is that too soon for you?"

"Oh no, the sooner the better."

"I thought you might hang around for a bit. It's been so long since you were home."

"I need to get back. I've already stayed longer than I intended."

"Somebody pining for you over there?" He says it lightly but I know he's been waiting for an opportunity to ask.

"No significant other, if that's what you mean." I match his tone: we are Ms Bright and Mr Breezy, dipping and swerving around our history.

"And you can send in your work by email, can't you?"

"Mmm."

"Well, then…"

I shrug.

He levels off the Guinness, tops it into a perfect ring of white topping a glassful of black and holds it up for me to admire.

"Not bad," I say. "For a first attempt."

"Cheers."

I lift my drink to his and we clink glasses, our eyes meeting. The air between us becomes charged and we drink and swallow and put our glasses down with an unnatural awareness.

"I was telling Margie about your mother and her bequest… the suitcase, I mean…and she dug out this for you."

Margie is his sister, one of the O'Donovans who was most vigilant about never speaking to our family. What could she have for me, I wonder? He reaches over to his briefcase. He puts a yellowing newspaper cutting on the counter between us. "It seems our two uncles, Barney and Dan, were great friends. Did you know that?"

"No."

"Friends and comrades. They ended up in an English prison together, for drilling IRA soldiers and for playing the Sinn Féin trick of the time, carrying on as if the British courts had no jurisdiction over them."

I smooth it out on the counter, careful not to tear the brittle paper, and he starts to read:

Unprecedented scenes of excitement accompanied the trial of two Mucknamore men, Ibar Parle and Dan O'Donovan, at the Wexford Assizes on Tuesday last. A large crowd of onlookers congregated outside the courthouse before the trial, and the District Inspector billeted 20 local RIC police to the building to keep order.

The two prisoners were brought out and put in the dock and immediately began to speak amongst themselves. They also ignored the order for Hats Off. The police were forced to remove hats from the prisoners, leading to shouts and jeers from some among the assembled crowd and it took some time for the magistrate to bring the court to order.

The magistrate said he would bind them over in sum of £50 to be of good behaviour for twelve months, in default of which to go to jail for six months.

Magistrate: "Do you intend to go to jail?"

O'Donovan: "We do not recognize this court."

Rory interrupts himself. "Do you remember the background to this?"

"Not really. What year are we in?"

"Spring 1921, just before the British Empire agreed a truce."

"I don't remember. I think our history classes in school leaped straight from the glorious Rising of 1916 to the glories of living in a theocracy."

He laughs. "I can't quite hear the nuns putting it like that. And they must have taught you that after the rising, Sinn Féin won a landslide election, declared the Irish people had voted for an independent Republic and set up a 'Republican' government to run the country."

"Ignoring the minor detail of the English government that was already there?"

"Exactly. And all the Irish who had voted for any other party. The Brits were scathing, of course, but plenty of the Irish too thought the whole thing a joke, especially the older people. Their laughter stopped when the IRA got going."

"Which, I'm guessing, is where the great-uncles come in? Soldiers of the Irish Republican Army?"

He nods. "Here. You read on."

Ibar Parle made the following statement: "We do not recognise any authority in this courtroom. The only authority we recognise is that of Dáil Éireann, elected by the free will of the Irish people. The British Government may dub it a crime to drill soldiers for the defence of Ireland but it is no crime in the eyes of the authority we recognise and to which we owe allegiance."

At this, widespread applause broke out in the court. There were cries of "Up the Rebels!" – "Good on you, Dan!" – "See you in six months, Barney!" Some members of the public began to sing 'The Soldier's Song'. The magistrate ordered the court to be cleared and an ugly conflict broke out as the police set to do so with baton freely used. Many were injured in the mêlée.

"So they were comrades together in jail?" I ask.

"In jail and out. Comrades and best friends, Margie says. But they took opposite sides after the treaty with England was signed. You and I talked about that, do you remember? Back in college?"

"Did we?"

"Yes, don't you remember? My family voted for Fine Gael, yours for Fianna Fáil. And we wondered whether the bad feeling between them went back to the Civil War."

I feel good that he remembers something I've forgotten.

"But it didn't account for why they were so much at loggerheads," he goes on. "Other families were Fianna Fáilers and we weren't expected to shun them like we were to avoid you and yours."

"It was something to do with Auntie Norah."

"Possibly. Anyway, I thought you might want this, if you're going to dive into that suitcase your mother left you."

"Hmmm. Big if."

He opens his mouth to say something and, changing his mind, takes a long swig of his drink instead. "Margie showed me your magazine too, your column."

"What? Really?" My two worlds plough into each other. I never thought of anyone in Mucknamore reading Sue Denim, especially him. Eventually I say, "It's a living."

"A good one, I'd say."

"She's a character, the person who writes that column. She's not me."

"I wondered why you don't use your own name."

Because, I think, after the mess we made of everything, dear Rory, how could Jo Devereux ever give anyone advice? Instead I answer, "It was Lauren, my editor's, idea. Sue Denim. Get it? Pseudonym."

"Ouch!"

"I know. That's magazine land's idea of wit, I'm afraid. Lauren was so chuffed with herself, I had to go with it."

"What about the actual work? Do you enjoy that?"

"Enjoy? I don't know about enjoy. I find it riveting at times — you wouldn't believe the problems that arrive on my desk."

"Really? I always thought they were made up."

"Everybody thinks that."

But no. You couldn't make it up, the misery that people endure about sex.

"Quite flattering, I'd have thought, to have people see you as an oracle."

"What about you?" I say, wanting Sue Denim and her world out of here. "Are you still taking pictures?"

He shrugs. "I had an exhibition a few years back, in the Dublin Bay Arts Centre. Black-and-white stills of deprived kids on special ed. programmes in Dublin. 'Velvet Shoestring', it was called. Except the Irish Times listed it as 'Velvet G-String' so it didn't quite attract the audience we were hoping for."

I laugh. "You must show me the pictures. I'd love to see them."

"I don't know where they are, up in an attic somewhere. Those kids were something else, though."

"And now?"

"I thought the exhibition would give me impetus but the opposite happened…fewer and fewer pictures until…It's been more than four years since I picked up a camera."

"So? Pick it up again."

"I don't even take photos of my own children."

So he suffers it too. Block, self-sabotage, resistance. Forever failing yourself.

You wanna write? So write. That's what Richard used to say to me. He made it sound so simple and when he was alive, living around the corner from me, that's how it felt: not easy but simple. Just write, he would say and I just did. I filled notebooks with words and plans and poems. I had ideas. I was moving towards something, I could feel it. But now Richard is gone and I am all wound down. I have no writing, no man, no child, nothing I thought I'd have by now. No child. Ah yes, there's the rub.

"Begin again," I repeat to Rory, knowing there's nothing else for it, knowing — as only Sue Denim knows — how much easier it is to give advice than take it.

"I just might," he says. "Now you're here."

"Me?" I turn pink. "What's it to do with me?"

"I've been looking at these." He reaches into his briefcase again. "I brought them along tonight for you to see. You can add them to the other pictures in the suitcase."

He lays a large brown envelope on the bar counter between us.

The flap is unsealed. I reach inside and bring out a sheaf of black-and-white photographs, all of the same young woman, doing all kinds of things — in the park, at the beach, reading on a deckchair. And a set of black-and-whites where she is lying naked on a tousled bed. It takes me a minute to recognise her, then my hand flies up over my mouth. "Jesus, Rory."

He is laughing. "Don't you like them?"

"Look at her. My God, just look at her."

"I know. Gorgeous, isn't she?"

So young. So unguarded. So trusting. Me but not me.

"How can you say I haven't changed?" I say to him, staggered by her naivety, as I flick back through the pictures, faster than I want because I am aware of his eyes on both of us, me and my young image. Each of these black-and-whites shows me in a different position: lying, sitting on the side of the bed, sheet folded strategically across my thigh in one shot, thrown emphatically aside in another. I am flooded by the feelings we had for each other when he took them and I can't look up. Once, I knew every inch of this man's skin, the taste of his sweat, his spit and more. The time we had together is there between us but everything that happened since is also there, crowding it out. I feel like I am swaying on top of a wall.

I put them back in their envelope, shaken.

"Jo." His voice is gentle as he leans across the counter towards me. "Why don't you stay in Mucknamore? Stay for a while. Do what your mother wanted."

"I can't, Rory."

"Why?"

I repeat the objections I've already raised with myself and try to explain how impossible it is for me to stay a second longer than I have to in Mrs D.'s house. How memories I thought I'd sorted keep assailing me, hard and heavy as the day I put them away. How her spirit is so solid here, a boulder on my ribs. "I don't know if I'll even be able to last until the German couple come."

"What about staying at The Sea View? Or one of the B&Bs?"

I shudder. "Possibly even worse." The long looks of their owners slanting after me as I came in and out. Intolerable.

"You could stay at our place. We have a spare room."

Is he crazy? A flash of anger whips through me.

"OK, maybe not a great idea. Don't look at me like that, Jo. It's just that I'd say anything if I thought it would make you stay." He stares into his drink. "I don't want you to go."

"You shouldn't say things like that, Rory."

"I know. I know I shouldn't. But I hate the thought of you disappearing again. I'd like if you could...if we could..." He hesitates, takes a breath, plunges on. "I want to tell you something. I lied to you that first day. I don't love living in Mucknamore. My family does, but it's killing me."

"Too small?"

He nods. "Too Mucknamore."

My heart shudders. Stupid, treacherous heart. It makes me say, "I lied too."

"Did you? Don't you like San Francisco?"

"It's not that. I mean about everything being wonderful. Things aren't wonderful, they're a mess."

He waits.

"A while ago, I lost somebody."

"A boyfriend?"

"No. But a dear friend. A special friend." It incenses me that there is no title for what Richard was to me. Friend, yes. And brother and mentor and therapist and cook and minder…He was my lover, in every way but the sexual, and meant more to me than many husbands do to their widows. "I loved him," I say. "He loved me."

Over-worn words that feel threadbare but it's okay, Rory is looking past them, at me, and he understands. "So your mother dying now was a double blow?"

"For a long time, it's been one death after another." I check his face again. It's still okay: no false sympathy, just a clear face held open to me. "Mrs D. now," I say. "Richard a while back.' More than a while, much longer ago than I want to admit. "Auntie Norah. Before her, Gran. Daddy. And…you know…back then…"

That brings on a flinch so small that few would see it. I do -- but I also see that his eyes are with me, still. And his hands folded across the bar counter are open, small hairs curling round the edge of his shirt cuff. What if he were to touch me, I think, and as I think it, that's what he does. He runs the outer edge of his index finger along my cheek.

"Don't," I say, pulling away, though I want to take the hand and hold it there forever.

How easily my traitor body rises to meet his but another part of me is appalled. He makes these moves so easily, as if he is not married at all, as if our not seeing each other for twenty years was some kind of accident.

I try to fold myself back into place. I decide to tell him what I have told nobody yet except Dee. "Rory, you should know… Remember when you came into the bedroom, yesterday? And you remarked that I don't look sick?"

He nods.

"You were right, I'm not sick. Just vomiting all the time."

He looks at me, blank. A woman would know immediately

what I am trying to say.

"Especially in the mornings."

Still vacant.

"Morning sickness."

"Oh..." The message gets through. "Oh. Oh my God, right. Yes. I see." His brain winds slowly around all the implications. "So that was why you threw up at the funeral..."

"Yep. Happens every morning. Not usually on other people, though."

Lost in spiky thought, he doesn't smile. "The father?" he asks.

"Nobody. He doesn't know." Everything we are saying bumps into the past.

"Oh."

I put a hand on my belly though there's nothing to feel there, not yet. The changes are in other parts of me: the chaotic stomach, the tender breasts, the seeping tiredness. "I feel like that line of Oscar Wilde's that everybody's always misquoting. 'To conceive once, Ms Devereux, may be regarded as an accident but to conceive twice...'"

He is staring at me.

"Even if there is twenty years between the two," I add.

AFTER HE'S GONE I go to the sitting room and slide the pictures out of their envelope, to look again at the face and body that seems so clean, so clear. One picture in particular draws me and, as I'm looking, it blurs. I squeeze my eyes shut and it clears but then mists again, and now I find I can't keep them down, these tears of mine that live in my chest these days, forever waiting for their chance to erupt.

I let them come. Encourage them even, feeding them memories of the old heartache until they become loud and harsh and ugly, the sort of sobs that nobody wants to hear.

I cry and cry until eventually I fall asleep, staring into the wild and glittering eyes of the girl who used to be me.

Hours later, I wake with the dawn, cold and cramped, with stomach churning, still holding the photo. I go to the kitchen to make some toast, though I have no appetite. If I don't have something to throw up, I'll soon be retching on bile, which is worse.

After I've pushed down some food, I go upstairs and open the blue suitcase and take out the notebook entitled *Diary 1922*. Slipping the photograph in between the last page and the back cover, I bring it outside. For a walk.

I ignore The Causeway this time and walk eastwards along the beach towards Rathmeelin, for two miles or more. I keep going until I reach the green slope of land studded with crosses and gravestone, that is the old cemetery. For a moment, I stand on the beach with my back to it, looking out over the water at a world where everything is horizontal and vast, except me. Then I turn and walk up, diary in hand, to the very top, to the Parle graves.

I crouch in front of them and they stare back at me. Auntie Norah's little cross. The family grave that holds so many, Gran's parents and grandfather and herself — Margaret Mary Bridget Parle. 1900 to 1989 — and now Mrs D too. And the big, strutting Celtic Cross that commemorates Uncle Barney, her brother, her hero.

What am I to do? I ask Granny Peg. Tell me?

Please?

But I hear nothing. Nothing but blood rushing around my head, in time with the waves.

Weary, I lie down on the stones. From up here, I can see over the other graves, over the wall, over the waves. I can see all the way out to Coolanagh and beyond, to the horizon. I lay down my cheek. The stones are sharp. But beneath them is the smell of earth.

I close my eyes. The chip-stones stab my skin but still I lie there, like that.

PLASH: NORAH

1925

*H*ere comes Useless John, skulking up Mucknamore's main street. Every evening the same time: twenty minutes past seven. You could set your clock by his leaving. Straight past this house he'll go, walking another three full miles to Ryan's of Rathmeelin for his nightly imbibement. Five bottles of stout and a couple of whiskies he'll have – or more, if somebody else is buying.

And here comes young Cissie Cummins running up to have a go at him. "Hey, Useless!" she shouts up the road in his wake. "You're useless!" She keeps a safe distance, mind, in case he might turn and give her some of his talk about Coolanagh.

Coolanagh. The word alone is enough to frighten Cissie out of her brazenness. I can hardly bring the ink out to write the name of it myself. "Do write it," Peg says. "Write all the words. Get them all down onto paper."

Like I used to before.

It was good, right enough, when I used to do that. But then I got afraid of where my mind went, when let on the loose. No need for fear, Peg says. Just write it. The best of it and the worst of it. Put it all into a secret book only for myself. It's what she does and it always helps her.

And that woman has faced down enough, Lord knows, and come up only the better.

So. Coolanagh.

Coolanagh that night.

December 1923, two years ago already, if you can believe it. The December of the big fog. None of us had ever seen a fog like it, the way it clung, shrouding the sky and the water, pressing thick and white against our windows. People were shadows moving about in it. Everyone's talk fixed on it. Where had it come from? Would it never pass off? And what were we to do about the herring?

The shoals, long awaited, were in. A bay swarming full of fish we had, but every fisherman in the village grounded.

Six dreary days of this, morning, noon and night, until, on the seventh day, it shifted. Within an hour of daylight, the air started to stir. Hopeful men got up and sat by their windows, watching the mist peel back and the sea reveal itself, inch by slow inch.

John Colfer was one. As he tells it today, from his high stool in Ryan's public house, when he saw the island emerging, like a big battleship creeping into the bay, he knew it was over. He left his house, went down to the hut, and dragged his, as the fisherfolk do, across the sand and shingle into the water, then clambered in, trousers wet to the knee.

Off he set, boat slicing through the water and the patches of mist, small fallen clouds, that floated on it still. Just as he was about to pull right of Coolanagh, to steer his way out into the bay, one of those billows shifted, revealing a shape on the flat sands close by.

Colfer stared. Shreds of mist teased his eyes. Was it...? It couldn't be...? Even as he was asking, he knew. By the hammering of his heart, he knew.

He steered his boat across, as close as he could go without danger, close enough to confirm. Yes, it was a person, jutting up out of the sands like a rock sculpted. Like a bust of himself. Face bulging blue and smeared with sand but unmistakeable. Dan O'Donovan. My brother.

It was his eyes that were the worst of it, Colfer says, when launching his horror tale to the audience. Wide open, apparently. Crusted with a grainy glaze of sand. "One look at them eyes and I knew I was dealing with a corpse," he'd say. "No living person could stand it."

Shameless, not Useless, is what John Colfer should be called, for that is what he is, flourishing his finding of my brother in exchange for drink. But for all his bar-stool blather, he has at least held his lip on the question everyone was always asking: what was Dan O'Donovan doing out on Coolanagh sands on that night, in that fog?

Colfer's reply to that question is alway the same: three heavy-fingered taps to the side of his nose.

In the main it's admired, this reluctance of his to put words on his thought. "Not so useless in that department, thank God," Peg says. They know what he thinks all the same, with him footing it all the way up to Ryan's each day. He hasn't come here since it happened and we all know he never will again. Nothing is said of that. Even the nosiest has to admit that Mucknamore has had enough talk.

Wasn't it talk that unhinged the country, words like 'betrayal' and 'honour' and 'principles'? Principles, my eye. Wasn't it talk that turned our young fella's guns on each other? So if another young fella was dead, where was the use in asking why? Wouldn't the answer only lead to another question? Wasn't the country riddled with why?

Cruel it was, all the same, to see what John Colfer's queer mix of story and silence has done to him, how the gap between what he said and what he could have said has grown so wide that he's fallen right into it. His only pleasure now is turning on the children who jeer him, frightening them with his stories about Coolanagh, and the voices that can be heard calling from out there, on a quiet night, when the wind blows a certain way.

He's never married and now he hardly will. The bit of a farm his mother left him lies neglected. His boat rots in the hut from lack of use while he walks the village drunk, or fixed on drink. Finding Dan the way he did, knowing what he knew, not being able to do anything with the knowledge: that's what turned the man useless.

My brother did that to people.

PART II
REFLUX

1995

They are unmaking the house. From the door of my shed, I stand and watch the diggers trundle around it: forwards and backwards; claws up, claws down; buckets full, buckets empty.

Drills puncture the walls and bricks that have supported each other for more than a hundred years fall apart.

On and on it goes, day after day. Inside, steel struts brace the structure they want to retain, stop the whole from collapsing.

I watch the work from my shed.

Here is where I'm living now, inside a strange hiatus. The accommodation is primitive. I have an oil lamp for light, an oil stove for cooking and each morning, before the builders arrive, I draw water from an outside tap beside the house, lugging it across the garden in two enamel buckets. Calls of nature are answered between the dunes.

Primitive, yes, but the walls and corrugated iron roof are sound. And it's what I seem to want. I feel like I'm being purged.

Most days, I spend my time around the other side, facing the sea, but every so often I come round here to view progress. Across the lawn from me, the new owners Hilde and Stefan watch too. Their gaze is fond. Arms entwined, they stand and stare, smiling at the work and each other.

To them, these labourers are wonder-workers, making concrete the dream that sustained decades of desk-bound years in Düsseldorf.

One of the workmen in the distance sees me and waves. He is a show-off who likes to go naked to the waist, to roar along to songs on the radio. His wave is really for the other men, not me. I don't return it.

The builders agree with my sister, that I am unhinged. By grief, perhaps, or maybe just by nature. Most of the village agrees. Eyes lift skywards or slide away from me as I pass. Behind my back, index fingers are circled around temples.

I don't care. I can be mad if that is what they need me to be, if it means I can live in my shed and forgo explanations.

Fifteen black refuse sacks were filled with rubbish to clear this shed, then Rory helped me carry some furniture across from the house before the Germans came — the single bed from my old bedroom, a long table I use as a desk, one wooden chair, one easy one. And a rug for the floor by my bed.

The kind weather makes it possible. Each morning, the sun comes up shining, and as warm as California. I leave the steel sliding door open during the day as I work; sometimes a small breeze lifts my papers so that letters or notes or newspaper cuttings have to be weighted down with stones. But mostly it is calm and clear. And set to stay fair, according to Hilde: June, she tells me, will break all records.

Under Hilde's hands, Mrs D.'s front-room shop is to become a substantial business, serving food as well as alcohol. Upstairs, what were family bedrooms are to be renovated to provide guest accommodation: six rooms – "all en suite!" cries Hilde with delight – from which tourists will rise each morning and come downstairs for "the Irish breakfast" – fried eggs and sausages and rashers of bacon.

She has supplied me with breathless details of her plans.

Stone floors, wooden tables and stools, walls decorated with replicas of old advertisement boards: "Guinness is Good For You"; "For a Smoother Smoke – Smoke Sweet Afton"; "Drink Lyons – the Quality Tea". Tankards and bottles and musty old books scattered on high shelves, in calculated disarray.

"A real Irish pub," she says, hugging herself. As the Zimmermans' ideas about Irish pubs were acquired in Europe, truly traditional features like outside toilets, men-only access or sawdust on the floor will not feature.

Hilde is a large woman, lavishly warm, and my reaction to her plans is a great disappointment to her. "Your dear, dear mother," she says, bringing her face, a round melodrama of sadness, close to mine. "What you must know is that we, Stefan and I, love this place as much as Máirín did." Hilde gets everything wrong. She mispronounces my mother's name: Mayreen she says every time, instead of Maureen. And my reservations about their schemes have nothing to do with Mrs D.

I cannot explain myself to Hilde but I like her. She has spoken to my sister, has heard the talk of the village, has been informed about my performance at the funeral. Her response is kindness. Every day at one o'clock, she comes to my door with a dinner tray held out before her.

"Hello, hello," she calls, the same words each day, the same cheery tone. "Are you there, Jo? I have brought for you a little food."

She tries not to shudder at my choice of accommodation. I live in a shed while she and her husband overthrow my old home: she is shocked at that. Shocked at me, that anyone could choose to live like this, but especially a woman in my condition. Shocked at herself: she still can scarcely believe she has allowed it. The house is legally theirs; I had no rights to it. Still, she acts like I have done them a favour.

So I eat her food, all of it, although it is not to my taste – pot roasts, frankfurters, gravy. I even drink the accompanying glass of milk. To Hilde, Irish milk is something wonderful, and for a pregnant woman, essential sustenance.

She knows I want to stay in Mucknamore until I finish what I am writing, though I haven't explained why. What reason can I give for not returning to San Francisco with the blue suitcase and doing the work over there? None, except that I know it would never be done.

At first I slept badly here in my shed, my sleep perforated by noises of the night. The door has a big bolt and is secure but still I would jerk awake at certain sounds, heart pounding. Or I would turn over, thinking myself in my double bed in San Francisco and wake against this mattress's narrow edge, with a sensation of being about to pitch out onto the rough, unsanitary floor.

All this has passed. I have learned to turn in a smaller space, got used to the snaps and rustles of the outdoors, so they now bother me no more than the night-time creaks of an apartment building.

Each evening, while the sun is going down in a flamboyance of oranges and reds that bode well for the following day, Rory comes to visit. He waits until then, knowing I won't see him earlier. He brings drinks, wine or beer for himself, orange juice or Coca-Cola for me.

I look forward to these visits, I admit it. As the light seeps out of the day and I push my tired brain through another diary entry or document or letter, I listen for his footfall and, when he arrives, I fold away the papers and we go and sit on the rug I have already set down behind the shed for us. It's private there, overlooking the night water, high enough and far enough back from the edge to be cloistered from passers-by on the beach below.

We sit close for two or three hours each evening in velvet darkness and talk, our voices low, moths swooping in to knock themselves against the oil lantern set between us.

We talk: we do not touch, except when he is leaving to go home, when he bends and places a swift, soft peck on my cheek.

Each time, as I tilt forwards to receive this almost-kiss, I think about turning my head to allow his lips to meet mine. That would do it, I know: one gesture from me and the rest would follow.

He is glad that I don't. He loves his wife, his children. He is afraid of what sex with me would do to his feelings for them. As for me, I don't have his belief in — his awe of — the sexual act. That he comes here every night is betrayal enough, surely? Yet I too hold back.

Become Rory O'Donovan's other woman? Unthinkable.

So I accept the peck, keep my eyes steady front. And after he is gone, I wash and brush my teeth by lantern light, turning my thoughts away from him and back to the doings of young Granny Peg and Norah and Barney and Dan. They are who I take to sleep with me.

Sometimes, I think of my empty apartment in San Francisco, its curtains standing open to foggy summer days and street-lit nights. I think of the agony letters I left lying beside my computer, unanswered, dust settling over them. I think of Dee and Gary and Susan and Jake and all the others who continue to meet in Benton's or Araby's or Café Crème without me. I find it hard to believe it's all still going on while I'm not there.

A replacement has been engaged to cover my column. "She won't be the same," Lauren said when I called, "but she'll do us fine until you get back." I was not to worry about work. I was to take all the time I needed. Lauren lost her mother two years ago; she thinks she understands. I trade on her sympathy to win myself this interlude.

I am content to be here, for now; I don't want to go back, not yet. It's all very temporary. As soon as the construction work on the house is done, the builders will turn their attention to terraces and gardens and my shed will go. Hilde tries to reassure me with terrible promises about what will happen then. The guest bedrooms will be done, she says, and I can join her and Stefan in the house. I will be most welcome, I must stay as long as I like.

Her generosity terrifies me, so I work hard, harder than I have ever worked in my life. Up in the morning with the sun to write out the previous day's findings. A break at nine for food, again at eleven for a run on the beach. Once, I was able to run for miles and I am taking this opportunity to do what I have been pledging to do for a long time: regain my lost fitness.

After the run, it's back to my shed in time to wash and eat Hilde's lunch. The afternoon I spend writing until I can write no more. I make myself a light meal and after that, read something from the cache in the suitcase. Read and unravel until Rory comes, when we talk and talk, piecing together what happened to him and to me and to the people who made us.

It isn't always easy; often I worry that I'm getting it wrong, or over-interpreting. I don't fully trust my own recollections any more than I believe everything I read in the papers. Memories are like dreams: putting them into words makes them too solid. Even as I'm doing it, a part of me is thinking I shouldn't.

But I do. To my own mixed feelings, I stay on in Mucknamore, in a crumbling, run-down shack of a shed, and I write.

1922

On Monday afternoon, Peg Parle came out the side door of Mucknamore National school, and saw him immediately, sitting on the schoolyard wall with his back to her. He had his jacket off in the sunshine, his shirtsleeves rolled up. She spun round on her heel the second she saw him, to face the door she had just closed behind her.

It was she who locked up the school each afternoon, as Master Cole flew off home like a hare out of a trap as soon as the three o'clock bell came, and she was glad of the duty now. It bought her a minute to hide her infernal blushing — and to think.

Was he waiting for her? He must be. What else would have him sitting there like that, at this time of the day? The key shook in her hand as she tried to fit it in the keyhole. Look at what he did to her, it was desperate. His simple presence two hundred yards away…The key clicked in the lock and now she had nowhere she could go but about turn and forward, to see what he wanted.

She put on what she hoped was an ordinary smile, as if it was no great surprise at all that he should turn up like this, as if he were nothing to her but an ordinary friend well met, as if there was no blush pumping through her face and forehead.

At the sound of her footsteps approaching, he turned, got up. Stood facing her, with his jacket looped on one finger over his shoulder. "Hello, you." He was grinning, enjoying her confusion as he always did.

She fought for her voice to be normal. "What has you down here? Is it thinking of going back to school you are?"

"There's a thought," he said, putting his head to one side as he pretended to consider it. "Sitting in a little desk every day and you leaning over me telling me what to do."

"I'd say it would be old Cole you'd have. You being a big boy." Dark hairs coiled all along his bare forearms, she could see them from the edges of her eyes and something about them made her dizzy. She hardly knew what she was saying. He opened his mouth to make some smart retort but she cut across him.

"Be serious. What has you here in the middle of the day?"

"The ould fella wanted me to fix some fencing in the upper field but I couldn't stay to it. Everything was telling me it was a day for a walk on The Causeway so I made my escape. And as I was walking down, I saw the children coming from school and I thought to myself, I'll go down to the schoolhouse and see does Peg want to come along with me."

A walk. Out in public, in front of everybody. Her insides warmed, she hoped it wasn't showing.

"So do you?"

"They're expecting me at home." That was true. And her mother wouldn't be one bit pleased to see her walking the roads with Dan O'Donovan. Only this morning she'd been spitting fire about him bringing Mucknamore Band to the Michael Collins rally in Wexford.

"But they'll manage without you for half an hour?"

She could tell Mammy she took the opportunity to question him, to sort out where he stood.

"It is a lovely day," she said, with a show of reluctance.

"And who knows when we'll get the next one?"

He started walking in the direction of the strand and she fell into step beside him. "I won't be able to stay too long."

Without discussing it, they walked towards the gap between Lambert's farm and Dillon's to get to the strand, rather than going down to the Hole in the Wall, which would take them too near to her house.

In the ditch opposite Lambert's, some crocuses were peeping up purple and white, and bunches of daffodils, tall beauties, were flaunting their flamboyant yellow heads. Was there anything lovelier than a lovely spring day, especially after a tough winter? For weeks, they'd had an east wind with the waves hurrying to the shore with veils of spray blown back, like an army of angry brides. Now the wind had dropped and the water settled to sleek.

As they turned onto the strand, the brightness and beauty of it all laid itself out before them.

"Do you ever wonder about heading off out there," he asked as they walked down towards the shore. "Off beyond the sea?"

She hadn't. Which wasn't very adventurous of her, when she thought about it. "If you go up to Forth Mountain on a day like this, you can see Wales," she told him. "Did you ever do that?"

"I didn't. Maybe you'd like to take me up there sometime."

"I might," she said, matching his tone. "If you're good."

"Oh, good, is it? Good at what?"

He was the very devil of a man. He always bested her because he never minded going low.

"We went across once, when I was about thirteen," she said. "Mammy brought us on the ferry from Rosslare and we stayed in a boarding house."

"What was it like?"

"The people talked funny. We took a coach into the mountains – their mountains are huge – but it rained all day and we could hardly see a thing."

He nodded. "When I said about going away, what I meant was for good."

"Oh, emigration. No, I never considered that."

"I suppose why would you?"

He was right, why would she? She was one of the lucky ones, with her good job and her nice house where she could live happily until the day when, please God, she'd meet a good man and make her own home and family. For him, it was different. He was a second son, doing jobs about the place at home but knowing that his brother John would get the farm. He wasn't a man to play number two.

"You're not thinking of leaving us, are you?"

If he were, would she go with him? He'd make something of himself wherever he went. Would he ask her?

"No," he said. "I might have, before. But this Treaty we have now, it changes everything. There's hope for us all now."

"I don't want to get into an argument about the Treaty, but—"

"Good," he said. "Then don't."

She'd better ask him the hard question so, get it out of the way. "What's all this carry-on with the Mucknamore Band?"

"Listen, I know your mother has me blamed for that, but she's all wrong. The band members are ten men with minds of their own."

"But you're not coming to the Sinn Féin meetings any more. And neither are they." She kept her voice light.

"There's no point. There's only room for one opinion in Mucknamore Sinn Féin."

"Mammy's." She laughed and he – looking relieved – laughed along.

"That's right."

"But if you want your opinion to get across to the other members, you can't go isolating yourself."

He stopped. "It's the other way round, Peg."

"What do you mean?"

"It's ye who are isolating yourselves. Your family needs to be more careful. You've a lot of influence around here. There's no good hoping your mother will calm down but you – the schoolteacher -"

He was looking into her face, as intense as she could ever wish him to look. "This Treaty gives us the freedom to win freedom, Peg. We work within it for the time being, keeping our eye on an all-Ireland Republic down the road, when the time's right. Everything doesn't have to be done at once."

"But Dan, our oaths."

She took an oath of allegiance to the Irish Republic when she joined Cumann na mBan, as did Norah. As did he and Barney when they joined the Irish Republican Army. They couldn't now go and take an opposing oath of allegiance to a so-called Free State, as this Treaty demanded. Or to an English King.

"The Irish Republic lives. It was brought into being by the Irish people in 1918. Nothing but the decision of the Irish people can dismantle it."

"That's what I'm trying to say to you. When the election comes, the Irish people will do the sensible thing and vote yes to the Treaty."

"We'll see about that."

"Why wouldn't they? Every English soldier is to be shifted out of their barracks and shipped back home. We're to have our own army and our own government and our own judges and our own police. They're gone, Peg. It's over."

Dan bent to pick up a flat stone, and tossed it across the water so that it skimmed the surface once – twice – thrice – four times before sinking. How was it that boys could always do that, Peg wondered, and girls couldn't? It was a paltry skill, one that didn't need strength or any other masculine quality to succeed. It must just be that girls didn't bother with it. Because it was a boy's thing, boys became good at it.

She wondered what it would it be like to be a boy, to do what Dan did today, just decide that you wanted to spend time with somebody and turn up where they were. Imagine if she were to do it the other way round, call up to the O'Donovan farmhouse when she felt like seeing him. Just imagine.

"The Treaty applies to 26 counties only, Dan. The Irish people won't vote for half a Republic."

"I hope you're wrong. Because if they vote no, what then?"

She wasn't sure what to say to that and he swooped in.

"We all know we've been sold a pup, Peg. The question is, do we put it down now or do we rear it until it can use its teeth for us?"

"Michael Collins' argument."

"Collins was the hardest man of the lot. What's good enough for him is good enough for me."

"It was he who let the English outfox us. If Mr de Valera…"

"Don't mind that nonsense. Dev knew well a Republic was never going to be granted. That's why he stayed at home and didn't go to the Peace Talks. So he'd have someone to point a finger at."

She had an answer but she kept it behind her teeth because she knew he wouldn't let it go until he had the last word and what she wanted, more than anything, was for them to have a nice time while they were out and not to spend it arguing. It was such a beautiful day and what she would most like was if the intense looks he was giving her were for her, and not for politics.

Earlier on in school, in a marvellous mid-morning moment, she had felt what she hadn't felt in months — warmth! — and rattled up the winter-grimed windows to let in the soft, fresh air. At break time, she'd happily gone on yard duty under trees that were on the point of puffing open into leaf. The birds, she could see, were feeling what she was feeling, spinning fast, circling high, getting as close as they could get to the sun.

The children felt it too, scurrying around the schoolyard, in and out of the glare and shade, laughing and screaming. It made them skittish when they were back in the classroom so she'd swapped the sums she was going to do for story-time, the best way to settle them. The story of Maeve, the ancient Irish Queen of Connacht.

Peg enjoyed story-time herself and especially loved to tell the children the stories of old Ireland, that were once, before the coming of the English, known to all the Irish people and cherished as the crucible of their heritage and civilisation.

In the same spirit, she also taught them some of the Irish words she was learning in her Gaelic League classes – simple words and phrases like hello, Dia dhuit (literally "God be with you"), and thank you, go raibh maith agat ("may good be yours") – and demonstrated to them how an awareness and love of God suffused the Irish language.

The books that Master Cole taught from did none of this. They were full of English propaganda, about the supposed benefits that being part of the empire brought to the Irish. Once – a while back, admittedly, but still – she had heard him teaching the children to recite: "I thank the goodness and the grace / Which on my birth has smiled / And made me in these Christian days / A happy English child…"

Well that day was over now, at least that much was a job well done. No Irish master would ever teach the like of that again.

Master Cole wasn't exactly hostile to her Gaelic League activity – how could he object to the children being taught their native language and lore? – but he wasn't what you'd call encouraging either. And, as theirs was a one-roomed school with his big desk only forty feet or so away from her own, she liked to draw the children in close to her for story-time.

This she did today, moving everybody except Tom, Paddy and Nancy into the front two rows and bringing her own chair down off the platform and up close to them. She had promised she'd tell them more about Queen Maeve, the fiery woman at the centre of the epic tale Táin Bó Cualainge, a great queen, daughter of the High King at Tara, very rich and very beautiful, as all the great queens always are.

She began quiet, drawing them in: "You remember last day,

children, how Maeve was arguing with her fourth husband King Ailill over who had the most riches and how riches at that time in Ireland didn't mean money, but meant land and cattle?"

They all nodded.

"And how she needed to get her hands on the Brown Bull of Cooley, the best bull in all Ireland, if she was to have the winning of that argument?"

Again, nods all round. Some of the eyes were already widening, just two sentences in and already ensnared.

"All right then. So Maeve got together friends and allies and soldiers into a small army and off she set to win this bull away from the men of Ulster. The journey took a long time and they were tired out by the marching. One night, while stopped for sleep, a seer appeared to Maeve and told her that the men of Ulster were all sick and weakened with labour pains."

Peg looked around her young audience. "Do you remember what labour pains are, children? Do you remember that other part of the story that we did before Christmas, when the curse was put on these men for their bad treatment of a woman with child? Making them feel the pain of birth all the time, day after day?

"Well, you can imagine Maeve's delight at being informed about this, but the sorceress then told her about one man who had been spared from this curse, a young man called Cúchulainn, a skilled warrior, champion of Ulster, ruthless and strong. The sorceress told her that if Maeve persisted in going to Ulster, Cúchulainn was going to defeat her army. Maeve was very angry to hear this and—"

The schoolroom door opened, stopping Peg mid-sentence. All the children's heads turned. The doorway was filled with Father John, his coat off in deference to the fine day, a big patronising smile fixed in place above his white collar. He came in and bade her a good day and a good day to the children and how were they all on this fine day, thank God, thank God, making his way as he was talking down the narrow aisle between the desks to where Master Cole was coming forward through the senior children to greet him.

The two of them would now go and stand in front of the fire, Peg knew, to warm their self-satisfied posteriors, smoke a pipeful of tobacco each and, in their own minds, put the wrongs of the world to right. The priest often dropped in like this, supposedly on an inspection but really looking for company. Not the company of the sick and dying, mind you, but that of the only man in the village he considered his equal.

Master Cole set the senior children a passage to copy out of their readers and led the priest across to the fire. Father John would probably come over when he'd finished his pipe and start asking the children questions about what they'd been learning. This now made her feel self-conscious as she picked up near where she'd left off.

"Maeve decided to march her men on, despite the warning," she told them. "And she sent a message to Cúchulainn, who agreed to fight any of her Connacht champions man-to-man, in single combat. And this is what he did. Each one he met and each one he killed, until in the end there was only one remaining warrior. Ferdia.

"Do you remember Ferdia, children? Cúchulainn's oldest friend and foster-brother who had gone to work for Maeve? Well, naturally, Cúchulainn didn't want to fight him. He tried to persuade him not to, reminding him of the days they had spent together as boys, training in arms, when both were students of the great female champion, Scathach.

"'We were heart companions,' he said to Ferdia. 'We were companions in the woods, we were fellows of the same bed, where we used to sleep the balmy sleep.'" Peg loved the musicality of these lines that she had learned by heart and welcomed the chance to quote them.

"But Ferdia feared h..." Peg's voice faded as she saw Father John coming through the classroom towards her. She stood in deference to him.

"Good day, Miss Parle," the priest boomed in his big public voice, the greeting for the whole classroom, not just her. "Hello, children."

"Hello, Father," the children chanted.

"So what are we working on today?"

"We're learning some of the ancient Irish legends, Father."

"Are we now?" He turned to the class. "So, who can tell me something about one of Miss Parle's ancient Irish legends?"

Katy Rowe's hand shot up first. Little Katy was bright as a military button, though being a Rowe, she'd be lucky if she got to stay on in school past the age of ten.

"Yes, Katy." Father John was smiling at her enthusiasm.

"We were learning about Queen Maeve, Father."

"And who is Queen Maeve when she's at home?"

"She had four husbands, Father," said Katy with a how-about-that face. "And her army killed bad men from Ulster. Hundreds of them she killed, 'cause she wanted this bull...er..." Seeing Father John's forehead folding into furrows, Katy stuttered to a stop.

Peg knew that Father John was an Ulsterman himself, from the county of Monaghan, but poor Katy didn't. Thinking she hadn't explained the story well enough, she tried again. "The queen was able to kill that many of them because they had labour pains, Father."

The priest's eyebrows disappeared into his hairline.

Katy elaborated, helpfully. "That's the pains you get when you're pushing out a baby, Father."

The priest turned to Peg. "What sort of a story is this to be telling small children?"

"Katy got the wrong end...She...It's one of the oldest Irish legends, Father. It dates from the sixth century."

"It's a pagan story, by the sound of it. I'm surprised at you, Miss Parle."

"You have to hear it in its entirety, really, to understand it."

"I'm thinking Bible stories would be a lot more elevating."

"I didn't tell the children anything wrong, Father.' She had, in fact, withheld many things about Maeve contained in the original tale: that she first tried to win the great Bull of Cooley by offering its owner the "friendship of her thighs", for example. That after she left her first husband, he came to her home place in Tara and violated her while she bathed in the River Boyne. That it was her boast that she was never without one man in the shadow of another. But Peg knew she wouldn't win any credit from Father John by telling him any of that.

"You cannot go wrong with a Bible story, Miss Parle."

"Yes, Father."

He turned to the class. "We'll forget about Queen Maeve, children. Let me see now, who can answer me this: Who made the world?"

All the hands went up, Katy's first, waving furiously. Martin Dunne was nearly halfway up the aisle, waving his hand, calling, "Father! Father!" It wasn't too often that Martin had an answer to anything.

"Well, Martin?"

"God made the world, Father."

"Good man. Good man." Father John put his hand in his pocket and took out one of the lemon sweets he kept for the purpose and fired it at Martin who, when he caught it, couldn't have been more delighted if it were one of the crown jewels.

"And who is God?"

This one was Katy's. "God is a Spirit Infinitely Perfect," she chanted in her sing-song way, once Father John gave her the nod. "God Always Was and Always Will Be, World Without End."

A sweet came flying through the air at her and her hand shot up, fast as a cracking whip, to catch it. Instead of eating it straight away like Martin, she folded it away into her fist.

On it went, the priest asking the children the well-worn questions and the children restoring Peg's standing with their rote-learned grasp of their Catholic catechism. At the end, just before he left, Father John filled his two fists from his pockets and threw both handfuls of sweets up in the air for the children to catch. This was something he always did to conclude his visit and Peg hated it. He would laugh as he watched the children jumping and scrambling, elbowing and pushing each other, but when he was gone she was left to deal with the disappointment of those who were unsuccessful and the agitation of them all.

"It took me a full half-hour and a blackboard full of sums to quiet them back down," she told Dan, as they walked, companionably, along the strand. All talk of the Treaty was now set aside, her intention when she'd started to tell the story.

"I'd love to have seen the priest's face when the young one said that about pushing out babbies."

"You should have heard the helpful little voice on her. You could tell she thought a priest might not understand such things."

"So does this mean you'll have to stop telling the Irish stories?"

"Indeed and it does not."

He laughed at her vehemence.

"Once the English are gone out of the country, all Irish schools will teach those stories," she said. "And our own native language too."

"You're right there. Once we have our own Education Department, they'll look after that."

She had meant: once they had a Republic. He was implying that the Treaty had it all fixed up already.

They were halfway out to Coolanagh now, where the sands were treacherous if you stepped off The Causeway. The tide was retreating, leaving rippling undulations and sand-puddles behind, in which gulls waded with slow, high-footed steps, ignoring their reflections.

He went back to talking about the Treaty. He just couldn't leave it alone. About how when the boys around here woke up to the fact there was a war on, the Truce was called, and now that it was all over, they were dying for a bit of action. "We can't do much about the real hotheads but there's plenty who don't know what they think and they are waiting for someone they respect to tell them. I'd include my own sister in that."

"Norah?"

He nodded. "You could moderate the message going out to the village, Peg. This Treaty is what the people of Ireland want and the sooner that's accepted, the better."

"Norah knows her own mind," Peg said, aware that this was not quite true. "And the arguments you're making... You do realise they are the self-same arguments the people used to make against us when we were fighting the English. You must know that if we went on what the people wanted, there would never have been a shot fired."

"If ye had to go out and be shot yourselves, ye women might be a bit more careful what ye said."

"What?"

"You heard me."

"Dan!"

He shrugged.

"Dan! How can you say such a thing? While you were in jail, where nothing worse could happen to you, we were the ones who had the soldiers raiding the house, never knowing what time of the day or night they might show up, and what they might find or what they might do to us."

In the months coming up to the Truce, they had got ever more vicious. Peg had lost count of the number of times they came swooping into Mucknamore, turning everyone out of the pub onto the road while they wrecked the place, pretending they were looking for something. Molly had the same thing up at hers and the O'Donovans too. And Lama White's house was burnt out because his mother said the wrong thing to one of them.

Families had started to vacate their homes at sunset, to sleep out in barns or in fields so as not to be in bed when the soldiers came swinging in, banging on doors, letting off bullets or grenades, threatening to set houses and farm buildings alight, or to shoot or bayonet people in their nightshirts.

And she had had to balance her work for the movement with her schoolteaching and her home duties. More than once, she had imagined what a relief it would be to do what only boys were allowed to do: go on the run with a band of others of like mind and carry out ambushes and raids on barracks. To have nothing only that to think about, and to receive the honour and glory given to those who go out and fight, seemed like luxury.

Her role was more humble and she accepted that and tried to be cheerful and to rise to any task requested of her. But now to hear him say she and the girls were little better than cowards, stirring it up from the sidelines...That cut deep, so it did.

Not wanting him to see just how deep, she hung her head, and in so doing noticed that she had chalk-dust marks all across her skirt. She bent to brush them away and what did he do then only reach over as if to help her? Through the fabric of her skirt she could feel his hand, rubbing against her leg. Blood flooded her face, a blush so swift and so absolute that it was nearly sore against her skin as she pulled back in fright.

When she'd composed herself enough to look up, she saw he knew exactly what he was doing. His mouth was stretched up on one side into that devilish half-grin of his.

"I'd better head back," she said, still blushing.

"Ah, come on, walk on a bit. We'll take a rest further out."

She knew what that meant. "No."

"'No'," he said, imitating her voice. "Why is it all 'no' with you these days? You were willing enough before."

She straightened out in shock when she heard him say that, as much at his tone as at the words. This was even worse than what he said a minute ago, the derision in his voice each time.

"I'm only joking," he rushed, when he saw how she was taking it. "That came out all wrong."

She turned as if to go back.

"For Christ's sake, woman. Don't make a meal out of it."

She started to walk away.

"All right, suit yourself. I'll go on ahead so. If you don't mind."

"No, I don't mind," she said. But she did. It would be much more gentlemanly of him to accompany her back. She felt like a servant, dismissed.

"It's going to be a lovely night," he said, coaxing, his voice softer now. "I might call down to your house later."

"To the house?" Her heart leapt. She turned back, caught his expression. "Oh, you mean, on the sly."

"I'll throw a few stones up at your window. Around half twelve?"

"I don't know, Dan."

"I'll bring a lamp. We could come back out here then with more time. And no one to bother us."

"I don't know," she said again.

"Don't make up your mind now. I'll drop down and you can see how you feel later."

The walk back away from him, along the sandy Causeway path, was awkward, feeling that he might be watching her from behind and also aware of the windows of her own house, knowing that if her mother was upstairs in her bedroom and looking out the window she could see them both. She walked mindlessly, snarled in thought. Respect was lacking in him, she had to face that. He was far too presuming.

Then again, he had called up to the school for her, that was a good thing...

But no, it was too small a thing to hold up. She wanted him to like her for all to see and any to know, not this hole-in-the-corner business. She spun around and quickly retraced her steps. If her mother was watching, she'd be wondering what on earth was going on.

She marched back towards him with determination, not letting herself think too close. He was still standing where she'd left him, looking out across Coolanagh sand, towards the island and the water in the distance.

"Don't call for me tonight," she said when she finally reached him. "I won't be coming out."

Was that amusement glinting in his face?

She carried on. "I don't want any more sneaking around. I don't see the need for it. If you want to call for me, come to the house. Tonight or tomorrow night. Around eight o'clock would be perfect."

He burst out laughing.

"That's funny, is it?" she said.

He just kept laughing and she could think of no other way to keep her dignity but to turn and leave again. So that's what she did.

He called after her – "Come back. Come back for a minute. Aw Peg, come on!" — but she let the words slide off her back as she retraced her steps all the way back to the village.

She was dead late back to the house and had to get straight into helping her mother prepare the tea. They fell, as they so often did, into talking about the Cumann na mBan work. This time it was all about Mr De Valera's visit to Wexford to round up support for the anti-Treaty side. "Will the lads make a guard of honour?" her mother asked, "To lead the car from Enniscorthy to Wexford?"

The question, the implied criticism in it, stopped Peg in the act of laying the kitchen table. "No," she said, knives and forks pointing upwards in her hands. "No, Mammy. We won't have time for them to walk all that way."

Máire folded her lips, purposefully.

Peg was stung but knew it was frustration at her own weakness that was making her mother critical. Three weeks ago, Máire handed over to Peg her part in organising the great day because she just wasn't able for it. She strained for patience. "The Enniscorthy meeting opens at three," she explained. "By the time Miss MacSwiney and the others say their bit, it will be

nearly four before Mr de Valera gets to speak. They have to be in
Wexford for five so there's not time enough to walk it."

"But you'll escort them into the town, surely?"

"Ah, Mammy, of course we will. They'll motor as far as
Ferrycarraig where the troops will be waiting to lead them
through."

And after the public meeting in Wexford there would be a
reception in the Talbot Hotel, and it was there that she, and two
other girls, would make their presentations. Máire turned back
to her frying pan, and was leaning into the press as she stood by
the cooker, turning meat. Always now if she was standing, she
had to rest against some surface to steady herself – a hand on the
table, a hip against the chair. And she moved slowly about the
place, as if weighing the wisdom of each step before putting her
foot down. These changes had advanced so gradually that Peg
hardly noticed them, until something reminded her of her
mother's old bustle, the way she used to come swinging through
a door with five times more force than was needed.

A lot of her mother's strength went into trying to hide her
weakness, in ways that turned Peg's heart over. She tried to
catch Barney's eye behind their mother's back, but he had his
face dug into the newspaper so she went back to setting the
cutlery.

"It'll be a great occasion," Máire said, trying to make amends.
"I might make it in myself."

"Are you serious, Mammy?"

"What do you mean, am I serious?"

"I never thought for a minute that you'd not come."

Her mother frowned. "I'll do my best."

"You have to come, Mammy. Every Republican this side of
Enniscorthy will be there."

"All right, all right," she said, short with her again. "I'll do
my best, I said. Don't pick me up till I fall."

Every time Peg thought of herself handing that statue to Mr
de Valera, she felt dizzy. To think of him taking her hand in his,

probably addressing a few words to her. Whatever would she say back? How would she answer him without blushing?

"It will be so strange to see him in the flesh," she said.

"He has a powerful presence all right," said Máire from the cooker. "And Miss MacSwiney too. They say she's a great speaker."

Barney lifted his head. "They say she'd talk the hind leg off a donkey. Two and a half hours she went on for during the last Dáil debate. Two and a half hours!"

"I know, but worth listening to, wasn't she?" Peg said. "All that stuff about blades of grass and dragon's teeth..."

Máire picked up the quote, word perfect: "'If they exterminate the men, women and children of this generation, then the blades of grass, dyed with their blood, will rise, like the dragon's teeth of old, into armed men, and the fight will begin again in the next...'"

"Strong stuff, Barney," Peg said. "You have to admit it."

But of course he wouldn't. None of the men liked Miss MacSwiney; she frightened the life out of them. And Barney, once again, was in a disagreeable mood. "Will the dinner be long, Mam?" he asked, drumming his fingers on the table. "I'm in an awful hurry."

Peg said, "Aren't you always in a hurry these days?"

She wouldn't mind if it was movement work he was going to but it was only an old game of hurling, not even a match, just a friendly. Her mother crossed the room and put his plate of food on the table, pinching his cheek as she passed, like he was still a child.

Peg laid the potatoes in front of him. "Surely they'll not start the match without the great Barney Parle? If you gave us a hand, it would be quicker for us all."

"Don't start, you two," said Máire. "Leave the chap alone, Peg, and run out and see can your daddy come in for his."

"Do you want me to take over the shop?" It was Saturday, a day that had a different routine to weekdays. Peg had no school and Pats, the hired help, had a half day. It would get busy but not usually until later on.

"See is it quiet enough to leave the door open." They did that sometimes; the customers tapped on the counter with a coin if they had a need. Máire liked to get everybody fed at the same time, so the food didn't spoil, but she didn't approve of them eating behind the counter like some publicans.

The dinner was fried pork chops, one of JJ's favourites, and he came in rubbing his hands. "Looks good and smells better," he said, taking his seat at the top of the table. Barney was steadily advancing through his meal, his first chop shorn to the bone already. He and JJ had two, and the women one. Máire's own plate held the smallest helping but Peg knew she wouldn't finish even that.

"So," said Peg to Barney, "are we expecting the Rathmeelin girls again to cheer on the heroes of the hurling field?"

He ignored her, carried on working through his plate of food, barely stopping to swallow. His cup of water sat beside him untouched.

"Some girls want their heads examined," said Peg, "To stand for an hour-and-a-half on the side of a hurling pitch on a day like this."

"If you had an eye for one of them," said her father, "I'd say you'd be out there too, same as the rest."

"Not if Pádraic Pearse himself was playing."

"Where is the game?" Máire wanted to know.

"Creel," Barney said, his mouth full of meat.

"You'll be going on the bike, so. Did you get that brake fixed?"

"It's all right."

She frowned. "Is it fixed, is what I asked."

"I'll manage all right for now."

"You didn't manage too well when you hit that hole on Rathmeelin Hill last time, did you? Weren't you lucky not to break a limb? Daddy, tell him."

"Your mother's right, son. You need the brakes to be in order."

"I'll fix it later. I've no time now."

"What has to happen to you before you get sense? What do you have to be inviting accidents into your life for?"

"I'll fix it later, Mammy. Honest I will." He gave her one of his humouring smiles. "Honest."

Close under her chiding of them these days was an anxiety like gone-off milk under a film of cream. They all sensed it but none of them wanted to poke through to it.

Barney pushed back his chair.

"Are you not waiting for a cup of tea?" Máire said.

"I haven't the time." Already he was at the door.

"What hour of the day or night will you be back?"

"Around six. Bye." And he was gone, leaving a space behind him.

Peg stood to gather the side plates and pile the potato peelings and the dirty cutlery. She too needed to leave – her meeting started at two thirty – but she didn't like to take off too quickly after Barney's sweep-out. Time was when her mother used to be the one always off somewhere in a hurry.

"Are you finished, Mammy?"

"I am."

JJ looked up. "Ah, Máire, eat another bit, for pity's sake." But she shook her head.

Peg scraped her plate, stacked it with the rest, carried them over to the board. She put the kettle on the fire. It had boiled earlier and only needed a minute. As she stood waiting for it, she felt herself wilt in the heat of the fire and realised she was tired. Between teaching in school, helping out at home and her Cumann na mBan work, she never seemed to have a minute these days. Steam and water came hissing through the spout of the kettle and she lifted it off, made the tea.

"Good girl yourself," said her father, as she put down the pot.

"I need to go as well, Mammy," she said, soft as she could.

"You've no time for tea either?"

"I'm sorry, I have to be in town by half-past two. But I'll be back in time to give you a hand with the supper."

She replaced the butter and salt in the pantry, put the dirty delph in the basin, poured boiling water into it.

"Leave it, so," her mother said. "I'll do them myself."

"Are you sure?"

Her mother made a cross face. "You have to go is what you said."

That wasn't fair. How was it allowed for Barney to trot off to a hurling match without a word said about it? You couldn't but feel for Mammy, her weakness went hard on her, but how was it Peg was always the one to get the lash of her tongue?

"Go on, then, if you're going," said Máire, standing up quickly, too quickly, which brought on one of her coughing attacks. This racking immediately transmuted Peg's anger into fear. She stood, unsure whether to cross over to help or whether Mammy would rather it ignored. God, but this was a long one. Would it never stop?

Máire was scrabbling at the fabric of her dress trying to reach into her pocket – for the flask she kept there that was small enough to spit into without making a fuss, or for her handkerchief – but before she could, a spout of blood burst from her mouth. She put her hand up to try to hold it.

"Mammy!" Peg cried, rushing to catch her. She steered her towards the armchair, snatching a tea towel off the chair at the same time and pushing it into her mother's trembling fingers.

Her father stood, helpless.

"Get water, Daddy."

He turned to do it while Peg held her mother's shaking frame. The eruption had eased the cough and the worst of the shock was subsiding. The scarlet stain screamed out of the grey towel. Máire tried to fold the fabric so it couldn't be seen.

As soon as her control returned, she pulled away from Peg.

"I'm...all...right," she said. She tried to smile, unaware of the blood smearing her teeth and the ghastly look it gave her. Peg wanted to turn away from the sight of it. "Your...meeting..."

"Never mind the meeting." Peg took the glass of water from JJ, held it to Máire's shuddering lips. "Can you stand at all? Can you get up the stairs, do you think?"

Using the arms of the chair to lift herself, Máire moved to put weight on her feet. From the shop came the sound of a sharp rap-rap-rap on wood, followed by a yell: "Anyone at home?"

In the agitation, they had forgotten all about the customers.

JJ stood transfixed, like he was the one stricken and Peg saw that it was going to be up to her to take charge. "Daddy, go out and serve whoever needs serving. Then see who you can send for the doctor."

Máire tried to protest. "No...need for a doctor."

"We're getting the doctor, Mammy, and that's that." She turned back to her father. "As soon as they're looked after, come back in here to me. I'll need your help to carry her upstairs."

Máire opened her mouth to object again. JJ dithered, to see what she'd say.

"Quick, Daddy," said Peg. "Go on. What are you waiting for? Go."

So there they were, catapulted into the next stage of Máire's illness. It wasn't that she hadn't coughed up blood before, they all knew she had. They knew she had been losing weight and that she'd been struggling for months with a continuous secrecy and each morning, for months, had broken with the sound of her raucous, distinctive cough. Now even JJ was going to have to admit the truth of what was happening. After months of circling around it, of never saying certain words aloud (they might as well say them now: TB, tuberculosis, consumption, phthisis, the white plague...), of making small advances and retreats from the edge of all that it might mean, the illness had reared up and insisted they face into it.

After getting the patient up to bed, and admitting Dr Lavin, and listening to his diagnosis and administering his prescription, and seeing Máire off to sleep, Peg and JJ – and later, after he came home from his match to be told the news, Barney too – did what everyone usually does in the face of death: they kept life going. Peg, her Cumann na mBan meeting now unfeasible, cleaned the kitchen and, while she was at it, gave the back pantry a good going over.

JJ tended to the customers and, when Pats came in, spent an hour with Barney in the bottling store, filling bottles of stout from the big vat, stocking up for the weekend rush. And Barney, as well as helping his father by putting the caps on the bottles and sticking on the labels, also, finally, fixed the brakes of his bicycle.

All the things Máire would have had to nag them to do if she was in the whole of her health were done without having to be asked and without complaint.

Máire's eyes flickered open. Half-caught in a dream about her Aunt Hannah, her father's sister who, years and years ago, lived in their house at home on the mountain. In the dream, she was a child, light as air, helping Auntie Hannah with the hanging of clothes in the back yard, picking pegs out of a bag and handing them up to her, as she used to do. For a moment, she lay prone and confused in a dusky room, unsure of where she was.

Turning her head towards the light of a candle, she found her daughter sitting on a chair, sewing, a basket of mending beside her. Then it all came brimming back: she was at the end of her life, not the beginning.

When Peg saw her move, she laid down her work. "You're awake, Mammy. How are you feeling?"

"All right. Better for the sleep."

"Are you hungry? I've made some soup."

Soup? The thought of it turned her stomach. It had been months since she knew what hunger was. It was the way with her always now, to be neither hungry nor full.

"Maybe in a while."

The blinds were pulled, but she could see it was dark outside too. "What time is it?"

"Nearly nine."

"I've slept for hours."

Peg nodded. "Are you sure I can't get you something? You really should eat."

"Is Barney home?"

"He is. Do you want him?"

"No. No, just wondering."

The way you always wondered, even when they were great strapping lads of twenty-two. Soon, she wouldn't be here to wonder. She knew it and was not fooled by the evasions of Dr Lavin this afternoon. The black knowledge that she was going to die reared up in her and she gagged on it.

Sweet Jesus. Almighty and Everlasting God, preserver of souls...help me. She clutched the two sides of her bed like she was adrift on a raft. Help me. Mary, Queen of heaven, most blessed virgin, holy Mother of God, help me. In the blood of Jesus, in thy intercession, is my only hope. My life is over. Over though it feels like it hardly started. Over. Help me Holy Mary to deal with that.

She started to recite prayers inside her head to try to bring calm. An Our Father, a Hail Mary, a Glory Be. She fixed on the rote, familiar words, using them to drive other thoughts away. It worked, her panic subsiding enough for her to lie there without screaming.

In the clearing of her mind, something began to niggle at her. Then she remembered, and was glad of the distraction: "I'm sorry," she said to Peg. "For the way I was with you earlier."

"Oh Mammy, stop. No bother."

"No, I am sorry, Peg. It's foolish anger that gets me that way sometimes."

Anger at my sickness, anger at God, anger at everyone who's well, everyone who doesn't yet know what it's like to wake in the morning walloped by a black wave of nothing. To inhale the ash-grey, sour-water taste of death with the opening of your eyes.

"No one could blame you, Mammy."

She was a good girl, Peg, the one the other two would rely on now, while thinking themselves in charge, the way men do. It was wrong of her to get irritated with her the way she did, for no good reason. Maybe that was the way a mother always felt about a daughter: a bond too close for ease.

Or was that just her, not able to get it right, not having known a mother herself? Her own died the day she was born, died in the having of her. Was that why her feelings for Barney had always been easier, even these days when he was acting as though her condition was a personal insult to himself?

Yet a daughter was someone you could talk to and she was gripped with the need to talk, while she still could.

"I hated this place when I came here first. I never told you that, did I, Peg? When we came home here after our honeymoon in Killarney, every customer in the place was lined up along the counter to have a look at me. I was only eighteen and I found it awful hard. Only eighteen, younger than you are now. That's why they were so curious, your father being so much older."

It had always stayed with her, the way their male eyes had all harboured the same low thought, their curiosity like another body following her around all through those first weeks. "They could be as ignorant as they liked to us but I had to have a smile for all and never let on what I really thought about any of them. You know how it is, you've grown up with it, but I had never set foot in a pub in my life."

"It must have been hard, all right."

"I had to learn everything. But I did learn. I kept my side of the bargain."

"Bargain?"

"A marriage is a bargain, isn't it?"

"I suppose." Peg looked pained, wearing the face she used to make as a child when you'd give her her cod-liver oil. Oh, young ones and their notions. She hardly expected her mother and father to be a pair of turtle doves, did she?

What sort of a face would she make if Máire was to tell her that she had spent the first months of her marriage making lists in her head of all the things she hated about her new husband, this old man who up to then had been nothing to her but her own father's oldest friend?

A fine lengthy list it was too: the pink scalp that beamed through the combed-across streaks of his papery hair; the explosion of red veins across his nose and cheeks; the long, yellowing teeth, his breath blowing hot and stale between them; the fuzz of grey hair like moss across his chest; the bulge in his long-johns like a small animal curled up between his legs; his toenails, thick and tough as bone...

What if she was to tell her daughter that for years she was haunted by the image of the two men shaking hands over their deal, as JJ had told her they'd done? If she told her that he himself knew she had been wronged? That as she was passed to him at the altar, he wasn't able to look her in the face, wasn't able to raise his eyes any higher than her eighteen-year-old neck?

If she told her that a year into their marriage, she went to a priest in town about it?

"Does your husband mistreat you?" he'd asked.

"No, Father."

"Is he perhaps too fond of the drink?"

"No, Father."

"A gambler?"

"No, Father."

"Have you any complaint against the man?"

I can't bear him to touch me, Father. I can't bear the touch of him.

But how could you say the like of that to a priest?

What if she were to tell that after she became pregnant with her, Peg, she had turned her back on him, only allowing him the run of her one more time, when she wanted a second child?

And what, oh what, if she was to tell her daughter of the flirtation she ran herself into with Billy Ffrench, one of the customers, a fascination that nearly ruined them all, only Lil Hayes pulled her back from the brink? Young Billy, wiry as a whippet. Nothing special to look at, with a face that looked like nothing as much as a skin-shrouded skull, but very tall, with a certain strange presence. And young.

Young.

One day she found herself wondering what it would be like to have someone like him kissing you, putting his hands on you, and once the thought had been allowed, she couldn't rid herself of it. After a while, she didn't even bother to try; it gave her solace. After another while, she found that she was going over to him whenever he was in the shop, leaning into the counter to have a laugh and a joke.

Harmless, she'd told herself. She was just being agreeable the way JJ explained you had to be with the customers, but she knew it was a lie and that the truth was Billy coming into the shop more often, his eyes skimming the counter to see if she was there, an echo of her own eyes scanning the place whenever she came through from the house. Soon they were the butt of talk. Trouble so distressed her husband that now it was she who wasn't able to look at him straight — but on she went, making a fool of herself for the bold Billy.

Until word of the carry-on got back to his father.

The night Mr Ffrench heard what was going on he beat Billy with the leg of a kitchen chair, beat him until every part of his body except his face and hands, was a bruise. Beat him and then forbade him from going "next, nigh or near Parle's" until he had sorted matters out.

It was her friend Lil Hayes who told her what had happened, not Billy himself. Lil was kind about it, in her straightforward way, kinder than any other woman in the village would have been, but blunt. Told her straight out that she had been a fool, that every man in the pub, every woman in the grocery and others too who never came near the place were talking about her.

Maybe the priest. Maybe even her own father, above on the little farm towards the mountain had heard. It was altogether possible that word had stretched that far.

Nothing had happened between them, she told Lil. "Even bigger fool you, then," was Lil's reply.

And nothing had, nothing more than their hands touching for a second too long when she'd be giving him back his change. For that, she had thrown away her reputation because once there was talk, people always thought the worst.

It was as if that conversation with Lil tore a film from her eyes; everything afterwards looked different. Her admirer did what his daddy told him to do, got engaged, then married, and never came near her with a sincere word again. She saw that he had little real feeling for her, that the thrill for him had been in having a woman, a good-looking woman and a married woman at that, making it obvious that she had a fancy for him. He had loved not her, but the winks and nudges of the other men.

It was the lowest point for her, lower even than her engagement, or the black hours of her wedding night. She took to her knees. Weeks and months she spent praying, asking God to show her how to live, how to make amends, how to do right. And, in time, her prayers were answered. She came to understand her flirtation for what it was, a foolishness born out of resentment for her situation. Weakness might have made her consent to this marriage her father forced on her but now she came to believe that the way to show strength was not by resistance but resignation.

She didn't stop sleeping with her back to her husband but, in every other way, she struggled to accept her lot. Rearing two children, looking after the house and doing her share in the shop would be enough for most women to be going along with but she also started to take an active part in the movement that was shaking up the country, her generation's response to the ancient problem of English rule in Ireland.

Now she looked across at Peg, whose head was bent over her mending. "He let me do what I needed to do," she told her. "That was the best thing about your father. He didn't push his will on me. On you children either."

Peg lifted her head and nodded. Go on, her eyes said. Tell me. "He hated it when I joined Sinn Féin. He didn't mind the work for the Gaelic League so much. Teaching Irish-language classes was one thing but canvassing for the new political party, that was quite another, he being Irish Party himself.

"As for encouraging Barney to go raiding the farmhouses for guns, or training you into Cumann na mBan work – well, you know yourself how he hated that. But he let me off.

"Only one time, when I took money out of the leather purse under the floorboards unknown to him, to buy Barney a Webley rifle, did he lose his temper with me. And he was justified in that. It was wrong of me but our boy had to have a good gun if the others were to look up to him as they should."

It was JJ's shame at what had been done to her at eighteen that made him acquiescent, that was another thing she didn't say to Peg. Neither did she explain how the work she did for Ireland restored her self-respect after that misguided business with Billy Ffrench, gave her back some pride in herself.

Those years as the impossible unfolded into reality and the English were put on the wrong foot, were the best years of her life. On the day that Barney was sent to an English jail with Dan O'Donovan, she came back to Mucknamore from Wexford town and went on her knees to God. With the sound of tin-drummers and the shouts of rioters ringing in her ears, with a bruise on her chin from where she had caught a flying police baton, she had made straight for the chapel to kneel and give thanks to God that her struggle to accept had not been in vain. Through her son, and her own efforts, something greater than herself was born.

What she never foresaw that day — now almost a year ago —

when Barney was dragged off in handcuffs was that he might need more than ever to be kept on the right track after he came out. Half of County Wexford might think him a hero but she was his mother and she knew the truth: he wasn't nearly clear enough about how this Treaty was a betrayal.

Peg had a much better grasp of the principles. "I need you to speak to Barney," Máire said to her now. "His thoughts are everywhere but where they should be."

"So you have noticed, Mammy. I didn't like to say."

"I think he might be suffering for love."

"Love? Really?" Peg looked at her over her darning, eyes popping to hear her mother use this word.

"Maybe I'm wrong but I believe he has a fancy for Norah O'Donovan."

Had Peg really not noticed? Too caught up in her own fascination for the brother, maybe. Neither O'Donovan appealed much to Máire and she cursed the day they arrived in the village, setting hearts a-flutter.

Oh, she could see why her children were impressed: all that family had the looks. The girl Norah was like something in a picture and as for her brother, with his jaunty walk and talk… what young girl wouldn't be dazzled?

But young O'Donovan was inclined to make little of those who hadn't his brains or advantages: she had seen him have a go at poor Tipsy Delaney more than once, flattening him with a fancy phrase. He was the kind who'd use a rock to smash a fly instead of swatting it away.

"Norah's father is very strict," Peg was saying. "Then again, he can hardly expect her to stay single forever. She won't say a word against him, though. She's very private about things like that."

Máire could see Peg had the idea of Norah and Barney well turned over in her mind. Time to put a stick in their spokes. "I don't think she's the right girl for your brother," she said.

"Really? Why not?"

"Those O'Donovans are too cocky altogether."

"Ah no. You couldn't say that of Norah. Dan, maybe. But not Norah."

The foolish girl blushed every time she said his name.

"Peg, there's a copybook and pencil above there on the shelf. Will you take it down for me?" Peg laid down her mending, did as she was bid. "I'd like us to make a list of those who are likely to stay sound in the weeks ahead. Forget the flag-waggers and the would-be warriors, think on those who were with us in the hard times."

"Tipsy, Lama and those?"

"Go through them," Máire said. "I'd say you're right that the White boy is firm. And the Moran boys I'd nearly swear on. The three Fortunes. The Leacys. Jamsie Crean. Jack Kelly. The Connicks. And you think young Delaney?"

"Tipsy? Definitely."

"It's just he's such an eejit sometimes. He could be talked into anything. Though I suppose," Máire arched an eyebrow, "he listens to some more than others."

Peg was writing the names, allowing her to ignore that jibe.

"The O'Donovans?" Máire then said, lightly. This was the real question, the one she'd been building up to. "Dan and his sister?"

"They're staunch."

"You're sure?"

"I was only talking to Norah last night. As staunch as ourselves."

"And her brother?"

"Of course, Mammy. You know he was the most fervent of all."

"John O'Donovan had been making ratification speeches all round the village since the day we heard the word Treaty."

"We're not going to start judging men by their fathers, I hope." If they did, where would she and Barney be? Wasn't JJ himself less than eager?

"Let's hope you're right," said Máire. "O'Donovan is a sharp lad, if not quite as sharp as he thinks he is."

"He's an asset all right." Peg couldn't keep her face from rising red.

"I just wish he'd be a bit more respectful."

Barney was captain of Mucknamore Company when Dan arrived to live in the village from Cork but by the time they were sent to prison, Dan had almost usurped the leadership role.

In fairness to the chap, it was not a deliberate appropriation, more a consequence of their two natures. Though he was a stranger, the other boys instinctively gave him a grudging regard. A regard of a different sort to that given to Barney, which had more to do with the Parles' social position in the village and him being such a good hurler. "He'd take more than a few with him if he went."

"Went where?"

"Joined the Green and Tans." This was the name true Republicans had put on the new Free State army that was in the making.

"Dan? Never!"

"I'd like to think not, a ghrá, but I fear anything might happen now our principles are being watered down."

"It seems to me there's as many opinions on the Treaty as there are people to have them. And even if we do differ on some of the details…well, we can agree to differ, can't we? They are our friends. And we're all Republicans, that's the important thing."

"That's what I'm trying to tell you, girl. Anyone can call themselves a Republican but if this Treaty carries, the Republic dies." Máire pulled herself up in the bed, holding her breathing steady against a paroxysm she could feel forming inside, crawling up her windpipe. "You can't be for the Treaty and for the Republic as well."

"Ah Mammy, that's not –"

"It is that simple, Peg. You mark my words. Watch how it unfolds now in the weeks to come."

She broke into a cough, discharging her beyond talk, beyond thought even, or any thought other than getting back out of the spasm's malignant clench without too much damage done. It took her longer and longer each time, now, and after it was past, she was left fractured and scattered on her pillow. Knowing next time, it would take longer again, and so on, and on, until the time would come when she'd reach in vain, grasp for a settling, returning breath that would not come.

"I want to see this Treaty defeated," she declared, as soon as she could trust her lungs again. She said it loud and clear into the darkening room so Peg could not misunderstand.

The way she said it stopped the girl in the act of biting a thread, made her look up with eyes full of what was not being said. But why keep it unspoken? It was too important. "I want to leave something worth leaving behind me."

"Ah, Mammy. Don't."

"We'll say no more. But I can count on you? To keep up the struggle and the work? To fight for the Republic, no matter what?"

Peg leaned across to her, fervent. "You know you can, Mammy. Of course you can. Of course."

1968

My birthday, ten years old. For the first year in my memory, Mrs D. hasn't baked a birthday cake. When I come home from school, in the place of my favourite home-made chocolate sponge is a square, shop-bought, fruit cake. She has slathered some icing across the top as a disguise and stuck in ten candles but I recognise it: O'Connor's Fruit Cake, which we eat often, with the chewy raisins and the plastic red cherries like clown's noses cut in half.

She is sitting at the table with Gran, half-smoked cigarettes squashed into zigzags in the ashtray in front of her. I suppose she hasn't baked because she hasn't the heart for it.

That's what she says about everything these days. Some mornings she hasn't the heart to get out of bed. When she is up, she doesn't bustle and boss, but stays hunched over the ashtray, her eyes a world away. Everybody is kind to her. Gran and Eileen cover her hours in the shop. She has flu, the men in the pub, the women in the grocery, are told.

Yesterday Granny Peg told her that people are starting to suspect. "You'll have to put your face out there," she whispered, glancing across at me doing my homework by the fire in case I'm listening. I keep my eyes on my books. "Otherwise, what's the

point in trying to get him back before anyone's the wiser?" Gran
says. "You might as well write it up on the walls for all to see."

Mammy tries: plucks up a face, plasters on a smile, takes it
out to the shop. Later I'm out there myself getting milk and Mrs
Cummins is in the grocery, telling her how great it is to see her
about again. "Flu, was it?"

Mammy agreed that it was.

"It must have been a bad dose." Mrs Cummins' eyes are
flecks of bone. "To have you missing Mass."

A terrible dose, Mammy agrees, holding up a small red
notebook. "You'll want those -" she points to the groceries on the
counter – "in here, I suppose?"

Mrs Cummins nods, slapped back into place by her debt.

In the shop, Mammy keeps up her front, but in the house her
gloom is thick and sour and dumped all over us.

"That's a lovely birthday cake," I try now, coming into the
kitchen and sitting down beside them. "Thank you, Mammy."

She rolls her eyes. "Why did I ever bother baking a proper
one for her before? She doesn't even know the difference."

I cannot win. To punish her, I say: "Will Daddy be home for
my party?"

"No, your daddy's away."

Can she really believe that I have not noticed days of red eyes
and snuffly noses and cloudy whispers steaming out under the
kitchen door?

I make my voice clean of knowing, ask: "Will he be here
later on?"

"No."

"When, then?"

"Ask no questions," she says, "and you'll be told no lies."

"Tell me," Gran puts in, "you didn't happen to see my
scissors, did you? I've been looking for them all day."

If they were not so busy covering up, they would see through
my questions. Why should I suddenly expect Daddy to be at a
party of mine? He never was before. My party is unlikely to

attract him; always a slack affair, not really a party at all. Just Coke with my dinner instead of milk and an overdose of sweets from the shop afterwards. Then Mammy lighting the candles on the cake and Gran shouldering her and Auntie Norah through 'Happy Birthday To You' and 'For She's A Jolly Good Fellow'. Just the four of us, nobody else. Same as last year, and the year before.

I never bring anybody from my school to the house. Nobody wants to come, and anyway, to bring someone here and let them see how we live: it would be like handing bullets to your own firing squad. What if Mammy flared into one of her tempers? What if Auntie Norah took off her underwear like she did the other day? It stopped me in the hallway, her panty girdle and skin-coloured stockings bent right and left across the floor like a pair of fractured legs, her underpants open to the world, showing a stain. Yellow water oozed across the tiles and I knew what had happened just by looking at them. She had had one of her accidents and walked away, pretending it hadn't happened.

I wanted to slink off too, but I was afraid for Auntie Norah in case it might not be Gran who found her leavings. So I got the rubber gloves and picked up the hateful underclothes and dumped them in the wash. I wiped the mess with a cloth that I put into the bin when I'd finished. I made it like it never was and didn't tell anybody about it, not Maeve, not Gran.

I hate our life. I miss Daddy. No matter how hard I listen at doors I cannot find out where he is or why Mammy thinks he's not coming back. I miss him but I don't blame him for going. I know what drove him away.

I am walking out The Causeway towards Coolanagh. Ahead are three other girls my age, two from Mucknamore – Mary Cummins and Sally Rowe – and the other is Louise Farthington, home on holidays from England. The desirable one, the one we all want.

Our hands are full. Louise and Mary and Sally each carry a long stick but they have made me carry a heavy stone. A rock.

This is my punishment, though I'm not exactly sure what I am being punished for. These girls are my new friends. My friends.

Though Louise's mother is from Mucknamore and her father from Donegal, she was born and lives in London. Her skin seems softer and whiter than ours, her hair glossier, her accent shinier. She calls her mother Mummy and makes ordinary things sound fancy with her way of saying them: caah for car, ba-nah-nah for banana; hat and tomato with the 't's clipped tight. Louise's school has uniforms and bells, assemblies and school dinners, a PE hall and a headmistress, just like the schools in the Mandy and Bunty comics we all read. Everything about her is dazzling.

Mary won't admit this. She and Sally jeer Louise's way of talking. "Very lah-dee-dah," Mary says, but still she has taken her away from me. Louise was mine first. Her grandmother is Mrs Redmond, my mother's friend, and she was happy to play with me until Mary and Sally came along. Now the three of them have me under orders to stay back, ten paces or so behind, carrying this stone. Louise's long dark plait swinging against her spine as she walks makes me ache.

The sands around Coolanagh is our destination. The sticks are for poking, the stone for sinking. This has been our craze for days: investigating the sinking sands. Our experiments are teaching us the character of the place: that the sands are erratic; that a heavy stone will sink in a certain spot one day but stay on the surface there the next. Each time we talk about going out further and testing more, but in fact we cling close to The Causeway. We are not as brave as we pretend.

I hold the stone as if it's a baby, cradled in one arm supported by the other. My muscles ache from its weight so I have to keep changing arms. Up ahead, I can hear Mary explaining my inadequacies to Louise in words that are really aimed at me: "just not good enough", "giving her too many chances..."

Foul glances are torpedoed back at me, over their shoulders. The day before yesterday the problem was the way I walked ("the state of her, like Quasi-bloody-modo"). Yesterday, it was something I said. ("No, we won't tell you what it was. You can just think back and work it out for yourself.")

It seems especially unjust that they are mean to me here, when it was my idea to go out to Coolanagh in the first place. I told them the stories about it, the stories Gran told me — about a bad man who met his deserved end out there, confessing to all his sins as he went down. About a woman who was too fearful to go to the aid of someone in trouble out there, and never had a lucky day after. About the special liugh that people are supposed to send up if they go astray out there, a particular shout for the purpose, high-pitched and staccato, that everybody recognizes, so that anyone passing on The Causeway knows the meaning of it and comes to help. About the ghosts of such screams that can be heard echoing through the night, when the wind blows a certain way.

Coolanagh belonged to me while I was telling them those stories. Now it is theirs, the backdrop to my torment. Halfway out the Causeway, the three of them stop, turn to face me.

"Can't you keep up?" says Mary. "Why are you so slow?"

"It's heavy," I say.

"It's heavy," she mimics. "Of course it's heavy. It's a rock, isn't it?"

"She doesn't want to keep up with us," says Sally. "She thinks she's too good for the likes of us."

"You're right, Sal. She thinks she's better than us but we know the truth, don't we?"

I protest. "You were the ones who told me to stay behind y—"

"The Devereuxs think they're something but everybody knows what they really are."

"Except her."

"She's so stupid she doesn't even know that."

I look across at Louise, who is appalled and fascinated.

"But we all know, don't we, Mary?" Sally looks across to Mary for approval.

"You don't know the half of it, Sal," Mary says.

Sally bites her lip. Mary always does this, has to be the best of the bunch.

"I do so," Sally says.

"I bet you don't."

"What? What don't I know?"

"I can't say," Mary replies, narrowing her eyes at me and shaking her head with pretend sorrow. "Sorry Sal, you're too young."

Louise's eyes shine wide with curiosity. Something real lies under the jibes, it seems. "Tell me, then," she says. "I'm older than Sally."

"I might tell you sometime," says Mary.

"Why not now?"

"You'd never talk to her again, that's why. Isn't that right, Jo? We shouldn't even be talking to you, should we?"

A few days later, Mary suggests we should go further, to the other side of the island to examine the stream that runs there into the sand. Fairies are supposed to live in the water under the rocks. Tiny fairies, impossible to see unless you get down close enough and are really lucky.

We walk all the way out. I am wary of them now and I no longer believe in the picture we make, four friends walking out to Coolanagh together, but still I'm glad to be seen with them. On the island, Mary leads the way to the stream, and we lie beside it staring into the water. Mary lifts a rock and Sally shouts out, "They're there. Look."

"Oh my God, Sally," cries Mary, excitement jumping from her. "You're right. Can you see them, Jo?"

Is she serious? Fairies don't seem like Mary's kind of thing but her face is all puffed up with delight.

"Look, Louise, look. We're after finding them."

"That's super," says Louise, but she stays where she is, lying on her back, her eyes closed to the sun.

Mary whispers in my ear. "Are you able to see them? Look closer. Look now or you might never get the chance again."

Stones and silt and plants swaying in the water. She points, at what seems to me like tiny blobs of black. Dirt maybe? Or some tiny form of water slug?

"I can't believe I'm actually seeing fairies," she says. "Can you, Sal?"

"I can't. I really can't."

"Janey Louise, would you get up off your bum and come and have a look?"

"It's all right. I don't need to see them."

"But it's beyond all, isn't it, Jo? Louise should come and look, shouldn't she?"

I decide to join in. "You really should, Louise. You won't get a chance to see something like this again."

Louise says, "Oh, Mary, give it a rest. You don't really believe in fairies. You're just trying to trick Jo."

Mary looks at her through slitted eyes and I feel a sinking in my gut. Why did I pretend? Why, why, why?

"Or perhaps you do?" Louise says with a laugh. "Perhaps you think they're leprechauns?"

Now it's Mary's turn to be stung. She takes a step back to stand between me and Sally and says: "We don't want any English bitch coming over here to laugh about leprechauns, do we, girls?"

Louise sits up, shocked. A word like that would never be allowed to cross her lips. Mary decides to hurl another bad word at her. "Why don't you fuck off back to England with yourself? We don't need any English lah-dee-dahs here."

I look at Louise, her eyes swelling wet with offence and hurt, and I am glad. She did nothing to help me: she only told about Mary and the fairies because she didn't want to get up, not because she cared about me. Now it is her turn to suffer and I rejoice.

It doesn't last. Next day, I'm in the wringer again. Louise cries too easily and is too likely to tell. Louise's mother would not stand for anybody giving her girl a bad time. She would bring it into the open, tackle Mary and Sally's parents, get them punished. I am safe. I take what they dole out and wrap it up inside.

Louise goes back to England and the other two stop calling for me. I feel myself dimming in their eyes. Even bullying me isn't interesting enough to hold them. All that summer I feel something leaving me, draining out of me, like water down a plughole.

Back in school in September, Mary tells everybody that I believe in fairies. I have never been popular but now the others sense a new weakness and round in. Mary leads the pack, guides the moves. Water is poured into my schoolbag, ink onto my hair. My books are scribbled on with indelible marker. I am held down behind the bicycle shed and the boys are lined up to look at my knickers.

Each evening, I am first out of school, like a hare out of a trap as soon as Mr Walsh says we can go, but a hare who must appear to dawdle. The five-minute walk home is torture, with what feels like the whole school behind, firing jeers and occasional pebbles. Aching to run, I glue slow, indifferent steps to the ground. I bite the inside of my lower lip as I walk, a habit I have taken to. My teeth gnaw on the soft pink flesh until salty blood runs to the back of my throat. I swallow it down. Sometimes adults pass us on the road, see what's happening. We all — me too! — smile at them, as if it is a game. They are unconvinced but nobody does anything to help me.

Mammy is glad Mary and Sally have stopped calling for me. The Cumminses were never "in the book", she says, her phrase for respectable. "You were right to drop them," she says. "Why would you want to be going around with the likes of Mary Cummins?"

I think about telling Granny Peg, but tell her what? I have no bruises to show, no war-wounds to flaunt, and anyway Gran's days are full of trouble already, balancing Mammy and Auntie Norah. She knows I am not popular and she says it's because I'm too brainy, that the other children are jealous.

She gives me a saying: "Sticks and stones may break my bones, but words will never hurt me." It doesn't sound right but I try it anyway, hurling it at them one day, when they are doing their worst. They laugh it right back to me.

So I don't tell Gran, or anyone else, the things they do to me. A bunch of spiteful girls is all they are. I am shamed to silence by how much hurt I allow them.

Maeve comes home for half-term. "What's wrong with Mammy?" she wants to know, making new again what I have got used to: the scrunched-up eyes and jagged face, the lying in bed with the sheet pulled over her head like she's a corpse, the cigarettes half-smoked then crushed into little elbow-shapes, piling high in the ashtray.

"Daddy's gone," I say, "and she's broken-hearted."

It's Gran's word I use but it's not the right one. Mammy's sorrow is not pure like the princesses in fairy tales. It skulks around the house, claws curled in, waiting to pounce.

"Gone?" Maeve says. "What do you mean? Gone where?"

"Nobody is saying."

It feels good to have someone to tell. I know that once Maeve is back a while, we will be squabbling again but today, the first day of her holidays, we are almost friends.

"I don't think he's coming back," I say.

Maeve says I should know whether he is or he isn't. So should she, we have a right to be told. So we go to Granny Peg.

She laughs us off. "Not at all, Whatever gave you a notion like that? Of course he'll be back."

"Are you sure, Gran?" Maeve asks.

"It's been so long," I add.

"You know your daddy. Doesn't he always turn back up like —" She stops herself saying it. Like a bad penny.

"But when, Gran?"

"Soon, girls. I'm sure it will be soon."

"Very good," says the teacher as I write the correct answer on the blackboard. On the way back to my desk, I feel Mary Cummins's attention calling me. I try not to look and immediately regret it when I do. I pull my eyes from hers but too late to avoid her index finger pointing at me and jerking upwards to indicate that I am shot, and her malevolent lips blowing on the gun-barrel finger like a satisfied assassin. This is not just annoyance that I am able to solve the sum. She has some new taunt; it swaggers in her face. Daddy? All morning she keeps pointing back over her shoulder at me, miming my shooting with a sadist's smile. I sit on my own in my double desk, gnawing my inner lip, cutting through the healed-over scab with my teeth, reaching for the familiar.

I miss him badly now. Each morning I get up on my own, breakfast alone in the hush of the quiet kitchen, looking out to a distant grey sky pressing down on the distant grey sea. I wish he would come back for a little while. He could go away again, if that was what he wanted, but I wish he would just check in with us, bringing the glow of the outside world he always used to bring to the house. Mammy is too much for me, for us all, without him.

At break, Mary bears down on me with a gang of cronies behind her. Eyes swimming in their heads with excitement, they form a circle around me. I am backed up, hugging my ribs, against a wall.

"Her da's after leaving home," Mary tells the others, as if they didn't know. "Gone off with a fancy woman from the town."

I make my face blank to the sneers and staring wonder.

"Have you nothing to say for yourself? That's a mortal sin he's committed. He'll go to hell."

"You can hardly blame him, though, Mary," says Sally. "Who'd want to see that ugly mug sitting across from them at the table every day?"

Everybody laughs.

Silence is my only defence. If I don't speak, my voice can't tremble. If I don't shout, my face doesn't turn red. If I don't feel my feelings, my eyes don't fill.

Mary starts to sing, a song with the words changed, just for me. So tell me Jo Jo, when did you see your daddy do? And the others join in with a laugh-along routine they must have planned, maybe even practised. Daddy, daddy, do, do.

Little Jack Breen comes home for his holidays from Birmingham and tells everyone that he met Daddy, that he sees him often in the Irish club over there. He is with Mrs Larkin, except she calls herself Mrs Devereux now, and the two of them are living off the money she got from the sale of her pub. Living the life of Riley, if you want to ask Little Jack, going to race meetings and hotels and dinner-dances, out on the town every night of the week.

Each of the customers finds their own way of letting Mammy and Gran know that they know.

I am outside the front of the house collecting the milk when Bartie comes along with the post and gives it to me to bring in. Between the brown window-envelopes, there is a pale blue one that sticks out. The head of the English queen is on its stamp. I pull it up to the top, insides already churning, even before I recognise his writing.

Like a thief, I look around to see if anyone is watching me. I go round the back of the house where I can't be seen. I think about hiding it, steaming it open later like I have read about in books. I consider this for a long time, but in the end I slip it back into the middle of the pile and set out to find Mammy.

She is upstairs, making beds. "Post," I say, handing it over as if it were a normal bundle. I stay and watch as she files through them. She stops when she comes to it and flushes from neck to forehead, then looks at me, hard. I shrink from the slap that's certain now she's seen through me. The slightest thing these days brings on a slapping. Shoes abandoned in the living room:

Slap. Clothes not laid out on Saturday for Sunday Mass: Slap, slap. Spat-out toothpaste not rinsed off the wash-hand basin: Slap, slap, slap.

I point at the unmade bed. "Will I give you a hand?" I ask, wiping my face clean of anything but the willingness to straighten sheets and blankets.

"Since when did you turn into Little Miss Helpful?"

I cower but the blow doesn't come. She folds backwards so she's sitting on the bed, shrivelled into herself. "For the love of God, what are you trying to do to me? Are you trying to send me over?" she says, eyes splintered, shaky fingers clutching the blue envelope. "Get out, child. Go on, go."

Later, when she has gone into town to the cash-and-carry, a trip that always takes hours, I search for the letter. It's not in the desk in the living room where important papers are kept. Not in the kitchen drawer with the bills and notes and parish newsletters. Not in the little side locker beside her bed. I have to go to more secret places. Her underwear drawer. No. Beneath the account books in the sideboard where I once found a book of mine she had taken and hidden as a punishment. No. Under the mattress. Yes.

Under the mattress, out of its ripped-open envelope, lying flat and open. One sheet only, writing on one side. Blue ink. I take it to the bathroom, lock the door, sit on the lid of the toilet seat. For a minute I am blind, unable to see. Blackness floods in through my eyes, turning me cold all over. I shiver and my vision rights; I can read again.

It has no address or telephone number at the top. It says:

Dear Máirín,

You're to stop sending people after me because it will do no good. How you found out where I was, I don't know, but we can get lost again if that's what we have to do, go to Coventry or London or some place where there will be no tracking us down. We'll change our names if necessary.

What I'm saying to you is, sending people to see me will not change my mind and only wastes your money.

You must know by now that I took nothing with me. Everything I left behind is yours, for you and the girls. I hope some day you'll tell them I did that.

This is for the best, Máirín. You mightn't think so now but I'd say you will come to see it that way eventually.

Yours sincerely,

Christy Devereux

I read it and read it and read it again, until the words have parted from sense. Then I slip it, letter and envelope, back under the mattress just as I found them.

The knowledge of the letter follows me around all the time, summoning me to look again. Next day, while Mammy is in the shop, I take a chance and scurry up to her room, slide my hand into the chink beneath the soft mattress again. It is back inside its envelope, telling me that she too had had it out for another look. I read it again and find I know it, word for word, off by heart.

Next time I return, it's gone. My hand pats and rummages and feels around but comes out empty. For weeks afterwards I search the house, trying to find its new hiding place. If Mammy moved it because she suspected my investigations, she gives no sign. I search and search but turn up nothing. It's as if it never arrived, except for the words that are branded in my brain.

1922

*J*ig music skittered out the open windows and doors of Fortune's farmhouse, the tum-te-tum of Dandy Rowe's accordion chased by a couple of fiddles. The sounds came jumping down Rathmeelin lane to meet Peg, enticing her forward from the stillness she had stopped to savour. On either side of the lane, two hedges of shrubs and trees were coming into their spring flowering and the evening air was cool on her face and hands. A balm. She could feel something in her rising to meet its sweet solace.

For a moment she was confused by conflicting urges – to stop? To walk on? – then it came to her that she was in the middle of a perfect moment. She had the delights of presence here in the lane, with the ash and the sycamore and the yellow ribbons of primroses all along the hedge, their hearts yawning open. And ahead, the delights of anticipation.

For Dan had sent her a message by Molly Redmond, saying he hoped she'd be coming along to Johnny's shindig tonight. This, surely, was the sign she'd been waiting for, that they could now go public.

In Mucknamore, all the young people kept their love affairs hidden for as long as possible. In Mucknamore, love was a joke, a fever of delusion requiring vigilance from those who were not ailing. Otherwise it would surely lose the run of itself. Jeering and mockery was what awaited any couple revealing a fancy for each other, so a relationship had to be firm established before you admitted to it.

Norah and Barney had told nobody yet either. Barney would shout it from the chapel steeple if he was let but Norah, like her brother, was more set on keeping it quiet. Maybe it was a family thing?

But now, it looked like Dan was ready to make a statement. Peg surely was, now more than ever, what with all the political talk going around, arguments springing up, everywhere. If she and Dan were out as a couple, then Norah would surely follow and the four of them would be able to go where they wanted, at last. No more sneaking around or pretending. And politics kept in its place.

It was nearly a week since she'd seen him. Last Saturday night, he'd sent Barney up to her room to get her at two o'clock in the morning. She had snapped awake and, against her better self, dressed and gone, boots in hand, stockinged feet whispering across the creaky floorboards outside her parents' room, excitement cutting through her fug of sleep. Months it had been since she'd done anything like that. Life just hadn't been the same while he was away in that prison.

They'd walked out The Causeway to Lovers' Hollow, the spot on the Coolanagh side where there was a dip, like a giant hand had taken a scoop out of the earth. There, she'd let him kiss her. Her face hotted up now at the thoughts of it, the sour tang of stout on his mouth and the things she let him do...And, worse, that thing she did herself, without him even asking, without her even knowing such a thing could be done.

"Ohahh!" she groaned aloud, into the quiet of the lane-way, waggling her head to try and cast the memory out.

Tonight, she'd put everything right, so she would. She'd be full of possession, in charge of herself and so on, and he'd be impressed by her dignity. It was going to be a great night, so it was. The primroses were heralds to that. She could feel their own living essence, their nearness. "Glory be to God," she murmured, making the sign of the cross on herself and kissing her thumbnail. Then she skipped on to meet her evening.

The crowd was already spilling out of Fortune's house into the yard; their parlour, one of the biggest in the neighbourhood though it was, too small to hold all who had come for Johnny's American wake. Peg passed through the group, greeting as she went — "Hello Miley…Hello Cat…Lovely evening…Isn't it splendid…? Hello Jack…" — on through the kitchen, where Mrs Fortune sat weeping, surrounded by female relations and friends.

The big table was pushed to the side and all the chairs of the house were arranged in a circle around the edges of the room. On a high stool in the corner, Patsy Cogley played his squeezebox high on his chest, with Tipsy Delaney and Johnjo Gregg on two upside-down crates at his feet, bows bouncing across their fiddles.

Mrs Fortune and her girls were great cooks and they had gone all out for Johnny. A big ham in the centre of the kitchen table and, around it, plates of white and brown soda bread spread stacked into towers. On a side table set up for the occasion batches of square scones dotted with sultanas and the warm seedy cake that was Johnny's favourite, spicing the air so that everyone who passed commented on it. Dishes of butter and blackberry jam occupied the spaces between the plates. Also flowing was a plentiful supply of snuff and tobacco and, of course, drink. Stout and whiskey for most of the men and some of the women. For the others, the children and the Pioneers who'd taken the pledge of no drink, bottles of minerals and cups of tea.

The set was just finishing and the musicians were putting down their instruments for a few moments' rest. When he saw she'd come in, Tipsy Delaney stood up on his beer-crate and asked for a bit of hush. When they'd quietened down, he said, "Thank you ladies and gentlemen and now I'd like you to put your hands together, please, for this composition from our very own Peg Parle."

And what did they do only start up 'The Boys Are Coming Home', the ballad poem she had written when Dan and Barney were released from prison at Christmas, set to the tune of The Ballad of Father Grey. She couldn't have been more surprised, especially to see some of the others in the room who were reciting along, knowing all the words. They must have cut it out of the paper when it was published at Christmastime.

> *Hear the rousing cheers around us*
> *For the boys are coming home*
> *Mothers, sisters, sweethearts greet them*
> *The dear boys now coming home!*
> *And Erin's bitter story*
> *Of her fight so long and gory*
> *Ends in sunburst of bright glory*
> *For the boys are coming home!*

That homecoming night was the last time the whole village of Mucknamore had turned out for each other. A very different night from this: black dark and bitter cold, with frosted stars and a swollen moon dangling low over the railway station. She'd never forget that night, not if she lived to be a hundred. She could still smell the burning crackle and spit of the tar barrel and see the tricolour flags of green, white and gold hanging from windows and gables and lampposts all over the village, dancing in the orange light of the flames and making it feel like a different place, a brighter and altogether better place than their old Mucknamore.

Nothing showed how matters had changed in Ireland more than the show of support that night. When the light of the train carrying Dan and Barney had appeared under the bridge...oh, the entire crowd had gone wild, jumping and cuffing the air, waving little flags and hats and handkerchiefs, banging kettles and tins with spoons.

Sentiment had begun to change in the village after the 1916 uprisings in Dublin and Enniscorthy and had gathered more steam, especially among the young, during the Conscription crisis of 1918. But, even as late as this time last year, when Barney and Dan were convicted for their "crimes" of drilling volunteers, even as recent as that, you had plenty in the village who turned their backs. So many stopped coming into the shop that Daddy had worried for a time about the effect on business. Then all changed forever with the Truce.

"None of them ever thought that boys the likes of Barney Parle or Dan O'Donovan could bring the Great British Empire to its knees," Mammy had said. Well, it was hard to blame them, when the Parles could hardly believe it themselves. Wasn't it a miracle that a band of ordinary Irish boys with a stash of rusty guns were able to bring the greatest power on earth to a Treaty?

So the night they came home, even the elders turned out to honour that miracle. Even Mossie Whelan was there holding up a large framed picture of the Easter Rising men of 1916 and Mrs Whelan beside him holding a framed copy of their Proclamation: Irishmen and Irishwomen, In the Name of God and of the dead generations from which she received her old traditions of nationhood, Ireland, through us, summons her children to her flag and strikes for her freedom…And Mammy's friend, Lil, her apron on over her coat, unfurling a banner she'd been working on for weeks: "Welcome home to the Mucknamore prisoners" in green writing decorated with harps and shamrocks.

Oh, what a night. The verses they were reciting now in this room brought it all back. Dan and Barney up on the shoulders of the crowd, the band belting out 'A Nation Once Again' and everyone elbowing everyone else out of the way to stretch up and shake their hands. And herself going across to them and being welcomed like nobody else, Barney saying, "Here she is."

And Dan giving her his grin, and calling her "the woman herself'" as she stepped between the two of them.

She had taken that central place not as Barney's sister, certainly not as Dan O'Donovan's sweetheart, but as president of Mucknamore Cumann na mBan. It was respect for the job that fine organisation of women had done, in supporting Mucknamore IRA Company, that had them all listening to her on that night, gathered in a great circle around her.

"Before we go into the pub to celebrate," she'd said, "I'd just like to recite a short poem I made up for us to honour this occasion tonight. It's called 'The Boys Are Coming Home' and it goes like this…"

And it was the same respect that had them singing along those very words now, as Tipsy led them through it, all seven verses.

Then it was back to the dance music. As she made her way towards the food, she saw him up on the floor. Dan. Dan, who by his own admission had a pair of left feet, who never once could be coaxed up to dance with her, was there with a girl… with Miss Agnes Whitty, no less. Nothing untoward was passing between them. He was attempting to follow her directions for the dance and both were laughing as he exaggerated his blunders for her amusement. Oh, but Agnes Whitty, of all people. He surely knew that she was over the Wexford branch of the new women's organisation, and that she had written a letter to the paper condemning what she called the "wild and unwomanly ways" of Cumann na mBan.

Where was Norah? She needed Norah. No sign of her but Molly was waving from the far side of the room. She skirted around the edge to her, bypassing the food table but, as she approached, the zeal on her friend's face made her want to turn back. It was too late, so she allowed her arm to be pulled, endured the wet hiss of Molly's questions in her ear. Had she seen? What was he playing at? Agnes Whitty? What about him and Peg? Had they had a fight? Peg waved her hand to dismiss it all, trying furiously to remember how much she had said to Molly before. "I don't know what you mean. We're nothing to each other this long while now." She stretched her mouth wide into what she hoped was a smile.

"Oh, really?" said Molly.

"Yes. We never went back the same way after he was inside."

"So what was he doing sending you messages, then?"

"I don't know. Pulling the wool over your eyes, maybe?"

Molly looked indignant at this attempt to turn the tables. "You looked fairly surprised when you saw him with Her Nibs."

"Surprised?" said Peg. "Not at all. She might do for a bit of dancing but he'll find she and her like are not much use when it comes to the fight."

"A crowd of milksops," laughed Molly. "All Cumann na Saoirse girls are the same."

Peg had pulled her smile so wide she didn't know what to do with it. "Is Norah about?" she asked.

"She's not. I haven't seen her anyhow. But tell me—"

"Did you see Mrs Fortune on the way in? Isn't she in an awful state?"

Molly set upon on that subject as Peg hoped she would. "Oh, Lord, the poor woman. I was in the kitchen earlier. She's broken-hearted, broken-hearted. I don't think she'll ever get over it."

Johnny was his mother's favourite – everyone knew it – but even allowing for that, Mrs Fortune's distress over his going was considered excessive. For weeks now, she had been cracking into tears in front of anyone and everyone. Nobody knew what to be saying to her, for tomorrow, Johnny would be gone. He would take the train to Cork, then to Cobh, where he would board a ship, leaving behind this farmhouse and a future as flat and firm as a future could be, to switch to a new life, unimaginably different. His mother would probably never see him again but he had to go, even she knew that. The farm was Jem's, the eldest boy's, and there was no living for any of the other five sons. Pat, the second, was already at the seminary in St Peter's but the priesthood held no attractions for Johnny.

Hard to imagine him in big, bad New York all the same. It was said the winters there would freeze your blood to ice. That the tenements were worse crowded than the worst of Dublin's, with the Irish huddled together close as rats in a nest. That in the noise and rush, the poorest got trampled to death. Not that Johnny would be reduced to that level. Mary, his sister, who left four years ago, had sent across his passage money and had a job and a bed lined up for him. With that kind of assistance, Johnny could make something of himself over there.

Given the choice, here was where he'd stay, they all knew that. He wasn't one of those who were driven to get out, get up, get on. A few acres and his own girl and he'd be happy for life. All of which made the letting go of him harder. And so, an emigration wake, to honour their sorrow and their good wishes for his future.

"Miss Parle!" A booming voice behind interrupted them and Peg felt her back being slapped. "A cure for sore eyes to see you. We knew our humble festivities were lacking but now our evening is complete."

It was Jem Fortune, Johnny's eldest brother, a boy so smooth he'd plamás the teeth off a saw. Enjoyable to play along with, you'd never take him serious.

"He said the same to me earlier," said Molly.

"Ladies, ladies. Don't be getting particular on me. What's this I see? An empty fist, Miss Parle? Have those strawboy brothers of mine been neglecting you?"

This was Jem's way of asking would she like a drink. "I've only just got here, Jem. Have you a lemon soda?"

"Don't budge from where you're standing. It will be with you before you knew you wanted it."

The music stopped again to allow the musicians to take refreshment. Agnes and Dan retreated to the side. Peg could see them out of the side of her eye. Dan never looked her way once but Agnes, flushed with exercise and triumph, kept throwing looks over and one or two reached their mark.

Jem came back with the drink as Johnjo stretched out the squeezebox on a new tune, a reel. "Would you do me the honour of stepping it out?" Jem asked her. So she did, playing at smiling and laughing all through, as if she was having a great old time. When that set was over, Dandy took out his French fiddle and started up the plaintive old tune, 'Mary Browne's Favorite' by Carolan, usually a favorite with Peg too. But, tonight the melancholy pull of bow across string was like salt in a sore to her.

Her eyes went on a furtive search for him and found Isla Moriarty, from the town, talking to Agnes Whitty and Dan gone, nowhere to be seen. Gone out the kitchen door, probably, or else she'd have seen him go. And now that she thought of it, couldn't she do with a snack? One of Mrs F's nice seedy-buns?

She got up and edged her way towards the kitchen and, as she came in one door, he was nudging his way through those gathered at the other. Meant to happen. Looking backwards, crossways, any way but right at him, she made her way across through the clumps of bodies and only when he was almost flat up against her did she turn to face him. She tried to pack surprise, friendliness and nonchalance all into the one smile.

"The woman herself," he said. That was a good start, anyway.

"I need to talk to you," she heard herself say.

"You talk too much, woman. Has anyone ever told you that?" He said that bit loud, too loud, so others might hear. But he was smiling. "So out with it then, what sweet nothings have you for me?"

Sniggers seemed to rise behind the blank faces around them. Seeing her discomfort, Tipsy jumped in. "Don't mind him, Peg. He's had one too many."

"Mind him?" She crowed a disdainful laugh. "I'd as soon mind one of the little boys in school."

"Well, you're always saying how fond you are of those children." He leaned back on his heels, killed her with a slow grin. "Does this mean there's hope for me yet?"

While the others were laughing at that, he slid her a look that nobody else saw, that seemed to pierce through her skin to the sadness she'd wound her hopes around.

"Are you not listening to Gregg?" He inclined his head towards the parlour. "I thought you loved that auld banshee music."

"It's too sad for the night that's in it. With Johnny going so far away from us."

"Ah, yes. Johnny."

"I've known Johnny all my life," she said, tongue tripping over dry teeth. "No one would expect you to feel it the same."

He ignored this jibe. "Is Barney not coming down tonight?"

"He's working. He'll be along soon, I'd say."

A pause.

"What about Norah?" she asked. "I was expecting her to be here before me."

"Norah's not coming."

"She told me she was."

"Well, she's not."

And that was it. He turned away from her then without so much as a goodbye and headed back into the parlour. Back inside, to Agnes Whitty.

At two in the morning they were all still there. "The night's young yet," Jem Fortune kept saying, every time anyone looked like they might be thinking about taking their leave. Some, like Barney, had come along late, after the pub closed, and were only now getting into their swing. Others were too drunk to know where their homes were. Young Johnny had passed out on the floor and some wag had put his mother's hat, the one with the peacock feather, on his head. He'd be sick tomorrow for his travels but maybe that was as well.

The sing-song was starting up and Peg was still dancing and

making merry with the best of them, smiling, smiling. Lama kicked off the proceedings with 'Kelly the Boy from Killane'. Lama had a voice like an old jackdaw, but to his own ears he sounded good. Enniscorthy's in flames, he crowed, and old Wexford is won, the veins standing out in his high, balding forehead as he reached higher and louder. By the time he'd finished, he'd moved himself close to tears.

"Good man, Up Wexford."

"Let's have another Wexford one. What about 'The Boys of Wexford'? Come on, Denis."

That song was known to be Denis Mernagh's and he began it suddenly from where he stood, one elbow angled against the shelf.

'We are the boys of Wexford / Who fought with heart and hand / To burst in twain, the galling chain / And free our native land…'

Peg sang 'The West's Awake' and when the turn was Dan's, whose singing was no better than his dancing, he gave his recitation, 'Dangerous Dan McGrew'. It was new to some here and even if you'd heard it before, as Peg had, you'd enjoy again the way he performed it, speaking loud and soft, sometimes going fast, sometimes slow, pulling them in like a fisherman with a reel. At the end of each verse, all joined in the last line and the laughs and yelps increased as the silly story went on.

By the time he was finished, laughter was all over the room. Agnes Whitty's face was creased with pride as she joined in the applause, nearly clapping the hands off herself, looking up into his face as if she were his mother. "B'God," said old Nick Cummins, wiping his eye, "that was better than a play."

After the applause died, Peg called on Tipsy. "What about one of your Percy French's, Tipsy? The one about the motor car?"

She smiled across at him and, to her horror, saw him glance

from her to Dan. He knew. Somehow Tipsy knew, though she had done everything right all night, talking, singing, dancing and smiling, smiling, smiling until the back of her throat was sore.

And if Tipsy – a semi-eejit who didn't know what was what half the time – knew, that must mean everybody else did too. Behind her back, were she and Dan all the talk?

She should never have said anything about him to anyone. For so long, she had kept the thing quiet, then when he came back from prison, after all that waiting, he became too big for her to keep inside herself, so she told Norah more than she should and also some things, not as much, to Cat and even – God alive! What was she thinking? – a bit to Molly, knowing surely that if Molly Redmond had it, half the country would be in the know. All for the small pleasure of having his name in her mouth.

She was so tangled in thought that she barely heard what Tipsy had begun to sing, aware only that it wasn't a Percy French. Slowly, the atmosphere of the room began to penetrate, drawing her out of the gnarls of her mind. Faces all round around the room were tightening at what Tipsy was singing in his fine tenor voice, with greater gusto than usual:

...'Tis traitors vile who damn our Isle
Prolonging here the tyrant's sway
They've taken up the Saxon game
And keep its dirty rules in play...

These were new words to an old tune, indicting those who supported the Treaty. Such songs had been doing the rounds, whispered between those you could be sure were true Republicans but not, until now, sung out in this way. Sung into the faces of those who were known to favour the Treaty.

Dan and Agnes were by no means the only people with a leaning that way, but both had gone public: Dan in persuading the Mucknamore Brass Band to go into Wexford for the coming visit of Michael Collins to the town, Agnes in setting up this alternative women's auxiliary. So it was to the two of them that everyone turned, the whites of their eyes showing.

Dan was sitting forward in his seat, frowning. Miss Whitty looked like a turkey, Peg thought, her neck red-swollen with indignation.

…For filthy English lucre
They've sold their race and sod…

At this Dan jumped up. "You're going too far now, Tipsy," he shouted across the song. "You'd want to watch yourself there."

But Tipsy kept on singing to the end of the verse:

…They play the role that Judas played
When he betrayed his God.

When he finished, nobody clapped and the tick of the clock on the parlour mantelshelf could be heard.

Dead fury lined every letter of Dan's words when he finally spoke. "Who are you calling a traitor?"

"Ah, now, Dan, old pal," Jem Fortune said. "Take it easy there."

"It's only a song," someone else said.

A few other voices joined in the persuasion, telling him to calm himself, that no offence was intended but others, those who'd quite welcome a fight to finish off the evening's entertainment, said nothing. Tipsy's eyes were locked onto Dan's and not a sign of apology on him. Peg couldn't believe it of him. Usually Tipsy didn't know what to think, never mind what to do, until someone told him.

Agnes Whitty leaned across and tried to whisper in Dan's ear but he pulled away. "I'm not letting any fucker call me a traitor," he shouted and he jumped out of his seat at Tipsy and made a go at him. It was a drunken, half-hearted effort and easy for the other boys to hold him back.

"Let him go, lads," cried Tipsy, putting up his fists. "Let him go and let's have it out."

Dan pulled himself free of the hands gripping his clothes. "Twenty to one, is it?" he asked, looking into the faces gathered around him. He swivelled round to face Tipsy again. "When there was English soldiers to be fought, you weren't so quick off the mark."

Most of the room was already on Tipsy's side and this remark of Dan's put more over.

Barney said, "Steady on there, Dan."

But he was beyond calming. "That's it, back-clap each other. That's about all ye're good for around here." He blundered across the room away from them. In his anger, his Cork accent was very strong. "If you're all such great Republicans, how come when HQ had a job to do in Wexford, it had to be given to outsiders to do?"

"God, are you ever going to let go of that?" Barney said. "Just because the job went to a Corkman. We've heard you tell that one twenty times over."

"And I've not heard you answer it once. It's ye that are the traitors and ye haven't even the wit to see it."

Peg had to speak then, though her voice was shaking through the interjection. "Now look here, there are no Irish traitors in this room. You're right Dan, more could have been done – we can always do better – but even if we were not as active as fellows further west, we're every bit as keen...and is it not –"

"Keen now. Now it's too late. Now the fighting's finished."

"Ah, hold on. Wasn't Wexford one of very few counties outside Dublin which turned out for the Easter Rising in 1916?" she said.

That got a cheer from around the room. She could go on. She could ask him where the Cork boys were for that rebellion. Or go a bit further back and remind him of all the Boys of Wexford who died for Ireland in 1798. No county did better than Wexford in that revolt. Instead she said, in what she hoped was a unifying way. "We're all Republicans, Dan. That's what matters. Let's not allow ourselves to be divided."

She knew what others didn't. That he was not as defiant as he sounded. That he had been delighted by the turn of events in the past year, the opportunity that finally saw him accepted around here. He didn't want to be an outsider, though you wouldn't know it to look at him now, his face hopping out of his neck with belligerence.

He made a noise, something between a snarl and a sigh and then he turned and stalked off, leaving the door swinging open behind him. Every piece of her yearned to follow but instead it was Agnes Whitty who got up and click-clicked across the floor after him in her hard-nosed boots.

They left behind a second of pure silence, then Jem Fortune, with face and voice deadpan, said: "Who's been eating his porridge?"

Tipsy guffawed. Guilty laughter spread around the room. There was still no love lost for Dan among these people, her people. It wasn't only the politics. For some, it was probably no more than the fact that he was from County Cork, an outsider with a funny accent and a different way of looking at life, but not everybody was that closed-minded. Mainly it was that he didn't bother with the few soft words that made all the difference to people. He was a big man and he made smaller people feel their size.

It was like looking at the same scene painted by two different artists. Yesterday she saw people looking up to Dan, as a fighting man, as a man who made things happen; today she could see how that regard was tinged with hostility for many. Nobody had it in for him exactly, but nobody, not one person, not even Barney, was sorry to see him challenged. In the unity of the room Peg felt something close in around her, and she gave way to it, let it enfold her like a prickly blanket on a cold night, comforting and irritating, both at once. She thought of her bedroom, her bed with its white coverlet, her pillow soft and warm.

She said, "I think it's time we called it a night."

"I'll go with you," Molly said.

But Jem Fortune wouldn't let them. "No, no, no," he said. "The night's young, only a pup. You can't be going home yet, not until we get this bad taste out of our mouths. Tipsy, give us an encore there. Something a bit lighter this time. Something that won't drive any more guests down the road."

Tipsy started on 'Are You Right There, Michael?', Percy French's song about the West Clare railway. So Peg sat put for a while longer, thinking. She would pretend they fell out over Ireland. Tipsy's performance, by bringing that question out in the open, made it easier for her. Maybe he even did it on purpose? He'd love to play her Sir Galahad, she knew that. But he'd hardly have the wit to work it out, would he?

From across the room, he smiled at her through his song and she didn't know whether she should smile back or not. She hoped he wouldn't start mooning over her again, like he used to before Dan came on the scene. Fatigue was pouring through her limbs, hot and sticky, and she didn't know what was the right thing to do anymore. It was as much as she could manage to sit there and sing along with the silly chorus of Tipsy's silly song – "Are you right there, Michael, are you right?"

PEG'S DIARY 25TH MAY 1922: I never got such a fright as I did this evening with Norah. We spent the evening locked together in the grocery, having sneaked into the shop after it closed. She'd told her parents she was working late, which wasn't quite a lie – she was working, though not at her job in Furlong's department store as they would presume. Instead, she laboured for the cause we both hold dear, helping me to collate the new election leaflets that arrived in two big cardboard boxes this afternoon.

From the minute she arrived, she was jumpy, all "ssh" and "keep your voice down" and "Your mammy might hear".

Neither Mammy nor Daddy would dream of betraying her but she is more apprehensive than ever. In the pre-Truce days, when Dan – the old Dan, the loyal Dan – went public about his volunteer involvement, it led to the most dramatic fights in the O'Donovan house, the sort of hostility gentle Norah finds unbearable. Her dedication to Ireland's freedom was earnest but she kept it hidden in the shadows of Dan's rebellion. Now Dan is no longer of the same mind and she is going to have to make a stand for herself or give up altogether.

All those pre-Truce arguments her father had with Dan are now forgotten, "as if they never happened", she said. He's taken up the Free State cause as he once supported the Irish Party who kept things constitutional – which is to say, achieved little or nothing — for thirty years before the rising. Of course, his politics are really only self-interest, driven now as then by fears that instability might affect farm incomes. He's hardly alone in that. Most of those on the pro-Treaty side are thinking about commerce, jobs and the like.

Mrs O'Donovan is so delighted to see her husband and son getting on again that she's falling in with everything that's said and, with none of the younger children old enough to understand or care, poor Norah is isolated. She has to endure her father reciting the latest statement from Michael Collins like it's the word of God, when he once called him a guttersnipe and a corner-boy. Or, worse, quoting the latest opinion of her brother at her.

"I'm afraid I might explode into argument with him some day at the table."

"Maybe that would be the best thing you could do," I said. "You're twenty-two years old, Norah, not a child. You're entitled to your own mind."

"'Honour thy father and thy mother'," she said. "Isn't that what the priests say?"

"Oh, the priests. The priests say more than their prayers these days."

The hierarchy has spoken out against us again, urging the people to support the provisional government, until the outcome of the election is decided.

"Sooner or later, if you're determined to keep up your involvement, they'll come to know. All I'm saying is that sooner will be easier, for them as well as yourself."

As we talked, we collated leaflets into piles for delivery. We've been waiting for days for this new material to come from Dublin, ever since Michael Collins and Mr de Valera agreed the electoral pact. With this last minute agreement, Mr Collins has finally redeemed himself. Both pro- and anti- candidates will put themselves forward as Sinn Féin nominees, forming a coalition panel of candidates for the election who will form a coalition government afterwards. It's a sound move that will prevent the division that was setting into our ranks and we've had to rush through new leaflets that tell the people what to do.

The intention was that the latest leaflet should replace the first, but Mammy suggested we might as well distribute both together. The boys are also on election duty, going round the same houses with their guns on show, giving people a little "persuasion" in doing the right thing on voting day.

"Daddy says the pact is biased towards Republicans."

Oh, he would. You can be sure he won't be saying too much about the dirty dealings of the other side, refusing to update the electoral register that leaves me, and Norah, and Barney without a vote. No woman under thirty on it and no boy who attained his majority since the last register was drawn up. We were sick of talking about this unfairness and now we have a new grievance.

"Had he anything to say about them not publishing the Constitution of the new State yet, with the election nearly upon us? It looks like we'll be voting on a document we haven't even seen. Did he have anything —"

"I'm not arguing with you, Peg," Norah interrupted. "I'm

not defending Daddy and of course it's all wrong about the Constitution. As wrong as anything."

The tone of her voice snapped my mouth shut. I had been shouting without realising it and what was I shouting at poor Norah for? She was gripping the folded leaflet so tight her knuckles jutted out white. None of this was easy for her, especially confiding in me about her family.

"I know it's easier for me, Norah," I said, sifting out the words, as gentle as I could make them. "Our own father has never been too keen on our activities but – " I hurried on as I saw she was about to speak – "Barney and I have never had to face Daddy down because we've had Mammy to do it for us. Still and all though, I think you're going to have to face up to them. Don't misunderstand me, Norah. I know that's not easily done. We're girls, for God's sake, trained from the minute we're born to do what we're told. But I also know that doing what is right – no, don't look so stony-faced – doing what's right has a habit of making the unexpected happen. Look at what we have gained so far. We can gain much, much more if we hold onto our courage. I'm sure of it."

I did pause at that stage to let her respond. When she didn't, I went on. (Oh how I went on!) "The old have had it all their own way in Ireland for too long, Norah. That's why this country was so low for decades – the young people either having to emigrate or else be bullied by the older people into submission. All that is changing now. We've changed it, our generation. And we can change a lot more, if we hold onto what we know to be right."

"So I should go home tonight and just tell him my opinions?"

She looked at me as if the suggestion was that she should dance naked with the devil down the village street. "Knowing that there will be a storm, but knowing too that once they've finished huffing and puffing, you can get on with doing the work you want to do for Ireland. Yes, Norah, I think if I were you, that's what I'd do."

Norah let out a bitter laugh that hurt to hear. That's when I knew I'd done wrong. "Maybe if I were you, Peg, I might do the same. But we're not all the same in this world, however much we might wish to be. You can lift that bag of sugar over there with ease. I couldn't if I tried for a week."

She turned her eyes on me, two big jewels of green in a tiny skull that looked at me like I was some class of a dunce. "You can talk to your mammy and daddy. They look at you and they see Peg. Mine look at me and they see another O'Donovan, who does and says what O'Donovans are supposed to do."

I knew what she meant but I knew too that she was probably stronger than she believed. With courage, she could break that grip they had on her heart and soul.

"What if you weren't to think so much of your family? What if you think about your country?" I hesitated, but I had gone so far, I felt I might as well get it all out. "What about Barney?"

"Barney?" She stopped what she was doing. "What about Barney?"

"Norah, you know. Surely you must know."

"Do I? Oh God, do I? I suppose I do."

I thought that was a strange thing to say and I think that I knew, by then, from the look on her shrivelled face and the way her fingers were twisting each other crooked, that I might be going too far. But on I went again. "Norah, have you any time for him at all? I only ask because he has it bad for you, so bad. If he's wasting his time, you should tell him. Really you should because....Oh, Norah, I'm sorry, stop. Don't cry."

Norah burst into shuddering tears. 'Peg, I don't know...I just don't – I don't—"

"Oh, don't cry, Norah. Don't. I'm so sorry."

"It's not you...You're right. Everything...you say...is right."

I put my arm around her, feeling terrible. "Here. Take this." I pressed a hanky into her trembling hands and she buried her sobs in it. When she recovered a little, she said in a voice washed empty, "You're right. I'm a coward."

"That's not what I said."

"That's what it amounts to…And you're right, you're right."

I knew then that I wasn't. Who could say what I'd be like if I grew up in Norah's house? Bolstering her is what I should have been doing, not making her feel worse than she felt already.

"Look, Norah, forget what I said. Only you know what's right for you."

"Me? Stupid, useless me."

And that's when she really shocked me. She started to hit herself, to punch herself on the forehead, hard.

"Norah!"

She broke into a flurry of blows, beating herself around the head with both hands.

I caught hold of her wrists and for a minute she resisted me, then her arms went limp and she gave in, looking up at me with a face that turned a fear in my stomach. It was that fear that made me bluster: "Dear God Norah, what are you doing? Stop that nonsense. I never saw the like…"

She was crying again, quiet tears this time, down frozen cheeks. "Don't shout," she said, in a dead voice. "Don't shout, please. You'll have them out after us."

I let her arms go. "Then stop crying. And stop talking about yourself like that. Come on, Norah, blow your nose. Dry the tears. There, that's better." I kept on saying things like that, trying to soothe myself as much as her. I never knew the strength of feeling she kept hidden behind her pale, quiet face. Now that I did, what could I say, only advise her not to listen to anyone else, not her family and not me either. To examine her own conscience, and let it tell her what to do.

"It sounds so simple when you say it, Peg," she said, padding her eyes with the puckered handkerchief.

"Underneath it all, under the confusion and the pressure from all sides, it really is that simple," I said.

I'll be a lot more careful about how I speak to her in future.

DIARY 21ST JUNE 1922: So we lost, thanks mostly to the traitorous acts of Mr Michael Collins, who — with only hours to go and at the behest of the British — reneged on the pact he had signed with Mr de Valera. That man will surely perish in hell for this grave sin to comrades and country. It's clear what consorting with the English has done to his morals, he who was once our leader. And the old-timers and the respectables, the farmers and the shoneens, the gombeen men and the merchants got in behind him and voted our Republic away. 239,193 votes to the pro-treaty candidates, 133,864 to us. (And 247,226 to the rest between them — Labour, Farmers and Independents).

Mammy got up out of bed to go to the polling booth on the day. We didn't even try to stop her because we knew we'd have no hope and she managed fine. She got excited at being out and about with people coming over to her and making a fuss: all enquiries about her health were brushed aside and she concentrated on the politics, getting herself rightly worked up. Once we saw the Constitution, we knew why they'd waited until the morning of the election to publish it. Every nail of the treaty was driven home in it.

She was still complaining about it tonight, as I helped her get ready for bed. Apparently Mr White, Lama's father, made some remark to Daddy that the result expressed a wish for compromise among the ordinary people, a concern about social and economic matters. That was why the Farmer's Party and Labour did so well, he held, because people wanted the fighting put aside and for the new government to concentrate on things "that mattered", like jobs and land reform and housing. Daddy had passed this on to Mammy, hoping, I think, that she might take some notice of that point of view (it being, to some degree, his own) and take it as a consolation.

If that is what he hoped, he must have been sorely disappointed. She ranted and railed against the Whites as a crowd of Bolshevists sheltering under the name of Republicans. Then she moved on to all the self-seeking people who put their own welfare above the noble cause of the nation. ("Who were the Farmer's Party anyway? Only a string of Orangemen and Freemasons.") And then she went back to denouncing the provisional government and her outrage that people in general were now taking up their label for anti-treaty soldiers – "Irregulars" — though these were mostly the men who brought the government into being in the first place, while most of those joining the new "National" Army had never seen a day's service in their lives.

At first I feared she might strain herself if she got too worked up, but after a while I came to feel it did her good to fume and think of something besides her own poor health. It was a change from the reminiscences that have made up so much of her conversation lately and to see her so excited and alive to the present again…it made me hope…

If we, the women and young men, had had our vote, we'd have won it, that's what gets me most. That's what I can never forgive them.

Well, they needn't think that it ends there. I don't know what we do next, but we won't be lying under this injustice, of that they can be sure…

Diary 1st July 1922: I was supposed to be going to Ring College in the Gaeltacht for an Irish course. All the arrangements are made, I've paid my money and Father John is agreeable and has sponsored me. He won't be too pleased when he hears what I'm going to do instead. This afternoon I leave for Enniscorthy, where our troops are preparing for war against the Free Staters. Outright war has come to Wexford.

Since Michael Collins took two 18-pounder guns from Winston Churchill and used them to blast apart the defences of the brave men holding the Four Courts for the Republic, the rest of us have been waiting for orders on how to react. All Dublin is said to be a shambles: the heart, liver and lights torn out of the city by days of bombing and shooting.

There's a song going around that just about sums it up:

Oh Churchill dear, did you hear, the news from Dublin town?

They've listened to your good advice and blown the Four Courts down.

And likewise with O'Connell Street, the worst we've ever seen

The guns the best (as per request) and the lorries painted green.

When they turned those English guns on the Four Courts, they blasted to high heaven six centuries of documents and records, and charred scraps of paper were carried for miles beyond Dublin, like leaves on a storm wind. My head and heart are full of these burnt fragments of British rule blowing about the place. And of course of our men, so many of them, who lie dead, dying or wounded.

We don't know how many yet, only that we've taken a fearful hammering. The fighting is dirty and we are outgunned by English weapons. And outnumbered by men who were nowhere to be seen when it was the English we were fighting, the type who are all for it now there's a salary going and free uniform and boots.

"Official IRA" they have painted on their lorries and armoured cars. Meanwhile, we are nothing but "Irregulars". Mammy is right: it is beyond belief.

So there's an end for any hopes of unity. We can forget any notion now of being able to work together. They've declared war, and war they shall have, and though they may have might on their side, we have right. They'll not find country boys as easy to defeat as in the city. They won't find their way around woods and mountains as handy as avenues and streets.

And down here, outside the Pale, it is the Staters who are outnumbered, by at least four to one. In Wexford, all the main towns – Gorey, New Ross, Wexford town and Ferns – are now held by us. Only Enniscorthy is not ours, not yet, so it must be taken. Barney has gone ahead, so have Tipsy and Lama and Molly, and I'll be leaving myself as soon as Daddy gets back from the station. I will be able to stay as long as is necessary, as we began our school holidays yesterday. I haven't told Father John of my intentions – I wasn't in the mood for one of his little talks and would prefer to face that music when I get back. Even if school was still on, I would be going. This thing is bigger than any one of us.

Mammy is delighted to see us off, only wishing she could join us herself. When Barney told her what was planned, and of the concerns we had about leaving her, she waved them away. "Go. Go with God's blessing and mine. Your father's too. Go save Ireland." I don't know about blessing, but Daddy is being better than brave about it all. Even he is sickened by what's going on.

Barney spoke to me before he left about Dan. There's more than a few on the Stater side who are sickened by this betrayal and have declared themselves unwilling to shoot at old friends. We both feel Dan is likely to go this way, even though such men of honour are no longer required by the Stater Army and are being rounded up and arrested. We both know Dan wouldn't be able to actually turn out for the army and turn an English-sponsored gun on us. Now he can see what true treachery looks like in action, he's bound to come back to us.

I hear George's hoofs pulling into the yard. Daddy is back. It is time for me to go. My next entry will be when I come back from Enniscorthy. I should have plenty to report by then. God bless the work.

(4PM) Well now, as they say: the best-laid plans...

Here I am still in Mucknamore having taken you back out of the drawer in which I so carefully locked you away. I was about to leave my bedroom, giving it a last go over, making sure there was nothing untoward if Mammy or anybody else should decide to pop in while I was gone, when next thing I heard a call from Tessie downstairs. "Peg, are you up there?"

"Yes."

"Someone to see you."

I went out of the bedroom and hung down over the banisters to see who it was and there stood Norah, her eyes like two big green lamps shining up at me. "Come ahead," I said to her and she took the stairs two by two, most unlike her, bursting to tell me her story. I've never seen her so agitated.

All day long, she had been stuck behind the counter in Furlong's, listening to the hearsay being carried in by customers visiting the store. Furlong's had no shortage of customers, it being a Saturday, and no shortage of rumours about the goings-on in Enniscorthy: the fighting had started with an all-out attack launched on the courthouse where our boys are; the fighting had started with the Republicans besieging the Castle where the Staters are lodged; the fighting had not started yet but wouldn't be long now.

It was torture for poor Norah, listening to all this, not knowing what was true, what was false. Then through the window of her office, she saw that Mrs Redmond was in, Molly's mother, and that she was deep in conversation with Miss Ellen Bolger at the millinery counter, whose sympathies are in the right place. Under pretext of making notes about the gloves and umbrellas at the next counter, she managed to listen to their conversation and to hear that Molly had gone up to Enniscorthy to get involved. Mrs Redmond was upset, hadn't wanted her to go, but Molly had been insistent. As Norah listened to this, something in her just clicked.

"I knew this was the moment," she said. "That if I didn't go to Enniscorthy like Molly, I would regret it for the rest of my living days."

So she went back to her office for her coat and hat and went to find Mr Carr. She found him in men's footwear and told him she had to leave, and when he asked why, she told him out straight. And he said to her, that's not a reason I'd allow any of my girls to leave work. And she, brave as can be, said it was as good a reason as she could think of, the future of Ireland. And he says, if you leave now, you needn't bother coming back. And she didn't have to even think, not even for a second. "I'm sorry you should say that," she told him, "but I'm afraid I have to go." And she went.

"I went," she said to me in my bedroom, amazed at herself. "I just went." At this she burst out laughing and I joined her. It was the kind of laughing you do after you've come round from jumping out of your skin and find out it was only someone shouting boo.

"So I'm going with you," she said. "But first I have to go up home and get my things."

"What will you tell them?"

"I don't know yet. As little as possible, maybe. I'll see when I'm up there."

I was afraid for her when I heard her say that. "Come ahead now instead and say nothing. I'll lend you clothes and whatever else you might need. Face them when you come back."

But she wouldn't hear of it. On up she went and she's been gone nearly an hour now. I hope to God they haven't talked her out of it. I hope to God she'll be back soon and maybe, just maybe, her brother with her?

I turn twelve. That September, I leave Mucknamore for the first time, am driven into Wexford town by Mrs D. to boarding school. Convent boarding school. The routine there is rigid, every hour accounted for with prayers, meals, classes, study, exercise or pastimes. The nuns are strict, towering over us in their stiff black habits, shrinking us to silence with their expectations of The Highest Standards of Behaviour.

Our day begins with the dormitory bell and the high energy of Sister Elizabeth. We call her Busy Lizzy, she never stops, go, go, go, work, work, work, watch, watch, watch. Every morning in her up-and-down voice, she wakes us with the clang of her big bell and her loud voice, chanting: "Good morning, girls… Seven o'clock…Mass at half-past…Praised be Jesus."

Then she goes round from cubicle to cubicle, thrusting a font of holy water round through our curtains with a Latin blessing. If we don't want big trouble, we have to be up before she arrives at our cubicle, to dip our fingers in the font, make the sign of the cross, and answer her with an "Amen". The girls at the far end of the dorm get a precious extra few minutes, clinging to the mattress.

All the way round Busy Lizzy harangues us to get up and

strip off: "Take off your night clothes now, girls, and wash yourselves properly..." Deirdre Mernagh says she only says this so she can get a gawp of us in the nude as she goes on her holy water round. Lezzy Lizzie, Dee calls her. Dee is always saying things like that.

Once we are washed and dressed, we have to strip our beds to the mattress, folding blankets, sheets and under-sheets across our chairs to "air" our beds. Then it's downstairs for Mass, mantillas clipped onto our hair. The priest comes down to us from the local boys' school and the nuns play altar boy, passing him his chalice and cruets, servants of the servant of God. Mass can take anything up to an hour, depending on which saint's day it is. Every few weeks one of the girls, overcome with hunger, falls into a faint.

After breakfast, we are joined by the outside world in the form of day-girls and lay teachers for the school day. The lay teachers are not so strict, but the nuns are said to be better teachers.

"They've nothing else to be thinking about, that's why," says Dee, rolling her eyes. "No family, no boyfriends, no sex. Imagine."

Dee loves saying the word Sex. Or Fuck. Or Ride. Or Bollox. Any word she's not supposed to say. I am learning other words from her too, words that are not taboo, but that I never heard in Mucknamore. I now describe girls I like as "dead-on" or "the business". Those who are boring are "drips". Good things are "desh" or "deadly"; bad things are 'woeful'. These words come from the town via the day-girls, but Dee picks them up and makes them her own.

We like to think we have more in common with the girls from town. As Dee puts it, we might be from the country but we're not culchies. She comes from Oulart, a village in the north of Wexford that sounds even worse than Mucknamore. Her father is an "alco", she says, and her mother worn to nothing trying to pretend that he isn't. She turns them into a joke, laughing at her father's drunkenness and her mother's attempts to cover up.

Mr and Mrs Mernagh, she calls them, when she is telling these tales. I begin to refer to my mother in a similar way – first Mrs Devereux, then we shorten it to Mrs D. and Mrs M.

One day Dee tells me that she's afraid to give her mother advice anymore, since she suggested to her mother that she leave her father, and her mother cracked apart, saying she would have left long ago if it hadn't been for the children.

"All out frantic, she went," Dee tells me. "She was clawing at my wrist, saying, 'Tell me I did right, tell me I did right.' Jesus!"

I listen and nod, marvelling at how she lets it all spill out so easy. Somehow, she seems to like me. I overheard her describe me to Monica Rowe, another girl, as her friend. I want to give her something back. At night, I plan how I will share some Mucknamore story with her, but in the light of day I can never get one past my teeth.

I have other friends too. Friends! They know nothing about Mucknamore, about hero uncles, absent fathers, mad aunts or abandoned mothers. I shove my difference down deep under my skin and – miraculously – they don't smell it out. They believe in this manufactured, ordinary me.

I am happy in the convent, though sometimes I have to lock myself in the toilet or go to one of the other secret places I have hunted down – behind the grotto in the corner of the grounds, at the bottom of the slope beyond the far end of the hockey pitch, under the stairs on the way up to study – to sit tight and empty my mind, to breathe deep and hard, until I am able to breeze out wearing the same broad smile I brought in.

Terms pass, my life parcelled out between school and home. I have breasts now, and hips that elbow out beneath the red sash that knots around my gym-slip. My legs have sprouted and it feels good to be tall, to look down on younger girls. Dee and Monica and I skip hockey games by going to Fanny-Jo (Sister Frances Joseph) and asking for aspirin. Fanny-Jo is enthralled by periods. "Your monthlies, is it?" she whispers, when you turn up at her door, clutching your forehead or your abdomen. "You poor dear," she will say, guiding you to the high, hard bed, never seeming to notice that it's only been a week since you were there last time.

It is widespread among the nuns, this fascination with bodies and the secret things they do. Soupy – Mother Superior – takes over one of our Home Economics periods to give us The Talk, an event that older girls have warned us about since we joined the school. She stands in front of the blackboard with her face set around her duty, to tell us all about the making of babies. She draws a picture of our insides on the blackboard with neon-pink chalk: womb and tubes and ovaries.

Embarrassment twitches around the classroom as she talks. She tells us what can happen after a bath, when you are drying yourself. It's not a sin, she says, to feel yourself as you towel yourself dry, but to linger over such a feeling would be a grave sin indeed. Some girls are weaker than others in such matters, more subject to immoral impulses. Each girl listening will know where she falls; her own conscience will tell her whether she is vulnerable.

Soupy's eyes flick around the classroom as she talks. I try hard to meet them but my gaze keeps sliding away from her words. If we examine our consciences and decide that we are in danger, she suggests precautions: wear a vest when having a bath; sleep with hands outside the blankets at night; avoid love stories in books and magazines. I feel Dee's shoe pressing against mine.

Afterwards, when she has finished and gone from the classroom, we crack into laughter. "I hope you always wear your vest," we joke with each other, in shaky voices. Underneath the jokes, we are looking at each other in new ways, wondering who does what. We mock the nuns but we are just as bad, twisted inside our own silences.

PART III
SWELL

*a*s they came into the outskirts of Enniscorthy town, Peg, who was cycling upfront, made to dismount. "I have to have that drink," she said. "I can't wait another second."

Norah, who was coming up fast right behind her, pulled over too, braking hard, then swinging onto one pedal and jumping off. "Best idea I heard all day."

"And what a day. Could we have picked a hotter one to come cycling 23 miles?"

After so long on the bicycle, the ground felt unsteady underneath Peg's feet, but she hopped up the two steps into the shop with Norah just behind. It took a minute for her eyes to adjust to the darkness inside the small premises, so small that a third customer wouldn't get in beyond the door frame. Flies buzzed, loud and insolent above shelves that were half bare. Behind the counter an enormously fat middle-aged man sat, leaning over one of his newspapers, ignoring them.

"Em…Good evening," Peg said. "Are you open?"

He lingered on his paper a long moment before dragging his eyes up.

"I am if you're paying," he said, with a significant look at their Cumann na mBan uniforms.

"Of course we're paying. We only want two lemon sodas."

With sighs and wheezes he lifted himself down. Leaning heavily on the stool, he bent from his hips, turning his vast, shop-coated rump up towards them. Peg widened her eyes at Norah and they both folded their lips to stifle rising giggles. Straightening up, the shopkeeper held the two bottles aloft between his fingers. "You're part of the shenanigans going on above?"

No answer to that was possible. He could see their uniforms; he knew right well what they were doing here.

Slowly he drew the corks from the bottles. "I had your lot in here this morning. 'Commandeering' by their own account. Eggs, potatoes, butter, bread."

"Soldiers must eat," said Peg.

"Stealing more like."

Peg said, "If they were genuine Republicans, you'll have been given a receipt."

"A Republican receipt won't feed seven children."

Peg could feel answers rising in her. That if the rest of his family were the size of him, they could live off themselves for a year. That he should be proud to feed the soldiers of the Irish Republic. That many people with a lot less to give than him had given a lot more. But she put two coins on the counter and left it at that.

Back outside, they crossed to the riverbank. "Wouldn't they drive you up the wall?" Peg said, after they'd drawn the first long, delicious draughts down their throats. "The way they don't see past their few greasy pence? We should have tried to find McDaid's. At least they're Republican friendly."

"Don't mind him," said Norah. "Just wait till we win them back the Republic. Then their old talk will turn."

Peg smiled at her. It was the first time she ever heard her friend say something like that. Norah was full of surprises today, in a state of high excitement ever since they left Mucknamore, whooping up at the birds in the trees, freewheeling her bike down the hills with her legs sticking out each side.

"So who's going in with the empties?" Peg asked, when they'd finished.

Norah looked at her, wide-eyed. She hadn't changed that much.

"I'm only joking, give it here."

The shop man was stuck in his paper again.

"I'm bringing back your bottles," she said, placing them on the little counter.

"Do you know what I'm wondering?" he said. "I'm wondering how two well-brought-up girls have got yourselves tied up with them rowdy boys above. Do you know the type you're dealing with at all?"

He held the tuppence he owed her for the empties aloft between two fingers, like a priest holding up the Communion host. When Peg reached for it he pulled back his hand, swallowing it into his palm. "As low a crowd of corner boys as Enniscorthy ever produced, demanding salutes from respectable people."

"They're the cream of the country," Peg said, and as soon as she'd said it, she was sorry. She'd never get a money-grabbing huckster like him to understand, not if she talked to him for a twelvemonth.

"The cream of the country, is it, and they wrecking the same country from end to end? Do you even know what you're fighting for?"

"For the Republic, of course. For the future. For the coming generations."

"To grow up in a country that hasn't a bridge or railway or decent building left intact. The coming generations are not likely to thank you, I'd say."

"You can keep your old tuppence."

She found Norah talking to two young men in trench coats with guns slung over their shoulders and it took her a minute to work out that one of them was Tipsy. The other fellow she didn't know, a tall, thin chap with a helmet of tight curls.

Norah looked concerned. "What's the matter?" she said. "What did he say this time?"

"You wouldn't believe the go-on of him."

"Is that so?" said the stranger, putting his hand to the strap of his rifle. "Do you want me to go in and have a little chat with him?"

"Steady there," said Tipsy, fidgeting his feet at the thought.

"We can't have it said that we stood idly by while the women of the Republic were insulted."

"Don't be soft," said Peg. "He just annoyed me, that's all."

"Oh well, if you're sure," said Tipsy, now that the chance of it was past.

"Stop, I said. It would be more in your line, don't you think, to be making introductions."

"Denis Heffernan," said the stranger himself, lifting his cap to her and a second time to Norah and giving Tipsy a puck with his elbow.

"Miss Peg Parle," said Tipsy, with the air of a gallant that didn't suit him. "And Miss Norah O'Donovan."

"Two fair and fatigueless fighters for Ireland, I gather."

"We do our bit," said Peg. "Tell us, is it true? We've taken over the Portsmouth Arms?"

"Aren't we on our way there now ourselves? You should see if you can stay there. It's the heart of the action. Here!" He took the bars of Peg's bicycle and jerked his head towards Norah's. "Hey! Delaney!" and they started to walk. He seemed all right, this boy, a little bit full of himself maybe, but it was nice to be meeting new people instead of the same old faces from Mucknamore. She was surprised it wasn't Norah who'd pulled his interest. Norah looked even lovelier than usual this evening.

"So tell us what's been happening," Peg said, as they began to walk towards the bridge. "There's that many rumours about we don't know what to believe."

Heffernan filled her in. The two armies, Free State and Republican, were pouring into the town and setting up quarters, an uneasy tension between them as each awaited news and orders from Dublin. The Staters had taken over Enniscorthy Castle, a castle built on the height of the hill, overlooking the town. Built by Anglo-Normans in the 1200s, Peg knew, and owned at one stage by the Elizabethan poet, Edmund Spenser. This stronghold had been besieged by Cromwell in 1649 and used as a prison during the 1798 Rebellion. It was now a private home belonging to a Mr Roche and his family.

"The same Mr Roche was full of haughty protests at being turned out," said Heffernan. "Apparently he kept saying over and over, in his West Brit accent, 'I'm as Irish as you are, man. My family has lived in Wexford for three centuries. I'm as Irish as you are.' But not even he could argue with a battalion of National Army rifles."

Heffernan was laughing through the posh English voice he affected.

"They've set up a machine gun," Tipsy shouted from behind. "On the roof."

"Hey!" Heffernan said, throwing a look back over his shoulder. "Who's telling this yarn?" He turned back to Peg. "He's right," he said. "We've not been idle ourselves. The courthouse has been fortified and tomorrow we're going to take over a photographer's place beside it and a couple of other adjacent houses. And at the moment we've a troop clearing out St Mary's."

"St Mary's?"

"The Protestant church."

Peg laughs. "No! You're codding?"

"I'm not. The church has a fine belfry. With the Staters up on the roof of their castle, we needed to climb up there to meet them."

"And the Proddie church is the only other building in the town that's high enough." Tipsy laughed.

"Have you been up there, Tipsy?" Norah asked.

"No, but—"

"Tipsy?" laughed Heffernan. "Tipsy! Is that what you call him? He told me his name was Martin."

Just then, a sound like thunder approached from behind. Two military motors rumbled past, each packed with men, Republican flags fluttering from all sides of the vehicles.

"They're Tipperary men," Tipsy said, bringing up his hand in a salute. Peg and Norah followed suit, tipped their fingertips to their temples.

"Reinforcements are pouring in," said Heffernan. "We've at least fifty men from Tipperary already. More Dublin boys are on the way too."

Tipsy was leaning on the handlebars of the bicycle to look after the disappearing lorries, his mouth hanging open around his too-big tongue. You could drive both military lorries through that mouth, Peg thought.

"We'd better move on," Heffernan said.

As they got into the heart of the town, they found people standing at their doors to watch the activity. Peg felt self-conscious walking past in her uniform, her first-aid knapsack on her back, flanked by the two boys with rifles. They were like actors on a stage, all eyes turned their way, with a scrutiny so silent that she could hear the tick of the bicycle wheels turning.

A barrier blocked entrance to the hotel lobby, fortified with sandbags and barbed-wire, but one of the two volunteers standing guard knew Denis and helped them to climb in and lift the bicycles over. Inside, soldiers swarmed all round, their activity contrasting with the luxury of their surroundings. Tables and chairs had been piled high behind the windows. The dining room was now a store for ammunition, grenades and other explosives. The bar had been sealed off. At the reception desk, two officers Peg had never seen before pored over a map of the town, one making lines on it with a pencil. Denis Heffernan lifted Peg's bicycle up over his head and led them through to the back yard as if he had lived in the place all his life. Tipsy copied him. When the bikes were safely put by, Peg asked, "Where are the girls, Tipsy? Have you seen Molly?"

"She was in the basement earlier."

"That's where most of the women are holed up," said Heffernan.

He pointed the way down the narrow back stairs and they parted ways. Down in the basement too, activity was humming, women in groups performing various tasks: washing and drying dishes, making bread, mopping the floor, wiping down shelves and tables, cutting up bandages and making first-aid dressing packs.

They found Molly in a corner of the kitchen, blacking a cooker. "Ah, girls, it's great to see you. D'you want some dinner? What's left is going to the pigs." She upended a huge pot to show them the remains of a stew down at the bottom. "They ate well, but I could heat this up for you. Do you fancy?"

They declined.

"I'm surprised to see yourself here, Norah," Molly said, with her usual directness.

"I had to come," Norah said.

"Isn't it amazing? I have to keep pinching myself, so I do. Cat is coming up too. She sent a message with Jim Healy that she'll be up in the morning."

A soldier came in and slapped a heavy brown cardboard box on one of the long tables. "Anyone got a knife?"

Molly had and she slit the box open. It was packed from base to brim with sausages, pounds and pounds of them, wrapped in greaseproof paper. She picked out one pack, held it up for the others to see. The volunteer slapped his hand down on top of another box. "Rashers of bacon," he said. Another slap on another box: "Black pudding."

"Aren't you the right little hunter-gatherer?" said Molly. "Where have you been?"

"Buttle's meat factory. Provisions for the Irish Republican

Army, I told the supervisor. He wasn't too inclined to do his patriotic duty until I made him acquainted with Betsy here." He tapped the barrel of his revolver.

"We'll have a feast and a half in the morning," Molly said. "We'll get up early and make brown bread for it. You'll help, girls, won't ye?"

"Of course we will," Peg said. "Isn't that what we're here for?"

"If you're not busy now, you could take over the last tea round. Mary-Ann Maloney said she'd do it with me, but we could do with a bit of a break. We've been hard at one thing or another since the forenoon."

She showed them where the cups were kept and told them to put the milk and sugar directly into the big teapots. "Leave it to us," Peg said. They made the tea as instructed and carried it up, Peg in charge of the big teapot with the two handles, Norah following behind with a tray of cups. Everyone was delighted to see them.

"Here comes the tea," the shout went up. "Good girls." They saw Barney in a corner with a group and he came over, but there was no time to talk; everybody wanted refreshment. First the tea ran out, then the cups, then the tea again. It took five journeys to the kitchen before all were catered for.

Collecting the teacups afterwards was an altogether more relaxed task, with time for a bit of banter, meeting up with old acquaintances and being introduced to new, so many new people they couldn't possibly remember them all. When the crowd around them thinned out a bit, Barney slipped across, taking a place beside Norah.

"Any bit of news from the front lines?" Peg asked.

"Nothing much," said Barney. "Just prep work, still."

"But we're definitely going to make a strike?"

"Definitely. But not tonight. We need the church back before we strike at the castle. The vicar sent a representation to Fleming, asking if he could do Sunday services as normal, then we could have it back."

"That's gas," Norah said, flicking a little smile at him.

"Isn't it just? A Protestant minister bowing the knee to the likes of us."

"I never thought I'd see such a thing," said Peg.

"Anyhow, we obliged him," said Barney. "The lads made good the defences and have vacated the church until noon tomorrow so the Protestant prayers can be said."

"I think it's a generous gesture," said Peg. "It shows our finer instincts have not been blunted."

"It might be more of a military motive," Barney said. "Reinforcements are still coming in. The more we have the better, before we make our move."

"So it'll be tomorrow, you think?"

"That's what everyone's saying. Tomorrow afternoon, probably."

Tipsy bounded over to them, like an over-keen hound. "I've got a room for ye, girls."

"Do you? Thanks,' said Peg. 'That's great."

"It's number 27. On the second floor. Ye'd want to be taking it now to keep it."

"We've cups to collect yet, Tipsy. Is there a key you could give us?"

"The key for it can't be found, which was how I got it. I'm after putting a few sandbags on the beds but if ye don't stake your claim, somebody else will take it over."

Peg frowned. "We don't want to be putting any men out of their beds. Norah and I can bed down anywhere."

"No," he said. "It's yours."

"But it's the men need their sleep, more than us. If there's action tomorrow they'll want their wits about them."

"No. It's for you," he said, in the tone of a stubborn two-year-old.

While this one-sided conversation was going on, Norah and

Barney had drawn together. Now Norah whispered in Peg's ear to ask if she'd mind if they went for a walk. Barney stood apart, pretending not to listen.

"Go on ahead," Peg said. "I can finish off here."

"Are you sure?" she said, her back already turned. And then they were gone, leaving a lonely moment behind. If only…But there was not time for any of that here. And just as well.

Tipsy piled some empty cups onto her tray. "So, will I go up and mind it for you? Until you're ready?"

"Really, Tipsy, there's no need to go to all this trouble…"

"Not a bit of trouble." Specks of saliva spattered out of his mouth on each "b".

"All right, so. Thank you."

It was three-quarters of an hour later before she got upstairs, but he was still standing guard outside the door as she knew he would be. His face spilled into his slack, sloppy smile to see her and he threw the door open as proud as a bridegroom on honeymoon night.

Two twin beds, one under each window. Neat brown bedspreads. A sink with running water. "It's lovely," she said, feeling a compliment was called for.

"Ye'll need to put that dressing table against the door to keep it closed. Otherwise they'll be coming in on top of you all night."

"We'll be grand."

"And you're at the back here, so even if there is shooting…"

"I don't think there will be, not tonight. Where are you sleeping yourself?"

"Downstairs."

"On the floor, I suppose?"

He shrugged.

"I meant what I said, Tipsy, there's no need—"

His big wet smile disallowed any more objections.

She shrugged. "All right, so. If you're sure. Thanks again."

She had her hand on the door handle when he said her name – "Peg" – and she heard in his voice that he was marshalling his courage to say something. Something she knew she didn't want him saying.

"Goodnight, so," she said, and made to close the door behind her.

"Wait," he said, putting a foot in the doorway. "Wait a minute. I—"

"Yoo-hoo!" came a voice. It was Molly, bustling along the corridor, waving a key at them. "Yoo-hoo! Look! I got one too!"

Peg was never so glad to see Molly in all her life.

"Have ye heard the news? Fleming is on the rampage. Pat Simmons and his lot got into the store and started passing bottles of stout around after strict orders that no drink was to be touched. Carty caught them and raised the roof."

"Carty did right," Peg said. "It's a war we're here for, not a leisure camp."

"Marky Field and Pat Murphy have been put on guard duty, to stop any more being taken."

"Yerra, no harm was meant, I'd say," said Tipsy. "Haven't they had a long old day of it?"

"Don't be talking daft," replied Peg. "If they start on the drink, discipline will go out the window."

"That's what Carty said," Molly nodded.

"That's right, of course, when I think about it. Of course that's right," Tipsy agreed

"I don't know about you two," Peg said, "but I'm exhausted. I'm off to bed now. Goodnight to you both." And she slipped in and shut the door on Molly's surprise.

Peg leaned back against the door. She could hear their voices, Molly saying, "Is she all right?"

"I don't know," said Tipsy.

"Where are you going?"

"Duty calls."

"Does it now? No sign of it calling you a minute ago, before I came along."

"I was only showing Peg her room."

"Of course you were." Molly's tone was facetious and, from the other side of the door, Peg could feel Tipsy's confusion. After a long silence, he said, "I'd better go."

Molly burst out laughing. "Goodnight, Tipsy," she said, as his footsteps retreated. "Don't go getting yourself shot now."

As far as Peg could hear, only one set of steps moved away. She imagined Molly outside the door, looking after Tipsy's disappearing back, mulling over possibilities. She moved away from the door and, sure enough, a moment later heard a knock-knock and Molly stuck her head in. "Did I interrupt something there?"

"What's that supposed to mean?"

"You left in a mighty hurry, that's all."

"Did I? I'm just tired. It was a long cycle we had today."

"You don't look that tired."

Peg wasn't going to answer that.

"Maybe yourself and Mr Delaney are becoming more than friends?"

"Molly, don't talk daft."

"I suppose he's no great shakes. But it would do you good to be with someone else. Get you over Mr D.O.D."

"Oh, I'm well over that, believe me."

"So why not give poor Tipsy a look-in? He has it bad for you. You must know that. Everyone knows that."

"I'm only going to say it to you once more, so open your ears, girl. Not a chance in God's Heaven."

Molly rolled her eyes.

"Listen, Molly, I'm awful tired…We'll see you in the kitchen in the morning, Norah and I. About half-six, isn't it?"

"Between half-six and seven."

"Grand. We'll be there." Peg sat down on the bed.

"Speaking of Norah, where is she?"

Did the girl never give up nosing? "I'm not sure."

"Oh?"

"There's no 'Oh?' about it. She's off doing some job."

"Is she? What job?"

"Molly, will you give it a rest? I don't know. She didn't tell me what job. Are you going to go -- or do I have to throw you out?"

"You are throwing me out, grumpy-drawers. All right, I'm gone. Goodnight."

On Wednesday morning, Barney woke with the dawn. He could feel his skin and muscles sore from sleeping on hard ground, but it didn't matter, not a whit. Not a smidgeon, not a damn. The beat of his blood was humming. Norah O'Donovan's boots were beside his face on the floor, as she took what sleep she could on a hard chair. Jesus God, that face, so female. Even the way it was, all leaned over to one side against a first-aid pack he'd rolled up into a rough pillow for her, her mouth slightly open, a sliver of wet visible on her bottom lip, tendrils of hair escaping their clips, even like that, she was the best looking girl in the place. By a crooked mile. Wake up and look, he wanted to shout into the room full of bodies that lay still caught in sleep, angled into every kind of attitude and position about the place. That's my trench coat the best looking girl in the place is using as a blanket, tucked around her arms. And look at me too. This morning, he was in on a job, a proper mission, with Ernie O'Malley, no less. The famous OC, fresh from the fieriest battles in Dublin, sent south to organise Wexford. With Ernie O'Malley on their side, they surely could not fail.

From his worm-eye position, he surveyed the room. Since Monday, they had spent their nights and much of their days in this storehouse on the river, the property of a Mr Yates. The only action so far had been half-hearted sniping from a safe distance, the only casualty a young fellow hit by a ricochet off the hotel wall. Peg and Norah had been off kitchen duty, allocated to communications and despatch. Republicans had seven different posts around the town, all needing to be kept in communication with each other. It was dangerous work, cycling through streets with bullets flying, but of course they were proud to do it.

Unlike some of the other girls, no complaint passed their lips about scarce food, roughly served, or sleep that had to be taken in snatches, fully dressed and booted.

Look at us. Soldier and the auxiliary. Fighting side-by-side. He had told Norah how he admired her bravery, especially after Dan's defection. He had told her everything, everything, in snatched whispers, surrounded by others, the noise of sniper-shots clacking. Things he never thought he'd reveal to a living soul, things he hardly knew he thought himself. And she was entrusting him the same way. And allowing him to hold her, and kiss her, and touch her. This was one outcome of the fight he hadn't expected. In Mucknamore, it would have taken them months – years, maybe – to get to where they were with each other now. Here, away from the watchful eyes of parents and elders, in the hub of danger, the usual reservations and protocol had melted, even for the most circumspect girl.

Everybody knew about them now. She had shoved her worry about what her parents would say forward into the future and he had promised her he would protect her in whatever ordeal she might face back in Mucknamore. That had been the only time she seemed to waver in her belief in him, turning two gooseberry-green eyes on him, that were fogged over with questions. It wasn't idle talk with him, he meant it all the way. He was quite prepared to marry her and keep her, or take her, from anything that might be trouble to her. But he was shy to say that out so soon, afraid he'd frighten her off.

It was a wonder she could sleep like that on that wooden chair. He pushed himself up on one elbow to get a better look at her. Her breathing was heavy, almost but not quite a snore. For comfort, she'd loosened the top two buttons of her blouse and he could see a white V of skin at her neck. He followed the line of it down her clothed body. Her figure was neat and soft and tantalising. Sleep made it look like it was on offer to him, relaxed in a way she would never be when her waking self was in control. He checked the clock: quarter-past five. Time to rise. He stood, and bent and tucked the trench coat up around her shoulders; he'd do without it. He dropped a small kiss onto her forehead and she moved in her sleep.

"Oh— Is it – Barney…?"

"It's morning," he whispered. "Time's come."

Her eyes sprang open. 'Oh, Barney, God keep you safe. Don't forget to come back."

She reached her arms up and around his neck and kissed him full on the lips with the kind of kiss they'd got used to in recent days. The kind of kiss that made him want to stay, but they were surrounded by others, some already waking, and besides, duty called. Proper military duty. He detached her hands from behind his neck, placed one kiss on each bracelet of wrinkles round her wrists and tucked her arms back under his coat.

Gun in hand, canvas ammunition sling across his shoulder, he picked his way between the bodies down to the back exit. The door squeaked as he opened it. No firing to disturb the morning. Not yet. He sat on a doorstep to put on his boots, attached the ammo sling to his waist, checked his supply. These first minutes of the summer day were beyond lovely, bright as a coin new-minted, and he stopped for a second to breathe in the sweet dewy morning air, feeling the life within himself expand.

He set off again. Turning into the next empty street, he saw two fellows up ahead: Lama and a chap called Denis Heffernan. They were headed where he was going – it was Heffernan who put the job their way. He ran to catch up and jumped in between them, slapping each of them on the back. "We're on, so?"

"As on as we'll ever be, boy," said Heffernan.

Lama just nodded but Barney could see excitement rising off him like steam off boiling water. Frank Carty had got a tip-off that the enemy had secretly occupied the post office, planning to ambush Republicans from there. But the surprise would be the other way round: instead of them being ambushed, Ernie O'Malley was to lead them in an attack on the building, putting a brake on the army's plans before they even had a chance to get them going.

Eleven men met at the corner of Friary Place. Ernie O'Malley and another Dublin-man, Paddy O'Brien; Paddy Fleming, head of the Third Eastern Division and Frank Carty, adjutant; five Enniscorthy volunteers, Denis Heffernan, Dick Sullivan, Thomas Roche, Michael Kirwan, Andrew Redmond; and Barney Parle and Charles (Lama) White, the Mucknamore men. Good men, true men, one and all. Rifles and pistols to the ready, and a plentiful supply of ammunition and grenades.

O'Malley – a wiry redhead, terse and intense – outlined the plan. They would rush the narrow lane leading to the back of the post office, smash the glass in the windows and, through the holes, throw in a series of hand grenades.

"Bit rough, isn't it?" Heffernan whispered, out of the side of his mouth to Barney. "Lobbing grenades into a room full of sleeping men?"

Barney shrugged. O'Malley burned with the sort of single-mindedness usually seen in missionary priests, but wars weren't won by the fainthearted. And the aim was to win, wasn't it?

Down the hill they trooped, directing their rifles right and left as they went, but encountering no trouble. Turning the corner, they passed a pub that commanded a view of the lane, but none of them took any notice of that. And why would they? It stood as shuttered and silent as the other buildings around it. Past it they marched, down the lane, steady and quiet as they could be in their boots, towards the red-brick post office that faced them at the end. The windows were barred, but O'Malley managed to shatter the glass with the butt of his gun and Fleming, Carty and Sullivan copied him. Smash! Smash! Smash!

O'Malley took the catch off the first grenade, lobbed it in. Then a second one. Everyone stopped: they heard the pop of bursting cases and they pulled back, leaned away from the building, hands over their heads to the blast. But the blast didn't come. In its place, silence lengthened until it became obvious that it wasn't going to shatter.

"Fuck it!" said Fleming. "Don't tell me. More faulty ammo."

The attention of all eleven men was on the red-brick building with the smashed windows. They didn't hear the window of the public house behind them sliding open, nor see the barrels of three guns nudging out and the crack of rifle fire behind them came as a complete surprise. Denis Heffernan fell instantly to the ground, folding like a concertina. Another series of cracks and Paddy O'Brien staggered and sprawled forward, his collar shooting red. Michael Kirwan shouted, "I'm hit. Jesus, I'm hit."

O'Malley turned and emptied his pistol in the direction of the fire. Tom Roche and Barney copied him, while at the same time trying to move towards safety. The others had scattered, as fast as their love of life could carry them. Kirwan too, despite his wound, was running.

Fleming and Carty, the two nearest the wounded O'Brien, lifted and carried him between them, hauling him back along the lane behind the protective fire of O'Malley, Roche and Barney Parle. Roche took a graze in the face, cried out but carried on, retreating backwards, firing all the way. Somehow, they succeeded in getting the injured man around the corner without being gunned down. Barney and O'Malley took cover in a shallow gateway in the wall near where Denis Heffernan had fallen.

The shooting ceased. Barney could hear Heffernan trying to say an Act of Contrition. "Oh…my God…" Slowly he spoke, haltingly, the sound draining from his voice. "I am…am heartily…sorry…"

"It must be a habit with him," O'Malley said, "to be able to say it like that when he is dying."

Barney stared at the young man on the ground, struggling with his last prayer. He wanted to turn his eyes away from the sight but they were riveted onto the contorted body. "Is he? Dying?"

"I'm afraid he is."

Heffernan never got to finish his prayer: he let a small shuddering gurgle and his voice stuttered to a stop. O'Malley hesitated, but as no more shots came, he went out into the lane. Barney followed. O'Malley put his fingers on the wrist pulse.

"Nothing'" he said, and he dropped the arm, in a careless way that made Barney flinch. Why be squeamish about it? Heffernan didn't know what was done to him now, but still…

A thread of blood leaked from the corner of the dead boy's mouth.

"Did you know him?" O'Malley asked.

"I only met him first a few days ago." Yet he felt nearer to him than others he'd known his entire life and he was vibrating with a strange sense of disbelief. This was happening. It had happened. And now they had to pick him up. O'Malley took the legs so Barney grabbed him under the arms, took the weight of him on his chest. The head fell to the side, the neck at an impossible angle, but they proceeded, back down the lane, hugging the side of the wall as they went, nervous in case of more shots.

O'Malley's talk was all about Paddy O'Brien. The two of them had fought side by side against the Tans, he explained to Barney between breaths, and had been together in the Four Courts in Dublin since last April. When the Four Courts was attacked, O'Brien was one of the worst injured but he was determined to get back into the fight. As soon as he could walk, he had joined them in Enniscorthy, his head bandaged to hold it together. He was unfit for service, really. "But…" puffed O'Malley, "his eagerness to help…was greater than his strength…His weak and wounded body…was made to…obey."

It was clear to Barney that this was what Ernie O'Malley admired, the same sort of never-say-die courage for which he was himself renowned.

Around the corner, they laid Denis Heffernan's body on the path. Sullivan had notified first aid and said they were on their way with stretchers. Paddy Fleming came up to them on the street outside with Dick Sullivan. "The post office wasn't occupied at all," he said. "We were set up."

"Fuckers," said Sullivan. "That's not war."

Michael Kirwan lay half-upright, against a wall, a hand supporting his wounded side, face bunched with pain. O'Brien was bleeding badly from the chest. O'Malley went over to him. "Paddy, are you all right?"

He got no reply.

"I think he's been shot in the lung," Fleming whispered. "Best not to talk to him."

The lull in the shooting brought spectators onto the street, already carrying the rumour that there had been a fatality.

"Oh my God, it's true."

"Who's dead?"

"Who is it?"

"It's Denis Heffernan."

In seconds, it seemed, the crowd grew. Even the children were out, staring round their mothers' legs. There was a ring around the body, a circle people didn't dare to cross. They stood, awkward with shock, all their looks fixed on the same spot, as if there was nothing else in this world to look at but poor Denis, lying there on the pavement, his face open and pale as water, turned up to the sky. Barney took off his own jacket, put it over the dead face, wanting to shield him from the probing eyes. This isn't a show, he thought, wondering whether to let a crack of his rifle into the air to scatter them all.

Then he heard the sound of a bell, its determined ring drawing closer. The ambulance came flying around the corner and the doctor and the Cumann na mBan girls with their medical armbands were jumping down, bristling with duty, organising stretchers and bandages and other first aid. But what was that other noise, that other, more terrible wailing? The crowd parted to allow a woman of late middle age – hair half put up, clothes half put on – come running through, shrieking.

She fell to the ground beside Denis, threw Barney's jacket off his face. The crowd stood still, very still as Mrs Heffernan lifted her son's head onto her lap. Her words were indistinct but the sounds she made were unmistakable as she rocked him back and forwards, just as she once used to rock his little, baby self.

*I*t is evening, recreation time, the half-hour between study and bedtime that is one of the few unstructured times in the convent day. Tonight is November 1st, All Souls night. Dee, Monica and I are slumped over a radiator, thrilling each other with ghost stories. Monica is in the middle of a complicated tale about a ghost ship that can sail on land when the rec. room door opens and Sister Martha, the parlour nun, comes in. Sister Martha is the height of most first-year girls but many times wider and rounder. She looks around and starts towards us.

"What's this about?" Monica says. "Who's been doing something they shouldn't?" If a nun is looking for you, it generally means trouble.

"Jo Devereux, you're to come to the parlour."

"What's wrong, Sister?"

"You have a phone call from home. Come quick now and don't be wasting your father's money."

The last time somebody got called to the telephone, it was for news of a dead relative. Granny Peg? Dear God, please God, no.

I follow Sister Martha through the clumps of brown-uniformed girls scattered around the hall. In one corner, a record player spins out Elvis Presley and eight pairs of girls jive through 'Blue Suede Shoes'. At the games table, the Doyle sisters are once again beating all challengers at chess. Usually Dee and I are among those fighting around the record player, queuing to take off the show-band music favoured by the culchies, and replace it with the latest 45 by Marc Bolan or David Bowie, or LP by Bob Dylan or the Rolling Stones. We deride their dum-de-dum country music – Bogman Shite, Dee calls it – and their foxtrots, waltzes and jives. When we dance, we dance alone, letting our bodies go with the beat of the music. Head-bangers, they call us, but the insult has no sting. We feel superior: a new experience for me.

Music is a seal on friendship. Under my pillow, I keep a small radio so I can listen to the pirate station Radio Luxembourg after lights out. Dee, her bed just three cells down from mine, listens to the same programme and we communicate by sneezing when we like a song, coughing when we don't. Sometimes I cough even when I like something, if I think Dee might jeer. Singers like David Cassidy and Donny Osmond and David Essex – fancied by most of the other girls – are dismissed by Dee and Monica and me. Too clean, too nice, more like girls than boys.

We look for something else in our pin-ups and I find it in Marc Bolan. He is beautiful, with his slush-brown eyes and long curling dark hair, but it is not just his beauty that makes me shiver. Something else swims in the liquid brown of his eyes, something I acknowledge but cannot name. In the posters it is under my control; I can use him as I want. In real life, I know it would be the other way around.

I haven't told Dee or Monica about Rory. I could never gossip about him, giggle over him, drop him into our talk. Instead, I concoct crushes on good-looking boys from St Peter's College. One in particular I swoon over, a boy called John Foley. It is true that the set of this boy's jaw sends my heart fluttering down into the pit of my body. That before we go out walking, I belt myself into my gabardine coat and adjust my beret with the thought that we might see him on the way and he might look at me. That at night I do deals with God: Get John Foley to talk to me and I will give up the bedtime probing of my body that I have recently embarked on, the secret fingering that had me looking forward guiltily to lights-out.

I have become a cauldron of sensation and John Foley and his jutting jawline is part of that. But neither he, nor Marc Bolan, nor the churning explosions I barter with God, have anything to do with Rory O'Donovan.

The corridor is dark and cold after the activity of the rec room and my loafer shoes sound loud on the linoleum. In the parlour, Maeve is already on the phone, called down from choir practice. She pops her eyes wide at me as the phone spills a long string of squeaks into her ear. Nobody is dead, anyway; I can tell that much from her face.

"OK, Mammy," she says, after a little while. "Jo's here now. I'll put her on."

She pulls another unreadable face, hands me the receiver.

"Hello," I say.

"Siobhán." It is Mrs D., clipped and businesslike. "I'm ringing because we've a bit of news here. Eileen is getting married."

"Oh."

"The thing is, she wants you to be bridesmaid."

"Me?"

"Yes. The wedding is in three weeks' time. I've told Mother Superior and she's given permission for you both to come out for it. And I'll be in next Saturday afternoon to take you off for a few hours, so we can go down town and buy you a dress."

"All right."

"So I'll pick the two of you up on Saturday around twelve o'clock."

"All right."

"I'll see you then, so. Bye now."

"Wait...Who is Eileen marrying?"

As I ask the question, Maeve's head sinks into her shoulders, like she's ducking something that's been thrown.

"Séamus Power," Mrs D. says, after a pause.

"Séamus Power?" Does she mean the same Séamus Power who is first cousin to the O'Donovans?

"That's what I said," she snaps.

"Gosh."

"I know...I know. What can we do only make the best of it?" The words sound weary, like she has used them before on herself and others. "I don't know what she was thinking of...After all we've done for her."

"It's happening very fast, isn't it? A wedding in three weeks?"

A yell punctures my ear. "What are you saying, you foolish girl? Did anybody hear you say that? Did any of the nuns hear that?"

I look at Sister Martha. "No."

"Keep your mouth closed about this, for God's sake. Say nothing, do you hear me? Nothing to anybody, especially Geraldine Kehoe." Geraldine Kehoe is a girl in the year above me, from Rathmeelin. "There'll be talk enough without us advertising the thing."

"All right. 'Bye."

I replace the receiver and Sister Martha dismisses us back to our routine.

"God Almighty," Maeve hisses, as we walk back along the corridor. "What made you say that? Do you do it on purpose or are you just plain thick?"

"You shut up."

"Of all the men in County Wexford, Eileen had to pick Séamus Power," Maeve says. "What a wedding it's going to be, us on one side of the room, dozens of O'Donovans on the other and the bride's family stuck in the middle."

"Do you think they'll go?"

"Of course. You know the Powers and the O'Donovans: they're like that." She holds up her middle and index fingers, fixed together. "Mammy said they're definitely going."

"What about Auntie Norah? Will she go?"

"Oh my God! That never struck me."

"She'll have to be invited," I say. "She's connected both ways."

"Why don't you ask Mammy about it on Saturday? That should make for a jolly afternoon."

I make a face at her and we part. As I am walking back to the hall, the bell rings and the corridor suddenly swarms with faces heading towards the refectory for bedtime orange and biscuits. I decide to slip away to the dormitory for a few precious minutes alone. The loose knot of fright brought on by the ghost stories has gone, unravelled by a fiercer feeling. A feeling I want to have and hold, to take with me to bed, where I can hug it close.

Hope. A delicious, finger-crossing, heart-piercing hope.

HE IS THERE. As soon as I walk into the church, I know. I know even before I see him, on the aisle-end of a pew, almost halfway up. He faces the back door through which we, the bridal procession, have just entered. Turned round in his seat by the pounding organ announcing the coming of the bride.

So many times I have sat, rooted to one of these seats, a spectator. Now it is his turn to watch. I smile as I step up the aisle behind the bride, not at him but at everyone, like an actress beaming for the press. Eileen is the chief exhibit in this spectacle, but I too am on display, and I look good in my long blue dress, my face scrubbed and polished and made up, my hair scooped into a floral headdress; as good as I have ever looked. As we approach his seat, I slide him a look and let it rest on him for a second before sweeping past.

Up on the altar, I perform my bridesmaid duties as required: prettily. With my hair up, cool air teases the back of my neck. I imagine his eyes resting on the pale skin there and I shiver. The awareness that he is behind me is branded into my every move.

Afterwards, in the hotel, most of the men ignore the sherry reception and line up at the bar instead, three-deep, shouting for pints of stout and large whiskies. The women take the sherry and sit in sets around the reception area, little stemmed glasses pinched between their fingers. Between swallows, their lips twist sideways to one another with comments on the ceremony, on the cracks in Séamus's whispered vows, or the finery of Eileen's dress.

It is the women who are keeping the closest eye for any clash between the two families. We are in the corner nearest the door, the O'Donovans occupy the furthest end of the room and between us lies a gulf of hotel carpet that nobody intends to cross. I sit in Mrs D.'s female circle, with Maeve and Granny Peg and Mrs Redmond, who played the organ and sang in church. Auntie Norah, to everybody's relief, has stayed at home. Also in our group are Mrs O'Neill, Eileen's mother, and her sister, Mrs Maher.

I drink Coca-Cola, bottle after bottle of it put down in front of me by one person or another, while the hotel delays the meal to increase the profit at the bar. The sweet fizz adds to the excitement already popping inside me. From where I sit, I can I watch him without seeming to. He is at the far end of the room, in a circle of men that mirrors ours: with his older brothers and his uncles. I see him trying to join in when they burst into laughter, or slap his back, or spout asides into his ear.

On our table the glasses of sherry sit, barely sipped. Mrs D., as she tells everyone, would prefer a cup of tea any day. She feels awkward here, with all these people she half-knows. At home, in the house and the shop, she is the boss. Here she is exposed: a woman without a husband, a deserted wife.

Her friend, Mrs Redmond, admires my dress, addressing her remarks to Mrs D. "That's a gorgeous shade of blue she's wearing, Máirín. You have her lovely."

"Ah, now," says Mrs D.

"And what about Eileen's dress?" says Gran, mindful of Mrs O'Neill beside her. "I never saw any dress as nice."

Mrs Redmond slants a look across at Eileen, who is talking to the priest. "It's very fancy all right. Was it made or bought?" she asks, knowing well that the rushed wedding left no time to have a dress made.

"Bought," says Mrs O'Neill.

"In town, I suppose?"

"Some place in Dublin, I believe."

"Dublin?" Mrs Redmond's eyebrows disappear up under her perm. "Is that right? Imagine that."

"I knew as soon as I saw it that it hadn't been got around here," says Mrs D. "No local dressmaker ever produced that likes of that."

Mrs D. and Mrs Redmond are scandalized by the dress. Excessively expensive for Eileen, they think, and in the face of her shame, nothing short of brazen. This is what they said in our house last night. Now, in front of Eileen's mother and aunt, they let the set of their faces speak.

Mrs O'Neill's cheeks are pink. "I felt myself there was no need for it," she says. "But…"

"Girls like to go all out for their weddings these days," says kindly Gran. "And why not? Aren't you only married the once?"

"Thank God for small mercies." Mrs Maher takes the bite out of the talk by making everybody laugh but above her half-smile a pair of narrowed eyes have hooked into Mrs D.

"Ah, now, Mrs Maher," says Gran. "Don't go putting off the young ones."

"That's right, don't." Mrs Redmond touches Maeve on the leg. "This girl has probably got her eye on the bouquet later. Have you, Maeve? Will you be jumping for the bouquet?"

Maeve smiles at her. "I haven't thought about it."

"She's way too young for any of that, Mary," says Mrs D. "She has her studies to finish first."

"Of course she has. I'm only joking with her. And how is the study going, Maeve?"

"All right, thanks."

"Maeve is hoping to get into Carysfort College," Mrs D. explains to Mrs O'Neill and Mrs Maher. "To be a national schoolteacher."

"Oh. Like her grandmother was, once upon a time," returns Mrs Maher, and the words are drenched with significance. The shot, obscure to me, finds its target. Mrs D. shrinks back in her chair, away from her pride in Maeve.

"Oh, yes," says Mrs Maher, thumping her glass down on the table. "I was one of your mammy's pupils, many moons ago."

"You're going a long way back there, Margaret," Gran doesn't seem bothered and Mrs Maher's smile shows her argument is not with her.

"You never forget a good teacher," she says. "And at my age," she swivels her eyes back round to Mrs D., "You remember things that went on years ago better than what happened yesterday."

A prickly quiet settles around this pronouncement.

Protected by the audience, I dare to play innocent. "You never told us you used to be a teacher, Gran."

"It was a long time ago, lovey. Before I was married."

"Maybe Maeve will be lucky," says Mrs Redmond, twisting the conversation back to the present. "Maybe she'll get a job back in Mucknamore when she qualifies."

"Wouldn't that be great?" says Mrs D. "That would be just too good to be true."

"Give Father Pat a dance later on, Maeve," says Mrs Redmond, "and he might look after you when the time comes."

Again Maeve smiles, as if Mrs Redmond's blather and the possibility of coming back here is pleasing to her, as if the snarls in the conversation are not happening. Is it possible that her smile is real? Or is her face like my own, a lid that seals off pickled thoughts? I imagine their faces if I were to do what I long to do: walk away from their cryptic baiting of each other, grab Rory O'Donovan by the hand and run out the door with him.

The day draws on. I buy cigarettes and sneak up to the ladies' room to smoke. Dee has taught me how to inhale, drawing a fraction of smoke back through my nose. It's a neat technique that we both consider to be sophisticated, but I need practice. The ladies' room is empty, with a partition in front of the door that allows me plenty of time to drop the evidence down the plughole if someone comes in.

I like smoking in front of the mirror. "Let's face it," I drawl to my reflection, "I need a cigarette, the day I'm having." Everybody has a way of smoking: it is a stamp, like your signature or your way of walking. It can look sophisticated or sad, cool or anxious. I practise Dee's new method, feeling the nicotine jolt my brain. Inside me, a vein of frustration throbs.

I go back downstairs, endure the day bleeding on. I dance with Séamus, with each of Eileen's brothers and with every other male who feels he has a duty to take out the bridesmaid. When not dancing, I sit quiet in Mrs D.'s corner, peeping across. How can anything happen here under the drilling eyes of our families? I feel my hopes for the day splinter and die.

Towards the end of the night, on my final visit upstairs to the ladies', I let down my hair. My scalp is aching from having it pulled so tight, for so long. I take my comb from my little bridesmaid's bag and run through it through the spring of red fuzz, unsnarling the knots. When I am finished, I lean across the basin, rest my scorching cheek against the glass. Tears swell behind my lids but I push them back. Later, in bed, I will cry. Not here.

The door creaks open and I jump back, as if I have been doing something wrong. I turn on the tap to pretend to be washing my hands. Mrs D.'s face appears around the partition. "There you are," she says. "We were thinking of sending out a search party."

The soap revolves around my clean palms.

"You've been gone so long Eileen's gone up to her room without you. It's one of the bridesmaid's duties, you know, to help the bride change into her going-away outfit."

"I didn't know it was that time. I'll go up to her now."

"Forget it, it's too late now. I sent Maeve instead. What were you doing up here for so long?"

"Nothing, really."

"You took your hair down."

"It was giving me a headache."

"It's not half as smart down."

"It doesn't matter now, though, does it? It's nearly all over."

"Thank God. As soon as the going-away bit is done, we can get on home." She sinks down onto the red-velvet chair in the corner, unstraps one of her shoes, kicks it off. "My feet are killing me," she says. "On fire, so they are."

She crosses her knees, brings her ankle up and takes her foot in her hands. It's misshapen, rutted with bumps and blemishes that are visible even through the sheath of skin-coloured nylon. I loathe that foot, I realize, loathe the cracked skin, the protruding bunion, the slug-like toes, the moist feel and the stale smell that doesn't reach me here, on the far side of the room, but that I know surrounds it. And I detest the other foot too, sitting there still encased in its shoe, its flesh bulging beyond the straps. And the ankles above the feet, so puffed up with their pain, and the two shins, snaked by jutting varicose veins, and the knees like a pair of angry knots in an ancient tree and... and...and...? All of it. Yes, all. Every piece and part of her fills me with distaste.

Swinging my revulsion away before it shows, I carry my wet hands towards the towel machine in the corner. The exposed section of towel is soiled, already used. I tug at the loop, trying to pull down a clean piece, but the machine grunts and cranks tighter, refusing to dispense. As I yank, I feel something rip underneath my skin. Why do I care if she finds out about my smoking? About Rory? About anything? Why should I care about her disapproval? She disapproves anyway. Always has, always will.

"I'm going on down," I say, my hands still damp.

She looks up, surprised by something in my voice, squints hard at me through her glasses.

Outside in the corridor, as I am approaching the stairs, I see Mrs O'Donovan and her daughter May heading up. His mother, his sister. As soon as they notice me, they avert their eyes, turn in towards each other so they can pass without acknowledging me. I want to stop them, explain that I am different, that I don't care about the family row, but we pass in the usual way. They will walk into the toilet just as Mrs D. is washing her hands or walking out. I imagine them stopping a moment, before swinging away from each other. Let them at it: I am going to find him.

And then I look down to the bottom of the stairs and find that it's going to be easy, so easy. Because he has come looking for me. There he is, standing just inside the front entrance, waving up at me. The lobby is empty, apart from the receptionist with her head bent, behind the reception desk. Something quivers inside my chest and I begin to hurry down the stairs. He takes a second to smile, then he walks out the door. I slither out after him.

Night has fallen and a dark breeze is deliciously cool on my cheeks. My ears are pounding with the echo of the band's bass drum. He leads the way: down the road, around the corner to the back of the hotel, where we stop, between two cars. The boom-te-boom of the music reaches us, muffled, playing 'Little Arrows'.

We are shy with one another. He asks me whether I smoke, offers me a cigarette, lights a match for us, making a cup of his hand against the breeze. I dip my face into the flame, shake back my hair on the way up. I inhale nicotine deep, feel my light-headedness. He begins a conversation: about his uncles, how they had started drinking before the wedding Mass that morning, how many pints each had, who's holding up the best. He has had a few himself, he says.

"What's it like?"

"Fairly disgusting, to tell you the truth. But you get used to it."

He calls me Dev, short for Devereux, but also a nod at my family's political preferences and at our disdain for such things. He has no more time for Fine Gael than I have for Fianna Fáil.

"Is that why they don't talk?" he asks, meaning our families. "Politics?"

"I think there's a bit more to it than that. Something that happened in the old days, some dirty deed your family did on us," I say, smiling.

"I heard it was the other way around." He is smiling too. For the first time, I look fully at him. My eyes are wholly open to him but it's OK. I don't feel unsafe. When he speaks again, his voice is husky. "I had to fight to come here today."

"What do you mean?"

"They didn't want me to come, said Séamus would understand with me being away in school. I had to feed them a story about not wanting to miss the family occasion and really wanting the day out."

"So what was your real reason?" I want to hear him say it.

"I heard you were going to be here."

I let out a breath I didn't know I was holding and, with it, the small, deep-down fear that I had not acknowledged to myself, that our connection might exist only in my mind, might only be a yearning of my own. A reasonable fear — but I had been right not to admit it.

I lean across and kiss the lips I have touched so often with my eyes. I find them gentle, softer than they look. It is a light kiss I give him, our mouths barely touching, and when I pull my head back, we are both smiling still. He takes the cigarette from my fingers, drops it onto the ground with his own, and grinds both under his shiny black toe. The long, unsmoked tubes split, spilling their tobacco guts over the ground.

He pulls me close and this time our kiss is firmer. As our mouths tighten on each other, our bodies follow, burying deeper, until we are pressed full length against each other.

We kiss for a long time. Afterwards, we keep our heads close, our breaths mingling. He whispers, "If our mammies could see us now," and we laugh, both of us, together. For that moment, our foolish families – like the rest of the world – are nothing.

We talk then, our first real talk. I tell him about the convent, what the nuns are like, DeeDee and the trouble she sometimes leads me into. He tells me all about a vicious priest who has it in for him. Then we kiss again. This time his hands move across my tight blue dress bought with him in mind. I knot my legs against his and through our clothes I feel it, hard and unmistakable, delightful and alarming. I pull my mouth away.

"I better go back," I gasp. "They'll be wondering where I am."

"Never mind them."

We kiss some more but anxiety bears down on me now. If anyone was to see us…If Maeve came looking for me…

"Really. I'd better go."

"All right."

I step away from him. Night air cuts in between us, cold as metal.

"Aren't you coming back in?" I say to him.

"Better let you go ahead. In case anyone sees."

"Oh…Yes. Of course."

I walk away, backwards, still looking. I know I will rerun the moment a thousand times in my convent bed. As I reach the door of the hotel, he bows, pretends to lift a hat from his head in a flourish, smiling, smiling. A smile as wide and deep as the sea.

I go back in to my relatives, wondering what I will hope for now. For so long, all I have dreamt about is being with him, talking to him, kissing him. Now my dream has come true, I'll have to change it.

1995

I wake in my shed, to the knowledge that it is Sunday: no building noise, all is quiet. Up at the house, the machines lie silent, abandoned since tools-down yesterday. Summer weekends are busy in Mucknamore, when visitors arrive from early morning. I hated running through the crowds last Sunday, weaving my way between watching faces, then arriving down at the far end of the beach, beyond the curving cliff and finding other people there, walking or swimming, enjoying the solitude that is usually all mine.

It will be good, I tell myself as I unzip my sleeping bag, to be out in the earliest hours, while the sand and sea are empty and morning-clean. The best part of the day, Granny Peg always said. So that's what I do. I jog out slowly at first, through the churning, soft sand to the harder surface down near the water. After a few minutes, I pick up my pace.

It feels good to be fit again. Five daily miles is my average distance now, as it was when Richard was alive. It was tough at the beginning, struggling with breathlessness and sore muscles, but it didn't take me long to build back up; those earlier years were there, waiting for me to return.

The sun drops a dappled path across the water. This ongoing

heat wave makes me feel like I'm not in Mucknamore at all. Oh, we had days like these when I was a child, I know we did, when Mrs D. or Gran hung plastic buckets and beach-balls outside the shop and day-trippers came to visit, but so seldom. This part of Ireland might be dubbed "the sunny south-east" because it is warmer and drier than the rest but, to me, rain was always the spirit of this place, rain that could bear down on us at any time, in drops or sprays or showers or mists or slanting, angry strings; its absence always marvelled over ("Glory be to God, another lovely day!"), its inevitable return hovering behind every clear horizon.

Whenever I go to Murray's Supermarket for food these days, the talk is of the weather. Fanning their faces with newspapers, they look skywards. The temperatures are perfect, rarely reaching the eighties and almost always accompanied by a seashore breeze, but I heard the heat described by a woman the other day as "pure persecution".

I run until I come to the rock that tells me I've done my distance, then turn to retrace my steps. My footprints are the only ones in the fresh sand. In this direction, the offshore breeze fans my face and I inhale it deep, lengthening my stride as I draw it down into my lungs. I'm going to have a baby, I catch myself thinking again. A baby. Day after day, the idea reverberates round my head, like my mind needs to catch up with what my body already knows. My feet beat the word into the sand as I run: bay-bee, bay-bee, bay-bee…

I have left the early stages of pregnancy behind, the breasts that hurt as I turned over in bed, the churning sickness that made mornings a misery. Food still doesn't taste as good as it should – I am told it won't until after the birth – but physically, I feel better than I have in years, even better than the last time I was alcohol-free and training daily. I don't remember this surging energy running all the way through me: into my face, my fingers; into the feet that whip my legs along through strong focused strides. Maybe it's second-trimester hormones or maybe the contrast with the first, gruesome three months.

By the time I'm back at my shed, visitors are starting to arrive to Mucknamore. Some have come equipped as if for battle, with cool-boxes of food and drink, stripy windbreakers and sun umbrellas, sunscreen lotions and games for the children. Others bring only their swimsuited selves and a towel. Back in my shed, I watch them, but once I settle to writing, they fade away as the past rises up through the page to claim me. When I glance up, I am surprised to find them still there, sprawled across the sand or bobbing about in the sea, calling to each other.

In the afternoon, with the best of the day's work done, I am more distractible. A family walking by the edge of the water draws my eye from the page. A good-looking family: dark father, fair mother, matching son and daughter. The little girl wears a pink-striped swimsuit. Her hair, longer and blonder than her mother's, streams behind her as she and her brother trot ahead. She carries two buckets and spades and can hardly see over them, running so determinedly that she looks as if she might tumble headfirst. The boy wears a baseball cap the exact blue of his swimming trunks. His fat little legs pump him along as quick as they can, but not quick enough to keep up.

Ahead, the girl suddenly stops and bends to look at something. A pretty shell? A stranded sea creature? Buckets and spades slip from her fingers. She calls over her brother and the two small heads come together, crouching all their attention on it.

Father and mother are dressed alike, in blue jeans and white T-shirts. His hands scrunch in the pocket of his jeans, as if fisted; hers are folded under her breasts. Both bodies are bent to their walk, two question marks gliding across the sand towards The Causeway, a small but constant gap between them.

When they realise the children are not following, the father turns and calls, his hand a cup around his mouth. The wind carries his shout up to me in my shed: "Ella! Dara! Come on!"

No response. He begins to walk back towards them, his calls growing louder and testier, until at last the children look up and acknowledge him. "Come on," he says. They pick up a bucket and spade each, rush to follow him. Behind him, his wife waits, arms still folded, smiling indulgence.

They catch up. The man takes their daughter's hand, the woman, their son's, and the four turn onto The Causeway. Out towards the island they walk, breaking in and out of their foursome like a dance. I watch until they are specks too small to see and, when I can no longer see them, I watch and wait for their return.

And that night, Rory comes to see me and tells me that he was thinking of me as he walked on the beach, past my shed, with his family. "I knew you'd be at your desk," he says.

I let him tell me this, though I don't know what I'm supposed to do with it. For a while, we sit marooned in one of our silences. To break it, I talk to him about what I was writing about today, a picture that I've carried in my head, all my life: Daddy stepping off the boat in Fishguard, his suitcase in one hand and Mrs Larkin in the other, all a-quiver at what they have done.

From that small image, a whole gallery of pictures unfold. The pair of them on the train to Birmingham, sitting side by side, holding hands maybe, gazing out at the new sights churning past: rows of back windows of back-street houses in backward towns, all bigger than Ireland's capital. Nuclear-power stacks. Factory pipes pumping arrogant smoke into the sky. My father, taking it all in, gusty with confidence about what he has done, what he and his new woman are going to do.

Then the actuality of finding themselves in 1960s England. I tell Rory: "It would have come as such a shock to him to be looked upon as just another Paddy. At home, he was the big fellow who didn't mind coming down a level."

Rory moves in the dark, takes another bottle of beer from the sand where he has burrowed them to keep cool. Usually we use my oil lantern for light but, tonight, he has brought along one of those big scented garden candles that keep stinging and biting creatures at bay. It tinges the night with the tang of lemon.

He takes a long draught from his fresh beer and waits. "They only lasted a year. After that, he lived alone in some Birmingham bedsit. I picture that too, though I never saw it: one room high over a busy road, traffic snarling below."

I pull some grass out of the ground I sit on, make a little pile and pull some more. I don't tell him how I see my father sitting in a sleeveless vest, smoking and drinking tea at a formica table, one toe peeping through a hole in his sock. A black bin-liner full of fish-and-chip wrappings. An aluminium sink and a two-ring counter-top cooker. Copies of the Wexford Weekly and other Irish newspapers growing in a pile beside his armchair. Sometimes, the amount of details in my imaginings frightens me. I'm afraid of sinking into a place where I mix up what is real and what I have made happen in my head.

"What became of her, the woman he went with?" Rory asks.

"We never heard another word about her. Maybe she got tired of him when he wasn't Mr Devereux of the National Bank any more."

"What was he over there?"

"He never got himself a proper job, as far as I can make out."

"I only have a vague memory of him," Rory says. "He was nothing more than a face to me."

"I know so much more now than I knew then, especially about being Irish in England. There is so much I'd ask him now, if I could."

"But would you, actually?"

I sigh, knowing the truth. "Maybe not."

"When my Dad was dying, I wanted more than anything to tell him I loved him. One evening, near the end, I was left alone with him in the hospital. He was on a breathing apparatus and I sat in silence beside him, thinking: I'm going to say it, I'll say it on the way out, so that I'll be gone before either of us had time to get embarrassed. But I couldn't. When the moment came, all I got out of me was, 'Take care.' 'Take care', for Christ's sake!"

I laugh. "And my English friends think the Irish are so unbuttoned."

He lies back down, hands behind his head, his elbows two arrows facing away from each other into the dark. "We are, though. Compared to the English."

"Are we?"

He turns his head at the challenge in my voice.

"You know I don't believe in generalisations like that," I say.

"But there is a difference between the Irish and the English," he replies. "You said so yourself, that you felt it, living in England. That your father felt it."

That is true. I have felt the difference, and so have countless others, but that's only one story. There is another: all the people I met in England who are more like me than many of the people I met here.

"And what about this child you're expecting?" he asks. "How will you feel about it growing up American?"

"I'll feel fine," I say, surprised. This is the first time since the night in the pub that he has referred to afterwards. I don't see why that should bother me at all but perhaps he – being a parent already – knows something I don't. Generally in these night-time talks of ours, I have the advantage — he can't reach into the places I have been the way I can unreel his life in my head — but parenthood is where he has gone ahead.

We lie in silence again for a while. I am feeling it strong tonight, the awareness of each other that's always there, lying just underneath the talk. Our memory of how we used to be: young, lusty, careless.

"Gimme a kiss," he says, lightly, like it's a joke.

"Feck off." I match his tone.

"Don't be such a miser. It wouldn't kill you, one little kiss."

"There's no such thing as a little kiss."

He starts to sing, Bogie style: "You must remember this, a kiss is just a kiss…"

I don't laugh. "Stop it, Rory. You shouldn't. We shouldn't even be here, like this, each night. It's—"

"OK, OK, forget it. I was only kidding around."

I close my eyes, trying to steady myself. Behind the whoosh of the sea are other sounds: car doors banging, voices calling, somebody heading out into the night. With our pub closed, they have to drive up to Ryans of Rathmeelin for a drink.

After a while he speaks into the dark: "So…never?"

"No."

"You've gone right off me?"

"That's it."

"Jo, you don't have to be so rigid. I'm not going to jump you if you show a moment's feeling."

He is right, but I'm afraid of what will happen if I let go. I feel like I'm the one holding the line for us both, but I don't know how much longer I can last. Sometimes I fear he is the real reason I came back to Mucknamore, the reason I didn't rent a cottage down the coast. Is all this acting the hermit here just to keep him in my sights?

My grass pile is growing, into a mound. I keep plucking away, adding to it. He says: "After you cut us short, did you never wonder—"

"I cut us short? Me?"

"Come on, Jo, I wasn't the one who disappeared off to England without a word."

"You could have followed me if you'd wanted to. Maeve knew where I was."

"You left the country, for God's sake. You made it clear you didn't want to…' Then he stops himself. "Oh, maybe you're right. Everything was different then. I was so young. It was all too much for me."

That was the truth. That was what I found so hard to take. It was all too much for me too but I hadn't the choice to opt out. If I could have, would I? Would my love have let me? Old questions that once revolved round and round until my whole self was spinning.

"It doesn't matter now, does it?" I say. "I hate thinking about the young me. She was such an idiot."

"She was wonderful."

"Don't."

"She was. She still is. You are."

"Rory. Don't."

He starts to pick at the label of his beer bottle. "What are you trying to say, Jo, that we're just friends now? Is that why you think I come up here each night, putting my marriage under strain…"

"Then don't come, Rory. Don't come. I don't want—"

"You do want, you know you do. Don't say what you don't mean."

That takes me aback. That's my line.

"We know each other, Jo. Nobody knows me like you."

Nobody? Not even her? "Oh, Rory. We're different people now."

"Not inside."

"Yes, inside. Inside and out, every way. I am not that eighteen-year-old girl."

"I still see her in you."

"What do you want, Rory? What do you want from me when you say things like that?"

"You know what I want." His voice is low.

"Then why? Why do you want that?"

"Why?" The question surprises him.

"What, seven-year itch? Wife doesn't understand you? Midlife crisis?"

"You don't have to play the cynic all the time, Jo. Is it so hard for you to believe that I…want to be with you? You don't know how coming up here each evening is keeping me sane."

He reaches across, stops my hands from plucking grass,

holds them in each of his. His palms are cold from the beer bottle, so cold they feel wet. "Ever since you've come back, I feel like we are playing out a part. All these things you are finding out about our families, all this history before we came into the story. It's like we have unfinished business, like we have to play it out…"

He hesitates, shakes his head. "Does that sound crazy?"

"No," I whisper.

"See," he says. "You understand. I couldn't explain something like that to anybody else.' After a small silence, he goes on: "'Wife doesn't understand you…' You fire it off like it's a joke, but let me tell you, it's no joke when a marriage is going awry. I'm not saying I'm blameless in it, I know I'm not, and I know she feels every bit as bad as I do. We haven't been good for a long time. There: that's the first time I've said it out loud to anyone."

He lets me go, leans back. "We haven't. So when your mother approached me last year about looking after her will, and it meant I was going to see you again, I felt like a small light had been switched on for me. I didn't think you'd come back here, so I used to imagine going across to California to you, what I'd say, how you'd be…I fixed on it, held onto it, and that got me through. Seeing you, I thought, would sort me, take me out of the terrible paralysis that was squeezing me dead. I'd know what to do next. And now you're here. And I—"

He has looked into my face and what he sees there makes him falter. My wrecking-ball anger. I pull my knees into my chest, wrap my arms around my legs to try and hold it down.

"You talk about unfinished business, Rory," I say, speaking slow and low, winnowing out words that won't say too much. "You talk as if we mislaid something and now we can reclaim it. I could never, ever see it that way. For me, that time…what happened…it was a cleft. I can no more take up where I left off than I could go back to being a toddler."

"That's not what I meant." He untangles my fingers from

their grasp around my legs, takes my hands in his again. "Look at me, Jo. Please. I know I let you down before. But now...Now we're here and we're together. I'm not saying our feelings are the same as then, or that there aren't complications. But the feelings are there, you know they are. Can't we just concentrate on what might come next?"

1922

PEG'S DIARY 4TH JULY 1922: Independence Day in America --
and now in Wexford too.

It's Wednesday, very late. I'm sitting in the ladies' room of
the Portsmouth Arms, locked into one of the water closets with a
candle, the only place around here that it's possible to be alone. I
can't think right after meeting Dan. He's thrown me into a heap,
as he always does. I need to set my thoughts down to steady
them.

But before I get to Dan O'Donovan, let me first write these
glorious words: The Republic lives! Enniscorthy's fight is over
and the so-called National Army lies defeated!

It didn't take us long in the end. We had a shambles of a
morning during which we received a number of injuries and lost
one man – that boy Denis Heffernan that Norah and I met with
Tipsy the other day. After that, Mr O'Malley got decisive and
gave orders to collect all the petrol and explosives we could get
our hands on.

The plan was to blow in the yard-gate of the Castle, the
army's stronghold, then fire the building. A deputation of
priests, hearing of it, went to ask him to reconsider, to withdraw
from the town so further bloodshed might be prevented. Mr

O'Malley told them he was here as a soldier and under orders. If they really wanted to prevent bloodshed, it would be better to interview the Free State garrison and tell them to surrender. What he could do was arrange a ceasefire for an hour, to facilitate that.

The news went around the town in no time and the people piled onto the streets to see what would happen. After the hour was up, a Free State soldier carrying a white flag was led blindfold to our HQ, and that was that.

We'd won.

The Republic was — is won. I am pleased, of course I am, delighted. Though it feels different to what I expected and I can't stop thinking about Denis Heffernan. What a foul thing to happen, especially when it was all going to end like this the next day. A sneaky lie to pull our men into a sneaky ambush.

Watching the soldiers in their fancy Free Stater uniforms making their surrender was very gratifying, especially hearing them swear they would never again be disloyal to the Republic. It was decided to permit those who had fought in the War of Independence to keep their arms, on condition they took an oath swearing they would not use them again against us. Our side doesn't have anywhere yet to house prisoners, so all we could do was march them out of town. Within a few hours they were back, green uniforms turning up everywhere on the streets and in the pubs. They were greeted magnanimously: our lads are not men to be haughty about victory, especially against old comrades.

And that's how we came to meet Dan. Norah and I were walking up through the town, talking about going back home to Mucknamore to face into our ordinary lives. I can't imagine how I'll settle back down. And if it's bad for me, what about poor Norah? The past few days have been like a place apart for us all, but for none more than her. How she'll face her family, she doesn't know. She is nothing short of petrified. The thoughts of a

Republican victory will sicken her father and the thoughts that she was part of it…fighting against her own brother…

And now that everybody knows about herself and Barney, she's terrified he'll get wind of that too.

I tried to console her as we took a walk out The Prom. Right to the very end of the river-path we walked, then all the way back, and afterwards we sat on the grass, reluctant to return. These fighting days have really brought her out of herself. She's much freer than she used to be.

But there are still things she finds it hard to talk about, especially her family. You have to respect her privacy. And admire her loyalty.

We sat for ages. Lack of sleep had caught up with us and we were too tired to move. The sun took a long time to set and, even after it went down, the sky held onto the light, as reluctant as we were to let go of this great day. For a time we stayed, murmuring into the dusk, and saying a prayer for Denis Heffernan. Then darkness settled in for real and we knew we had to make a move.

As we were turning into Slaney Street, at the top of the hill, we saw two men arm-in-arm, one tall and dark, wearing the green uniform of the Free State Army, the other shorter and fair, in the trench coat of the IRA Volunteer. We recognised our two brothers, arm-in-arm, their free hands holding a bottle of porter. Leaning into each other and singing: Soldiers are we, whose lives are pledged to Ireland…

Dan looked down and saw us. "There's the girls," he called and – foolish! foolish! – I felt my heart take an excited tumble as he began to drag Barney down the hill towards us, laughing, nearly knocking him over, he took it so fast.

"Look at the state of you," I said to Barney when they righted themselves. I ignored the other fellow.

"Ah, Peg," Barney said, wheedling me. "Don't be like that…"

"Barney, you're drunk."

"G'way out of that. A few drinks, is all…a few drinks with my friend here…"

"Friend now, is it?"

You'd think he'd never heard what Dan O'Donovan has been going around saying about us.

"'Tis a good thing, surely?" he slobbered. "Men who were shooting at each other earlier today are now able to enjoy a drink together. That's a grand thing. Don't you think so, Norah?"

Norah didn't answer.

Dan's eyes were too heavy-lidded, though you'd need to know him well to see it. Barney was visibly stocious, barely able to stay standing. He was looking at Norah with his feelings all over his soft, silly face.

"What separates us is nothing…nothing compared to what unites us. It's Ireland we all love. Isn't that right, Dan?"

"Sure, Barney. That's it. Good old Ireland."

I could have slapped him, and my fool of a brother too, who hadn't even the wit to see he was being laughed at.

Then what did Dan do only lean across and whisper in my ear, so the others couldn't hear: "It's grand to see you. You're looking fine tonight."

My traitor heart twisted inside me.

Out loud, he said: "I think the four of us should go for a bit of a walk, to sober up this fellow." He elbowed Barney in the chest. "What do you say, girls?"

My insides took another roll. "No," I cried, so the three of them looked at me in surprise.

"No," I said again, more controlled this time.

"The Prom by the river is lit all the way to the end," Dan said. "It makes a nice walk."

Barely lit, as Norah and I knew, having only just come back from down there. Full of shadows and trees along the way. And part of me was tempted, but – thank God! – I had it in me to resist.

"No," I said a third time. "We wouldn't be caught dead with you two, the condition you're in."

I looked over at Norah and was pleased to see her nodding her head in agreement. I thought she might have been keen to step out with Barney, but I should have had more faith in her decency. Only an eejit like myself would even consider it.

"Ah, now, Peg." Barney fumbled around his sodden head for words. "Ireland is…Ireland will be…"

"I'll tell you about Ireland, Barney," I said, without looking at Dan. "Enniscorthy's battle might be won today but we've Wexford town and the other towns still to be freed. And even here isn't guaranteed safe yet. The Provisional Government isn't going to take defeat lying down. But here you are, on the side of a hill, consorting with the enemy. Go home to your bed and sober up and be ready for the work we need to do tomorrow. I shouldn't need to remind you, Barney."

And before he — either of them — could answer, I turned back up the street. Norah followed and we never looked back, not even when we heard Dan make one of his remarks. I know it was something facetious by the tone of voice. And by the way my brother let out a guilty laugh and then tried to swallow it.

*M*rs D. is late. By the time her car pulls into the convent car park, I am the last girl waiting by the recreation-room window.

The nuns have started to let us go home at weekends. Every second Saturday, we can leave after study at one o'clock and stay out until Sunday evening. It is optional, this home visit, and I'd rather stay in school. I'm pretty certain Mrs D. would prefer that too, but she'd never leave me here like some parents do: whatever would the nuns think of that? So I play my part, lining up with the other girls at the window, calling out, "There's me," when I see the blue Ford come in through the gates, swinging down to her with my weekend bag slung over my shoulder, as if Mucknamore is my idea of a good time.

Today, she is not hunched over the steering wheel, but out of the car and walking up and down beside it. Smiling. It's like seeing a clown's smile. Too painted on.

"Sorry I'm late," she says, as I approach. "Maeve is getting in on the half-two train, so there was no point in coming earlier. We'd only have been sitting in the car, waiting." If it was the other way round, she would have welcomed the time with Maeve, but sit in the car with me for half an hour? Intolerable.

Maeve has left the convent now, gone to Dublin to teacher-training college. I had forgotten she was coming home this weekend, but surely it is not this that has Mrs D. beaming?

"By the way," she says, getting back into the car. "We have a surprise at home."

"Oh, yeah?"

I open the passenger door, throw in my bag, nonchalant. Every cell in me resists her mood.

"Don't fall over yourself asking me what it is, anyway."

"What is it?"

"Well now, it wouldn't be a surprise if I told you, would it? But you could show a bit of interest."

We sit into the small car, Mrs D's perfume heavy, and she jerks into reverse, making the medal of St Christopher swing wildly on the end of his chain. It takes only moments to drive down to the station. She parks and, before getting out, replaces her driving shoes with a pair of slightly higher heels. Does she not realise that in either she looks just what she is: old? And old-fashioned. Mrs Moran, when she collected Martha today, was wearing gypsy pants and a cheesecloth shirt, but Mrs D., twenty years older than some of the other girls' mothers, has worn the same clothes all my life. Knee-length skirt, sensible blouse or sweater, skin-coloured stockings. An outfit that surely was never in fashion.

I move into the back seat, leaving the front free for my sister, take out my transistor radio, turn it to BBC Radio 1. It's the Golden Oldie Hour and they're playing Dusty Springfield's 'Son of a Preacher Man'. I adore this song. The lyrics and Dusty's ardent tones perfectly capture my fervid feelings for Rory O'Donovan. I lie down on the car seat, turn up the volume, holler along with the words. The song ends just as the puffing train pulls in. As my mother and sister approach, I sit up and turn off the radio before I'm told.

They are full of talk about Mrs D.'s surprise. "At least tell me, is it good or bad?" Maeve is pleading as they sit in.

"Oh, good," Mrs D. says. "Definitely good."

As if her smirking didn't already answer that. Maeve is such a suck-up.

At home, Mrs D leads us into the house like a tour guide, then stops us outside the kitchen door. "Are you ready?" she whispers and, when Maeve nods, she reaches in front of us to flourish the door open. Our surprise sits at the kitchen table: Daddy.

Daddy, drinking tea.

Daddy, with long straggles of hair tickling his shirt collar and two big, new sideburns. Looking up at us through a squint that is also new.

"Hello, girls," he says.

He doesn't get up, carries on nursing his mug of tea. Clinging to it like a raft.

"What are you standing there for?" says Mrs D. "Go on in and say hello to your father."

We sit in chairs opposite him. Maeve says: "Hello, Daddy."

I can't say anything. It's too sudden. The man I remember is still in England. The person in front of me is someone else.

"My God, you've grown," he says, to both of us.

"I'm nearly eighteen," Maeve tells him. "And Jo is fifteen."

"My God," he says again. "Imagine that. You're a real pair of young ladies."

He takes a mouthful of tea, peers over the rim of his cup with two hunted eyes. I notice how old his shirt is: the thin blue stripe is faded at the collar, the cuffs are frayed. My head rattles full of things that can't be asked.

Later, Gran fills me in. He turned up on Wednesday evening without a by-your-leave and got a welcome from Mrs D. as good as the prodigal son's. Had his feet back under the table by supper-time and now goes around the place like he was never away at all.

"Been good for business, mind you," Gran says. "Every man and woman in the parish has been in for a look."

That evening, Mrs D. sends me out to the shop to get some cooked ham for tea. I have to walk through the bar to get to the grocery and, for this ordeal, I always let my hair fall forward to shield my face. I hate this small journey: twenty-two steps of torture if certain customers are in, those who see me as a target. The ones who jeer my name ("Shove on your knickers...") or my clothes ("Nice blouse," they'll say, their eyes poking through it). If I respond, they'll mock my voice or my words. Any part of me is open to their taunts.

They are farm labourers, mostly, or fishermen or tradesmen. Lower on Mucknamore's carefully calibrated social scale than me, the daughter of the public house owners, whose father wore a white collar to work, whose mother was a nurse before she married, who attends boarding school and is intended for university. But the advantages are not all mine: they are grown men and I am a teenage girl. Their family histories hold no shameful secrets. And they are our patrons. We have to be nice, whether we like them or not. My shyness is a chink through which they can funnel submerged feelings about our family and their resentment of the money they have to spend to get drink.

I'm not supposed to take it all so seriously, I know. I'm supposed to pretend their teasing is a game.

I wish I could be like Daddy: indifferent. He is seated on the high stool behind the counter, arms folded and his eyelids drooping over their talk, in just the old way. While I'm waiting for Eileen to cut the meat, I stand where the customers can't see me, on the grocery side of the divide, listening. Easy chat slides across the counter and back in a way that it hasn't since he left. Man-to-man talk, about last Sunday's hurling match.

The bell rings and Pat Rowe comes in, stopping in the doorway with showy surprise.

"Well, well," he says. "Boys, oh, boys. Look who's back in town."

The other customers stand to attention, hopeful of a bit of

excitement: Mr Rowe is known for his direct talk. "Well, well," he says again. "Christy Devereux, back in the saddle. And there was us thinkin' you'd turned your back on this no-good town forever."

"Ah, now," says Daddy. "We all know what thought did." This is an old joke. What thought did: stuck a feather in the ground and thought he'd grow a hen; peed in his pants and thought it was raining.

Mr Rowe won't be diverted. "So where have you been, stranger?"

"Ask no questions, Pat, and you'll be told no lies." Daddy holds up a big glass. "Pint, is it?"

"Birmingham, was it?"

"Mmmm. Birmingham," nods Daddy, his eyes narrowing above the word in a warning to back off. And it works. Something in him – what is it? What? – stops Mr Rowe's advance.

"Did you see Mulcahy's tackle?" John Buttle asks from the lower end of the bar, when the silence gets self-conscious.

"Tackle, how are you," says Daddy. "That was nothing but a dirty foul."

Talk of the match resumes. Mr Rowe pulls up a stool.

Gran is right. Daddy's slipped back into his life as if it were an old jumper he found and decided to start wearing again. His armchair is pulled out of its resting-place in the corner, his boots slump in their old place inside the back door, tripping everybody up. His razor and toothbrush have reclaimed their spot in the bathroom. The only change is that he has his own bedroom now, in the second spare room. His comb is in there on the dressing table and the faint tang of Old Spice smarts in the air. Under a pillow are his pyjamas and a book: The Honey Badger.

On the cover, a woman with gold skin holds a sheet in one hand to cover her pubic bone. Her eyes are turned away, but two pneumatic golden breasts stare hard at me. It looks like the kind of book that has dirty bits, something that would get passed around in my school with giggles and page numbers. It gives me a strange feeling to find it here, in Father's bed.

In the wardrobe, two pairs of trousers hang, one over the other, beside a small row of shirts and jumpers. One shiny suit. And down at the bottom, his red canvas travel bag, empty and flat, like a deflated balloon.

Sunday morning over breakfast, Mrs D. announces that we'll be having lunch in the dining room today for a change. It's a celebration, we know, though she doesn't say so. After Mass, while Daddy looks after the shop, she and Gran and Maeve juggle pots and pans in the kitchen. I stay in the sitting room, avoiding them, stretched on my front across the rug in front of the fire, reading. Auntie Norah too ignores the cooking fuss. These days, what's happening on TV seems more real to her than the events in our house. She has not commented on Daddy's return any more than she seemed to miss him while he was gone. Gran has turned on her favourite program for her, The Addams Family, and aside from one thumb rapidly revolving around the other when Gomez kisses Morticia's extended arm, she seems relaxed. Smells of roasting meat and bubbling vegetables fill the silent room.

Close to serving-up time, Mrs D. bursts in on us. "Siobhán, make some gravy. I'll be back in a minute to serve up."

In the kitchen, Gran is mashing potatoes in the big pot. A roast leg of lamb sits in the dish, its bone sticking up like the handle of a club. I mix gravy powder with water in a cup, stirring it to get the lumps out, and when it's smooth, I add it to the meat juices. Mrs D. comes back. She has taken off her apron, brushed her hair, put on make-up.

"Lipstick now, is it?" Gran says when she sees her. I'm so shocked I stop stirring. The only time Gran differs from Mammy is on her Matters of Principle. I have never heard her vexed like this.

"A daub of lipstick is a sin now, I suppose?" Mrs D. puts on a pair of oven gloves that make her look like a boxer, picks up the meat dish and sweeps it off to the dining room.

When she's gone, I sidle across to Gran. "Are you not glad that Daddy is back?"

"As I've been told, lovey, it's nothing to do with me."

I pull close to her, searching out her softness. "Please, Gran."

She looks at me and shrugs. "Your daddy disappears off with himself, then turns up four years later as if he only went out to bring in the milk. He just—" She breaks off.

"But it's good that he's back, isn't it?"

"What would happen in the world if we all did a bunk when we felt like it?" A shard of envy seems to spike through her words. Is that possible? "If you bring children into the world, you do right by them. It's that simple."

But if it was so wrong for him to go away, why is she not happier that he's back?

"Gran, can you not just forgive him?"

I'm thinking of all the times she forgives Mrs D.

I'm thinking if we can forgive Daddy, why can't she?

"Oh, Jo, don't give me the hard face. It's only that I'm afraid for us, that's all."

"Afraid?"

Under her pounding, the potatoes turn to mash.

"You think he might go off again? Is that what you mean?"

She looks at me through glasses that have steamed over. "I'll say one thing to you now, and listen to me good, because this is one of the best bits of advice you'll ever get in your life. Don't interfere. Keep yourself to yourself. Let the Lord above look after what's to happen and stay out of matters as much as you can."

What is she talking about?

"I mean it," she says. "It's when you think you're doing good that things end up all wrong."

"What do you mean, Gran? I don't understand."

She sighs. "I suppose you don't. But think about it all the same."

She turns off the cooker, points towards the bubbling gravy pot. "Now get that into the sauce boat, like a good girl. This food won't serve itself."

*T*he air in my shed is thick and stuffy, like a hand over my face. I'm coated in the dream that just spat me out. A woman whose voice I knew but could not place was in the newly renovated house, calling across to me from one of the upstairs windows. "Come," she entreated, her voice a dry whisper. "You know why you're here. Come on over."

"In a minute," I said.

"When?" she asked. "You don't mean it. You're not coming." Then she leaped from the window and hurtled through the air towards me, so fast I couldn't see her face. Through the night and in through the window of my shed she flew, frightening me out of sleep.

"Noooo!" I screamed as I jerked upright in bed, heart thrumming.

I'm still in my terror for a second or two longer, then I come to. A dream, that's all. I look around: nobody else is here. My shed's whitewashed walls, my few belongings, the broken furniture at the end, Mrs D.'s suitcase: all are here, less distinct, less separate from the world and each other than in daylight. If I can see like this, there must be a moon outside. I look and look, settling myself with the actuality of things. They are here, I am awake, I'm OK.

Through the shed window, I can see the new version of the house, its outer shell complete except for doors and windows. The remodelling has been extensive: our old house used to hunch in that space but this new construction, not even finished, is already preening itself. I swing my legs out, slip my feet into their shoes. "All right then," I say aloud, to the voice in the dream. "I'm coming."

Outside, the night air is still and warm: no need for a jumper or jacket. Under the light of a full moon, my white T-shirt glows. My belly mimics the lunar bulge. I am now expanding day on day.

I am changing fast, but not as spectacularly as you, the life inside me. You are about a foot long now and already you have fingernails and skin, a nose and eyes, lips and ears. You have a heart and a stomach and kidneys and tiny ovaries containing all the eggs you'll ever need to have a baby yourself. Two days ago, I felt the first strange shudder of your movement, a quiver that was in me but not of me. It has come often since then, little seismic flutters that make me smile. Tonight I placed Rory's hand there.

"Isn't it amazing?"

"Amazing," he said, the intimacy of the act – the first time in twenty years that I have asked him to touch me – spiked with the knowledge that he has felt such movements in another belly. Not that we mentioned that. Since the night we almost quarrelled, we've given up such talk. He has stopped pushing me towards sex, which should have eased the tension between us, but hasn't. While he kept pressing for more, I held the line, but now he's stopped, I can feel my own need growing.

Up the garden path, past the machines that crouch in the dark, through the space that will be the back door. The stairs rising by the wall are naked timber blobbed with cement. I get cement powder under my nails from the banister as I climb, and I tighten my fist against its chalkiness.

I spy stars through the open slats of the roof. This is not the house I lived in. Concrete squares have elbowed out our unsymmetrical rooms. Eight squares, six doubles, two singles, each with a smaller square attached, the bathrooms.

In my bedroom, the little alcove where I kept my toys is gone. The walls are shorter than they used to be, squared off from each other. It smells of new plaster and wood, empty and open, not a trace of me in it. Nothing is the same except the sea outside the window, where it always was. I cross to the open rectangle, look out at the same old picture, milky in the moonlight, hear the familiar lullaby of the turning waves. I rest my elbows on the brand-new concrete windowsill and lean out and look.

I know now what Gran meant, all those years ago. That she regretted ever having arranged for her daughter to marry Christy Devereux.

It was in 1953, when she stepped in. Mammy had devoted her young life to doing everything right: becoming a nurse in Wexford hospital, tipped to become a ward sister — except that, by this time, she no longer cared about all that. She was tired of night-shifts and bedpans and it was all useless, anyhow, if it meant she remained single. Being good, working hard, getting on, she had done it all presuming it would help her attract a good husband. As a spinster, ward sister or not, she was nothing.

It dawned slowly on them both, that nobody was going to marry her. She was a good-looking girl, a qualified nurse, the only child of a family with a public house behind them: she should have been flooded with offers. Gran railed against the weak boys who showed interest but only for a while, who shrank from her sooner or later because of what they were told. Against those locals who took newcomers aside and explained why they'd be better off not getting involved.

Surely, there was some family out there broader in mind than the rest, able to get beyond the small talk.

But by the time Máirín was thirty, it could be denied no longer: none of it was her fault, but the consequences were hers to bear all the same.

That's what spurred Gran to action. Since it was the older generation who had brought stigma on the girl, it was up to her to mend matters. And while she was thinking this way, who should she meet in Wexford one day but the widow Devereux, an old Cumann na mBan girl, now a good Fianna Fáil woman, who had a son she wished to marry into money. For the sake of this boy, the widow had worked two jobs since her husband's death in 1938: as housekeeper in the mornings, serving in the public house on her street corner by night. Jobs that allowed her to be home when young Christy came from school in the afternoons, so she could have his dinner on the table and keep an eye on his schoolwork, while keeping enough coins in her red money-tin.

Out of her industry, Mrs Devereux was able to give her boy an education. She got him past the primary certificate into St Peter's College and people were starting to give him the same respect they gave to the sons of farmers and small merchants. Her plans didn't stop there: her intention was that he should go to the university.

Except the boy didn't cooperate. First he said he didn't want to go. Then he failed the scholarship. And not even the widow's sacrifices could support him at university without that. He could still have looked for a good job, an office position in Wexford or further afield, but instead he went to be a shop assistant in Doyle's Hardware, selling nails and the like to the tradesmen of the town. She was livid with him over it and frantic that he should correct his error before it was too late.

Sometimes she blamed herself, that's what she told Gran, one day in the middle of Wexford's Main Street. She had spoiled him, given him everything, and now he understood the value of nothing.

Back home in Mucknamore, Gran started thinking. Being married into a pub would be a great deal better for that young man than serving in a hardware shop. And she might, just might, be able to swing him an office job in the new building society that was opening in the town. A lot of Fianna Fáil people were involved in that enterprise and they were behoven to look after each other when it came to jobs and positions, after the way they had been treated by the Free State. The widow had done her bit for Ireland in her day, as had her dead husband – it was the treatment he was dealt in a Free State jail that had seen him off. The boy deserved help.

She wrote some letters and in time was able to call to the little house in Hill Street with a proposal.

The boy resisted at first, blustered and blew, never admitted then or since, to his mother or to Gran, that a part of him relished the plan. He knew that with a pub in the country and a job in the town, he could be a very fine fellow, might even, maybe, in time, be able to buy himself a motor car. The girl was older – thirty to his twenty-one – but not grey or fat or wrinkled and she seemed biddable enough. And – unforeseen inducement – Mucknamore was far enough from Wexford town for him to put distance between himself and his mother, who for some time had been a burden to him with her plans and ambitions.

So he did it.

He did it and when it didn't work out, Gran, you blamed him -- but you also blamed yourself. Is that what you were referring to that day in the kitchen, how that good deed of yours turned bad? Or were you thinking further back, to the days that began the trouble, to the things you had done that made your poor girl so unmarriageable in the first place?

I leave my own room, go down the corridor to the room my parents shared, and then no longer shared. Here was where I brought the post to my mother, where I searched for evidence of

Daddy after he came back, where he was laid out for his wake. Yes, Mrs D. moved him back in after he died. How I hated to see him where he hadn't been for years, knowing it was all for show. How I haunted this room, all the same, kneeling and pretending to pray while I waited for other mourners to go.

Here, right here, is where I ran my fingertips over his dead face and hands, searching out places that looked soft: the swell of his cheek, the pout of his lips. All unyielding; even his eyeballs under their lids were hard, like marbles. I didn't touch him while others were there, praying beside me. Then I would only look. His mouth was not quite closed, a tiny crack of black showed between the pink. I'd look at this so hard that I'd think it was opening, that his lips were about to part, pop open into a surprised O.

The room was cold for the wake, I remember that. No central heating in those days and, anyway, you don't heat a room that holds a corpse. I remember the smell of wax from the candles on either side of the bed and the taste at the back of my throat as I stared at what was left of my father. My first taste of death. I remember the look of Maeve, her young eyes hollowed out by shock, as my own must have been. And I remember Mrs D., sitting in her chair opposite, watching us watching him.

1922

PEG'S DIARY 10TH JULY: The days of our triumph are over already. As soon as news reached Dublin that we had the main towns occupied, a Stater Army column was dispatched from there. Down the Wexford road it snaked, a convoy of 22 lorries bearing 230 men and 16 officers, taking Blessington first, then Arklow, then Gorey, then Ferns and, at about three in the afternoon, they advanced on Enniscorthy. They approached the town in two strong lines, one up Nunnery Road, the other up Wafer Street, to converge in Market Square.

Our lads left, took to the fields and to Vinegar Hill, where freedom fighters had hidden in the 1798 rebellion. What else could they do, when the enemy was protected by more artillery and hardware than Ireland had ever seen before? Five armour-plated cars, two Lancias, more than 150 rifles, four Lewis guns. And an open "bird cage" into which they rounded us up, for their cronies to look on and jeer at us like we were animals in the zoo.

In each town along the way, the streets were thronged with town and country people both, cheering wildly and waving their hats and handkerchiefs. The press, now also an arm of our "National" government, is full of stories about these flag-waggers. Not a mention of those who stayed home with their heads in their hands, unable to believe what we've come to.

After taking Enniscorthy, the column moved on to Wexford. They took more than 100 prisoners, but plenty escaped and, before evacuating, we made sure to do as much damage as we could – setting fire to the courthouse and barracks and any other buildings that might be used to house soldiers, felling trees and digging trenches in the roads and bridges, to hamper progress as much as possible. So it's back on the run for Barney and the boys. The flying columns that won the Tan War for us are forming as I write. We beat the British once with such tactics, and can surely beat them again, even if they have Irishmen sent out this time to do their dirty work.

And dirty it will be, with 20 of their men to each one of ours, and every weapon and luxury that an army can have at their supply, while we'll have to make do with neither barracks nor base. This will leave us very unpopular as we'll have no option but to requisition goods and provisions from the shops.

But we must not despair. The challenge now is to carry the truth to the people in the face of falsification and censorship. The people must be woken from their slumber.

We know their vote was a vote for peace and, knowing all they have suffered, we can understand why. But the fact is, the Republic exists — and destroying it, trying to vote it away, cannot bring peace. With all the men on the run, the women will be needed to get that message across.

DIARY 22ND JULY: Norah came down to our place for a few minutes this evening, her first time out of the house since we came back from Enniscorthy, a full four weeks ago now. Her mother sent her to the priest's house for a Mass card and she was under orders to go straight there and straight back. They say she's locked in her bedroom, let out only to help with cooking or washing. She sneaked up to our place, coming up the back way from the strand and tapping on the back door. Mammy was in the kitchen and tried to get her to come in but Norah wouldn't, asking if I could come outside to her instead.

You could see she was frightening herself with her disobedience, the way her eyes were darting about the place, ready for the off. But she looked better than the last time I saw her, on our way back to Mucknamore from Enniscorthy. That evening, she'd been sick with dread. The sight of her disappearing up the road to her house, head bowed to the wind, back bent over the handlebars, face pale as candlewax... it nearly made me ill, myself to see her so.

Her disappointment tonight when she heard Barney was still away with the boys was deep. She had been counting on him to give her comfort and I thought how nice it must be to have your own boy you could lean on like that. Whatever their troubles, at least they have that in each other. I was near envious for a minute but then I caught myself on, remembered all that I have myself, and the awful things that Norah endures up at home, things I can only be guessing about.

"Has it been terrible?" I asked. She said she hoped the worst was over. I'm afraid to think what that might mean. She talked a bit about some of the things we did in Enniscorthy and I asked her had she any regrets. "No," she said, so vehement I jumped. "I'd do it again tomorrow."

I got little consolation from the words, the way she said them was so intense and strange. As if her life is already over and Enniscorthy was the high point, everything before leading up to it, everything after a downfall. As if she were already an old lady looking back on her childhood.

Her job is gone, for definite. Everyone in Wexford knows why she left Furlong's that day and, since the Staters reclaimed the towns, Republicans are next door to dirt in the eyes of the business community. So no job and no prospects of one. It's desperate to think of her confined to the house, with nothing to do but assist her mother. She's far too bright for that. I was lucky myself that the call to fight came during the school break or I too could have been facing unemployment. Father John grows ever less delighted with my activities but it's easy enough to avoid him during the holidays.

We said nothing about Dan and the ferocious things he has been doing and saying against us. He is firmly back in the enemy camp and even Barney is sickened by his duplicity. On Wednesday, he made a speech that's being quoted in all the Wexford papers, saying the country will not be "held to ransom by a crowd of blackguards masquerading as soldiers". So much for drunken ráméish about friendship.

With all the fretting Norah did about being caught, the few snatched minutes she had were hardly worth her while, though she said she felt the better for it. We have worked out a way to keep in touch. Going to the church to pray is the one thing her family won't disallow so we will leave notes for each other under a loose stone around the back of the chapel. I said I'd get a letter to Barney if she wants to write and leave it there. This should, I hope, prove some comfort.

DIARY 3RD AUGUST: Mucknamore was honoured today with a visit from a great lump of a Lancia military motor. It came sweeping down the village street at around eleven o'clock, driven by — who else? — Mr Dan O'Donovan. He's got himself a promotion and is to appear in a photograph in the Wexford Weekly next week alongside the big-wigs from Dublin, newly appointed Brigadier-Generals and the like.

When the Lancia arrived in the village, and people saw who was driving it, they trooped out onto the road like a herd of cattle to have a gawk. Even some of our own customers got off their stools and went out for a look. He sat off in it, taking in the compliments, letting the children climb all over the seats. After basking in the attention for a while, he drove on up towards his own place and we saw no more of him until the afternoon, when we heard the sound of the engine roaring down the road again. As he passed our place, he let a loud honk on the motor-horn. The nerve of him. We ran to the window and nearly fainted with surprise when we saw who he had in the passenger seat beside him: Norah! She looked tiny in the big front seat, shrinking down into the leather with her hand on her hat to keep it from blowing off, the look on her face speaking her humiliation.

Off down the road he drove, then he must have turned at the cross because in less than no time he was back, parading past our place again, blaring on his motor-horn once more, rubbing our noses in it, as well as Norah's. Up and down he went – fifty times if he did it once – until he made sure everybody in the village saw and heard him. We ignored the commotion that attended his passing and took good note of those who could hardly contain their glee at the insult to us.

DIARY 8TH AUGUST: In the paper today, a half-page picture of six Stater military men, including 'Lieutenant' O'Donovan, the six of them sitting up on the same motor Dan drove out here the other day. He is leaning back on the fan of leather that folds up like a squeezebox at the back and staring straight into the camera, his peaked military cap at an angle, but the face beneath as blank as the opening into a cave.

They all have the same look on them, the six army men in this photograph, with their strutting heads, their polished guns and self-appointed titles (Dan O'Donovan a lieutenant, Martin Hayes a captain!). They think they awe us with it all but it's the opposite. Their finery is English-bought and, for all their swaggering, you can see the knowledge of that in their eyes. They know their own perfidy and they have to live with it. Give me a battered trench coat any day, for the heart that beats beneath it.

DIARY 12TH AUGUST: Barney and the boys captured a barracks tonight, in Donore. We've been planning the strike for a week and they set off from here after tea aiming to get there around nine. It was after midnight before we got word of how it went. Daddy and I were counting the day's takings when the knock came to the bar window. We looked at each other and, putting the cash away in the strong box, he gave me the nod to answer it. I slid open the big bolt on the door and there stood Tipsy, all excited, the way he gets. "What are you doing out there?" I said to him, sweeping him in before he was seen. "Would you not go round the back?"

I knew by the look of him though that things had gone well. "Success?"

"Defin-I-tely," he replied, pronouncing the "i" in the middle as "eye" one of his little sayings.

"Come in, lad," Daddy said urgently. He made the offer of a drink, which — needless to say — Tipsy didn't refuse and we sat to hear how it went. Like clockwork, apparently. Barney opened the attack just after dark, firing at the two sentries on the bridge, two sensible men who lost no time in retreating inside the post. That brought the number inside to about fifteen, Joe Latimer commanding. They had a Lewis gun which they used to reply to our offensive and we focused our attack on that. More of our lads were arriving all the time, word having got out and, before long, we had over thirty, Tipsy said. By firing from four points, they soon gained access to the yard and from there it was an easy matter to lob in Mills bombs.

All the time, the enemy was sniping only half-heartedly, waiting for reinforcements from Wexford. What they didn't know was that we'd lined up Ballymolane Company to fire on

Wexford barracks, keeping the soldiers there occupied. That was my idea and it made the whole thing work, Barney insisted I was to be told so. Once the Donore boys realised they were not going to be rescued, they didn't take too long about surrendering. Up went the white flag on the roof and that was that.

Barney took the surrender and complimented Latimer on the good fight he had put up. The whole procedure took only two hours with no casualties either side. We captured the Lewis gun, which is faulty now but not beyond repair, some rifles and a fine haul of ammunition. Unfortunately, though, we had to release the men we took. Nothing hampers our work more than this inability to hold prisoners. All those men are now free to fight another day but if their side take any of our lads, it's inside with them to be interred in one of the old jails. Indefinitely. Without trial.

Oh yes, Mr Michael Collins and his followers have learned their English lessons well.

All the same, it was a sound evening's work. We'll sleep well on it tonight.

DIARY 13TH AUGUST: The Army sent a massive contingent today to clear Dunore outpost, led by none other than Lieutenant O'Donovan. We were apprised of their intentions in advance and our boys gave consideration to staying put and fighting it out but we knew we'd be outgunned and outnumbered so decided to get out in advance to spare bloodshed.

We cleared it of as much ammunition as we could on the way out and Barney, Pat Connors and Roller were still at it when the Staters arrived with a contingent twenty strong. Barney started shooting like mad while trying to get away and somehow made it over a high wall. He ran like hell until he came to a brake of bushes and hid there. Pat and Roller got caught. No-one stayed to put up a fight, which was sensible tactics as there was no point in causing unnecessary bloodshed. They've been taken prisoner and are in Wexford gaol.

So Dunore is in Free State hands again for the moment. The soldiers they have put in place are very jumpy, knowing they haven't seen the end of us. Several times a night, a mobile patrol is sent out from Wexford to provide backup, in case we decide to make a return call. As far as we can make out, the fools do it on the hour, every two hours. So punctual you could set your clock by them, according to Lama White. Can they really be that stupid?

Barney has sent a message that Molly and I are to go up there and find out. So we won't be long about setting up a welcoming committee for them. Let's see how Lieutenant O'Donovan likes that.

*T*he back road over the mountain to Dunore was the one they'd decided to take. It was longer and harder than the other two routes but it was the most isolated and thus the safest. Walking was far from comfortable for Peg. She had a canvas sling of ammunition around her waist and a bomb held in place by strips of an old torn sheet tight against her skin. The bomb was the bulkiest item, between the size of an orange and a small cabbage. The belt that held the pair of guns strapped down along her two sides also dug into her flesh. But the discomfort was like crown and robes to her.

It was a joy to be doing such work for Ireland. The stuffy worlds of home and school, rules and duties, were far away today. Today was about comradeship and adventure and she was going to allow nothing to be vexatious.

Since last week and the passing of the Emergency Powers, to be caught walking the roads in possession of a gun or ammunition was as good as walking into Wexford Gaol. Anyone convicted of possessing firearms or ammunition or explosives, of making any attack on "the National Forces", of destroying property, private or public – in short, anyone who believed in the Republic and was prepared to do anything to defend it – would get a spell in prison, guaranteed. And might be chosen for execution by firing squad.

In short, they were right back under the same martial law they had suffered under His Majesty's Government, only this time it was Irish men putting their heels on Irish necks.

It was Peg herself who suggested she should be used to carry the bomb to Dunore. If they were to be stopped by the army on their way to or from the job – a high possibility – there was a better chance that soldiers wouldn't search a girl. Barney had resisted the idea at first, said he was unwilling to involve her in danger, but she would have none of that. She was in as much danger any day of the week in their own house, she said, whenever the Staters came calling to raid the place, considering all the despatches and incriminating items she held there. Her brother argued it was quite possible the army's morals had degraded to the level of doing a close search on a female, but they all knew if one of the boys was caught, the game was up for certain. If he didn't want to use her, then they might as well to call it off altogether. "And wouldn't that be an awful pity, not to use those nice Mills bombs we got from the munitions raid, they being just the perfect size and type for the job?"

She persisted until he gave in. Bother to his reluctance, was what she thought. The men had had it all their own way for too long in Ireland. A new day was dawning now. The 1916 proclamation made Ireland the first nation in the world to proclaim the equal rights of women and men. The subjection of one sex to the other was a foreign institution, another inequity foisted on the Irish by the English. Unsurprisingly, it was the only iniquity accepted, you might even say cherished, by Irish men.

Now things were going back to the way they were in more equal, pre-English days. The time of Maeve and the Brehon laws that allowed women to own property and rule as well.

So on went the bombs and the guns, strapped to her body beneath her larger undergarments and an extra vest and cardigan for disguise and on top of all, her mother's old coat, too big for her normally but with her added bulk, almost too tight to close around the middle. Looking down at herself, she had a premonition of how her body might look twenty years hence.

"I'm like Ten-Ton Tessie," she'd said to Molly, who helped her dress.

"It's not that obvious, not really," Molly had said. "Just walk easy, else you might blow up."

The walk to Donore was a nice and easy one and for miles they didn't meet a soul. Clouds raised a little as the day progressed, seeming to promise a clearance, only to lower themselves and spill over again. The rainfall of the past week had had a terrible effect on the roads and, in places, they found themselves near ankle-deep in mud. At Hayestown, they heard the clop-clop-crunch of a donkey and cart coming up behind them, a farmer with a load of beet. He raised his cap without looking as he passed, his wheels throwing up dirt behind. They watched him pull ahead, the cart swaying left and right like the rump of some exotic beast, getting smaller and smaller as it pulled away, disappearing into what was ahead, giving her a strange sense of significance.

After that, many more miles of nobody and nothing. They walked mostly in silence, Barney with steady deliberation, something weighing down his steps. Norah, more than likely. Why couldn't he lighten himself on that? All that was asked of him was a bit of patience, you'd think the girl was dead and in her grave, the way he carried on. God made them and God matched them, the pair of them so intense.

A spattering of rain was beginning to fall when they heard the rumble of a lorry in the distance, sounding like it might be coming their way. Tipsy looked back first. "Oh, Lord! It's them."

"It's all right," said Barney. "Stay calm. We knew this would likely happen."

"We're only walking, remember," said Lama. "Not breaking any law."

Peg glanced back. "It's definitely them," she said. "This is it."

The lorry pulled in close beside them, revving. When they didn't look back, it pulled ahead and drew itself crossways up ahead, blocking their way. The engine stopped and a soldier jumped down. Dan O'Donovan.

"These are mine," Peg heard him say to the other soldiers in the car and he stood by the vehicle, waiting, his legs planted wide, his hand on his gun.

He looked fine, there was no denying it, six foot two of manhood in its prime, all shiny boots and buttons, the very picture of a soldier. She felt ashamed of her dilapidated coat and, if she was shabby, the three boys beside her were next door to tramps. One look at the contrast between them and him told the story of this war's injustices.

The other officer stayed behind the wheel, a man she didn't know. In the back, a third soldier petted a Labrador puppy.

"So," said Dan, as they approached, dragging the word out. "We're a little far from home, aren't we?"

Silence.

"What brings us to this vicinity?"

Barney gave him the prepared line. "We're visiting," he said.

"Of course you are. And the person to be honoured by this visit?"

"An aunt of mine who lives in Ferrycarraig. Mrs Roche."

"Looking forward to seeing half of Mucknamore village, is she?" This with a nod towards Tipsy and Lama.

"She's a hospitable woman."

This is witless talk, thought Peg. "Going for a walk is not a crime, Dan," she said.

He turned to her. "You know well I could take you all in for questioning."

His eyes travelled down her body and she could feel a blush rise in her cheeks. He was staring hard at where the bomb was pressed between flesh and fabric. She looked down, found a streak of whitewash down one side of the coat, which she had got one night painting wall slogans. "We're whitewashing the sheds at home," she said, then realised he hadn't asked the question.

"Is that a fact? I must around come and see them," he said. "To admire your handiwork."

Oh, this petty taunting: it was hateful. She was flooded with a longing to say so. If they were alone, she would say to him: all right, Dan, we are enemies now. All right, so be it. But let us, please, have respect for one another. Let us not have smallness between us.

He threw her another look like something you'd fling at a yapping dog, then turned his attention to the boys. "Hands up," he said. Six arms were raised. Tipsy started smiling like a drunkard, because the attention had turned from Peg. If he wasn't able to keep better control of his face, he'd give them away. Dan ran his hands down the torsos of the three men who used to be his friends – pat, pat, pat – in the most mechanical way, like he'd no expectation of finding anything. Then his eyes returned, slowly, carefully, pointedly, to her.

His face was quizzical as he let his look travel down to the centre of her again as if he could see right through her mother's coat.

How could she ever have thought it would fool anyone, and especially him, with his eye for the female form?

"New overcoat?" he asked.

She shook her head. "It's Mammy's."

"I was thinking it wasn't your style. And what might have you wearing your mother's coat, I wonder?"

"I don't need a reason, do I?"

She was done for. He was going to search her. He was well capable of it, the conventions wouldn't matter to him. One touch of his hands and he would know it wasn't flesh he was feeling through her garments but solid steel.

"Open it," he said.

That day on the Causeway came to her mind, the day he'd bent to wipe the chalk-dust marks off her skirt, and another flood of blood surged to her skin, and with it, the realisation that whatever it was they had had for one another was now gone, spoiled forever. In that moment she knew again, but only really for the first time, their estrangement. He and she were enemies.

This full and final knowledge made her want to bend over and close her arms across her chest. She was splitting inside. This must be what people meant when they talked about hearts breaking, she thought. She'd believed she'd understood that phrase but she hadn't, not until now, when she recognised just how precisely it described the feeling. Heart. Breaking.

Forbidden now from loving him, what felt like an irrevocable thought gripped her: I'll never love another. You were the only one for me. The tragedy of that, the knowledge of how deep it went, pulled her eyes up to his. Search me if you like, she thought, knowing the thought showed on her. Search me, do your worst, do whatever you want, because it makes no difference now to me. I'm bereft anyway.

He stared at her. He was going to do it. As the moment grew and grew between them, she saw him decide that he would. She saw him change his mind. Then change it back again. And again make a reverse. Indecision danced forward and back in him until, finally, he dropped her gaze.

He turned to the others, gave them all a peremptory shake of his head. "Go on," he said. "But ye'll stay out of trouble if you know what's good for ye."

At Dunore, the sunset was dripping liquid oranges and golds and the rain-filled potholes all along the bridge glowed full of its light, as if they were broken fragments of the sky that had fallen to earth. Peg went behind a copse of wet bushes to divest herself of her load. By now, her flesh was screaming. The indentations the weapons made in her flesh were pink weals turning red, so deep she felt no immediate relief on untying the straps and belts that held them in place. She placed the bomb carefully on the grass, the heat of her own body still on it.

She brought her booty over to where the boys were gathered on the bridge, smoking. Lama and Tipsy had a gun each and Bronco was complaining that he wanted one. "That's not fair."

"You're lucky to be here at all, lad," Peg said to him. "Remember that and respect your officers."

She handed the bomb – which seemed to be throbbing, as if it had a pulse – to her brother and they all took their places on the bridge, looking down on the flat road below. The sun was gone, leaving a fading shadow of pinks and golds behind all along the horizon. A wet star came out to shine. Then two. Soon there were dozens, and then too many to count. If the soldiers didn't come on quick, it would be dark.

With the thought, she heard it, faint, distant but unmistakable: the engine-sound of the military motor, chugga, chugga, chugga. On the bridge, they stiffened themselves, each making eye contact with all. Peg could see the twitch of that little muscle of Barney's that always flickered beneath his temple when he was nervous. Tipsy and Lama pointed their double-barrelled guns down to where the car would pass.

"Nearly too easy," Lama whispered.

It would all be down to timing.

The chug of the lorry drew nearer. With it came the sound of voices: the soldiers were singing, yes, singing. "A Nation Once Again", a song they had no right to sing. They took the bend that brought them into view. There were five of them, two in the front, three in the back.

No sign of Dan. A flood of relief swept through Peg, not entirely surprising her. Would she never learn?

The car approached, closer and closer. As it came under the bridge, Barney lobbed down the grenade. It fell with a clean arc and seemed, as far as Peg could see in the dusk, to land right in the middle of the vehicle.

"Bull's eye!" hissed Lama. "Bull's fuckin' eye."

The soldiers had time for a moment's surprise. In the dimness, they took the moment to look down at the bomb, then up to see where it had come from, before the explosion erupted, blasting them beyond thought.

The lorry veered off course. One body was flung clear. He might have had some chance of survival if he'd stayed where he was and played dead, but instead he picked himself up from the road and ran. Barney and Lama turned their guns on him, clack-clack-clack, and one or more of their bullets did its job: he crumpled onto the ground.

The vehicle, thrown off its steer, hit a wall. The driver had fallen sideways over his companion in the front seat, and both were apparently dead. The two in the back were also unmoving. Barney sliced the air sideways with his palm, his signal to the others to cease fire.

They stopped. The air drained of sound, became eerily empty. Above gulls cawed, casually, as if nothing had happened.

Peg was horrified but at the same time exultant. I am alive, she thought. They are dead now but I am alive. She could feel her blood moving. She could feel her skin and her fingernails and her scalp as if she'd never felt them before. Everything that she normally took as nothing was glowing bright in her; she was like something charged. The men on either side – her brother, their friends – were all looking to her and to each other, all bonded by the same wild and fearful and exhilarated awe. Now I understand, she thought. For the first time, I know.

Her brother shook his head at her. "You shouldn't have been here for this."

"Don't say that."

"You shouldn't."

He meant well but he was misguided, suffering from an outdated code of chivalry. The call to blood and dirt and sacrifice and glory was in her human heart as well as his. This was her world too, she wanted it just as he did. "Well, it's too late now," she said, not wanting to argue with him, but knowing that if he had the power to take this moment from her, she would fight him for it, claw it back from him with nails and teeth.

"Come on," he said. "Strap those guns back on under your coat. And lads, scarper. We'd all want to be getting ourselves out of here."

A quarter of a mile off, the Free State soldiers at the outpost had heard the explosion and were already jumping into their lorries, guns unlocked and ready, minds leaping with intentions of what they would do if what they had heard meant what they thought. Three minutes was all it took them to reach the bridge but they were too late. Only their five dead comrades remained at the scene. The killers were gone, swallowed by the rising tide of night.

*U*nleashed, that is how I think of myself. Like I am letting out a breath that I have been holding since I was born. I am almost eighteen, I am in Dublin, I am at university. Mucknamore is now, almost, my past. I have to hold myself back from throwing myself down on the soft grass, from throwing my books and papers in the air, from throwing a song up to the sky.

Underpinning my delight is the knowledge that Rory O'Donovan is here too, walking around this very campus somewhere. Early this morning, I saw him, standing outside Lecture Theatre M, a crowd around him. He looks good: long, straight, black hair looped behind his ears. A long military coat, down to his ankles, complete with epaulettes on the shoulders. Black jeans and black polo-neck jumper underneath. Compared to most of the other guys in their woolly jumpers and duffel coats, he is…oh, incomparable. For a while I watched him like I used to watch him at Mass when we were children, then I slipped away leaving him to his new friends. It won't be long, I know. We'll find each other soon.

He seems to have met a lot of people already. I am the only person from my old school in my faculty. Dee is doing science,

Monica has gone to Trinity College, the rest are training to be teachers or nurses or secretaries, the full gamut of our occupational options. But I will get to know people, I know I will: intelligent, amusing people. Books got me through my last two years in the convent and Mucknamore, reading and imagining other lives, the ways I might live once I got out. And now I am out. Released.

I walk circumspectly down to the lake that is the centrepiece at University College Dublin, a sunken concrete tub, square like a swimming pool but brown-grey, not blue. Leaves, papers, bottles, rusty tin cans, too-white plastic cups and other, less identifiable things lurk in its murky corners. Extinguished cigarette butts line the sides so it's hardly picturesque, but still the students are drawn to amble around the wide flat steps that form the perimeter, or loll on nearby benches. Couples lay down coats to lie on the grassy verge, limbs twisted around each other.

October sunshine skims the square of flat, still lake water, burnishing it to brass and my heart swells with the beauty of the day. Rapture cracks through my skin, turning my walk into a skip down the concrete path, red folder clasped to my chest.

Behind me, a shout roars out. "Oi, O'Donovan, get back here."

A stampede of feet and leaping yells comes hurtling my way. I turn to see him, Him, running towards me, his coat, that military coat, crooked over his arm. He runs a smoker's run, to the tune of gaspy breaths, and a group of guys running after him are gaining ground. "Well...well..." he pants, when he sees me. "If...it isn't...Dev." Then he grabs me from behind and swings me out in front of him like a shield.

Into my ear he whispers, "Sorry about this." Out loud to his pursuers he says, "Stop right there...or...the lady gets it."

"Rory. For God's sake!" I struggle to pull away but his grip tightens on my arms. His nonsensical "warning" has confused his pursuers. A tall guy, with arms so long they almost reach his knees, steps forward. "You'll have to do better than that, O'Donovan."

"I mean it. One…more step…and in she goes."

"What do you mean? In?"

He pulls me closer still, so the length of his body behind me lines mine. His hair tickles my face; it smells of stale smoke. And of him.

Long-Arms advances cagily and Rory bends me over, towards the water, as a response. I kick backwards at him and connect with his shin. "Ow!" His voice is wounded.

"Let her go!" insists Long-Arms.

Kick or no kick, Rory is resolute. "Lay off your yes-men and I'll think about it."

His opponent looks behind, gives a toss of his head, says, "All right, lads, you can leave him to me."

Objections murmur up but the group disbands, most moving away. One or two stay behind to watch, hopeful of action.

"Now," he says. "Let her go."

"Yeah. As soon as you clear off the same way your stooges went."

"I'm not going anywhere, pal. You owe me." He advances.

"I told you," says Rory again, leaning me towards the water.

"You can fuck her in for all I care. I just want what's mine."

I twist my mouth down towards Rory's hand, my teeth close around flesh and bone as I bite, hard. A yelp of pain loosens his grip a fraction, enough for me to slip away. As I pull free, I have one perching, teetering moment of disbelief – I'm going in? – then I'm falling, hands clawing the air.

I hear Long-Arms shout – "For fuck's sake, O'Donovan" – as dirty water slams up to meet me. Gasping, spluttering, I find my feet. It's shallow, only halfway up my thighs. Water streams from my eyes, my hair, my clothes. Water and rivulets of rage.

Around the lake, people are looking and pointing and laughing at us. At me. Rory's face holds surprise, stifled laughter and contrition. And something else entirely. I feel his eyes on my breasts, a look that plucks me out of my own body, so that I see what he sees: my wet top clinging and my hands up squeezing water out of my long red hair. I am Woman in Water, Venus among the Waves, Miss Wet T-shirt.

Long-Arms extends a hand to me, an offer of help. Rory sees this, crouches and proffers his hand too, and it is his I take, his palm warm and dry against my own. He tries to pull me up but my grip is loosened by slippery water.

"I can't," I say.

He bends closer. "Give me your other hand too." He leans forward onto his toes, penitent, keen to help. A sudden yank on both hands, as hard and strong as I can make it, and his weight slips. With a splash, he's in, and it's his turn to cry out. "Nooooo!"

"Yes!" is my answer, as I hurry towards the edge.

Long-Arms is jubilant. "Well done! Well done!"

Before Rory has righted himself in the water, I am hauling myself out. Trying to ignore the growing audience, I retrieve my folder and press my way through a tunnel of laughing faces, my knees turned out, cowboy-style, jeans dragging between my legs, socks squelching inside my boots.

I haven't gone far when I hear him coming up behind me, calling. "Hey! Dev! Wait."

It's the name that stops me, makes me look back, the name only he has for me. And the tone of his voice as he says it. He is clambering after me in wet clothes, insouciant to the crowd. Not ignoring them as I was, not even seeing them. His eyes are fastened on me. "Wait," he shouts. "Please. Wait."

As he reaches me, his index and middle finger are raised and crossed. "Pax," he pants, like we're a pair of schoolyard children.

"Pax?" I throw my eyes skywards. "Pax?"

"Ah, come on. We're evens now."

"We are not. What the hell were you thinking of?"

"I don't know. Nothing. I wasn't thinking, was I?"

"What did that guy want?" My voice is still cross but my anger is fading, overwhelmed by other feelings.

"Furry Freak."

"A magazine?"

"Mmmm. This month's issue, precious stuff." He nods, releases the laughter he's been holding.

"I ended up in the lake over goddamn Furry Freak magazine?" I am indignant and then, suddenly, find I'm laughing too. "Do you know how ridiculous you look?"

His hair is dry-black on top but wet-black at the ends, as if dye is growing out. His wool jumper is leaking runnels of water down his legs and around his feet.

"You look wonderful," he says. "Goddamn gorgeous."

The words stop the laughter bubbling in my throat. Then he is bending down and scooping me up. God, what now?

"Come on. You can't walk in those wet jeans. I'm bringing you home to dry."

He lifts me like I weigh nothing, settles me into place: my knees looped over one arm, the rest of me curled tight into his chest. His wet sweater soaks my cheek but underneath is the heat and smell of his skin. After a few minutes of carrying me, his breathing becomes alarming.

"You don't have to carry me. Put me down."

"No…Least I…can…do…"

"Rory, I mean it. You can hardly breathe. Put me down."

"…Nearly…there."

"Where?"

"Car…park. Don't talk…"

He has a car? He deposits me at the passenger door of a VW Beetle, grey and ancient. When he's regained his breath he asks, "Do you like it? My sister gave me an advance on my grant."

"You're on a grant?"

"Every farmer in Ireland gets a grant, no matter how many acres they have. Creative form-filling." He opens the door for me. "Hop in."

I sit in onto the leather seat with a squelch.

"If you spent your grant on a car, what are you going to live on?"

"The old man has given me some money and I've got myself a job. Barman at the Arrow."

"All in two days?"

"Not bad, eh?"

We drive out of Belfield, down the dual carriageway to Donnybrook, but instead of turning right for my flat in Sandymount, he goes left, towards Ranelagh.

"I live the other way."

"Do you want to go home? I was going to bring you to my place."

"Oh."

"Is that all right? There's a launderette beside me. They'll dry the clothes for us."

His flat is wonderful: two rooms and a bathroom all to himself. Like most students, I am sharing. Dee and I have rented a cramped bedsit with a mini-kitchen in the corner. Its flowery wallpaper and swirly carpet combination makes me feel seasick, but I love it because Mrs D. had wanted me to live in a university hostel run by nuns. The idea of Dee and me loose in Dublin with no supervision filled her with horror but Maeve and Granny Peg came in on my side and she had to give in.

Rory's flat is in a different league: smooth beige walls and floors, a suite of furniture that matches, a breakfast bar, a dining table for four. On one of the walls, he has put up a poster of 'Che' Guevara, on the others two Salvador Dali prints.

"This is lovely," I say.

"I spent all summer planning the sort of place I wanted. I've everything in place now. Well, almost everything."

He sends me a significant look that makes me shiver.

"Come on. We'd better get you out of those clothes."

Everything he says has two meanings. He doesn't seem to notice.

He plays the gentleman then: shows me how to use the shower; presents me with his dressing gown, soap, shampoo, towels. I undress. The water is strong and hot and I stay under its comfort for a long time. Afterwards, I wrap myself in his robe and find his smell wafting up to my nostrils every time I move my arms.

When I come out of the bathroom, he is sitting at the counter, wearing only a towel. Hair black and silky as a pelt covers his chest and weaves down his legs to the bare feet resting on the bar of the stool. He has a curl of black hair on each big toe. On the counter, a cup of tea is waiting for me, steaming.

"You can put your clothes into that bag over there," he says. "I'll bring them down to the launderette when I've had my shower."

While he is showering, I sip my tea, look at his books. Stephen King. Leon Uris. Zen and the Art of Motorcycle Maintenance. A Hitchhiker's Guide to the Galaxy. Lord of the Rings. Boy's books. On another shelf, beside a large professional-looking camera, are some photography books: some instructional – The Guide to Freelance Photography – others full of pictures. I flick through them for a while then I notice a brown manila folder with a black-and-white picture peeping out. I open it and lay the pictures I find out on the counter. At first they look abstract, a series of unusual shapes taken from different angles, then I realize I am looking at close-ups of animal body parts: a cow's udder, a horse's nostril, a sheep's tail, a pig's eye. I sit up on the stool to look closely. They are strange, these fragments of bodies, almost alien.

The bathroom door clicks and he comes back out. Dressed. Fully dressed: jeans, T-shirt, even socks.

"Oh, God, those pictures," he says, when he sees them laid out.

"You took them?"

"Guilty as charged." He is blushing, just a little.

"No, they're good. Different."

He shakes his head. "They didn't work. But I think I'm on to something. I need to keep working it out."

Uncombed knots of wet hair hang down his back, spattering a line of wet across his T-shirt. He sits beside me on the second high stool, close enough to touch. I smell on him the sharp soap that has also washed me.

"So," he says with a smile, "if our mammies could see us now."

What he said to me at the wedding. My heart leaps to the words and then – somehow – we are leaning into each other and kissing and I am off my stool and he is off his and we are wrapped around each other and I am straining towards him and one of his hands has slipped inside my dressing gown onto my bare body and is gliding across my skin.

He pushes the robe from my shoulders so it slithers to the floor. The buckle of his belt is digging into my belly, and the prod of his swelling underneath it. I am naked against him. Inside me, lust rears. I lean into him, wanting to swallow him up. I want to do everything with him, everything, anything. This is it, at last. What I have been waiting for.

PART IV
SURGE

1995

I know all about TB, or "consumption" as they called it in Gran's day. Hippocrates's "Captain of the Three Men of Death", it was one constituent in Richard's cocktail of killers.

Inhaled from the coughing or sneezing of an infected person, the bacillus lodges itself in the alveoli of the lungs, encasing itself within a waxy cell wall as the immune system and white blood cells rally to fight it, so that equal numbers of bacteria survive as are killed. This, the latent phase of the disease, can go on for years, even decades. An internal war rages but the body is unaware, feels nothing.

Then, for some reason – pregnancy, HIV, hunger, stress, age or, sometimes, nothing obvious — the balance tips and the bacteria begin to win, slowly but steadily replicating until each white blood cell is so full that it bursts. The alveoli fill, the walls of the lung become inflamed, begin to bleed. Now the disease is in the blood, able to swim to every organ: kidneys, intestines, brain, heart.

Today is Friday. I've been standing outside my shed for almost an hour, watching the tide come in. I think it's approaching its highest point now: the waves are lapping tight around Coolanagh and the wide expanse of sand that borders either side of The Causeway at low tide has narrowed to a strip. Perhaps it has already turned? From here it's impossible to tell the moment when its seemingly unstoppable advance goes into retreat.

What would happen, I wonder, if some day the mechanism that turns the tide faltered, if the water just kept on coming? We trust the ocean to do what it does, what it has always done, but what if one day the workings of our world failed us?

I sigh. I don't want to be here like this, staring out to sea, thinking strange thoughts. I want be in my shed, at my table, working on my writing. But my writing has rejected me. So I stare a while longer and think longingly of how it used to be when the words flowed through me as if they came from somewhere else, when all I had to do was turn up and catch them and write them down. Now memories hurt me in the remembering and the events of the past resist me, twist out from under my pen.

Every so often Gran writes in her diary how she would die – "just die" – if anyone were to read what she writes. Does this extend to her granddaughter reading her words after her death? I don't know, I honestly don't. For hours, I sit immobile, rearranging papers, staring at an empty page wondering if I should be doing this at all. Or standing like this in front of the ocean, feeling that the endless movement of the waves has a lesson for me, if I could only work out what it might be.

At least I can still run. I'm further up the beach than I usually go, and I run close to the little cliff, so I cannot be seen from above. Rory's house is set on top, a new build, with peaked dormer windows set into the roof, large windows and French doors overlooking the sea. What Americans call an "executive home". Her choice, he tells me.

I imagine her looking out from her window, a queen in her castle, and seeing me running past. That is why I hug the cliff. If she is queen of the castle, what am I?

It's another mile or two before the beach peters out and I run on, pushing myself faster than usual, stretching for something. I run until the beach turns shingly. Up ahead, I can see where it becomes too narrow and rocky to pass. I turn then, retrace my steps, pulling back the pace, settling into a gentler rhythm, more even breathing. From this end of the beach, The Causeway and Coolanagh look tiny, like miniature models of themselves. I feel like I could run through any limitation. It's only a feeling, I know. It won't last.

I've been spending a long time with Norah's notebooks and they are much harder work than Gran's — full of passages that lie flat on the page, unconnected to each other or to any clear meaning. Her handwriting is difficult, jerking into tight angles and sometimes ignoring margins and lines. This morning, I was furrowing through, copying out phrases that struck me, searching for something.

Now as I run, one of those disconnected phrases comes rising in my mind. Did it say what I now think it said? Or am I imposing a meaning? I race back to the shed and, without cooling down, go straight to the desk and, heart panting, rustle through the pages, trying to find the paragraph.

There. I read it again. My heart recognises its significance and starts to drum-drum-drum, a pulse of excitement that makes me go back and read the words yet again, this time with every sense keen and quivering.

My mind flings up thought after thought.

The day speeds past. When Rory comes on his nightly visit, I send him away. It is dark by then, too dark to write any more, but I don't want to sever the link to what I've just started to know. It's as though I've jumped off a cliff and have to concentrate on flapping my arms to keep myself airborne.

"I can't see you tonight."

"What? Why?"

"I'm sorry. I'll explain the next time. Please. Go."

Next day, I am steadier. I see that I had been trying to write the story straight, to outline and explain, draw conclusions, elucidate lessons learned: the Sue Denim school of writing, hard and clear and certain of its standpoint.

Norah is leading me to a new place. What she has revealed can never be contained within my well-wrought structure. I have to get out of the way, trust the words to arrive and place themselves on the page, know that the writing knows more than me.

1922

PEG'S DIARY 2ND SEPTEMBER 1922: Dan O'Donovan was in the paper, and the outrageous speech he made at the Dunore inquest was quoted in full. I'm copying it out here:

When the British forces were installed in Ireland, it was hard to find man or woman in Wexford with pluck enough to fight the foreign intruder. To my knowledge, no English soldier was fired upon around here during the whole of the Anglo-Irish war and I do not think I am wrong in stating that the present occasion is the first on which a soldier was killed in Wexford since 1798. The Truce begot a lot of warriors and those now attacking the National Army are just emerging from the burrows where the British terror drove them.

"*Hysterical young females are among the most active adherents to the Irregular cause because hitherto it has been safe to be so. They disfigure walls with lying propaganda and they are active carriers of documents, arms and ammunition. Some have been known to accompany men on expeditions of murder, concealing arms in their clothes until required and taking them back when used, relying for safety on the chivalry of those whose deaths they are out to execute.*

"*This ambush was a contemptible attack. Those who did these foul deeds may call themselves warriors but I would call them murderers.*

Jesus, Mary and Holy St Joseph, the superiority of the man.

He feels safe in vilifying us now because of the outrage and recrimination being hurled from all sides. As Mammy says, people haven't the brains they were born with. Can't they see it is one and the same cause as has been fought in this country since 1916, a cause they all claim to support? Can't they see it's one and the same tactics? Dan O'Donovan can't, it seems. What was brave and revolutionary when it was him is "hysterical" now.

Father John condemned the Dunore actions from the altar yesterday morning. Sunday after Sunday now, his sermon is nothing but a tirade of political abuse. It's getting very awkward. Mostly I avoid him and I've come to notice lately that the reason I'm so successful is that he is avoiding me too. He's no keener to have a conversation about the matter than I am. For all his huffery and puffery when he's protected by his pulpit, he's no brave-heart when he has to speak one-to-one.

What he, and all the others who find it so easy to condemn, fail to realise is that we fully understand the horror of killing. None understand it better than us, the ones risking our necks. How can a man of God ask another man or woman to ignore their most sacred oath? How can a spiritual leader — for that is what he is supposed to be — care so little for the principle of the thing?

No. I go beyond Father John to the good Lord Himself. Please God, do not forsake us, in our hour of need. Keep us safe. Deliver us onto the promised land. A free people in a free Republic -- that is what Ireland deserves. That is what we offer up our lives for, and if necessary, our deaths.

God save Ireland.

DIARY 4TH SEPTEMBER: The raid we'd been waiting for since the Dunore action came last night. At eleven o'clock they arrived, two lorry-loads of them, but no Dan, thank God. They started beating down the doors with their rifle butts. As well as ourselves, every man drinking in the pub was hauled out onto the road while they went through our goods and belongings. Even Mammy was brought out of her sickbed, shivering, into the night cold (but of course defiant). When I saw her there, like that, I could have run them through with a bayonet myself. I said nothing for the whole entire time, let Daddy do the talking for us, because I was afraid of what would come out of my mouth.

They gave the place an awful going-over, everything out of the cupboards and drawers again, though I'd only just got them back to rights after the last time. The locks on the bureau are busted and they butted in some of the wood panelling in the parlour. To fix it will cost a fortune. They even took the Sacred Heart down from the wall, the soldier blessing himself as he removed it. Another brave warrior took it upon himself to break some of the crockery in the kitchen. Black-and-Tans were gentlemen compared to some of these boyos.

Bad and all as the wreckage is, what worries me more is how close they came to finding my stash, including this diary. I had it in the usual place, which I've always thought of as foolproof, but they spent so long going through that particular corner of that particular room, it was as if they had a tip-off. So I've made the decision that tomorrow I will put some of the stuff into Molly's safekeeping for a while and find a new place, beyond their ken. It's harder with them than it used to be with the English, because our secrets were once theirs.

Barney is having a night home here for a change, which we're counting on as safe, please God, after last night's raid, as they'll hardly come again so soon. And it's a cold one, unseasonably bitter again. The poor chap was in dire need of a bit of comfort: after a wash, a shave and a feed, he put on fresh clothes and felt like a new man. He's sleeping now, on the settle bed in the bottling store. Norah managed a small while with him and promised a longer time tomorrow so he went to sleep happy.

DIARY 9TH SEPTEMBER: More reprisals for Dunore. "Lieutenant" O'Donovan arrived out from Wexford with a party that proceeded to set fire to a row of cottages on the Wexford road. The Whites own one of those cottages. I can pardon him for backing the treaty, but to be so zealous in the punishment of old friends, to watch Lama's mother who once fed him tea and welcomes, wailing in her daughters' arms? This is not the Dan O'Donovan I knew.

Lucky the worst of the blaze was put out before too much damage was done. Lama says his parents have a legal cause for action against the government, that no parliament could ever be seen to give its army the right to go around firing houses. He thinks we should also make a claim for the number of times we've been raided and smashed up but Mammy says no, she'd rather be homeless than ask that crowd for compensation. I told Lama to hold fast, that he would only be wasting time and energy, and that his best redress would come when we broke these tyrants as we broke their English friends.

Meanwhile, all classes of blackguards are taking advantage of the situation, even worse than before. We've got used to robbers holding up banks and post offices under the name of the IRA but for several weeks, a band of armed thieves has been terrorizing the Rathmeelin district, calling to houses late at night with masked faces, demanding money at gunpoint, claiming to be Republican soldiers. We had a fair idea who the culprits might be, but it took time to be sure. Saturday night, the lads went after them and made an arrest. They were brought before a Republican court set up in the Sinn Féin Hall and found guilty. On Sunday morning, the lads tied them to the front of the chapel gates and put a label on each of them saying: "Robbers Beware!

The IRA is on your track! Leave the Country within 24 hours!"
They also put a placard beside them, detailing the affair and
setting down their names and addresses.

After the Mass was over, anyone who wanted had their
chance to tell them what they thought of their dishonourable
conduct. Then they were run out, told to leave County Wexford
and never come back.

Diary 15th September: Disaster. Disaster. Disaster. I didn't go
to Redmond's out-farm last night as Mammy was feeling poorly
and I didn't like to leave her alone. Molly and Cat went up and a
friend of Molly's, a Miss Kathleen O'Brien. I don't think Molly
even asked Norah, presuming she'd be unavailable. They were
all together, with Barney and Tipsy and Lama and eight other
men, when Joe Breen came running in from cycling over the
fields to warn them he had heard the Stater troops were headed
out there after them. That very moment, they began to hear the
rumble of the lorries and all hastened to make an escape. Some
were lucky, but not all. Not Barney. Nor poor Tipsy, Molly or
Miss O'Brien either.

Also captured were sixteen rifles, seven revolvers, twelve
hand grenades, hundreds of rounds of rifle ammunition, two
mines, a bag of gelignite and a quantity of wires, cables and
electric batteries. The best of our stash.

But what is worse, what is truly terrible for us all, is that Dan
located Molly's papers, every last despatch and list in her
possession. The two large sack-loads of stuff I gave to her a few
weeks ago were found, hidden under a stack of hay. I cannot
believe her carelessness, hiding them all in the one place. Why
did she not separate it out and keep it in different stashes as we
have all been trained to do? Near everything was in those sacks.
A record of all our activities from January up to the end of last
month. The names of all our forces throughout South Wexford,

our strength and equipment, places of parade etc. And all the correspondence on the bank raids, the amounts taken and how distributed. In short, our entire scheme of operations and plans. I'd never have handed them across if I thought she'd be so careless.

Now we'll all pay the price.

The Gaol

    Wexford

    7th October

    Dear Peg,

    Thanks for your welcome letter. To answer your questions: 1. There are between forty and fifty of us here in the gaol. 2. During the day we're allowed out of our cells and confined to a large dayroom. 3. We pass the time as you might imagine, reading, playing cards, sparring. Our exercise is one hour walking round and round the yard. I'd give anything for a game of football but that's not allowed.

    One of our officers in charge is Lieutenant Dan O'Donovan. Likes his title a lot, I can tell you, and takes his duties very seriously. He's getting himself a name as a right hard man. Lucky, I don't have much to do with him. The odd time when he is in to do a check our eyes cross but we act as if we never knew each other. Neither of us knows what other way to do it.

    Thanks for the offers of help. We know you are "always there" and thank God we do know it. The only thing you can do for me is what I ask of you all the time, to look after Norah. She doesn't have your strength. I have written to her, as you know, but I'm not like you with the letters – my words never seem to say it right.

    My poor Norah, we had such great plans. Only God above knows when or if they'll happen. But our cause is just and that keeps us cheerful.

    Hoping, anyhow, that you're in the best of health. I'll write again when I get the chance.

Yours sincerely
Your affectionate bro
Barney

Kilmainham Jail

13 October

My dear Peg,

Well, you will have heard by now that they got me and how. So here I am in Kilmainham, where the 1916 leaders were brought to die. Could we ever have believed then that Irish men would stoop so low?

I am one in a ward of nine and each of us takes turns doing orderly for the room. The girls in single cells also take their turn, serving food, washing-up, etc. We have one bathroom to our floor and we share this amicably for personal use or washing clothes, but are forced to hang our washing over banisters or on improvised lines across the corridors to dry, an embarrassment in front of our male warders.

To keep our hands and minds busy, we study Irish, knit or sew and read. We have to be indoors by nine and have lights out at ten. A bit of a candle sometimes finds its way into our possession but, when lit, it has to be kept under the bed with the readers or card players squatting on the floor to avail of it. If the least glimmer is seen outside, the sentry roars in: "Put out that light" and if this order is not followed, he fires his gun in our direction. On the last such occasion, his bullet came in the window, leaving its mark on the wall opposite.

The Staters grow more insolent and shameless with every passing week. It's infecting even those who would never have been suchlike in the old days. You can see how it catches them, once the first wrong turning is made.

Friday night is the soldiers' pay night and we are usually treated to a musical watch. We too often sing in the dark to each other and sometimes we hear our men across the way doing the same. If one of us asks ourselves the question, why am I here, the answer comes then: because we are.

What did you think of the bishops and their announcement against us? You know the old good wish one Irish woman used to give another, "May you be the mother of a bishop"? Among us prisoners, it is now flung as an insult. Naturally, not a single one of us gave in to a decree that pronounced the FS the only government and ourselves nothing but unlawful rebels -- so we haven't been allowed to attend Mass or Holy Communion since.

What about you? Is Fr J. giving us a hard time still or has he come round? Whichever, it makes no matter. God hears our prayers one way or the other and if Cromwell and the Penal laws didn't succeed in breaking the faith of the Irish rebel, I don't hold out too much chance to the Irish bishops.

I hope this letter reaches you. We have been told we will be able to get out a stack of letters by a laundry van in a day or so. There's little point in writing through official channels – half our communications are not delivered and the other half are so censored they might as well not be sent.

Give my love to all and tell them to remember the poor convict in their prayers and to write to me. Even a few censored lines would make all the difference to…

Your affectionate friend,
Molly

The Barracks
Newbridge
15th October
Dear Sister,

This letter comes to you from Newbridge, where we are put up in the old British Cavalry Barracks. We were transferred two days ago, brought up by train. Conditions are not too bad, about twenty men to each room, and we all have a bed and enough blankets. Food, unfortunately, is not too plentiful. The Dublin boys are well away, able to get food parcels from home. They don't share with Wexfordmen but we fill up with the cuts of bread and cold porridge they don't want.

We spent a long day on the train when we were brought up, locked into one of those old-fashioned closed carriages with nothing to eat but tinned fish, and you know how I love that. It was dark when we got to Dublin and after a long wait we set off again. They didn't tell us where we were going. A rumour went round that we were being brought to the island of St Helena, where Napoleon saw out his days. Instead, we stopped at a wayside station about an hour from Dublin. From there they marched us towards a searchlight that scanned the skies and fields until we came to this place.

We were left standing for hours outside a group of low, dark wooden huts in the freezing cold while they checked us in, six prisoners at a time. It was early morning before I was shown my mattress. I fell gratefully into it, I can tell you.

Since then, it hasn't been too bad. Tipsy is here as well and Larry Crean, Joe Duggan, Paddy Doyle, Thomas Keogh and the Redmond brothers from town. Other "yellow-bellies" too that you wouldn't know so well. All are in good form. Tipsy sends his regards.

The worst, I suppose, is the slanders the press is putting about. Tell Daddy never to believe these stories that are used against us (I know you and Mammy wouldn't) and tell them both to pray for us. I have written to them too but saying less than I say to you. Take care of yourself also, Peg. We know the risks you take for us. It is only now that we have our backs to the wall and everybody against us, that we appreciate you girls of C. na mBan as the fine comrades you are. Without you, the fight would have died long ago. God bless the work.

Your affectionate bro,

Barney

DIARY 19TH OCTOBER: I had a horrible dream last night. I dreamt I was out with the boys, part of the column, with a gun in my hand looking for Dan O'Donovan. I saw him ahead of me and ran after him. He was faster than me and I would never have caught up with him but suddenly, as he ran down a long, narrow passage, he came upon this ten-foot-high hedge and he could go no further. I had him and he knew it. So he turned around to me and started trying to persuade.

"Now, Peg…" he started, in the same smarmy voice he used to me that night with Barney in Enniscorthy. "Let's be sensible…"

But I let him say no more. I shot him straight on.

He grabbed his front where the bullet went in and slowly folded to the ground until he was lying, flat on his face, dead. I went over to him and knelt down beside him to turn him over and when I did, I got the shock of my life, for I saw it wasn't Dan at all I had killed, but Denis Heffernan. And I woke up shouting, "No, no, no…"

Well, I couldn't get back to sleep for the rest of the night. Of course it was only a dream, but it left a horrible black feeling pressing down on me, a feeling that has stayed with me all day.

This evening I went up to Mammy's room for a chat. She was in bed early, having a rest, and I sat down on the side of the bed. She wasn't looking the best and I decided not to burden her with my worries. We spoke for a while of the decrees issued to the press by the government on how we are to be described from now on: we are "Irregulars", not Republicans; our soldiers are "bands of men", not an army; our engagements are "incidents", our battles are "attacks on property or people". They learned their English propaganda well.

After a while, Mammy sensed my mood and wheedled it all out of me the way she does. I told her about the dream and the heavy feelings I am carrying around with me. "Such feelings are only natural," she said, "considering all that's going on. What you mustn't do is let the worries turn you away from the work."

"No, no, the work is no burden, Mammy," I said, surprised at her misunderstanding. Yes, I had been up the last four mornings before dawn, painting slogans on walls: CALL OFF THE

MURDER GANGS. DON'T TORTURE OUR PRISONERS. THE IRISH REPUBLIC LIVES. Yes, as things get hotter, I've never been busier and with Molly gone and Norah a near prisoner in her house, it nearly all falls onto me. But I don't mind. It's an honour to work for Ireland.

"Work isn't just typing notices about informers or calling meetings, Peg," Mammy said. "It's coping with feelings the like of what you're having. Not letting such feelings deflect you." She touched my hand and I felt bad, because I knew she was thinking how much she'd like to still be up to such work.

She went on, explaining that reclining from the horrors and giving up now would be the easy thing to do. "You're missing your brother, that's part of the problem," she said. "You have to take too much on yourself while he's away in prison. But we mustn't let him down."

Again she didn't say it but I knew she was thinking of herself, of how hard it was for her not knowing when she might see him next or how she might be by then.

I hadn't thought about it in that way but she's right; I do miss Barney, and Norah too. She's only up the road but she might as well be in England itself for all I get to see of her. And though I know those who think like us were always a minority, that Boland and Pearse and Tone and Emmet and many more, all the way back, were always in the minority, still it can be hard to hold fast when press and pulpit and people unite against you as strong as they are right now.

Mammy is right: it was never going to be easy. Thank God that at least I have her to turn to. Whenever I am wavering, she is there to set me straight.

DIARY 6TH NOVEMBER: As I was walking home from school today, I came upon Father John at the end of the school lane. He suggested he walk home a bit of the way with me and, as I had little choice in the matter, I smiled nicely at him and fell in with his step. He took the scenic route in getting to the point, asking me first about Mammy's health and how was Daddy and how was the teaching going and would the children be ready for the parish concert in time. All very proper and almost pleasant, only we were both fixed on what was coming.

He started the subject by referring to the Rathmeelin robbers and asked me if I didn't think they should have been reported to the authorities.

"It was the people troubled by the blackguards who made the choice, Father," I said. "They went to those they thought best able to help."

"You'll agree, maybe, that they were at fault in that."

"I wouldn't be sure, Father."

"You wouldn't be sure. You wouldn't be sure. Tell me, Peg, don't we have a police force who could take up for them?"

"I don't think they put much pass on the new police, Father."

His eyebrows came down into that false furrow he puts on when he wants you to know he's cross with you. "You are aware of the statement of our bishops on these matters?"

"Ye-es."

"You know that it is a sin to take on the work of the government, to set up our own policing and armies and so on. You must know that."

I let my silence speak.

"And so you must know your duty in such matters?"

I looked down at my shoes, dusty from the bad condition of the road.

"Peg, your job as a national-school teacher brings responsibilities."

"I know my responsibilities, Father. I've always taken them seriously." He could have no complaint about my work, for since the start of the school year, I've made sure to be over-and-above diligent, no matter how tired I was.

"I'm not referring to your school duties, Peg. As I think you well know."

"You mean politics," I said.

He came to a halt on the road. "It's gone well beyond politics, Peg. You heard the pastoral letter of their Lordships, the bishops, read off the altar last Sunday."

To deuce with their Lordships the bishops, I felt like saying. The same bishops have deprived Republicans of the Sacraments. The men out there fighting – devout Catholics almost to a man – now go into danger without absolution of their sins. Knowing that if they fall in action or are captured or executed, they might be refused the Last Rites. If I ever heard of a sin, that is surely one.

"Am I not as entitled as the next person to what I believe, Father?" I said to him, quiet and polite as I could make it. "And believing as I do, am I not to work for what I believe to be right?"

He dropped his eyes and started fiddling with his cuffs, embarrassed. He can't take straight talk. I could have said a lot more only I was afraid of where I might take us.

"We must not be proud, Peg," he said. "Pride is a great sin. We must listen to those who know most about these matters. Follow the guidance of your bishops and you won't go far wrong."

It was pointless trying to explain anything to him. I nodded my head towards the house instead. "Will you come inside, Father?"

"It was my intention to go in and see JJ. Is there a need for me to do that, d'you think?"

"You mean…about what we've been saying?"

"Yes."

Was this his way of asking me whether I intend to give up my work? He stood like he was waiting for an answer but I wasn't going to lie outright to him, so I just stood there too. I killed a man, Father, that's what I was thinking as I stood there, looking into his comfortable chins. I've killed a man. What do you in your parochial house, and your lordships the bishops in their safe, hierarchical palaces, know about that? How can I look up to you, turn to you for guidance when I've done more, seen more than you in your safety ever will?

He sighed. "I'll leave it for today," he said. "Tell your mammy I sent a blessing."

"I will, Father. Thank you, Father."

"You think hard about what I said, Peg. And be sensible, like the good girl you are."

For God's sake! To think I once was afraid of him. I told Mammy all about it afterwards and she only laughed. "Don't mind Father John," she said. "All he wants is the quiet life."

DIARY 17TH NOVEMBER: Barney is home! Escaped from jail! He turned up tonight while Mammy and I were on our knees in the kitchen saying the rosary. I nearly died of fright when the two faces – himself and Tipsy – popped up at the window.

Oh but then I was up and away and so was Mammy. I haven't seen her this excited in weeks. It's that good to see them. Since the Staters executed those four prisoners the other day, we've been so worried.

I still can't believe what the Free State has come to. Four men taken out and murdered without trial, without word or warning, their relatives not even informed. They found out their loved one was dead by receiving a telegram saying: REMAINS OF _____ HAVE BEEN COFFINED AND BURIED IN CONSECRATED GROUND. SIGNED: GOVERNMENT, SAORSTAT EIREANN.

It is meant as a warning: nobody on our side is safe, that is what they're trying to tell us. Nobody. Not even – or maybe especially not – the ordinary boys. Thank God that Barney's out of their grip. We must keep him safely away from them now.

They escaped through a tunnel, with six others from various parts of the country, and then had to walk the whole way back, it being too dangerous to take any of the lifts they were offered– a distance of a hundred and fifty miles across hills and fields. Ten days of non-stop marching, poor things. They only encountered Army boys once along the way, near Arklow, so at least they were in luck there.

They've both lost weight from the long trek and from lack of food and had to change outside because their clothes were hopping with fleas and stinking from repeated wettings. Worse than the fleas, he says, is a rash that makes him itch all over. They both have it, God love them. They're downstairs now, in the usual place, putting in the night here. Probably not the safest but Barney will go nowhere until he sees Norah. He didn't say so but he wasn't fooling anybody, trying to pretend he wasn't like a hen on a hot griddle at the thought of having to wait until the morning. He wrote her a note and I took it down and put it under our stone. Yes, in the pitch dark. I could see it was what he wanted, that he has it so bad, he'd nearly go up there after her. Once it was sent, he fell into a dead sleep. Hopefully, she'll get to him somewhere, sometime in the morning.

I arrive back to my new flat, lips swollen, thighs aching. Dee looks up from the table where she has been writing, takes one look at me and lets out a shriek. "Ah, no," she says. "Not you. No, no, no."

I glance in the little mirror that hangs over the table. Is it so obvious what I have been doing? In the dappled glass, I see my face, split in two by a smile.

"I don't believe it," Dee wails. "It's not fair."

I have won a competition I didn't even enter. All through our last year in the convent, Dee moaned loud and long about her virginity. Leaving home launched her campaign to rid herself of her seventeen-year-old hymen, her tag of shame. She has a bet with Monica: whoever gets rid first also gets paid a tenner from the other.

"So come on, tell me all. I presume it was the mysterious Mr O'Donovan."

Dee knows a little about Rory now. She cannot understand that we allowed ourselves to be kept apart, living in the same village. Dee would knock aside barriers like boarding schools and vigilant families. She would slip him a note or arrange to "bump" into him or call to his house by night and throw stones up at his window. She is scornful of my weakness and even more of his. Is he a man or a mouse? Does he really like me at all?

I don't mind her thinking this way. It keeps her from realising how much I care. I'm not sure why – Dee is obsessional about her own crushes – but I'd rather she didn't know that through all the months and years of not being with him, my feelings haven't lessened at all but hardened and brightened inside me, like crystal.

Over cups of instant coffee, I tell her what I am happy for her to know, about the lakeside incident and going back to his place.

"You did it, didn't you?" she says. "You went all the way?"

I nod. I can't switch off my smile.

"Oh my God. Come on, tell me: what's it like? Did the earth move? Was there blood?"

"Dee!"

"I hope you were careful."

That turns my insides over. All the way home in the bus, I have been quashing that thought.

"Did he use a condom?" she asks.

"Jesus, Dee, you're unbelievable."

"Did he?"

"He doesn't like them," I say. I have no idea whether this is true or not.

"I wouldn't say he's too fond of squally babies either," Dee says. "You'd want to get yourself down to one of those new clinics for the pill."

"Clinics?"

"The family-planning clinics. That's what they call them but they're not just for marrieds. You don't even have to be engaged. All you need is your money and your health and they'll sign you up for a prescription there and then."

"How do you know so much about it?"

"I've looked into it. I intend going down there myself to get kitted out. I'll go with you."

"But, Dee, you don't even have a boyfriend."

"That, my dear friend, is a very temporary state of affairs."
She laughs at my face. "I mean it," she says. "I'll bring you
down. They're supposed to be really nice."

"I don't know, Dee…"

"You're not labouring under some thick notion that nice girls
don't, I hope. You're going. That's it."

In the afternoon, she skips her zoology practical so we can go
together and she is right, it is easy: no judgements or
disapproval, all so matter-of-fact that any embarrassment feels
childish. It takes just twenty minutes to fill out some forms and
see a doctor and then we're back outside with six foil-packs of
pills each. Six little packs of permission.

At the top of the steps, Dee already has hers out of the bag.
She selects a pack, pops open Tuesday's bubble. "Bless us O
Lord and these Thy gifts," she says, stretching out her tongue
and receiving the tiny tablet like it's a Communion host. She
gulps it down with a grin. "Amen."

I open my packet and copy her. The pill is small and hard
and sweet on my tongue, covered with a smooth coating that
makes it slide down easily.

I GET myself a job as a lounge-girl, in the pub where Rory works.
Three nights a week, I bring trays full of drinks to customers too
lazy to go to the bar. The hourly rate is poor, a pittance really, but
the tips are good, especially towards the end of the night as
alcohol loosens the punters' grip on their wallets. I dodge the
men's compliments and the occasional pinch; ignore them when
they try to look down my white blouse or up my black skirt; find
lines to spar away their slurred come-ons.

From behind the counter, Rory sends me looks that I hold
and post back to him: promises of later. We are a couple now: Jo
and Rory, Rory and Jo. After the pub doors are bolted and the
counters and tables wiped down, we sit with the rest of the staff
and have a complimentary night-cap or two. Then we walk

home, usually to his place; although it is further away, it is more private. Hand-in-hand we walk, heads blurry with alcohol, through empty Dublin streets where only the late-night chip shops and taxi ranks are awake. The wet tarmacadam is lined with little suns, reflections from the streetlights above, and the loud silence of the streets makes us feel like we are the last people on earth.

I love these walks, weaving from side to side of the pavement, stopping every so often for long deep kisses, not drunk but a long way from sober. Cider is my drink, sweet and fizzy. A bottle or two of Stag cider unclicks something inside me, dizzies me with possibilities. I have always known why men wanted to buy drinks for women; now I understand why women let them.

Back in Rory's bedroom, we astonish each other all over again and afterwards fall asleep, our limbs knotted. Next morning, we wake in our bed salted with sex and begin again.

He takes pictures of me: my fingers spread wide or rolled into a fist; the sole of my foot; one crooked toe and its painted toenail; my collarbone and the hollow above it; my elbows over my face; one breast, first in profile then face on; my pubic hair, zoomed so close that crinkles of hair fill the entire frame of the print and the pores of the skin beneath are visible. I am always surprised when the pictures come back: they are never what I expect.

Whatever part he wants to photograph, I make available to him. He does full-body shots too, usually naked, often after sex. These are my favourites, though I can see that the fragmented ones are more interesting. Even when I'm taken in full, I don't recognise myself as this girl with the wild hair and turbulent eyes who looks like somebody else, somebody I might like to know.

Soon we're spending every night together but still we haven't had our fill: our days are spent on the soft chairs outside the Student Union shop, burrowed beneath his army coat, hands under each other's clothes, fingertips on fire. We become known as the couple who are always at it. Everybody notices us, Dee says, her voice oscillating between censure and jealousy. Enfolded in our haze of love and lust, we barely notice them.

My clothes begin to mutate. The coloured V-neck jumpers Mrs D. bought me stay in my wardrobe while I wear grey sweaters or black polo necks hunted down in the Dandelion weekend market. My jeans fray and blanch to fit my new colour scheme of black or white or shades of grey. My skirts turn black, shrink up to well above my knees. Clompy boots weigh down my feet. I think about cutting my hair, short and sharp, but Rory asks me not to. He loves it long, he says, as he twists his fingers in its curls, buries his face in it, uses it to hold back my head when he wants to stare into my eyes.

Mrs D. hates my new image. I go home to visit and, when I get off the train, she takes a step backwards from the black net tights that climb from my Doc Martin boots up all the way up under my short, tight skirt. I knew she would detest this outfit but I wore it anyway. A small mutiny, pathetically small, but I have to try hard not to be nervous.

"Is that a skirt you have on you at all?" she asks, when we get into the car. "Or are you wearing a black handkerchief by mistake?"

At home, she uses this same line three times – to Gran, to Eileen, to Mrs Keating in the shop – as if it is the height of wit. Before I might have taken off the offensive clothes; now I pep-talk myself in the mirror, think of Dee and what she would do, of Rory and what he would tell me to say. Mrs D. does not realise that she and I have got by so far only because I have been switched to mute. Now I find myself drilling words in my mind, flexing and stretching them for combat.

When I get up next morning, it is the tightness of my stretch jeans that brings her eyelids down in exaggerated dismay. "Where in the name of God did you get those yokes? Where are the nice skirts we got for you when you were going to Dublin?"

I shrug.

"You must have had to jump off the bed to get into them," she snorts, and turns to Gran, who is drinking tea beside her. "Mammy, will you talk sense to her. She's losing the run of herself entirely."

"They're a bit tight, all right," Gran says.

"They're made to be like that, Gran," I say, bending into a squat to show her that they're quite comfortable.

"You have the figure for them anyway," she says.

"Oh, thanks very much, Mammy," Mrs D. says. "Encourage her, why don't you?" She turns back to me. "If you insist on wearing such things, you'll have to keep them to the house."

"Everybody's wearing them."

"Not around here, they're not. You're not thinking of going to Mass in them, or in what you had on you yesterday, I hope."

Ah yes, Mass. The clothes will be nothing to this. I take a deep breath and splurt it out: "I don't go to Mass any more."

"What!" Mrs D.'s jaw makes a sideways swivel. Gran puts down her cup. Fashion she can go along with, but this is something different altogether.

"Is this what I'm spending all that money on your education for?" squeaks Mrs D. "So you can come home with this kind of rubbish?"

"I don't believe."

"As long as you're staying in this house, you'll go to Mass. I don't want to hear another word about it." She thrusts herself out of her chair, out of the room, slamming the door.

Gran and I sit in the whirl of silence left behind her. After a while, she says: "Is it the truth, Jo? Have your really lost your religion?"

"That's not how I think of it, Gran."

"You don't believe any more, you said."

"No."

She looks stricken.

"It's not something to worry about, Gran. Some people do and others don't."

She shakes her head. "You'll come back to it," she says. "Father Matt was talking about this before, how the young people sometimes leave for a while. But they come back."

I say, as kindly as I can, "Maybe, Gran, but I don't think so."

"I don't want you to say that, Jo." Her voice sounds strange. "Some day not too far off, I'll be meeting my Maker. It would make it hard for me to go…if I thought I'd never see you…hereafter…"

If I go to the Hell set aside for non-believers, she means.

"Oh, Gran…"

"And for yourself…You'll make life very hard on yourself, Jo, if you don't have the Almighty God. When you make your mistakes, you'll have nowhere to turn. It's very few who don't go some way astray in this life. If you haven't got God in those times, you'll think you have nothing."

I look into the coals of the fire. I'll have myself, I think, my face hot. I'll have Rory.

"I was young myself once. I remember what it's like not to know what end of yourself is up. It's natural to question things when you're young. But you're a good girl, you'll return all right."

Back in Dublin, I get a phone call from Maeve. What am I doing to poor Mammy, telling her the truth about all sorts of things? Can't I do what everybody else does and tell a few lies? Do I think that she, Maeve, goes to Mass every Sunday? Is there any need to broadcast the matter? I endure her tirade without putting the phone down but I am not listening to her.

I start to miss lectures, because I am too tired to get up, worn out by pub work and late-night drinking and sex. I skip seminars and tutorials because no class can compete with the thrill of time spent wrapped around my love. I skip meals and appointments and duties.

I fall out with Mrs D. "Do you intend ever coming home for a weekend again?"

I fall out with my tutors. "You can't expect to pass your exams if you don't come to tutorials."

I fall out with Dee. "For God's sake, Jo. You'll have no friends left!"

I put all of me into him. All.

1922

"Slap your eyes on that one. What d'you think of that?"

"Fuck-ing hell."

"What's this? Dirty pictures is it?"

Jem Fortune had a supply of them, God alone knew where from. He wasn't telling. When not amusing himself with them, he liked to give himself a secondhand thrill from passing them around. And the freedom fighters of Mucknamore IRA, bored out of their brains sitting in an outhouse full of nothing but the smell of old straw, were even more than usually willing to give such matters their attention.

Seven of the column were there, in a rickety shed that once sheltered animals, had been there for over a week now, ever since Parle and Delaney escaped from the gaol. Seven brave soldiers of the Irish Republic enduring a miserable, wet afternoon that was turning into a dark, drawn-out evening. Rain fell like a curtain in front of the open shed door. Every so often, a gust of wind whipped the downpour indoors, so a wet semicircular patch guarded the entrance to the building.

Jem's entertainment was helping the time to pass. "Oh, man," said Lama, coming over to stick his head between him and Jamsie Crean, who was slow to pass them on. "Oh, man."

"Quite a baggage, I think you'll agree, gentlemen?" said Jem Fortune, as if he owned the girl. Lama plucked it out of Jamsie's hand, passed it on to Barney. "Take a look at this, Parle," he said. "She'll put hairs on your chest."

The girl was in a state of undress, lying back on a sofa with her vest up to her neck and bloomers pushed low down on her hips, showing some personal hair. Her dids were round and plump, with nipples big as saucers, and the way she had her arms folded underneath pushed them up and out at him. The bold-as-brass look on her face was as disturbing as her display of herself.

He tried to stop looking. If he was alone, she would have all his attention, but he was made uncomfortable by the presence of the others. He passed her on and sat back down on the upturned bucket he'd been using as a seat.

They had been brought to this place, eight miles from Mucknamore, by a suspected spy, a man called Browne. Tomorrow – it would have been today if the weather hadn't put a stop to it – Barney and Lama intended to dress up in Free State Army uniforms they had confiscated and hidden in old sacking in the back of the barn and pay him a visit, make him an offer of money for information about their own whereabouts. If he fell for the inducement, they'd have the proof they needed. Their own information had it that this Mr Brown pointed the way for the last military round-up. Twenty-two men got picked up in that – including their own Leary brothers, all three, and Jack Kelly and Gut Hayes – along with rifles, pistols and ammunition.

They were lucky the army didn't decide to do round-ups more often; it was their best tactic. Early as dawn they would come out from Wexford, assembling in bands of twenty or so, then moving systematically through the area, townland by townland, to search all suspect houses and hiding points. Regular round-ups could clear an area of Republicans in a matter of days, but lucky the Free State Army in Wexford were lazy, as half-hearted about this as they were about everything else.

What the column would do to Browne when they found him guilty had yet to be resolved. Jem Fortune said he should be shot. "May the gates of hell never screech for want of grease while there's marrow in the bones of a traitor," he had said earlier, waving his revolver in the air. Others were less histrionic. It was Barney's opinion that they should be merciful – punish the man, yes, but not shoot him. No agreement had been reached on the matter when Jem Fortune pulled out his pictures, the subject of which now seemed to exercise him a great deal more than vengeance on the informer.

Another photograph was placed in Barney's hand. "Perhaps," said Jem, "you are more of an arse man, my friend?"

The second picture was even more shocking. The same girl taken from the back, bent forward from the waist with her bloomers pulled down to the top of her legs, just below the large white globes of her rear end. Her legs were a little apart, showing the shadow between them. His breath stiffened in the back of his throat. He wanted to stop looking. He wanted to never stop looking. She gazed over her shoulder out of the picture at him, her long hair loose and hanging down.

"What do you think of that, Barney me boy?" said Lama. "Fancy running into that on a dark night, would you?"

"Give us a look," said Crean, snatching her away.

In the dim light, they huddled close to see. Cackling whoops of laughs were passed around. "Jaysus. Look at that."

"What I wouldn't like to give her."

"In your dreams, Delaney. What would a one like her want with a thick like you?"

The jeers were forced, a matter of making any noise rather than admit to the cramped urges the pictures stirred. Their laughter was lined with fear: fear of the sin of looking, but under that and stronger, fear of their own need.

Jem and Jamsie Crean retired to the back of the shed with

their pictures and nobody was under any illusions about what they were doing back there. Barney sat alone, as was his custom now, watching the grey light outside fade to darker grey. They had no lantern. The faces of the men around him blurred to moving shades, then disappeared altogether, as day become evening. Then, almost immediately, it was night. A night black as tar. Nothing but the palpitating rain, falling, falling. No more ogling now for Jem and the boys. No more anything, except empty conversation into the damp darkness, for anyone who could be bothered. They were sick of talking to each other: anything any of them had to say had long ago been said.

Nothing to do and fourteen hours of night to do it. It would be near eight o'clock in the morning before they saw daylight again. He got up off his upturned bucket, stiff and cramped, the damp of the rain in his bones. In the dim light, he felt his way across the straw, moving as far as he could from the others to the far corner of the shed. Settling there, heaping some straw under his head to make a pillow, he huddled down into his coat and took out his last cigarette, which he had been hoarding.

The match rasped loud and bright in his cupped hand and he dragged deep, ferociously, on the cigarette. Fortune's pictures had unsettled him. He couldn't stand much more of this. Only what was he supposed to do? He couldn't walk away from it either. The six men sharing this shed would see to that and, if they let him off the hook, he'd soon be hung back on it by the females at home. Jesus, the glitter in Peg's eyes that night on the bridge in Donore. But his mother too and even gentle Norah.

What he saw in Norah O'Donovan's eyes when she looked at him in Enniscorthy, that was what had taken him, all unknowing, to this place and now they'd put so many eggs into the basket of the Republic that they couldn't drop it.

Sometimes he felt like the world was drowning in human blood. Their own country's troubles were trifling compared to what other parts of the world had seen – the Great War, the revolutions in Russia, the goings on in Africa and China. All those men killing and being killed because that was what made him a man in his own eyes, or in the eyes of some girl. It was madness, especially when it meant you didn't get to see the girl enough to enjoy her admiration.

He had started out feeling like the hero of the show but, somewhere along the line, he turned out to be the fool.

The rain drummed down, relentless. Even his thoughts felt pallid and unconvincing, like his brain had been bleached. He squashed his cigarette butt out on the ground beside him, careful – with all the straw around – to ensure that it was extinguished. Then, hours earlier than usual, hours earlier than was good for him, he gave himself over to the squirms and spaces of the night.

He woke to find the rain had stopped and he pushed himself up off his bed of straw, stepping over the bodies of his comrades still slumped in sleep. His bones were sore but, as usual, morning thoughts were brighter and outside, the air tasted new and clean. He stretched, breathed in deep. The heaviest of the clouds had parted, allowing a gleam through the grey, and the grass was plump with rainwater. They'd get their man today, then he'd get to go home for a night or two.

He walked up the roadway that skirted the field to stretch his legs. He hadn't gone far when he saw Doyle's daughter on her bicycle, a pail over each handlebar, and he turned back. "Breakfast is on the way," he called into the shed.

Jem Fortune was out the door in an instant. He let a loud wolf whistle at the girl as she drew near. She dismounted from her bicycle and he moved to help her with the buckets and did his best to engage her in conversation. She was having none of it. A surly lump of a girl she was, with none of the hero-worship for freedom fighters that they liked to read in female eyes. And no time at all for Jem's brand of talk.

At the shed, she handed them two loaves of bread wrapped in a tea towel and a copy of the Wexford Weekly. "Mammy said you might like a read of that?"

"Thank your mother for us," said Jem. "And thank her too

for sending the vision of your fair self to open the morning for us."

She threw him a look that would wither a bush.

"If you can, bring the buckets back down to the house when you're finished," she said. "If not, I'll collect them later."

She turned away to pick up her bike.

"You look even better from this side," Jem shouted after her, his gaze pasted onto her rump.

After breakfast, it was down to the business of the day. Barney sent Tipsy and Bronco to the hideout to retrieve the army uniforms. They were found to be dishevelled from their time in the ditch so the column set to scraping the worst of the dirt off and brushing them down with damp leaves. If they were not smart looking, they wouldn't convince. While doing that work, they argued again about shooting the spy.

"I think what we should do is put a good fine on him," said Barney. "And send him out of the county, as we did with the Rathmeelin robbers. Let's not sink to the level of the Staters."

"Robbing is one thing," said Lama. "Informing is something else entirely."

"I'm in agreement with that," said Jem Fortune.

Barney combed his head for words. Even if it was Browne who gave them away – and that was what he expected – who was going to do this execution that they all claimed to want so bad? Not Jem Fortune, surely, who was known to have swallowed his lit cigarette the one and only time he saw action, at the Ardnacree ambush. Not Tipsy Delaney, who kept to the back of the firing in any encounter. Maybe Lama might have it in him, but what if he didn't? What if he funked it? Or worse, did it and never got over it?

"It's one thing to take a man out in an ambush," he said, "quite another to shoot him at close range."

"But if he's a spy…"

"I won't be doing it, anyway."

"What's wrong, Parle?" jeered Lama. "Not up to it?"

"I don't see the need for it."

"It makes sure Browne never gets the chance to inform again. It frightens others who might be tempted to do the same."

"Sending him out of the county won't send the same message," said Jem.

"What do HQ say?" asked Tipsy.

"Oh, HQ. Do those lads even know we're here?"

The argument lapsed into spiny silence. They finished brushing the uniforms and laid them out to dry. Barney picked up the paper that the farmer's girl left behind. When Jem Fortune blasted the left ear off him with one of his wolf whistles, he took no notice, thinking it was the girl come back for the dishes. He was stuck in an article about a lecture Father John gave at a meeting in town, disparaging the immodest style of dress now worn by women. All that was going on in the country, and this was what the man chose to lecture people about...

He was jolted by a nudge in the ribs.

Jem said, "Your visitor, Parle, I do believe."

He looked up and across in the direction of Jem's nod.

Norah. Norah, alone, standing behind the far gate as if she dared not come any farther.

His heart jumped, jerking him to his feet. Ignoring the jeers that were starting up behind him, he crossed the field to her, breathless. Lord, the force of his feelings! Lama showed no sign of being cuffed in the stomach whenever he set eyes on Cat Hayes. But then neither did he, Barney, let on. Did everybody feel this way and go around pretending they didn't?

When she saw him coming across the field, she pulled back behind the hedge, away from the inquisitive eyes behind him. He climbed over the gate and landed with a jump beside her but she was off, already walking down the lane, not giving him a chance to get near her, to kiss her hello as he would have liked.

"Are you all right, Norah?" he asked when he caught up.

She shook her head, like she was shaking out a dirty rag.

"It's great you've come," he said. Something had happened.

That shut face again, tight as a tomb. He pulled her into a gateway. How different this was to the sensations brought on by those pictures last night. Entirely different, even if it did bring on what seemed like the same stirring. The shocking beauty of Norah up close, every single time it knocked him over. The bones under the white skin of her neck were that fragile. He put his lips on the skin there and held the kiss. Dear God, the softness of her. And her glorious smell…

It was some moments before he noticed she was not responding. There was no reaching toward him today, no acquiescence even. She was gone, leaving him only the shell of her lovely face, her perfect body. He stopped kissing her. He took a step backwards. "What is it, Norah?" he said, but she just shook her head again.

He felt himself getting irritated: they didn't have the time for this, not when they only got to see each other once in a blue moon. She was stricken with some grief or fear, he could see that much. But why wouldn't she share it?

Peg had told him of this inclination of Norah's, lately, to retreat into silence. A quiet as cold as the grave was how Peg, with her liking for the dramatic, had put it. She said she could talk to Norah for whole minutes without being heard. Call for her attention, even wave her hands in front of her face. Then, after a while, Norah would surface, like a swimmer coming up from under water, looking around with pure puzzlement. Well, Barney couldn't be doing with that; they didn't have the time for it.

"What's wrong, Norah? You have to tell me."

No answer.

"I'll help you, whatever it is. Why don't you stay here for the night, forget about going back."

"Oh, Barney, don't talk daft."

"It's not so daft. What tie do any of them have on us if we don't allow it? We could go wherever we want, you and I. We could survive like men on the run until we got ourselves away from here."

"And the cause?"

He shrugged.

"Ireland needs all her men now," she said. "Especially men like you."

"Oh, Ireland."

Shocked at his tone, she looked up at him, took a step backwards. He'd said the wrong thing and now she was pulling back down inside herself, as if she shrank from her own skin. "It's all for you, Norah, do you not know that? I'd walk from it tomorrow if you gave the word."

Again, that shake of the head. Yet she had come to him, come all the way out here, eight miles on her bicycle with, no doubt, the threat of her family questioning her whereabouts when she got back. What was the point if they weren't going to speak truly to each other?

"All I want is you," he said. Maybe a man wasn't supposed to say a thing like that, but there, it was said. No sign of it melting her, though. "Come here, m'sweetheart. Tell me what's wrong. Come in here to me, my darling girl, and tell me what's wrong. I'm certain sure we can put it right."

1922

PEG'S DIARY 26TH DECEMBER: What a miserable Christmas Day we had yesterday. I keep comparing this year with last. The bonfires, the songs and celebrations, the vote on the treaty yet to be taken, that ballad of mine celebrating Dan and Barney coming home from the English prison. We could do anything, was what we thought then, for hadn't we already achieved the impossible? Only here we are this year, living in the "Free" State, as beholden as we ever were to the English Crown.

This year, Christmas is Barney absent from our table. It's Mammy trying to let on she's not as sick as she is. It's Dan estranged and Norah isolated.

All we have to hold to is the knowledge that our cause is true and right. Mammy gave us a small speech as we sat down at the Christmas table: "If Kevin Barry's mother could keep her eyes fixed on the tabernacle while the hangman's rope was round her boy's neck, and if Terence MacSwiney's sister could endure his agony as he starved himself to death in Brixton jail, and if Cathal Brugha's widow is instilling into her children the policy their father lived and died by, then surely to God we can put up with not having our boy to Christmas dinner."

All of which sounded twice as inspiring when you thought

about it and realised she may not even see another December 25th.

We would probably have taken the chance of having Barney here yesterday, only a rumour went round that the Army were going to use Christmas Day to do a big round-up. So the lads broke up into small groups, and while we were eating our meal, he was not a million miles away, eating dinner in a friendly hay-barn. In the event, nothing happened. It was probably a rumour started by the army to ruin Christmas for us. Even the Germans and Allies were able to acknowledge the spirit of Christmas across the trenches. But not the "National" Army, no.

And to cap it all, Norah never got down to see me. Dan is home for the holiday and she will have to endure her people fawning over him and the gibing he loves to give her. Is it any wonder she hasn't been herself lately?

DIARY 28TH DECEMBER: Still no sign of Norah and it's very awkward for me to call up her way. I thought about it, even set out this morning in my hat and coat, but I turned back. I'd manage her mother easy enough and maybe even her father. But Dan. If he's still up there on his Christmas leave, that I just can't face.

DIARY 2ND JANUARY: I finally took courage in hand and went up to O'Donovan's and how I do wish I'd gone sooner, especially as it was pure cowardice kept me away, nothing else. When I didn't see Norah at Mass on Sunday, I knew something was wrong but I thought only of sickness. Up I went to their place.

Norah's mother saw me crossing the yard and came to the back door and then just stood there with a face on her.

"I've come to ask after Norah, Mrs O'Donovan," I said, as if we'd no national question between us.

"Have you indeed?"

"I was worried she might be sick."

"She isn't."

"Can I see her for a minute?"

"No."

"I won't keep her long."

"She's not here. She's gone away."

"Away?"

"Away, yes. Now would you mind? There's work to be done in this house."

"When will she be back?"

She looked at me, hard, and when I didn't budge, she picked up the sweeping brush that was standing by the door.

"Will you not tell me?"

She let out a bitter laugh as she kept sweeping. "Norah's got herself a fancy job in Dublin. She left two days ago."

"But she never said goodbye. And she never mentioned anything about a job to me…"

"Enough! Now you listen to me, Peg Parle. We've had as much trouble as we can take from your family. You think about what I've just told you. Go home and think about it."

"What do you mean?"

"I don't want to see you or your brother near any of our family again. You should be ashamed to come near this house. Get yourself gone before her father comes back, for if he finds you here, I can tell you, he won't be as light on you as me."

Oh dear mother of God, I'm sitting here now with the most awful feeling. Would Norah not have told me? That is what I ask myself. If it was me, would I tell her?

Please God, please Holy Mother, let me be wrong. Let there be another explanation entirely.

Oh, my poor friend. Whatever the truth, you could have told me. I wouldn't have thought less of you. Never.

Not for anything.

DIARY 9TH JANUARY: This morning I was feeding the hens when two cold hands came round my face, covering my eyes. I knew straight away who it was. "Barney!" I cried, delighted first, then fearful.

Did he know something…? As soon as I turned round, I could see that he didn't. He was smiling a smile that broke my heart to see because I knew what I had to tell him would wipe it away.

"We're below in Colonel Taylor's," he said. "So near that I said I'd have to come home."

I bombarded the poor fellow with questions. "Are the boys around here now? You look thinner, have you been eating all right? Did ye get my despatch about the barracks job? Have ye a plan for it? Are you hungry?"

He laughed. "Which do you want me to answer first?"

"All, all. Oh, Barney, it's great that you're here. Christmas was awful miserable. And Mammy — "

"Is bad."

"Bad, yes. But she'll perk up now. She'll perk up now."

"A perk-up is what I'm in need of myself. I need a wash and some clean clothes. What I'm wearing is stuck to me and the itch is back."

I threw the last of the meal in a heap in the middle of the yard and the fowl leapt on it, clucking like the children over Father John's sweeties, beating each other away.

"Come on inside," I said to him, wiping my hands on my apron. "I'll put on the kettle. How does a feed of rashers and eggs sound?"

Only three weeks since we last saw him but he's grown even thinner. And he was filthy from face to foot. "Have a bit of a wash there in the barrel before I bring you up," I said, "Else Mammy will think you're the devil himself come to visit."

While he was doing so, I put on water to boil for a proper soak in the tub and got in food from the shop. Then the two of us went upstairs together. "Ah, son," was all Mammy said when she saw who it was. Two thin arms came up from the blankets as he went to her and they held each other in a way neither would have done six months ago.

When they parted after a long closeness, we each sat on the bed, one on either side of her, while she asked him questions that came slow out of her soreness, about the talk we were hearing that surrender might be imminent. He tried to fob her off, to talk of other things, but not a chance. She dragged herself up in the bed and gave us one of her speeches.

"At a moment's notice…this country produced…the finest politicians and soldiers, drawn from all walks of life. Six years ago they were nothing but they…they came to command the admiration of the world. Why?" Her finger poked the counterpane. "Why? Because they stood on the side of right… that's why. They had a principle…Now, the talk is of giving up that principle…or of watering it down but…principles can't be watered down."

We agreed with her, of course; you might as well argue with a goat on the charge and she wasn't able to keep it up for too long. Afterwards, back downstairs, Barney asked me straight if it was only a matter of time with her and I told him the truth: that it was.

"And how is Daddy about it?"

"Still pretending it's not happening."

"What are we at, Peg?" He gave a sigh I didn't want to understand. "What are we at, at all?"

"Don't say things like that, now. If we lose faith, we're surely doomed."

He let his head fall into his hands and I knew nothing I might say would reach him. It was like he had been to another country and come back to find he couldn't describe it to me because the mountains and fields there were nothing like ours.

And I had yet to tell him about Norah. I took a deep breath and did it.

"Gone away to Dublin?" he said. "That can't be right. She'd never do that without telling us."

"That's what I said. But she is gone, Barney. I've been up there, asking after her."

"And...?"

"If there was anything to tell, it's not me who'd be told it, you know that."

When he was leaving, I told him I'd see if I could talk to young Martin, Norah's little brother. He might give away some information. "I'll get a message to you tomorrow at the Colonel's," I promised, "one way or the other."

DIARY 10TH JANUARY: What a morning. Tipsy arrived before the dawn, with a letter from Barney marked "private and confidential", which he was told to put directly into my hands and no other. Dear diary, I was never more surprised than I am after reading this letter.

I hadn't time to think properly about it because I had to bring Mammy up her breakfast and, next thing, while I was up there, four lorry-loads of Army boys went honking up through the village in the direction of Colonel Taylor's, making sure to slow down as they went past here, and to hoot their horns at us.

Mammy shook her fist at the window and shouted after them. "Go on out of that, you might be good for taunting women — but our boys will soon silence your hoots."

It's been months since she had a shout in her. It's Barney's visit yesterday that's given her the lift. Honest to God, if she knew how he was thinking, I do believe it would kill her.

Letter from Barney, 9th January 1923, Derriestown, Co. Wexford.

Dear Peg, I'm writing this shortly after saying goodbye to you. It's for your eyes only, this letter. Destroy it when you've read it. You'll see why.

I hope you'll soon have news of Norah for me. You know as well as I do that something must be up. We'll get to the bottom of it, never fear, and soonest. To think of her having to sneak off without telling us is killing me.

And so I'm writing because I want you to face the truth. I hate having to say this to you, Peg, you who has done more than anyone. More than most of the women, because you've been in the fight itself, and are now living with all that goes with that. And more than me or any other man whose name is known, because the food, clothes, tobacco and all the rest of it from the home front might not be as heroic, but in the end matters as much or more.

When everybody else deserted us, you were there, facing the danger, shoulder to shoulder. Don't think what I'm about to write now means I don't know it. Don't think it will ever be forgotten.

But dear old Peg, I have to tell you, it's all up with us. It's only a matter of time before surrender is called. I know this is not something you want to hear and I didn't go through it with you today because our time was so short, but that's the truth of it, believe me. We are going through several kinds of hell with this fight, and continuing it is nothing but a spillage of blood.

When we were fighting Black-and-Tans it didn't matter that we were outnumbered, for they could hardly tell one of us from the other. We had the advantage of surprise, the ability to melt back into the countryside. All that is changed. The Enemy now knows every man of us. They know what we're planning to do before we know ourselves. They have all our areas overran and there's so many of them that killing a few of their side does not count. They can easily be replaced. Not so us. We're completely outnumbered.

Then there's the lack of money. Our arms are a joke; we have hardly any ammunition. Joe Sills asks HQ constantly for supplies but we get nothing. They're broke and anything they do manage to requisition gets sent down Cork and Kerry way, never to Wexford. Three of the lads who escaped an ambush last week had to leave their boots behind and have been going barefoot since.

I can't talk the truth of this around here. All the talk among these boys is as strong as ever for the Republic. They think if we destroy a railway line, we've won a major battle. They think if they're brave enough and stubborn enough that it will all come good in the end. Well, it won't. And it won't be too long now until it's all over and – I have to tell you the truth, Peg, I have to tell it to someone for keeping it to myself is driving me half insane – I'm glad, so I am. Surrender can't come soon enough for me.

What exactly will happen to me, I'm not sure. Prison, maybe, for a while but as soon as we can, Norah and I will get a nice little house and get married. That's all I think about now. It's not a lot to ask, is it? Other people seem to manage it without great difficulty. I will find her, wherever she is, if you haven't found her first, and tell her that whatever has happened, she shouldn't have run away from us. I will persuade her that the time for secrets is over and show her there's no need to be afraid. There is nothing anybody can do to her, not when I'm there to mind her.

Her family won't like it, of course, but if we have to, we'll go away. I'd give up the pub and the shop if I had to, or anything else. Anything. It wouldn't matter. And if there's no work in Ireland, then I'll take us to England or maybe even to America. We won't need much. We'll manage.

It was good to see you today, Peg, to see you so well and full of hope. It did my heart good. You're a great survivor. Look after Mammy and Daddy during the coming weeks. What they would do without you, God alone knows.

Like I said, burn this when you're finished reading. You can imagine the trouble if it fell into the wrong hands (which is anybody's but your own). God bless you and keep you safe.

Your brother,

Barney

Peg's Diary 10th January 1923: Was it only this morning I got Barney's letter and wrote the above about Mammy jeering the Army?

That entry reads to me now like it was written by someone else. I was someone else then. From this day forward, I'll be a new person, a smaller person, trying to live the same life.

It was Tipsy who brought the news to me, and he was that upset I was hardly able to get out of him what he had come to say. When it dawned on me what he was getting at, I let out a big scream. "No, Tipsy. No. You've made a mistake. No. You're not right."

But at the same time as I was denying what he said, I was starting to cry, admitting with my tears that I knew it was no mistake, that it was true. I'm crying again now as I write this, harsh out-loud crying that gets on my own nerves to hear.

Barney is dead, may the Lord have mercy on his soul. My brother Barney is dead.

Dead. No matter how often I say it and write it I can't get myself to believe it.

Barney is dead. We always knew it could happen but I've learned this morning the wide ocean of difference between imagining something and the real living of it.

Barney is dead and they're saying it was his one-time best friend Dan O'Donovan who fired the shot that killed him. God help us. How in the name of all that's holy are we supposed to bear this?

PART V
CREST

1975

"*R*ory, I've something to tell you."

The way I say it makes him put down his fork. "Ah no, Jo." How can he tell from what I have said? Is it in my voice or my face that he reads it?

We are supposed to be celebrating. It is my birthday tomorrow, my eighteenth. I am officially an adult at last and we are here, at the Granada Restaurant, at a candlelit table with linen napkins and a bottle of wine like a proper pair of adults. Soup finished, waiting for our steaks, which will be followed by Black Forest gateau.

Rory's treat, from his bar wages, and a fine treat for two impoverished students. Or it would be, if only…

"Yes," I say. "I'm afraid so. Yes."

"Jesus. Oh God, Jo. I don't believe it. Fuck!"

"That's what did it, all right."

He lashes me a that's-not-funny look. "But I thought you were on the pill," he says.

"Apparently, the pill is only ninety-nine point nine per cent effective. I – exceptional as ever – am one of the point one per cent."

Why am I talking in this strange, flippant way?

"Jesus!" he says again. "Fuck!"

"Will you stop saying that?"

"Sorry." He pushes away his plate. "What do you want me to say?"

"Maybe something like, 'Don't worry, we'll be OK'?"

"We will...but...just give me a minute, Jo. You've had time to think about this. I am really shocked. I just don't believe it. Jesus!"

Anybody would think he didn't know the facts of life. But how can I blame him? To me too, it seems impossible that our molten nights have anything to do with this cold, daytime reality. And I have had the connection pounded into me all my female life.

"You seem so calm," he says.

"I am anything but calm."

"Have you thought about what you want to do?"

What I want to do. Not we. "I only found out for sure this afternoon," I say.

"That's not an answer."

"What about you?" I hand the question back to him. "What do you think?"

"I asked first."

"Well...None of the options exactly thrill me..." I say, holding him off, while I take a clear look at what he is not saying. What he wants is there in the set of his mouth, oozing out from behind the shock in his eyes. He wants me to take it away, rewind the tape, make it like it never was. He won't say it, though, the ugly word. He just sits there, looking at me like I've suddenly become the opposition.

So I say it for him in my breeziest voice. "I suppose the old boat to England is the best of a bad lot."

He doesn't bother to hide his relief. "Are you sure?"

"I think so. Yes."

And maybe I am. Me, a mother? Eighteen years old, convent-educated, as immature as eighteen can be, with a degree to finish, a world to see, a self to find. A mother, me? How?

This is what I tell myself, and what I tell myself is true, but underneath I know another truth: that I would do it. I would follow my love into marriage and parenthood if he was willing. If he would come away with me – because the one thing I could never, ever do is bring this news home to Mrs D. – we could leave our families and their stupid quarrel behind and start over, somewhere else. The two of us. Then the three of us. Make our own family.

But such a thought isn't his. Not even for the tiniest sliver of a second.

And he's probably right. What he wants is what I too have thought, during fearful, sleepless nights, might be best: best for him, for me, for the baby-not-to-be. Neither of our families would forgive us, we would be on our own and what sort of life would it (she? he?) have with two cast-off, impoverished teenage parents, reluctantly and prematurely bound? This is what I have said to myself.

I'm sorry, I find myself thinking, addressing the beginning-to-live thing inside me. So sorry. Please don't blame me. How stupid.

Rory reaches for my hand. "What else can we do?" His fingers are bony.

"Nothing," I say.

"Nothing," he repeats, taking my word and setting it in certainty.

I say it again, his way: "Nothing."

Decision made. The boat it is.

Decision made, the tears come. What shakes me – what makes me get up from the table and hurry out to the ladies' room, to spurt my tears into a fistful of toilet tissue, to scowl at my crying face in the mirror and wrap my arms around my head – is not just the knowledge of what I – we – are about to do.

I didn't understand it then, but I was also grieving another thing that had just died. Our love. It was insufficient. It was not what I thought.

Next day is Saturday, my birthday. I travel down to Mucknamore by train to spend a night with my family.

At the station, I get into my mother's car, feeling I must emit clues like a stench. She looks me over in the usual way, seeing nothing but this student version of me that she detests. Her mouth creases against the good intentions she brought with her down to the station. It's my birthday, she wants to be nice to me but my clothes (skirt short and tight, Doc Marten boots), my eye make-up (black and heavy) and my hair (pulled high into a knot at my crown) won't let her.

"Did anybody we know see you on the train?"

I shrug the question back at her.

"I don't think Mucknamore is ready for this latest get-up."

Back at the house, a cake with eighteen candles and Happy Birthday Siobhán across the top waits for me and an envelope of money beside it, from Granny Peg and Auntie Norah. It's my birthday, my eighteenth. I try to care, try to be grateful.

Gran asks, "Are you all right, Jo?"

"I'm all right. Just a bit tired."

"Overdoing the celebrations, I suppose." She grins at me, her lovely old-lady grin. Could I tell her? But why would I do that to her? In a little while, it will all be gone. My tender breasts will return to normal, my morning nausea will dissolve.

Mrs D. is going through one of her phases so she heads to the sitting room with Auntie Norah. They have their television timetable worked out for the night. Our Great Nation. Starsky and Hutch. The Late Late Show. Gran is left with the washing-up and I volunteer to help, brushing away protests about it being my birthday.

As she washes the dishes and I dry them with a tea-towel, we chat. Her news from the village, my news from college. She wheedles out of me that I have a boyfriend. "Is he kind to you?" she asks.

I tell her he is.

"Good," she says. "Good, that's all that matters. The rest of it is nothing."

She wipes down the sink with her cloth. Could I tell her? Could I?

"Auntie Norah seems in good form," I say.

"They have a new doctor above and he's put her on different tablets. He said they'd suit her better and I think they do."

"She seems more alert."

"Definitely. Those other pills used to knock her out of it altogether."

"When did she get these ones?" Gran likes us to care about Auntie Norah, to ask.

"A few months back. It took her a while to settle onto them, mind. At first, she began the night-walking again, like she used to do years ago. She had your mother and myself shattered from broken sleep."

Gran tilts the basin as she talks and the plughole glugs down the sudsy water. Lifting the draining-board, she wipes down the sink underneath, then the counter-top, then the taps. "It brought us right back, I can tell you. She used to be a divil for that at one time, the night-walking. She couldn't be kept in the bed."

"I don't remember that."

"No, it was a long time ago. Anyway, your mammy and I put up with it for two weeks this time, until the three of us were near killing each other and it couldn't go on. I brought her back to the doctor and he fixed her up a stronger dose. And not a bit of bother since, thank God."

"That's great," I say, because I think that's what she wants to hear.

"I don't know. Sometimes I wonder which problems are caused by the thing itself and which by the side effects from those old pills." She folds the dishcloth over the tap, sighs. "But we can't manage her without them, that's the truth of it."

I put the last plate in the cupboard, hang up the damp towel on its peg. Our chore is done.

"Old lady complaints, Jo," she says. "Don't mind me, all's grand really."

I smile.

"Are you sure you're all right?"

I keep smiling, hard.

"It's not easy being young either, love, I do remember that. We move too fast when we're young, we don't stop long enough to hear the voice of God in ourselves. That led me very wrong onetime."

She drops her voice, low and gentle. "He only ever speaks to us in whispers, Jo, more's the pity. But He does speak."

This God talk is making me edgy. I nod and step away.

"Are you coming inside to watch telly?" she asks.

She would like me to, I know. It would brighten her night to have my company in a fireside chair beside her and Mrs D and Auntie Norah, sharing The Late Late Show with them, having a cup of tea at the ads. But I can't endure Gay Byrne's smug patter tonight, or Gran's patient explanations to Auntie Norah about what's happening on the screen. Not tonight.

"Later," I say, hanging up my tea towel. "I think I'll take a walk first. It's a lovely evening."

On the beach, cool air fans my hot cheeks. The sun dips towards the western horizon, throwing long shadows. No tourists yet, it's too early in the season. I walk by the edge of the water, the soles of my boots clinging to the sand, each step lifting with a small, wet smack. White-winged commotions of seabirds flap up, up and away as I approach, settle again further down the sands. I plough on, ignoring their flurries.

I walk to the end of the beach on the eastern side, where an outpost of rock crooks towards the sea like a long bony finger, barring my way, then I turn, follow my own footprints back. By the time I'm back at The Causeway, darkness has seeped across the sky and along the sea. I am warm and more than a little tired after being up all last night wrangling with Rory. I should go home, but instead I look up to the sky and find what I hope to find: a moon, dull-yellow, but there. And rising. I turn left, away from the village, out towards Coolanagh.

The tide is in and the waves rush past me in a hurry to get to the shore. I lengthen my stride, walk purposefully up and down the dips in the path, like somebody late for work. About halfway out, the barbed-wire fencing and warning signs that mark off Coolanagh sands begin: WARNING! they shout. DANGER! The Sands on this side of The Causeway are Unstable and Unsafe. Do not Diverge from the Path.

All the way out to Coolanagh I go, along the narrow neck where the sand turns to grass, then to rock, up the steep shelf that leads to the outer path around the island. The moon is now full-bellied white to light my way. I am going to walk all the way to the far side of the island, where the waves lash against hard rocks, exploding spray and spume. Only serious walkers and the occasional boater go out this far. Out there, on its far side, the island is granite hard, a completely different landscape to the flat land and sea around the village.

When I reach the plateau at the most southerly edge, I stop and sit on a rock, breathing hard from the climb. Below the cliffs, the water boils and bursts against the rocks. I sit, letting the noises of the ocean and the night settle around me. I know how not to be afraid. I know the trick is to close your eyes, not to peer into the dark, imagining what might be there, but to rely on your other senses. I let my ears and nose and skin tell me I am safe.

When I was a kid, afraid of what lurked in the dark, I knew the way to deal with it was get out of the bed and face those monsters down. Going after them was the only way to make them disappear, but I wasn't strong enough. Often, I lay rigid with terror in the bed, making myself say the Rosary, the longest, most tedious prayer. I knew how Maeve – happily asleep in the bedroom next door – would jeer me if she knew. Monsters! A part of me, and not a small part, knew they weren't real but that made them more powerful, not less.

And now? Now I pride myself on sitting alone on Coolanagh in the dark, refusing to be frightened of figments.

"THIS IS a fine time of the night to be coming in."

Mrs D. is not asleep, though it's 2.43 a.m. unless the clock is wrong. She's been sitting in the fireside chair and waiting through all these hours since she finished work at twelve, chasing thoughts that have stirred her to high temper and the disgust that's now spilling out her eyes. Sex is what's there. Her daughter, out God knows where, doing God knows what with God knows whom. Loathsome.

And if she is wrong about this particular night, she is not wrong in general. I have been having the sex that so disgusts her, it has led where she always feared it would. Inside me is her worst imagining, alive and growing. Maybe that is why, tonight, I finally speak.

"I'm eighteen now," I say. "When Maeve was eighteen, she used to come home this late."

"You can leave your sister out of this. I always knew where Maeve was. Maeve could be trusted."

"Good old St Maeve!"

"That's enough now. Your sister has nothing to do with this."

"Except that what was OK for her is not OK for me."

"If you're trying to imply favouritism, Miss…"

"I'm not implying, I'm saying. That's what it is. That's what it always is."

"You'll find anything you want if you go looking for it, Siobhán. But if you weren't always, and only, thinking of yourself, you'd see that—"

"I don't see why I can't stay out late if I want, that's all. What do you think happens when I'm in Dublin?"

"I don't want to even think about what happens in Dublin."

"Why? Are you jealous?"

"What sort of nonsense is that?"

A bitter red stain tracks up from her throat and I find myself feeling sorry for her. As Granny Peg is always pointing out, Mrs D. has had a hard life, full of bad things done to her. And I'm afraid, though I'm not quite sure of what. Of her withdrawing her love? Of the weight of the guilt if I went too far?

Knocking my corners off, Mrs D. calls it, when she snaps or slaps. She is the opposite of those mothers who compensate for their own hardships by striving to give their children what they never had. She wants to toughen us up, because life is hard and we might as well know it now and get used to it. "What is that silly comment supposed to mean?" she says, nostrils flaring, face ablaze.

Here goes. "I might as well tell you one of the things I 'get up to'," I say. "I'm going out with Rory O'Donovan."

"Rory who?"

"You know who I mean. Rory, John O'Donovan's son."

"No!"

"Oh yes, I—" But I don't have time to say any more. Her hand, clenched into a fist, swipes towards me. I duck to avoid it but it's too late: her knuckles catch the upper part of my cheek, just under the eye. I hear the crunch of bone on bone, then a wave of shock jounces through my face, ringing pain.

She has punched me. Not just one of her slaps, a punch. A punch in the face. Now an acid rage sears through my centre, flares into my head in flashing, hot thoughts. I'll box her back, I swear it. Box her face. She is smaller than me and old and I can punch harder…I can…

I want to brand all that she knows and does not know into her body with bruises.

…I will do it. It would give me pleasure. I can do it…I can. I will…

But I can't. I don't. No sound comes out except tears gurgling in my throat.

She has shocked herself. Her hand, her punching hand, is covering her mouth and guilty words bluster through her fingers. "What have you made me do? Dear God…What…"

I hold my swelling cheek with both hands. I want to tell her the rest, tell her the worst, but I can't even do that.

The door opens. We start and turn, like illicit lovers. It's Granny Peg in her dressing gown, her grey hair down.

"Máirín! Jo! I thought I heard…Good God, what's happening here?"

Mrs D. tucks her fists under her arms and when I see her face as she turns to Gran, my fury chills, congeals. I allow words to shape what my body has held close for so long. I speak to the side of her face, softly, as if I have just discovered it: "You hate me."

My mother's eyes swivel back to me.

"Jo!" cries Granny Peg.

I ignore her.

"You do, don't you? But you know what, Mrs D.?" I linger on the name that distances her from me, my first time to say it to her face. "You know what? It's all right. You can let it out now. Because I hate you too."

In that moment, it is almost true.

"Jo!" Granny Peg's eyes are as widely round as her glasses. "Jo, stop it. Stop. What are you saying?"

I take down my hand to reveal my face. Such pain must surely show? Shock jolts Gran when she sees it. She turns to Mrs D., back to me. She is a question mark, spinning between us.

"Ask her what she's been doing!" my mother babbles. "Go on! Ask her!"

Poor, poor Gran, who doesn't deserve any of this.

Mrs D. shouts, "No, she has nothing to say for herself now, has she? Oh, no. She's too ashamed to say it, and well she might be. Let me, then, be the one to tell you: she's only gone and taken up with young O'Donovan."

"O'Donovan. You mean…?"

"Yes. Yes! Him! Yes!"

"Oh, Jo. No."

"She picked it..." Mrs D. is turning hysterical. "She picked the thing that would hurt me most...Went out of her way to do this to me..."

"Now, Máirín, stop that. Stop. Of course she didn't. These things happen. Jo doesn't know..." She shoots her a look, a warning: Don't say too much. And that finishes everything off. It's a trapdoor opening under me, that look, and down I plunge. Forever.

Mrs D. starts to cry, fingers splayed across her face.

"No, no, Máirín pet, don't cry." Gran encloses her in loving arms. "Come here. Don't cry."

And there's nothing for me to do but leave them to each other, wrapped around their precious, protected secret.

1923

Peg's Diary 10th January, near on midnight. It was I who had to tell them. Daddy was in the bottling store and when he saw me come in, the state of me with tears running down my face, he just stood up from his work with the bottle still in his hand, and waited.

I didn't know how to say it so I just blurted it out. "Barney's dead," I said. "Shot in an ambush."

For a long, long minute he just stood there holding onto the bottle like a child asked to mind something without knowing why. Then he said: "I knew. I knew this was how it would end."

He got down onto his knees and began to pray. I couldn't just go and leave him to it, though I felt we should be telling Mammy, so I crossed myself along with him but couldn't pray for wondering how long he'd be.

After an Our Father and three Hail Marys, he got back up and said, "Have you told your mother?" and asked me to do the deed, saying he wouldn't be able. I didn't know if I'd be able myself.

She was out the back, coat and hat and scarf on, sitting on the bench she set up years ago under the apple tree, facing the sea. It was drizzling. She heard me coming and, when I got close, she spoke without opening her eyes. "I know you're going to tell me it's starting to rain and to come in," she said. "And I will in a minute when it starts in earnest, but it's so good to feel that wind in my face."

"I've bad news to tell you, Mammy," I began. She opened her eyes and made a short nod. I told her. She took it brave, not a word or a sound out of her. After a long while of a wait, with me not knowing what to be saying or doing, she spoke. "Leave me now, Peg, for a bit."

I said to her to come inside, that the rain was getting heavier, but again she told me to go and in such a way that I felt I had to obey. I went in and she sat on, under the tree, while the weather worsened and turned to a downpour.

Out I went out again and begged her this time but no. Daddy tried then but she refused him too.

Next, the military called to give us the news. When they saw we knew already, they didn't stay long. They've brought him to the barracks as they have to do a post-mortem. There will be an inquest to determine exactly what happened.

Then the word was out. People started to flood to the house, one after another, offering their sympathies. Father John came and, to his credit, didn't give any of his spiel against the Republic but just offered comfort and prayers and asked about arrangements. I sent him out, thinking he'd be the one to make her come in. I was really worried when he failed. The rain hadn't stopped and it would be bad for anybody to be out in it that long, but for her....

Lord, it was hard to watch her.

Tipsy left the column to come by again, at no little danger to himself. He says all the boys are broken-hearted. They are all talking of how brave Barney was, saying he died so the rest of them might escape to fight again. According to him, it was Dan who fired the shot that killed Barney. That he'd like it to be so is clear from his response when I challenged how he knew it.

Remembering how lenient Dan was on us that day in

Dunore, I truly doubt the truth of this. I know we've all got more bitter since then, but shoot his best friend dead? I could never believe that of him. It's as well there will be an inquest because the tongues that can't wait to be wagging around here would love nothing more than to have that one to pass on.

Tipsy was trying so hard to be a comfort, I found it hard to get rid of him, so he was there in the kitchen when Mammy walked back in, hair streaming around her face. "It is a glorious thing that happened today," she said. "The name of Barney Parle will go down with that of Pearse and Emmet and Tone. Greater love hath no man."

I ran for a towel and dried her hair as best I could. After a long time and the helpful persuasion of Lil Hayes, I got her into bed, shivering like a grounded bird. Dr Martin came over and gave her a sleeping draught. How we'll get her through the next few days, I just don't know.

I'm so tired. There's the wake to arrange and then the funeral. Daddy's distraught and it makes him worse to see Mammy the way she is. If only Norah was here.

Norah.

Holy God, what will it do to Norah when she finds out?

DIARY 11TH JANUARY: We had the inquest today and it was horrendous, listening to their soldiers, their lawyers and that doctor with his horrible medical voice giving details of what took Barney out of this life – "a large wound in the front of the abdomen with a knuckle bowel protruding. Death caused by laceration of the bowel and kidneys, haemorrhage and shock." More words to add to the torture in my head.

And Dan in the witness box, never looking at us once. Our solicitor, Mr Nolan, submitted that no-one was giving any evidence of how Barney was shot or who did the deed. Surely some of the soldiers must have seen him fall or come out of the outhouse? Dan replied that in the mêlée, with both sides firing for upward of ten minutes, it would have been hard to distinguish any particular man falling, let alone say who delivered the fatal shot.

According to him, when his troops had the house surrounded and he knocked on the door of the stable to take the surrender, Barney said "Wait until we put on our clothes" and then, a minute or so later, started to take shots at them.

Tipsy and the boys swear that what Barney shouted was "Surrender we never will!" And that the Staters were the first to fire. Barney hung back, they say, keeping up a defensive fire that allowed others to escape, until he made a break for the wall.

At which point Dan was seen by more than one person to have taken aim right at him.

I'm so confused. Dan was awful convincing, especially when he spoke of Barney being his neighbour and good friend. He said he had assured Barney from the outset that it was himself who was in charge and that, if they came out, he would see to it that they were protected.

He also made little of our solicitor's objections to the class of bullets used by the Staters, those ones that explode inside a body, like small bombs. Barney might have had a chance if it had been a fair fight, Mr Nolan said. If the Army used similar weaponry and ammunition to that used by the flying column, Barney Parle might be alive today.

The army used the equipment it was supplied with, Dan answered. Neither he, nor anyone in his command, had any choice in such matters.

The verdict came as no surprise. A Free State court with a Free State judge and the Free State Army giving the evidence were hardly going to bring a jury round to convicting one of their own. And so it was: the jury pronounced themselves satisfied that Barney had been shot by National Troops "in the course of their duty".

Mammy stood up then, saying she considered it a "poor

specimen of a national army when it was a case of fifty to one". She had seen the troops going past the house and there were more than fourteen of them, for sure. And they had used guns and bullets that were infamous throughout Europe for the excessive wounding they inflicted.

Dan rose to respond, and in a manner as superior as any English commandant, made a public spectacle of her, not caring an ounce for her grief. "Do the Republicans claim the sole right to carry on?" he intoned. "Are we to go to war as they wish? Are we only to send out three or four soldiers? Are we to use inferior ammunition? That is all bunkum, my dear woman."

Oh, God, thoughts wrestle each other in my head, throwing each other about without taking me any closer to knowing.

Is this a just punishment for what we did, Barney and I, at Donore? For making another family feel the way we Parles feel this day?

This is the real question, the one that won't let me go.

Weakness, Mammy calls this. Understandable weakness, but to be transcended. She's asked me to write something to keep Barney's memory alive. The Free State would like to make it as if men like Barney Parle died for nothing. Whatever the rights and wrongs of it all, whatever confusions and remorse I might carry, that cannot be allowed. So yes, I will write a ballad.

1995

"*I*f it weren't for the warning signs and the barbed-wire fence, you'd never know, would you?"

Rory is bent over a camera lens, looking out across Coolanagh. He has lived beside this place all his life, apart from his college years in Dublin, but he knows almost nothing about it.

We are out together in daylight in Mucknamore, for the first time ever. Walking out along The Causeway, we both felt exposed to the windows of the village staring into our backs, but out here, we're beyond view, in the dip behind the dunes that faces Coolanagh called Lovers' Hollow.

Oh yes, the irony is not lost on me. And as I look around at the wide flat expanse of sand and sea and sky, I get a strange, hall-of-mirrors feeling. I imagine Gran out here with his great-uncle Dan, and feel like their movements in the mirror are what is moving us.

He says, "You'd expect there'd be some sign, wouldn't you?"

"Sign?"

"That they were sinking sands?"

"I think maybe it's darker in colour?" I stand and point. "There?" He comes across to look at where I'm pointing.

"Where?" He steps in close, so that my bump nudges his back.

"There, where the stream comes off the island?"

"Hmmm...Maybe."

I move away, putting some space between us. He slings his camera over his shoulder and lifts the top rope of barbed-wire to slide through. "What are you going out there for?" I ask. "Be careful."

"I won't go far. I just want to get a close-up of that grass."

It's only ordinary marram grass but I know he sees something in it that I don't.

I take the cloth from the basket and spread it and our rug across the sand. "Another perfect day," I say, taking out food and utensils.

Each morning we wake and there it is again: the sun. Nobody can believe it.

He smiles. "I've never seen a summer like it. You're lucky you didn't come last year, when it rained nearly every day. We had the heating on all summer. You'd never have survived in that shed of yours."

"That's hard to imagine when it's like this."

While I lay out the food – sandwiches, fruit, cheese, chocolate – on plastic plates, and set out the cups and the knives and forks, feeling like a fifties housewife, he snaps, snaps, snaps picture after picture. Shhum. Click. Whirr. Sturdy thighs strain against denim as he leans in, rapt, every cell focused on his subject.

Just as I have the meal ready, the film reaches the end of its roll and the camera hums through its rewind. He slips back through the barbed-wire fence and joins me on the rug, stretching his legs to their full, long length.

I'm hyper-aware of those legs, their closeness to mine, the bulk of the body that tops them, but he seems blithe, pouring himself a juice and starting on some sandwiches.

"Jo, I wanted to ask you something. I wanted to ask you about" – he points to my bump – "about...the father."

I'm taken aback. "Why? I told you before, he was nobody. A one-night stand."

"Does he even know that you're pregnant?"

"He wouldn't want to."

"How can you be so sure? How come you get to make that decision for him?"

I don't want to talk about this. The happier I get about the idea of the baby, the less I want to remember how she came to be. That drunken coupling. That guy's anxiety to be rid of me, almost shouldering me out of his apartment. That time of wild panic afterwards. All the broken moments that had brought me to here are best left back behind me, locked up where they can't do any harm.

"Rory, let it go. You don't know anything about it."

He says, in the wary voice of one who's aware that he's saying something contentious, "Who would know better than me?"

"Ah. So that's it."

"I'm not trying to upset or annoy you, Jo. It's just I can't help feeling for the guy, whoever he is. I know how it feels not to be given a say."

"That's rubbish, Rory. You made it perfectly clear how you felt."

"Wrong. And what if you're just as wrong about this other guy now?"

"Rory, you made it obvious that..."

"I didn't, Jo. I did not. We barely discussed it, then – snap! – you were gone."

My mind leaps to the injustice of this. "You could have followed."

"You left without a word. You didn't want to be followed."

"Oh, but I did. I so, so did."

"Why didn't you just ask? One word from you, one single sign, and I..."

"But Rory, that was the point. I needed you to do it without me having to ask."

"Jesus!" he says. "Women!" He sits up and brushes crumbs off his T-shirt with force, as if they were our wrong turnings, our lost years. "Your entire sex should come with a mental health warning."

I am reminded of Richard, who always said he was glad to be gay for this very reason. Desire was so much more straightforward with guys, he said, because men just want. While women want to be wanted.

So I don't lob back any of the arguments waking inside me, the poisonous little vampires of exoneration and vindication, repeated to myself so often back then that I still know them by heart. What is the point in explaining or defending the viewpoint of that younger me? It's all too long ago. She was somebody else, with her convoluted desire to be desired, her need to be needed.

So I try to give him something true instead. "Maybe I should have had more faith in us."

"You should, Jo." His voice is vehement. "You really should."

But I was my mother's daughter. I had seen how it felt to need, to want, to crave what the other person could not give. If I didn't ask, I couldn't be let down.

Is that really how it was? Which is true, this new story of now? Or the hurt and angry tale that my younger self used to tell? My head begins to ache in the old way.

"Rory, I can't do this."

"I know it's hard for you, Jo. And I'm not bringing it all up just to make a point. It's that I...I..." He sits up. "It's that I've been thinking...about...about what might happen if I left my marriage."

I stop breathing.

"Jo, I don't want you to think...I haven't decided anything."

As if I'd asked him to. As if I'd said that was what I want.

"And your wife? Have you discussed it with her?"

There. That's the first time I've mentioned her, this woman who has started to spend too much time in my thoughts.

"Not that exactly. We have discussed you."

"I imagine you'd have to, with you going up to my shed each night."

"She didn't mind at first. But now…"

"She didn't?" This seems astonishing.

"She thought you needed a friend."

"Ugh!"

"Well, you were troubled, Jo. And when you moved into your shed and locked yourself away, like a hermit…"

"Oh, great. I got a pity loan of her husband."

He looks sheepish. "If I'm honest, that's the way I played it with her."

"And now?"

"Last night, when I told her I was coming out here with you today…she asked me not to."

"But you're here."

"I'm here."

Out on the strand, the seabirds splash in and out of sand-puddles. The angle of the sun is making each puddle a small mirror, holding and feeling the depth of the sky.

"It's not just about you," he says, after a while. "We – Orla and I – we haven't been right for a long time."

"Arguments?"

"No. That's not how it goes with us. Our relationship was always different to yours and mine. Never as…" He reaches for the right word.

"Intense?" I suggest.

"Yes, less intense. Less passionate, which was what I thought I wanted, then. She was attractive, clever, good at everything. She was…she is a good person. Everybody always likes Orla."

"But?"

"Oh, Jo, I'm so confused. All of that stands and the kids of course…But our marriage is not what it was. You might say, how could it be after so many years, but really it's that for the first time in my life, I know what I want. Not what my parents wanted, or what the world tells me I should do, or what the family need from me. What I want, for me. I fantasise about it all the time. At work, while I'm putting the kids to bed, all the time, except in the evenings when I'm with you."

"What is it? What do you want?"

"To leave here with you when you go back to the States, and to become a photographer. To start everything over and get it right this time."

I push down whatever thoughts I might be having about this, keep my voice even. "Does Orla know what you're thinking?"

"She knows more than I tell her."

That makes me laugh, I don't know why. A small, sniggery kind of laugh that I don't like but can't help. He doesn't rise to it.

"And, of course, there's the kids. That's one of the reasons I wanted to challenge you about what happened back then. What if Orla were to do that to me now? You see so many fathers get shut out when they…when a marriage breaks up."

Another laugh spurts out of me. Then I find I can't stop, gusts of laughter flooding up and out from I don't know where.

"Jesus, Jo. Stop it."

I try but I can't. I'm laughing and laughing and laughing.

"Christ!"

"I'm…sorry…Sorry…" I make a stern effort. I breathe deep. I focus. When I've got control, I say: "I'm sorry Rory. It's just that sometimes it all seems too ridiculous. All that wasted emotion, all that —"

He grabs my shoulders, kisses me on the mouth. A severe kiss, full of hard feelings and, oh yes, something in me leaps to it. My old self. We kiss and kiss and on we kiss, no other part of our bodies moving but our searching, accusing lips.

Oh, what a kiss. On it goes, all laughter wiped away now. My half-open mouth presses all I want to say onto his. You know me…you know me…I shouldn't have let you go…I want you…I want you but I'm afraid…Afraid to let myself love you again… Afraid of what might become of me…Afraid you are not mine… not mine.

Not. Mine.

I stop.

He stops.

We look into each other's eyes, ribs rising and falling over short panting breaths.

"Be mine," he says, echoing my thoughts, as he always used to. "Just for one day."

One day, in a vacuum, sealed off from his marriage and everything else. Oh I love the idea, I love the words in his mouth, I love the sound of him saying them.

Yet I'm pulling away. I'm standing up.

"Please, Jo," he says, jumping up too, gripping my arms. "Give me something."

That emotion in his voice, in the clutch of his hands – how can I know whether to trust it? To trust the way I thrill to it?

"I can't, Rory."

"Why? Why not? Don't pretend. I felt that kiss.'

'It's not that. You know I have… feelings—"

"Feelings!" His upper lip curls. "Steady on there, Jo. Take it easy, don't go overboard."

"Look at me, Rory. Just look." I shrug free, wave my hand across the front of my body. "I'm six months pregnant by a man who meant nothing to me. Less than nothing. I can't be careless again."

I step backwards, right out of his grip. When I'm at a safe distance, I look into his eyes and say, "And I can't be careless with you."

He stuffs his fists into his pockets, as if he is afraid he might use them. "So are you happy just to keep on playing this little game of 'will we, won't we'? Because I tell you, I can't stand much more of it."

My heart is still thudding from our kiss. It would be so easy to give in, but what I have told him is true. And it bothers me that he seems so ready to cheat. One conversation about how bad he feels and then...Bam! Never mind, let's do it anyway.

Then again, meeting every night, the way we do: is that not cheating already? When we're together, he makes me feel we are the love story and she is the one on the outside — but they have their own story that excludes me.

I can't get past my imaginings. And not just — not even mainly — of her. Of two others. Two small and silent children.

It is picturing them that makes me start to clear off the plates and shake out the tablecloth, to fold up the rug and pack away our day.

Two children, lying in bed, hearing the sound of their mother, contorted with loss. Two children, feeling their house fill up with betrayal and humiliation. Two children knowing their daddy has left. Gone out, gone off, gone away from them.

1923

Freedom's Sake: A Ballad
By A True Republican

State soldiers went round searching our countryside for days,
To flush out freedom fighters (or take them to their graves).
On this bright winter morning, you would have seen them
    creep
around the column's hideout while they lay in their sleep.

The stern command: "Surrender!" rang out o'er Derriestown:
"Surrender now Irregulars! To Free State! And to Crown!"
Bold Barney grabbed his rifle, his fighters did the same,
All jumped to strike for freedom, for dear old Ireland's name.

The crack of muskets broke out, a terrifying sound
of gun and bomb explosions went blasting all around.
Captain Parle was heard to call, above the piteous roar,
to rally on his comrades, as he often had before:

"Prepare yourselves to fight now, m'true born Irish boys
To make this dash for freedom, for Holy Ireland's cause."

Then he addressed the Staters (and made his comrades thrill):
"To falsehoods and English guns, Surrender We Never Will!"

So out they dashed to meet them, as sun rose on that day,
through shots and blasts of bullets, somehow they found
    their way.
Barney held the firing while the others scaled the wall.
The last one turned and witnessed the shot that saw him fall.

Sleep on, sleep on, brave Barney Parle, while we weep that
    you're gone.
We know that on your courage, God's brightest blessing shone.
On your soul His angels now bestow their kindest smile.
You've left and gone before us, but only for a while.

You fought the cause of freedom, like all brave Irish men.
You gave yourself to win it. God Rest Your Soul. Amen.
A Celtic cross now marks the spot where wounded body lies.
Fear not. We will remember just why you lived and died.

SURRENDER WE NEVER WILL!

PEG'S DIARY 12TH JANUARY: They didn't want us to wake
Barney at home. The doctor at the hospital suggested he be
brought direct to the chapel in a lidded coffin and, to our great
surprise, Daddy recommended the same. Mammy wouldn't
hear of it. Her boy would be waked in his own home, she
insisted. Her will, as usual, won the day.

The ambulance brought him out from the morgue and we
had the room all ready for him, clean sheets, a candle lit at each
side of the bed-head, a statue of Our Lady on the bedside table,
a font of holy water. The two attendants carried him onto the
bed for us on a stretcher, leaving the white sheet that covered
him in place. After they had gone, we stood over him, Mammy
and me, and found we weren't able to go on. She looked at me, I

looked at her, we both looked at the sheet between us, the lumps and bumps rising under it that we knew were Barney's nose and chin and chest and feet.

And the smell. As long as I live, I won't ever forget that smell.

I don't know what Mammy was thinking, but to me it seemed impossible that I could ever peel back that sheet and confront the remains of what used to be my brother.

Then we heard a step on the stairs.

"Quick," Mammy said. "That's Lil. She'll think we're a right pair of cowards."

She pulled back the sheet and, as soon as she did, I understood Daddy's motives in wanting to have Barney coffined straight away. Identifying the body, he had seen what death had done to our boy. His face was all twisted, the eyes bulging, showing too much yellowing-white. His jaw was knocked out of line with his cheekbones but it was his mouth that was the worst of it, all curled up in one corner into a leer. What would put such a face on a boy and he on his way out of this life? He looked like a man possessed. We could do nothing but stare at him in horror.

That's how Lil found us, stiff solid, unable to move, all sorts of dreadful thoughts flying through our heads. She took one look at him, then at us, then started barking orders, telling us what to do and how to do it.

Pull that sheet off entirely. Strip off that coat. Get hot water and soap and a couple of cloths. We fell to obeying her and, while we carried out the tasks, she kept up a long string of talk. It was a disgrace that he was left like that. Why had no one closed the eyes, straightened the jaw? She had seen many a dead person in her day but never one left that way. It was too late now, he'd have to do.

In any other mouth, her talk would have sounded like disrespect, but from her that day, it was a strange sort of comfort. With her matter-of-fact words, she brought us back down, made us see that it was nothing but a turn of the eye, a twist of the mouth. No more than that. We began to see our boy again.

He was wearing the clothes he had on him that day of the shooting, the clothes I had given him. Under the jacket, the jumper and shirt were stuck together with blood and other excretions that were part of the stench emanating from him and getting worse as we stripped him back to the skin. I turned right red as we took off the last of his clothes and came to his naked person. It didn't seem right that I should ever see my brother like this, though Mammy and Lil weren't making much of it. All eyes were on the job and I suppose they had bigger things on their minds than my foolish embarrassment.

An attempt had been made to dress his stomach wound in the hospital, but it was still a raw and bloody sight. Once we cleaned all off as best we could, and bandaged the wound as if he were still alive, we dressed him. The lads had done us proud getting together as good a Republican uniform as they could muster. A proper pair of army britches. A Sam Browne belt. A tall and shiny pair of boots. How Lil cursed those boots for the difficulty of pulling them on over the stiffness of his feet.

We got the job done and he's above there now, lying on his back, rosary beads looped around his dead hands, a couple of candles lighting either side of him. For all our efforts, he still looks tormented, like someone to fear. "Keep the light dim," Lil said to me on the way out when Mammy was hanging back and not listening. "A clear look at him could put the heart crossways in anyone with a weakness."

DIARY 13TH JANUARY: The military gave us a bag yesterday, with the things they took from Barney's pockets. Mammy asked me this morning would I go through it, as she was unable. Am I ever glad she did, for what was in it, only notes and letters from

Norah, rolled up in string? I don't think Mammy would have been able to stop herself reading those letters if they fell into her hands, so it was good for Norah that they didn't. I was curious myself but of course I didn't give in to such a low feeling. I've put them away where they won't be found by anyone else and will return them to her when I see her. Whenever that will be. Maybe she'll turn up for the funeral? Or maybe she doesn't even know he is dead? That's the worst to think of.

Tipsy was our first visitor this morning. He came to the back door before daybreak, knowing we'd be up all night. He asked for me and, when I went out, he said he had something for me. In his arms, he cradled a canvas bag like it was a baby. When I asked him what was in it, he opened it to me much as a mother might allow you to peep under a blanket at her child. It was a gun, a Webley pistol. The minute I saw it, I knew what it was. "Barney's," I said.

"I thought you might like to have it."

"It was a good thought, Tipsy. Thank you."

He took it out of the bag and handed it to me and I held it, the weight of its handle heavy in my palm. With two hands, I raised it, pointed it at the ditch, fondled the trigger with my index finger.

When Barney joined the volunteers, back in '17, before Daddy ever knew he was involved, he kept this gun and a rifle that Mammy bought him under a loose floorboard in his bedroom. As I stood there, pointing his gun at the wall, I tried to call up his face the way I remembered it that night and I couldn't. I could recall the bright, bursting expression he had on him but not the face itself. I reached for it in my mind – the arrangement of his nose and eyes and mouth, the real look of him – but they were no longer there, wiped out by the image of that leering corpse above. Only dead a couple of days and already his physical features were going from me.

"It's not loaded," I heard Tipsy say, and his voice sounded a long way off. I dropped my arm. The tears that are only barely held down were welling in me again. I was grateful to him for bringing me the gun, knowing how short they are of arms at this time, but he brushed away the thanks. "One pistol will hardly be missed," he said, but I knew better.

Outside the family, nobody cared about Barney more than Tipsy. That makes him dear to us in these dark days. He stayed for breakfast and we talked about the military account of the inquest published in the paper this morning – a pack of lies from start to finish. After he'd eaten, he helped us transport the coffin across to the chapel.

Barney will lie there for the rest of today, on a catafalque in front of the altar, giving those who have not paid their respects in the house an opportunity to see him and pray for him. Two of the boys stand to attention in front of him with their arms reversed. They are taking turns at it so he won't be left unattended between now and the funeral at 11 o'clock tomorrow morning. We're assuming the Free Staters will allow us to bury our dead unhindered but a ring of armed men surrounds the village on all roads, in case they get any ideas about calling by.

DIARY 14TH JANUARY: We've just got rid of the last of them from after the funeral – Lama and Andy White were last to go as usual. I thought they'd never shift.

Never in my life have I felt as tired as I am in this moment but still I can't sleep. Everything that has been said today about Barney is buzzing around in my head as if the words themselves were living things. And buzzing even louder is what's not being said at all. Nobody mentions Dan O'Donovan, though we all spent the morning wondering whether he would show up.

It was one of the largest funerals Mucknamore had ever seen. We are not the only ones spinning from the shock of how my brother died. Many you wouldn't expect to be there at all turned out to honour him. We held our heads high, didn't let our sorrow overcome us, even when Father John made that speech.

Who'd have thought he'd turn up so forgiving? It's true what he said, some things are bigger than a man himself.

Mr and Mrs O'Donovan were at the church, standing at the back with their younger children, but no Dan, thank God. And no Norah. People say to each other (not to us) that it was brave of the O'Donovans to come, given the circumstances. Behind their fists, they talk about the two who couldn't be there, the two who had most reason: Barney's sweetheart and his old comrade.

The secret of Norah and Barney's love affair is known to all now, common knowledge, passed around like an unaddressed parcel, together with recollections of what happened to James Tracey and Nellie Shiels two years ago, when the Shiels boys tarred-and-feathered James's private parts and Nelly was sent away to England to an aunt. They're saying that it is not unusual for the menfolk of a family to set upon a young man, if he's thought to be interfering with a girl of theirs. That it's not unknown for such a young man to have the life near beaten out of him. That such might have been in Dan's mind when he fired the shot that killed my brother.

The burial was the worst, desperate altogether. It was I who let the volley off over the grave, using his own gun, three shots of promise and warning. I didn't flinch from the task, kept my eyes open as I let the fire and didn't screw up my face to one side as I have seen others do. Oh, the sounds. The three loud cracks of the Webley. The cry Mammy let out of her as the coffin went into the ground. The thud of the first sods of clay hitting the wood. The sea-chant of the prayers, breaking in a holy wave across the headstones, down to meet the sound of the sea itself.

DIARY 20TH JANUARY: I can't write.

DIARY 28TH JANUARY: I want to, but I still can't write.

DIARY FEBRUARY 4TH: Dear Diary, Help me. I sit before your empty page and I feel you are censuring me. But I don't know how else I could have done any of it. Help. Help me to understand. If only Norah was here. Finding her, making up to her for all she's been put through, feels like the best way to commemorate Barney and make amends. But how, that's the question? How?

DIARY FEBRUARY 14TH: Dear Diary, I swear as I sit down here tonight that I'll stay seated until I manage to capture something of my wretched feelings, that I won't get up from this chair until I manage to write down something that comes close to the truth.

DIARY FEBRUARY 15TH: Another night of nothing. Blank. It's not like I don't have anything to say, but as soon as I hold the pen over the page, the opposite thought pushes itself up just as urgent. The page is not blank due to any blankness inside. Inside is a morass of nonstop sorrows and angers, a horrible sucking swamp of black that's pulling me down into it. Help me. Mary Mother of God, pray for me. Pray for us all.

DIARY FEBRUARY 20TH: I'm shaking so hard I don't know if I'll be able to write this and it's more than a day since it happened. He came down to us, down to the shop, and in, into the grocery. What he would never do in the days we were supposed to be courting, today he did, without a by-your-leave. I was up the step-ladder dusting down a shelf when the shop-bell went. When I turned and saw it was him, in his hateful uniform, the height and width of him filling the whole doorframe out, I nearly dropped off the ladder, my heart took such a wallop. Mammy was behind the counter, bristling like a feral cat, and I got down, with care and attention, and took my place beside her. I was glad it was one of her good days and that she was able to be downstairs and with me for this. Then the next minute I was regretting it, for it was sure to be bad for her.

In fairness, he didn't enter with any bullyboy tactics, just took off the military cap and said all formal: "I'd appreciate five minutes of your time."

What he wanted quickly became evident: that we would use Parle influence with Republican troops — higher than ever since our boy's sacrifice — to call a halt to activity. Mammy said immediately we'd do no such thing and launched into an explanation, to which he responded with the evil intentions of the Free State Army, how they intend to execute all those who go against them, especially ringleaders. Mammy said it should fill him with shame to stand there in that uniform and say such things and then the two of them were off, back down the back lanes of the sorry year we've just put in, the rights and the wrongs, the ins and the outs, with one of them saying black was white and the other the opposite.

White is white! I wanted to shout at them. Black is black!

Only I didn't know what I meant by that.

I switched out because it was pointless argument and, anyway, what I was most concerned about was Norah, whether I might be able to find out where she was. Or at least that she was getting on all right.

Next thing I knew, Dan was putting his hat back on, retreating. "You're right, Mrs Parle. Of course you are. Everything you say is right. You must be happy, so, with the outcome thus far and you'll be only over-the-moon with what's coming. Enjoy it all, then. I bid you both good-day."

And out he went.

"Yes, get out!" Mammy shouted after his back, so loud I'm sure the men in the bar heard her. "And don't show your face in here again."

I ran for my coat.

"Where are you going?" She looked alarmed.

"He needn't think he's going to get away with that," I said to pacify her, but that wasn't my thoughts at all. He had come to us and Mammy had blown it. He had come to us, and that felt like an opportunity to me, though for what I wasn't sure. Norah?

Persuasion? Resolution? Maybe, maybe. I wasn't sure. All I knew was I couldn't let him go like that.

When I caught up with him by Duggan's, he didn't look at me, just carried on walking in a temper down towards the sea, but I knew it was okay because he slowed his pace a small bit so I was able to keep up. We took the old way down to the back strand, across to the shoreline, then westwards, towards Rathmeelin where fewer people go. We needn't have worried, only two crazy people would be out on the day that was in it, freezing cold and with a sharp wind that didn't look too strong but would whip the ears off you.

We met no-one and were up nearly as far as the old cemetery before he'd calmed down enough to say, "Thanks for following. It was you I went to see anyway, not her."

"Nobody wants any more bloodshed, Dan. But that will need both sides to give in, not just one."

"You had the power to prevent all this from the start, Peg. Do you never stop to think on that? God Almighty, Peg, it wasn't like you didn't know where lazy talk of honour and principles led. You saw that young lad in Enniscorthy."

Denis Heffernan, the sky in his pale eyes. The cry of his mother up to the same dead sky.

Dan was still talking. "You were a good person, Peg, I thought that would stop you in your tracks. That was your warning from God. But no. Hyenas in petticoats."

"'Hyenas'...? What?"

"That's what the men call you. Even on your own side."

Hyenas in petticoats?

"A woman's job is to care and nurture. It's the greatest calling there is on this earth, but Republican females want to be men instead..."

Hyenas in petticoats. He'd shocked me to silence with that one. Were we as misguided, as ugly, as ridiculous as that? Every bit of my body and soul was outraged by this slur.

I wanted to think about it, what he was saying about

goodness and nurturing and caring, which I did think of as the finest calling, which was what I had thought I was doing with Barney and the boys. But if that was right, why had it all gone so wrong? I couldn't think it all through there in front of him and his certainty.

What I didn't want was to get into angry argument. That, I was positively sure, would solve nothing.

So I swallowed the insult. I let it go. "Dan, I would like to see Norah," I said. "I'd like to visit her, wherever she is, and let her know that we have not deserted her."

"Jesus, you've a nerve, woman. I'm not going to bargain over peace using my sister."

"That's not what I meant."

"Norah is where she can come to no more harm from Parles or anyone else. That won't be changing, no matter what happens with the Irregulars."

"Dan, it's me. I would never, ever hurt Norah. You know that."

"Do I?" he said, in a voice I'd never heard from him before, soft and quiet as a flick knife.

"What's that supposed to mean?"

"You won't even admit to how your family has hurt her already."

Was he saying what I thought he was saying?

"And —" he went on quickly when he saw I was about to speak, "that lying verse of yours that's doing the rounds, that'll be remembered and sung in mouths long after you and I are gone, that makes out I killed Barney."

"It doesn't. You're not even mentioned."

"It does and you know it. 'The last one turned and witnessed the shot that saw him fall'. Do you think I don't know what those boys of yours are claiming? Only it's all twaddle. And you lap it up and spew it back out, though --."

"Oh God," I groaned, but he went on.

"—Though you weren't even there. The truth is, if they had

surrendered that morning, as they said they would, there would not have been one shot fired. And the shot that killed him was not fired by me. I never even saw him."

"I believe you," I whispered.

"What you can't face is that you are the ones to blame for his death, not me. You and your mother and my sister, twisting his head round till he didn't know what he thought himself."

"Stop...Dan."

"You're at fault as much as the man who shot him."

"Please."

"Your mother, especially. She knows it too, under her bluster. She'll see her last days out in torment over what she has done."

"Dan. Stop. Have mercy."

"Yet you show none, Peg. As if you're the only one with feelings."

"Do you mean you? You grieve him?"

"Jesus, girl, he was my best friend."

I bowed my head. "I'm sorry, Dan," I said. "Truly. I'm sorry."

He left off then.

"Thank you Peg. It means a lot to me, so it does, to hear you say that."

We did more talking — but that was the gist of it. He explained how my determination to make contact with Norah was also selfish. She was much better off where she was, happy and well cared for and glad to be away from Mucknamore. The kindest thing I could do for her was to leave her be. She had expressly asked not to be contacted by the Parle family.

"And I think you can see why she would need to make such a request," he said. I bowed my head when he said that.

So it was true. Poor, poor Norah.

Her family, at least, have not disowned her, but obviously got a good place for her with some nice nuns and she'll come back, probably, in time. Changed forever. And the child, all she has — all we have — left of our boy, will go to strangers. That too I must now take onto my conscience.

I thought the urge I had to find her, and be with her, and make her part of our family — given that Barney would surely have married her if he'd lived — was good and true, but I can see now how it looks from an O'Donovan perspective.

So I bow my head. Not to Dan O'Donovan, no, but to the truth in what he said to me today. I have thought wrong, I have spoken wrong, I have done wrong. The talk going out of this house has to change.

As the Free State unleashes its worst on us, I have to work to cool the flames in the country. And the flames in myself. I have to let Norah be. Unless I want to leave this life looking as anguished as my brother, I have to make amends.

1975

*B*reasts tender as bruises. Nausea squirming in the pit of me like a nest of snakes. And tears, rivers and rivers of tears.

Hormones, I tell myself, mopping up. Just hormones. Once I have done the deed, they will disappear with the rest.

Deirdre thinks it is breaking up with Rory that makes me cry. I have not seen him for three days. I am home, snuffling around the flat in my dressing gown, or sobbing under my blanket. What happened? Deirdre wants to know. Are we finished? Can't we make up? Why won't I tell her? I want to tell but I can't. The word curdles in my throat: I cannot get it out.

I know I am (relatively) lucky, to have England next door. To have a safe, legal option to flinging myself down stairs with fingers crossed. To all the whispered things you hear that women do. Gallons of gin and a scalding bath. Wire coat-hangers. Knitting needles. I am lucky, I won't die of it.

If I could just get it organised.

I spend Monday hovering for hours outside the clinic where I got my ineffectual pills, walking up towards the door and walking away, like I am dancing a grim minuet. I can't go in.

Every time I imagine myself telling that helpful girl at reception and that kindly doctor what I want, I balk.

On Tuesday, I go looking around campus for a girl I have seen before handing out leaflets about "Women's Right to Choose". Beneath her alarming (green) hair, she looks kind, the sort of person who will listen, who will not judge. I find her and track her to the restaurant, the bar, the Students' Union. I even follow her into one of her lectures, sitting behind her for an hour of social policy, rehearsing the choice of words I will whisper to her when class is over.

I'll be direct: "I need an abortion. I thought you might know where I could arrange one."

No, I'll spare my blushes by lying: "My friend is pregnant and asked me to ask you how she'd go about getting to England for an abortion."

No, she'll see through that.

I won't say the word. I'll just throw myself on her compassion. "I'm pregnant. Help me, please."

When the lecture is over, I follow her out the door, but a guy comes across to talk to her and I am not brave enough to intrude myself between them. I let her melt away into the crowd.

I turn desperate. That word, that word, that horrible word. If I can't even say it, how am I going to be able to do it?

After another night of tossing and sobbing, I blurt it to Deirdre at coffee break.

"Oh, no," she says — just what he said when I told him. "Jesus, I should have thought of that. I'm so stupid. What are you going to do?"

"England."

"Oh, Lord. You poor thing. Is he going with you?"

I shake my head, a snap from side to side. "I don't want him to."

"Why not?"

I have no tidy answer to that. Deirdre stirs her coffee, probing my closed face. "Is this what you want or what he wants?"

"Both."

"Poor Jo." She puts her hand on mine. "Look, if you've made up your mind to do this, you have to just go and do it. You can't be condemning yourself all the way."

All around us, crockery clatters, spoons tinkle and voices talk. Happy talk, from laughing student faces, talk about essays or relationships or plans for tonight or the weekend.

"What about money?" she asks. "It costs a lot of money, doesn't it? And you'll have to get a boat and stay over there for a few nights."

"He has money, he's said he'll pay."

She nods, approving. "The least he can do."

I sip some of my coffee. Tepid and bitter.

"Do you want me to come with you?" asks Deirdre.

"Oh, Dee, would you?"

"Of course I would. Of course, if you want me to."

A wave of gratitude and relief breaks inside me. Everything flows out of me then. I tell her my trouble with the clinic, and the Right to Choose girl, and my worry that I won't be able to make it happen.

"What about an English telephone directory?" she says. "They stock them in libraries, don't they?"

"The directory would never be allowed to carry the addresses of places like that?"

"I'd say they might. They're a crowd of heathens over there. They're allowed do whatever they like."

She squeezes my hand under hers. "If not, we'll find a way. This doesn't have to be as hard as you're making it, you know."

"What do you mean?"

"You're doing what you have to do."

"I know. It's just I never thought—"

"I know, no one ever does. But you're a good person, Jo. Don't believe anyone who tries to make you think anything else."

She takes me over, hauling me off to the library to find a

London business directory. She places it in front of me, opens the front pages under the letter A.

"Wouldn't it be under Clinics or something?"

She upends the book and pushes it across to me. There it is, between Abattoirs and Abrasive Materials, two matter-of-fact words on a page: Abortion Advice.

We write down the names of the clinics and their telephone numbers, then take the bus into town, to the public telephone boxes in the General Post Office with their heavy, sound-proof doors. I squeeze in, line my £5 worth of fifty-pence pieces on the shelf, dial the first number on my list and am quickly through to a matter-of-fact English voice.

Certainly, she can give me information. Have I done a pregnancy test? What stage am I at? Am I certain that abortion is the option I want to take? In that case, as I am from Ireland, they can fit me in to do everything within twenty-four hours: counsel me in the morning, perform the procedure in the afternoon and I can leave the next day. I must, however, spend the night in England; that is a legal requirement. Would I like to book an appointment?

Clunk, clunk goes my money, dropping down.

I give her a false name for her appointment book: Siobhán Devoy. Her soothing voice drones on. Would I like details of bed-and-breakfast accommodation near the clinic, details of local transport? Have I any more questions? No? In that case, they look forward to seeing me on Saturday the 24th.

"It's all arranged," I say to Dee, coming out. "Saturday week."

"There, that was easy, wasn't it?"

It was. Too easy. Too, too easy.

LONDON. Immediately, I love it. Capital of Great Britain, still thinking itself capital of the world. Great big London.

Coming in on the train, I am shocked by its size. Dee and I sit staring through a rain-spattered window as mile after mile after mile of housing whips past, endless back views of endless backstreets. On and on it goes and still on, and on, until it begins to feel like somebody's idea of a mad joke.

The whole country is so different. As we moved out of Wales and through the middle of England with its giant power stacks, belching baleful ugly clouds at the sky, I thought of Daddy and wondered for the first time how he really lived during his years in one of these grim-looking towns.

And as we come out of Paddington Station and travel into the centre, everything tells us that we are in a new country. The red buses and pillar-boxes that to our eyes should be green. The awe-inducing buildings, taller than trees and wider than fields. Not just the touristy places, the palaces and churches that boom their importance with arches and turrets and carvings of impossible magnificence, but also the day-to-day buildings, the banks and offices and shops just sitting, resplendent, at the side of the street, thinking nothing of themselves.

I wish that Dee and I were what we seem to be: two young visitors with backpacks, here for the sights.

The sights. A group of boys our age jostling each other off the pavement, their dark skins and the whites of their eyes shining. A black woman at least six and a half foot tall, hugely beautiful in red and yellow. Another brace of boys around the entrance to a park, gravity-defying hair like cockatoo plumage, chains and spikes jangling. It has been raining and water is spilling from chutes, gutters are running, puddles lap like miniature lakes. Statues glisten, seem more animated to me than any statues I've ever seen, dead men and horses and lions invigorated by the rain, their eyes alive to the bustle about them and the washed, pale-blue sky.

I love it all but I especially love the people sliding past each other, unseeing, locked in the shell of their own thoughts. You could never do that in Mucknamore or even in Dublin. Here, I marvel, you can be no one right in the middle of everyone.

That's when I let it out first, the thought that has been there since the start. Could I stay?

Even the language is not really the same. In the pub at lunchtime, I ask the barman in a pub for a white lemonade and he hands me a biscuit. Three times I have to repeat myself, blushing redder each time, before he hears what I am saying. Dee is bent in two, behind me, laughing.

Afterwards, at the clinic, she tells the story to one of the nurses, an Irish girl from Carlow called Mary, as a joke but Mary doesn't laugh. She tells us that in England, there's no such thing as red lemonade. She tells us she had great trouble making herself understood when she came over here first. She tells us that the English think we talk like those stage-Irish people on TV and in the films. We all sound the same to them, whether we're from Wexford or Dublin, Cork or Donegal.

Mary has lost a lot of Carlow from her own way of talking. She speaks slowly and quietly, separating out her words; speaking not for herself but for the person who's listening to her.

She's a nice person and a good nurse. As she takes my pulse and blood pressure, only a shade at the very back of her eyes shows her awareness of what I'm doing. She is sorry for me, I know, for all the women here in the clinic. I know – even as she gently leads me into theatre, even as she offers me her hand to hold while the anaesthetic takes affect – that later on I will resent this pity.

Afterwards, when it is over and I wake up, she is there again, offering me tea, but I don't want to talk to her or to Dee or to anyone now. I wrap my arms around my empty body and ignore the look that passes between them, turn in my bed to face the wall, my back to them and the rest of the ward, the rest of the world. I feel scoured.

After a time, Mary comes over and taps me on the shoulder. I have to get up, she says.

"No. I can't." I am giddy with absence.

"You have to."

I try, but my legs are too empty to hold me up. I feel like a blow-up doll with an air-leak. "I can't stand."

"That's the anaesthetic," Mary says. "You have to help it wear off."

She gets Dee to walk me up and down the stairs.

While all this is going on, underneath I am thinking about staying, the idea hardening inside me while I try to pull back from everything else. But it's not until next morning over breakfast that I finally get the idea up and out. "I'm not going back."

Dee stops her toast on its way to her mouth. "What do you mean?"

"I'm not going back to Ireland."

"Yeah, let's stay forever."

"I mean it, Dee. I've been thinking about it ever since we arrived. I've made up my mind."

This is unfair to Dee, I know that. She has been good enough to come across to London with me and now I'm going to leave her to go back alone. And she will have to find somebody else to share our flat.

She tries to change my mind. I haven't got a job. I haven't got anywhere to live. What about my degree? My family? Rory?

"Rory and I are finished."

"You don't mean that."

"I do," I say, and I almost do. We're finished for sure if I go back. Our only hope is if I stay here and he proves himself, proves us, by coming after me.

As for Mrs D., I haven't spoken to her since the night I left Mucknamore. It's unthinkable that I should go back to living off her money, under her charge, and I know now that Granny and Maeve cannot help. The strength of Mrs D.'s weakness has us all in its grip — but not me. No more.

Dee thinks I am being overdramatic. The whole point of having an abortion, she says, is so you can step back into your life as if nothing happened. She says I'm overtired, a bit depressed maybe. It's natural, after what I've been through. Come to think of it, she should have expected something like this. This is no time for making big decisions. I should go home, see how I feel, and if I'm the same in a few weeks, I can come back.

It makes sense, what she is saying, but it terrifies me. If I go back, I know I will never escape again. While she is speaking, my feelings are banking up inside against her words and, for the first time in our friendship, she doesn't sway me.

After breakfast, we pack up our weekend bags and I go with her to Paddington railway station. Up to the last moment, she doesn't believe I'm not going with her. At the platform, I give her a hug, thank her for everything.

"You really mean it? You're staying?"

I nod, more nervous than I'm admitting.

"But what will you do? You've no job, nowhere to live, no money."

"I'll be all right," I say.

"Here," she says, unzipping the front pocket of her backpack. She presses something into my hand.

My fingers close around some notes and coins. I feel tears pressing against the back of my eyes.

"I owe you," I say.

She smiles, shakes her head. "It's not much. I wish it was more."

"I don't just mean the money." We look at each other, awkward with feeling. The train growls behind us, anxious to leave. "You'd better go."

"Yeah." She turns, strides down towards the second-class compartments.

A thought strikes me. "Dee!"

She turns back round and I see she is crying. For me?

"Don't tell anybody where I am," I call. "If Maeve or my mother ask, just play dumb. Don't mention England."

She frowns through her cloudy eyes. "You'll let me know where you are once you get set up, won't you, Jo?"

"Sure."

She walks back to me, to give me a fierce look through wet lashes. "Jo? I mean it. I want an address and phone number as soon as you have one. You're not to disappear, d'you hear?"

"I won't. Honestly."

"And you never know, you might change your mind and come back. Don't be stubborn about it."

"You'd really better go."

I watch until her red backpack climbs on board, then I leave. Walking away, I hear her voice behind calling my name. "Jo!"

I turn. Her head is sticking out the window. "Up the Irish!" she shouts after me.

I laugh, lift my hand in one last wave. The train revs up and begins its shunt and, before it has even pulled out, I've stepped away into a swarming crowd.

PLASH: NORAH

1923

Thirty-six hours she was in the coming. The pain of pushing my insides out, pain cutting me to blood. Two nights and a live-long day with no one to talk to. All I had was a cross old nun saying every few hours I'd be another while yet and getting annoyed with me because she wanted to be in her bed.

Curses to the Lord. Curses on curses and pain on pain, for a night and a day and another long night. And when she finally came, she didn't come easy. Push. Push again. Push, for God's sake, push would you, push I said, push can't you? Push.

At the very last, when I could do no more, Child took over herself.

"It's coming, it's coming," said the nun. Out my daughter slithered in a rush of blood.

She was given to me and — oh! — all curled over, she was, from being inside me, her back curved like a bowl and her hands and feet like little cups. A black downy head on her. Arms and legs purple and fleshy. Bits of my body and blood stuck to her.

And her eyes. Open so wide they seemed half the size of her face. I couldn't take my own off them. They drew me in.

"Look how she's looking at me," I said to the nun.

"Don't fool yourself," she said. "Newborns see nothing for weeks."

She was wrong. I was being seen and it was opening my own eyes wide too.

Too wide.

They cut the cord. All for the best, they said. Hush now, stop now, all for the best now.

They took her away as my bosoms were filling. Your milk's come in, the auld nurse said, when I told of the pain in them. Full hard fit to burst, longing for little lips to ease them.

And beneath, my belly was shrinking, closing in round the space where she used to be. And me, leaking. Oozing from every soft spot in my body, blood and milk and tears.

1923

*E*aster fell early and the schools started their holidays on the day before St. Patrick's Day. On the first morning of her break, Peg came in from a long walk and found her father in the kitchen, leaning over the fire. In the stoop of him, she could see how Barney's death, the manner of his going, had permanently affected him.

"Are you all right, Daddy?"

'Just a bit tired, a ghrá. Your mammy had a bad night.'

"Again. You must be weary."

He didn't deny it and she could feel it in him, beneath his bones. Born of lack of sleep, yes, but also of taking wrong turnings all his life. He began as a boy full of fear, for he had a father who was very hard on him, and he never outgrew it, that fear. It left him not knowing how to make his own life in his own image.

Everyone else had always led him, from his father to his daughter, and now here was where he'd come to. The horizons of youth narrowed to the hurdles of age and these latest — the death of his son, the illness of his wife — were most impossible to surmount, in the too few days he had left to him. He was too old and too tired to know what to do about any of it.

All of this Peg deduced from the way he stood over the fire. He straightened himself a bit and took up the teapot, and offered her a cup, and poured it for her.

"I think we'll have to take her into the spare room, Daddy. Then we could take turns leaving our doors open. You one night, me the next."

"Maybe so."

"Definitely. You can't go on like this. Next thing, you'll be sick too."

When he didn't deny it, she said, "Let's do it now, when we finish our tea. We'll have it all done before the shop opens."

They found Máire willing, which helped. She'd found it uncomfortable also, trying not to disturb him in the night, knowing she was keeping him awake. "But," she said, "Not the spare room, facing the back fields with no sun. No. Put me in Barney's."

Peg and her father looked at each other.

"Are you sure?" JJ asked.

She was, and Peg was sent in to prepare the room.

She walked briskly past the bed that two months before had held her dead brother and began polishing the windows, which were spattered with sand from winter winds. The fine morning was deteriorating; she had got the best of it for her walk. A wintery, watery sun seemed to throw no heat at all, but it did give the pleasure of light, especially where it struck the peaks of the waves further out. Five distinct clouds were following each other across the sky, thickening and darkening as they marched.

Once the windows were clean, she left them open a little for air, and swept the room out, and gave it a polish and, finally, set to dressing the bed. It gave her a queer feeling and she was glad she wasn't the one who had to sleep in it. Then she scolded herself. Most people in the village had slept in a dead person's bed and what harm did it do them? Few had the luxury of spare beds, never mind spare rooms.

She finished the job efficiently, went down and heated the bedwarmer, then went back to her parents.

"You're sure now?" JJ said again to Máire.

"I am. It's a nice little room. I'll sleep like the —" She stopped. "— like a baby in there."

He wrapped a blanket around her legs and two around her shoulders before picking her up. Watching them, Peg felt the mystery of a long marriage. The long melding of days and doings felt, in that moment, more significant to her than the melding of bodies to which everyone, including herself, gave so much attention.

All that seemed a small thing to hold beside her father's gentle lifting of his wife out of her sickbed, the lightness of her once-strong frame in his arms, the unexpected gratitude in the hands that slipped around his neck, the living, companionable togetherness of them, which Peg had sometimes felt but never before witnessed.

It was a balm to her now.

JJ carried Máire into her new room, set her down on the bed and Peg went to close the window, shutting out the hush-rush-hush of the sea. When she turned back, tears were streaming down her mother's face.

"The hurley," she said, pointing. "I forgot about the hurley."

Barney's hurling stick, that had won so many cups for Mucknamore, was atop the wardrobe. They were all, instantly, flooded with memory of him, the fitness and strength of him running and hitting and scoring. There was nothing Barney couldn't do with that hurley.

JJ still had his arm around Máire and Peg went round to the other side of the bed and sat in beside them, feeling her own tears high but not breaking, not this morning, for some reason. She passed her mother a handkerchief and the three of them sat quiet, facing the window, watching the waves.

"It's not a bad day," Máire said, after a while.

"It was lovely earlier," Peg replied.

"It's good that it's nearly spring. Conditions will be easing soon for those boys who are left to us."

"Now now," JJ said. "Let's not be thinking about any of that now."

"We'll have to get back to the work. We'll be needed more than ever now the army is…"

"They are our neighbours," JJ interrupted. "And maybe now is the time to find friendship between us. While we still can."

Máire fell back onto her pillow with surprise.

Peg found herself saying, "You might be right, Daddy."

Nothing happened at this saying of the unsayable except for a small sigh. The three of them sat on, in silence, until Máire spoke again to JJ, but kindly, not cross. "You'd better go down and open up."

"I will in a moment," Peg's father said. "The world will be met and its doings will be done. But let us just remain here, in the quiet, for another moment."

PART VI
BREAK

1995

A LETTER

Dear Rory,

I love you. Let's start from there. Neither of us used the word today so let's have it said. I love you — more than I've ever loved anyone else, before or after. Even that doesn't quite describe it. For me, there was no before you, there has been no after.

Do you know what I did when I left you today and got back here to the shed? I wrote to Sue Denim. Yes, to that version of me that other people come to with their problems. And do you know what she said? She told me to tell you that it's over.

So that's what I'm doing. Hence this note, pinned on the door of my shed, even though I said I'd be here tonight.

You were right, today. I was troubled when I arrived here. I did need a friend and thank you, Rory, for being that.

I haven't had proper friendship since the early days of Richard's illness. Those days, when we first realised he was going to die, were his happiest ever, he once told me. Mine too. Isn't that strange? We were always stopping in those days to admire a flower, or something in a store window, or an old lady's face. He used to say he had never really looked at things until he knew he was going to lose his sight, and never really lived until he knew he was dying.

I can feel him now, as I'm writing, frail on my arm as we walked around the city together, looking. So light, no burden. No burden.

After that, I went wrong. The papers you gave me, Gran's diary especially, has shown me how. And what I must do to put it right. Which is: let you go.

When we were young, I so wanted you to follow me, Rory. I wanted that long, long, long after there ceased to be any possibility that you might. I could follow that want of mine now, I could let it take me all the way into an affair. That's what you and I have been doing, by default. Letting our desire build and build until one day soon, we'd find ourselves overwhelmed. We'd "give in", and claim we had "no choice".

No. Not because I don't thrill to the thought, Rory, we both know I do. But no.

We missed our moment, my love. For reasons that were set in motion long before we came into the story, that love of ours failed to survive all that was ranged against it. You hurt me and I hurt you and, between us, we destroyed it.

Almost.

I'm leaving tomorrow and so I can tell you. As I say goodbye, I want you to know how in that place where there is no before and no after, I do still love you.

I am and will forever be,

Your Jo.

BEFORE THE FALL

VOLUME II OF IRISH TRILOGY

PART I
SPILL

1995

*M*idsummer is past. The days are getting shorter again. Sometimes, it feels like I've never lived anywhere but this tiny shed, in this tiny village, on the edge of the ocean. My busy days in San Francisco — so full of to-dos and appointments — used to seep past without me, but here, my life is stripped down to six basic activities: sleeping and eating, writing and reading, running and relaxing. Time is mine again.

Life likes to take it easy, it seems, and the only way to be properly alive is to slow your pace to match.

So I find myself less bored than when I was busy, and less lonely than I've been for years, though I've never spent so much time alone. Solitude soothes me, along with the fresh air, the sound of the sea, and the past that I'm excavating with my pen. All are helping me to heal. I didn't know that was what I was doing when I came here, but I know it now, and I tell myself that's why I've stayed on, why I haven't yet left as planned.

I'm reading an election leaflet of Gran's from 1923 when a voice from the door interrupts. "Jo Devereux, sometimes I think you're mad."

I jump. Then I see who it is. Irritation, instant and involuntary, coils in me.

I don't want to stop writing, certainly not to listen to my sister's views on my lack of reason. Yes, it is Maeve, come all the way down to Mucknamore from Dublin to visit me. She stands at the door of my shed, neat and slim in linen shorts and Ralph Lauren polo shirt, her car keyring looped over one finger.

Living here as I have been since May, centred on the secrets I've been finding in my mother's family papers, I've long ceased to notice the dilapidation. Now, following my sister's eyes, I see what she sees. Flaking walls. A concrete floor. An unmade bed on one side of the room. Debris piled into the opposite corner.

"What brings you here?" I ask.

"Lovely welcome, I must say. Can I come in?"

I hesitate, conscious of my shape and that I never did get round to telling her.

It wasn't intentional. What I had planned was to go to Dublin, to see her there, and explain. I never thought I'd still be here in this shed so many weeks on.

There's nothing for it now except to get up from my chair and step out from behind the table.

Her eyes fall on my body, swoop in on my abdomen, then swing back upwards to my face. "What —?"

She is stunned, her face so very shocked that I find myself laughing, that nervous laughter she always brings up in me when I've done the wrong thing.

"Oh my God!" she gasps. "I don't believe it. Oh my God!"

"Let's go round the back," I say, voice airy, as if I am a society hostess suggesting tea on the lawn. "That's the nicest place to sit."

I take my rug from the end of the rumpled bed and, while she's swallowing her surprise, I lead her to the grassy patch where Rory and I have been sitting most long evenings of this long, strange summer. It's private out here, between the shed and the edge of the little cliff, and the sea is singing a soothing song today, as if it's on a go-slow, not really wanting to turn the waves over.

"You should have rung Hilde to tell me you were coming," I say, flicking the rug out over the grass. "I'd have arranged to meet you somewhere a bit more comfortable."

"I've been expecting to hear from you every day, Jo. You've been down here for weeks and not so much as a phone call. But," she breathes, "never mind all that...What about this?" She leans across as if to touch me, then changes her mind. "Look at you. My God."

I gesture her to sit on the rug. "Would you like something?" I remember to ask when I'm down. "A drink? I only have orange juice."

"Orange juice would be nice." She puts a hand on my arm to stop me trying to push back up. "I'll get it."

"It's just inside the door, in the corner. The coolest spot."

She comes back with two plastic glasses and hands me one. "That's quite a mountain of manuscript you've got in there."

"I know. It keeps growing on me."

"Am I allowed read it?"

I shake my head. 'Not yet."

"When?"

"Soon. I have to type it up, and it needs a lot of tidying."

She opens her mouth to say something, but closes it again.

"Sorry the juice is warm," I say, when the silence stretches too long. "No fridge, obviously."

"I really thought I was beyond being shocked by you, Jo, but you've done it again. Why didn't you tell me?"

"I didn't tell anybody." Well, nobody except Rory.

"Not even the father?"

"No. Especially not the father."

She dips her head down to her plastic cup, trying to stop the disparagement that's rearing up inside her. She is thin, I notice, too thin; her hipbones jut against her shorts.

"What about you?" I ask her. "How have you been?"

"Fine. Fine. Nothing compared to this."

"Are you sure?"

Her face creases. "Oh, up and down, I suppose." Then she tilts her head towards the house. "Two shocks in a row. What they've done to Mammy's house, to the shop...It's so different, isn't it?"

"Unrecognisable."

Our mother had died just as she closed the sale of her house to Hilde and Stefan Zimmerman, an efficient German couple who'd pre-organised planning permissions. They'd arrived to live here within a week of her funeral. Work had begun immediately and was well advanced already.

"I wish it could have been kept as it was for a while," Maeve says. "It would have been nice to get used to Mammy being gone first, before we had to deal with this too."

"It's been easier for me, I suppose, being here. Seeing it change day by day."

"I still can't believe I'll never see her again. Can you? I think of things I want to tell her before I remember she's not here. And it hits me all over again."

"Time helps," I say.

"Is it helping you?"

"It's not the same for me, you know that. I hadn't seen her for almost twenty years."

"Still, she was your mother."

I try again. "I do know the feeling you're talking about and how awful it is. Time really does help."

"Your friend Richard?"

I nod, gratified that she remembers.

"Well, then, I wish time would just hurry up and do its thing."

We both fall into a silence, looking out over the sea.

How have I let this shed become my home-away-from-all-homes? That's the question my sister's arrival has thrown into relief.

I was supposed to depart for Dublin a week ago. Yet still I sit, day after day, at my makeshift desk, sifting through sentence after sentence bequeathed to me by my mother and grandmother, telling myself I need to be here to do it when I know I'm really here for Rory.

Though I told him I was leaving. Though I wrote it down to show him, to show myself, that I really meant it and though every word I wrote was right and true. If Rory's marriage was indeed so wrong for him, if our love — the first love — was what he wanted, then that had to be formally acknowledged. Properly done. Slip-sliding into an affair was not an option.

So, I wrote him. I was leaving. I was going to Dublin where my sister would help me organise an obstetrician. I would have my baby there and, as soon as possible afterwards, I was going to fly back to San Francisco to make a new home as a single mom.

My letter set him free. "We missed our time, my love," it said and I can still feel how good it felt to write that, to break the will-we-won't-we game we'd been playing since I came back here at the beginning of summer.

If his wife and family were not what he wanted — if what he wanted was me — then he was going to have to find a way to tell them and do what he should have done the first time, twenty years ago, when it was all less complicated. Come after me.

I didn't quite say all that in my letter, but it was implied. "When we were young, I so wanted you to follow me," I said. "I wanted that long, long, long after there ceased to be any possibility that you might."

Hint hint, Rory. Over to you.

When Maeve arrived fifteen minutes ago, I'd been typing out documents. A letter to Peg from her friend Molly, a letter to Norah from Peg that was never sent, and an election leaflet that seems poignant to me, that seems to carry in it all the yearning that my grandmother passed down the years.

Dear Voter,

We were told the Treaty with the British Empire would bring peace. If so, what is WAR?

We were told it would bring freedom. What, then, is SLAVERY?

We were told it would bring order. Then what is CHAOS?

They said this Treaty would fill Irish pockets. It has filled only Irish PRISONS and GRAVES. If the British Government is going to keep fighting and destroying us, we prefer that she should use her own English troops — as she does in the North of Ireland — and not our own misguided pretend-politicians.

People of Ireland, come back to us. Our country's future is now in your hands.

A REPUBLIC is the only basis on which we can build a proud and prosperous national life. Use this coming election to vote NO to this terrible Treaty. Then we can ALL share TOGETHER in the final victory over the British Empire.

Come back to us.

Vote for those who will yet SAVE THE NATION.

Vote Anti-Treaty.

IT GETS ME EVERY TIME, this leaflet put together by my grandmother and great-grandmother. It's those words: "Come back to us." Come Back.

People don't, do they?

We can't.

That's what I was trying to say to Rory, in my letter. Trying to reclaim what we had, to start over, to get it right this time, wasn't possible. No matter how much we wished it was.

So why am I still here?

"So tell me," Maeve asks, echoing my thoughts. "Why are you still down here? What have you been doing with yourself?"

"You saw that heap of papers in there. Reading and writing, mostly. Lying low."

"Is there anything of interest in those papers of Mammy's? Are they all rubbish?"

"Oh, no, they're not rubbish."

"Really? Tell me."

"I think you better wait until I've put it together."

She sits up, intrigued by something in my voice. "What on earth have you found?"

"All sorts of things."

"Deep dark secrets?" she grins.

"Yes, as a matter of fact."

"Things Mammy didn't tell us?"

"You're forgetting, Maeve, Mrs D. never told me anything."

That stops her smile. "Oh no, Jo, you're not going to write something Mammy wouldn't want known? Please tell me you're not."

I spread my hands and examine my fingernails.

"Jo!"

Above us a gull screams, slides across the air towards the sea. How much did Mrs D. know? That is the question. In her letter, she said she didn't read Norah's "scribblings" or all of Gran's diaries. I have read everything now, some of them many times, and still I'm not certain. Sometimes I find one thing in their words, especially Norah's. Sometimes another.

But what I hear in almost every sentence is the sound of their words shrinking from what they're saying, even as they say it. That's what speaks loudest to me across the years.

Maeve is annoyed with me again. "It's not your story, Jo, to do what you like with."

"Hey, calm down. I'll tell you in a while."

She looks sceptical.

"I will, Maeve, I promise. I just want to get it straight myself first."

"So you're not going against Mammy's wishes?"

I shrug. "Nothing I write can hurt her now. And if she really didn't want me to know — or write — about something, all she had to do was take it out of the suitcase."

"Maybe she wanted you — us — to know, but not the whole goddamn world."

I shake my head, though she's right, of course. That's possible.

Maeve takes off her sunglasses, blinks at me in the sunshine. "Jo, if you publish something she wouldn't like just to settle some score of your own, you'll be sorry later."

I don't think that's what I'm doing. I think I want to tell my family's story because if a story is to be told, it must be told as whole as we can tell it, not picking and choosing the bits that make us look good, as Mrs D. liked to do.

If I am to make anything meaningful of my life — and what else has this whole strange summer been about, if not that? — then I cannot let myself add one more drop to my family's unfathomable well of silence.

I know Maeve will never allow me all that, so I shrug and say instead, "There is no score."

She blinks even harder at this. I see her trying to calm herself, trying to find tactful, persuasive words to convince me. Just at that moment, you ripple inside me, then settle, like you are snuggling down.

I put my hand to where I feel you. Maeve notes the movement and, despite herself, smiles an indulgent smile. "Where are you going to have it?"

"I don't know."

"What does your doctor say?"

"I haven't seen a doctor."

"What? You're...how many months pregnant?"

"About six."

"Six months pregnant and you haven't seen a doctor?"

Here we go. I close my eyes, take a breath, wait for the next onslaught.

"That's just downright irresponsible."

This is why I haven't told her. Do all big sisters think they have this right to reprimand like this? It seems we don't have a single safe place to rest, Maeve and I, no matter how hard we both try.

"I'm sorry, Jo, but that's what it is."

"Correct me if I'm wrong, Maeve, but I thought this was my pregnancy?"

"When you're pregnant, Jo, you have more than yourself to consider."

"Yeah, well, I don't happen to think pregnancy is an illness. And I don't see why I need some doctor I've never met before to tell me I'm fine. I know I'm fine."

"But at your age especially..."

"Is this why you came, Maeve? To deliver a series of sermons?"

That works. "Oh God." She sighs and sags, like a pricked balloon. "How do you do this to me, Jo? Coming down in the car, I swore I wasn't going to criticise no matter what I found. But I never ever expected to find...this."

She's right, she can't help it any more than I can. Here we are, thirty-eight and forty years old, and as testy with each other as ever. We'll always be the same. The best time we ever had together was when she visited me in San Francisco, when we were on my territory, but here in Ireland, I'm her inadequate little sister again. Here, she'll always take liberties.

I try to appease her. "As a matter of fact, I am going to see a doctor soon."

"I'm glad," she says, trying to match my conciliatory tone. "Do."

"I will, I will."

I lie back, close my eyes to the sun. Should I tell her about Rory? What would I say?

That two days ago, I came out here, the day's work not so much done as abandoned for the evening, and found him sitting, his back to the shed, looking out to sea, waiting. He'd heard that I hadn't left after all and had come straight to me.

I knew that moment of seeing him there was one of the most important in our whole relationship. As important as the day when we were two children first spying each other across the village divide that separated our relatives. As important as the first time we spoke to each other properly, at a wedding, under the noses of our people. As important as the first night we slept together, twenty years ago, in his flat in Dublin. And yes, as important as the night soon after when I told him we were pregnant, and he responded so inadequately.

I hovered in the doorway of my shed, afraid to go forward. What would I say? Tell him to leave, to go back to his wife? Ask him to...Well, it doesn't matter now what I thought or considered saying, because all I did was go across and slip into sitting beside him.

We sat together for a long, long time, quietly watching the waves, afraid to speak. And ever since, it's been just as it was before, with him coming round each evening at sundown and us sitting, late into the night, talking, talking, talking.

It can't go on, I know. It has to stop, and soon.

While I'm trying to find words that might be able to explain some of this to my sister, she says, "You said 'her'? The baby's a girl?"

"That's how I find myself thinking. Of 'she', of 'her'."

"So you don't know for sure?"

"No, how could I? But right from the start, I've had the feeling it's going to be a girl."

And it's true. "She," "her": these are the words I used when talking about you to my sister — or to Hilde or Rory — but most of the time we're not with others. Most of the time we're alone together and the word I use is "you".

You are changing me, making more of me: swelling my breasts and my girth, expanding my heart and my lungs, ripening and plumping my genitals, filling and darkening my nipples, increasing the volume of my blood.

You have splashed my skin with colour, drawn a bold line of brown down my belly. Greased and furry, somersaulting and thumb-sucking inside me, getting firmer in the world: you rely on me. Soon you will be what they call viable, able to breathe on your own.

Still I can see how you will draw on me, body, heart and soul, for the rest of my days. For the first time, I see how a mother birthed every bird and animal and person on the planet. Everything, everywhere, has been mothered into being: how had I never noticed that before? I think of all the churches holding up their God the Fathers, the men who have insisted that children carry their names through the generations and, instead of my usual anger, I feel pity.

You've unpicked the me I used to be. I am going to join the band of mothers, those people who let themselves fade in the light of their offspring, those people — like my sister — that I used to slightly disdain. Now, as I sit here with her, as I look back up the tunnel of time at our mother's life, and our grandmother's, and our great-grandmother's, what I disdain is that earlier, unknowing me.

"Did you know this place used to be called Bastardstown?" I ask Maeve.

This was a secret of Coolanagh sands that I came across while doing library research. Coolanagh, Mucknamore, Inisheen: these names for our village, and the topography around it, came from the Irish language, but outsiders gave the area this different, ugly, English name, because it was famous as the place to go if you had a baby you didn't want, or were unable, to keep.

Infanticide. Thanks to its unique play of sands and tides, Coolanagh was where reluctant mothers came, according to legend — truth's abiding sister — to do their agonizing deed.

The book I read about it was schlock. It told its grisly stories, some of them going back centuries, without pausing once to consider the lives of those women, of why they were unable to rise to the demands of motherhood. To the man who wrote it — M.K. Trevalyan — they were ciphers, travesties of pure-and-holy womanhood: mad, bad and murderous.

Maeve shivers. "Bastardstown. God, I haven't heard it called that in years."

But she doesn't want to talk about that. While she embarks upon another long stream of sisterly advice, I look out to Coolanagh. It looks so innocent out there, on yet another beautiful summer day. The tide is so far out that the sands stretch almost as far as the island.

What age was I when Gran first brought me out that causeway to tell me her story about these sands having swallowed an entire town? The height of her hip, anyway. Auntie Norah was with us and the three of us stood on the tallest dune and I felt like we were on the high deck of a ship, sailing through an ocean of sand.

Gran's palm was rough, I remember, like the skin on a rock, but hers was the hand I most loved to hold. I can feel the damp of her swimming costume against my cheek as I leaned my face against it. Beneath the fabric was her soft old flesh and underneath that again, her tough hip bone.

She pointed in a diagonal from where we stood, towards the island.

"Look across now at that stretch of sand," she said to me. "There behind the barbed wire. Tell me what you see."

Hearing this, Auntie Norah took a few steps away from us. Gran looked back but, unusually, didn't follow. Instead, she pulled me in closer, gripped me tighter. "Do you notice anything strange about what you're seeing?" she asked again. "Come on, pet. Look a little harder."

I stretched my eyes for her.

"Can't you make out that double row of sand-hills near the edge and that long, straight dip running in between?"

All I could see was an undulating blanket of sand that looked flatter and flatter the further away you looked. The tide was way out that day, just as it is now.

"I wish we could walk across to it," Gran said. "If we could walk the length of it, you'd feel what I'm saying to you."

But we couldn't walk across Coolanagh sands. Young as I was, I already knew that.

"What would you say if I told you that what you're looking at is the rooftops of a sunken town?"

I turned my face up to hers, tried to read it.

"Yes, a sunken town. Under those bumps there, the ones that are so regular, all in a row. See? That's from the houses down below. And across there...that dip between them — " she pulled my hand up, pointed my finger — "that's the long main street."

She began to talk in her story voice. "Fadó, fadó – a long time ago – a big town stood on that spot I'm showing to you now. A city it was called, though smaller in them days than any of our cities now, but with its own charter to prove it. It was one of the largest sea ports in all of Ireland, and so rich that it used to send not one, but two, Members of Parliament to the government in London. I'm talking hundreds of years ago now, not long after the English first came to Ireland.

"What the poor people who lived in this city didn't know was that their town was built on sinking sand. From the first day those buildings went up, the sands were sucking at them — slowly, slowly drawing them down. So slowly that at first they didn't notice, but day by day it went on, until they came to know what was happening and to realise that they'd all have to leave.

"So they did. Still the city kept on sinking, until nothing was left of it above the ground only those bumps and hollows that you see before you."

At that, Auntie Norah, who must have been listening behind us, made an explosive sound, something like the harrumph of a horse. She started to walk away, back along the causeway towards home.

Let her go, the inside of my head pleaded to Gran, but

already we were turning after her. "It's all right, Norah," Gran called. "Wait now, don't be going on." We broke into a run, my arm pulled along, Gran calling after her back: "Ah, Norah, where's the harm in a bit of an old yarn?"

In the library, researching facts about quicksand, I was astounded to learn that Gran was right. There was once a bustling seaport town on this spot, five centuries ago. And it was sand that caused its demise. The inlet silted up and couldn't be navigated and that was the end of the trade on which the town depended. It declined and died and, eventually, disappeared. All of it, every building, into complete oblivion, until there was almost no trace of evidence that it ever existed.

Everything else she told me about Coolanagh, though, was wrong. Quicksand does not suck, it is not bottomless, it does not have a life of its own. It is a phenomenon, not a substance; any sand can become "quick" given the right conditions.

On Coolanagh, those conditions are a stream flowing off the island onto the sands, the stream in which I once pretended to see fairies to please a bunch of mean Mucknamore schoolgirls. That, and a layer of rock underlying the sand that slows drainage, keeps the sand grains in permanent liquid suspension.

As to the danger, the books I read were divided. One said it was impossible for an upright human to sink below the surface of such sand. The density of human body mass is less than that of any sand–water suspension and so they'd never get down far enough.

Yet people have died on Coolanagh. On the island, there's a cross which commemorates three people — a man and two women, who died out there in 1879 — as well as "all who fell victim to these sands". And there was Dan, of course, in 1923, the real source of my enquiry. They would have died, this book claimed, through trying to escape. It was their wriggling and writhing that would have pulled them face down into suffocation.

Another book disagreed. It held that a human body falling

into deep quicksand behaves as it would on falling into deep water, plunging down below the surface then rising back up again. Except in quicksand, the higher density elongates the down-and-backup motion, so that the lungs run out of breath before the body re-emerges from the depths.

On the tidal sands of Coolanagh, there was a third possibility: the sea. A victim who survived an initial immersion in sand, who succeeded in re sisting the urge to struggle, would remain stuck in the sand until the arrival of help, or the return of the next tide. Whichever came soonest.

Since reading that book on Bastardstown, my head is full of lonely women and their lost babies, and thinking again of them now, it comes to me. That's why I'm still here.

As Maeve and I run out of conversation, as we get up and she prepares to leave, I'm only half with her. Talking to her about you has brought it all together.

I see it now. I'm being held here by the loss that Rory and I never discussed.

He and I were doomed before we got started: we knew it back then and the family papers have shown me why. But none of that excuses how we behaved. Or accounts for what we ourselves destroyed, what we added to the loss. And the shame. And the silence.

We've talked about everything else, he and I. Everything I've discovered about his family and mine. All the events of our lives since we met and before. Everything, except how we came to fail each other so very badly that I ended up taking that boat to London, without him.

nock, knock, knock! Knock, knock, knock!

The sound had been going on for a while, Peg realised, as her sleeping ears woke to it. As it sank in that what she was hearing was somebody banging on the front door, like they were trying to rouse the entire county, she heard a voice calling. Her mother's, calling from across the hallway, from what used to be Barney's room, querulous in her weakness. "Peg? JJ? Peg?"

This was how they'd slept since Barney died: herself, her father and mother in three separate bedrooms, all doors open, in case Máire took a turn or needed anything in the night.

"It's all right, Mammy," she answered, already out of bed and shoving her feet into her slippers. "I'm coming."

Knock, knock, knock! again. Free Staters, no doubt, on another raid. Holy God, they'd been round twice already this month. They'd find nothing; they must surely know that by now. Nothing only the pleasure of persecuting true Republicans, a sport that never seemed to grow weary for them.

"I'm coming," she called to the front door as she hurried down the stairs, fast as she could without falling. Only when she opened the door, it wasn't soldiers on the step, but her neighbour, Mrs White, Lama's mother, and in a state.

All dishevelled, tears drying on her cheeks, with Tipsy Delaney beside her.

"I'm sorry, Peg," she said. "I'm sorry now to rouse you in the night like this, with you having the childer to teach in the morning."

"What is it? What's wrong? Come in."

"I didn't know where else to go. Tipsy suggested here."

No doubt he did. "That's all right, Mrs White. Come in, come in both of you." She ushered them into the hall. "What's happened?"

Her coat was on over her night clothes, and her hair was thrown up, falling out of its clips. In her hand, she was holding what looked like a letter.

"Is it...?" Peg stopped, not wanting to say her friend's nickname – Lama, so-called for his habit of saying "Lamb of God" every few minutes – to his mother. For a panicked moment, she found herself having a blank about the proper name of this boy she'd known her whole life long, who'd become a close friend in the experiences they'd shared over the past years, first in the War of Independence, and even more through being on the same side in this follow-up war.

This "War of the Brothers", as it was coming to be called. Only it wasn't only brothers divided. It was sisters, and friends, and parents from their children, and husbands from their wives.

John! she remembered, the name jumping to her mind. And with it her friend's face, long and angular and teeth forever stretched into a smile, like the wooden face on a rocking horse. A flood of feeling for him rushed in with the image, hot and soft.

When you shared a killing with somebody, as she had with Lama last October, it drew you close like nothing else. Even if the killing was something you knew you'd spend the rest of your days regretting, you were bonded to all involved.

And all the more so to Lama, with Barney, the third of the trio who'd done the deed, gone from them.

Killed in reprisal.

And now...? Was she in danger?

"It's bad," said Tipsy, his tongue, as always, a little too large in his mouth. Anyone looking at him would think he was smiling, but Peg knew better.

"Yes," wailed Mrs White, bursting into a fresh round of tears as she pushed the letter into her hands. "Yes Peg, it's John. It's the worst."

Dear Mother and Father,

I am very sorry to have to be writing what I know will be sad and shocking news for you. The Free State army has, without judge or jury, decided our fate. Tomorrow morning, at dawn, I am to be shot for my part in Ireland's fight for freedom.

This is a hard letter to have to write. But, if it were not for knowing how it will grieve you and Mattie and Janey and the little ones to receive it, I would not regret this way of leaving the world. I am proud to have served Ireland and I hope you, knowing I died to save the Republic, will be proud too.

I have seen a good priest, Father Carty from Kyle, and have made my peace with God. He who knows all has forgiven all and I, too, forgive the men who do this to us. Irish soldiers doing English work: they know not what they do.

I, and the three boys who will die with me, go to God in peace, knowing our blood — like that of Pearse and Connolly in 1916 — will bring new soldiers to Ireland's cause. For our cause is the cause of right and God is on our side.

So if you can, do not grieve me, Mother dear, or Father. We will meet again in Heaven.

May the Lord have mercy on us all.

Your loving son,

John.

JJ CAME DOWNSTAIRS, sent by Máire to see what the fuss was about and Peg, heart thumping as she read the letter a second time, sent him out to the byre to rouse George, the pony, and hitch up the trap. She sat Mrs White down in the parlour with Tipsy while she ran back upstairs to explain all to her mother. As always, Máire was roused out of awareness of her illness by Free State perfidy.

"You're right to go in," she said, when she heard what Peg intended. "Where there's life, there's hope."

"I pray we're not too late. And that they'll listen to reason. Surely even Free State soldiers won't sink so low."

"They've done it in other counties."

"But here in Wexford, Mammy. These are the selfsame boys who fought with us against the English. They surely won't do down one of their own."

"Take Tipsy in with you," said Máire. "They'll take more notice of a man, even poor Tipsy, than of a girl."

Would they? Peg wasn't so sure but the company would do no harm.

"Oh, I wish I could go myself, I'd give them what's what."

"We'll do our best, Mammy."

"I know you will, lovey. I didn't mean that. I just wish I was more use."

"You did enough, Mammy. You did more than anyone. We'd have no-one on the side of the Republic around here at all were it not for you. You rest yourself and we'll be back before you know it. With good news, I hope."

Peg kissed her cheek, as she always did now, whenever she took leave of her, and looked back for a moment at the door. Her poor mother, so reduced in size, and face so changed, it was hard to believe it was her and not an old aunt or relative in her bed.

No time for any of that now. Peg took the stairs down two steps at a time, and led Mrs White and Tipsy out of the parlour, into a night of high, tight stars, and a sliver of moon. Calm and clear and dry. That, at least, was a blessing. The night air was cooling on the heat of her thoughts.

As they climbed aboard the trap, she handed Tipsy the reins, so she could keep Mrs White company.

Peg had never gone into town by night. This was a new road to her. The trees and ditches were shadows of black on black, turned inside out in their night clothes. She didn't recognise any of them. For a while, she tried to keep Mrs White distracted by small talk, but then let them both settle into their thoughts. Oh, but that letter of Lama's. It had sounded so final. Would they even be in time? It was thirteen miles into Wexford: the journey would take them the bones of an hour, more maybe in the dark.

And of course the never-ending questions about Dan O'Donovan came slithering to the surface. Would he be there, in the jail? If he was, what was she going to say to him? Would he be moved to help? It was a measure of how things had changed between them that she hadn't a clue of the answer to that.

Surely he couldn't possibly be involved in this, the execution of his old comrade? If he was, then he was capable of anything now. And that, of course, was the real question, the one that rose in her still, hour after hour, driving her into a torment that let go of her only while she slept — and sometimes not even then. Had Dan fired the shot that killed their Barney, his onetime best friend? Was he capable of such a thing? And was that the real reason he was keeping her and Norah apart?

He had assured her not, told her the kindest thing she could do for Norah was to leave her alone, insisted that Norah had expressly asked not to be contacted by the Parle family. And while he was before her, handsome and bulky and seemingly sincere, she'd believed him. His flashing eyes, the fervour of his words, his sorrow about Barney all but convinced her.

All but. But. But.

Words come easy to some but it's actions that tell the real story. If his reported doings were to be believed, only a fool could trust him. Organising round-ups; stalking about the county making raids and arrests galore; putting Lama, Molly, Des Fortune and other good friends behind bars: all that she knew to be true, but could maybe be explained by politics and conviction. She mightn't like that he thought different from the rest of them, and was willing to go against them, but it was a long leap from there to the other thing she suspected.

And now, this. Lama, his friend and hers, to be shot at dawn. Executed — a word that was never made to fit any of them. If it was true, and Dan had any part in it, then she had her answer.

Trusty George clip-clopped on. Somewhere along the way, Peg fell into a place between waking and sleep. She was half-dreaming — Barney was chasing Norah down the strand with Dan running after them and Peg was looking on from the top of the cliff, helpless — when the sound of hooves and wheels hitting a harder surface jolted her awake.

A good road. They were coming into the town.

How did anybody live in a town at all, she wondered, as the houses started to cluster together and road turned to street. It was so unnatural. She wouldn't be able to breathe if her house didn't have field around it and the sea in its sights. She put her face up to gulp some air and saw that light was cracking a thin, faint line across the horizon.

Dawn.

At dawn, I am to be shot for my part in Ireland's fight for freedom.

Oh pray God, not. Not.

The buildings huddled, stern in the darkness, saying nothing.

At the bottom of Hill Street she said, "Pull over the side here, Tipsy," and he did as bid. "Mrs White, you stay here and look after George. Tipsy and I will go see what we can find out."

The older woman's frightened eyes were so like her son's. How had Peg never noticed that before? She handed her the reins.

The sound of their boots rang loud in the empty streets as they ran towards the jail.

"What should we say when we get there?" she asked, knowing as soon as the words were out that Tipsy wouldn't have any ideas to offer. "Should we ask for Dan, do you think?"

All she got back was a shrug.

At the jail, there was nobody about: just the big oak door, closed, and the thick stone around it.

"There's nobody here," Tipsy said, specialising as always in stating the obvious, but she, too, had expected somebody outside. A sentry. Someone.

Tipsy knocked on the door. Nothing.

They knocked together, hard as they could, but the slab of wood swallowed the thin sound of their knuckles.

What now? She sat on a stone ledge, trying to straighten out the snarl of her feelings, to decide. How had she ended up here, outside a jail in the middle of the night, with Tipsy Delaney? Her brother dead, her best friend gone from her? Had she brought it on herself?

Was it that she liked being a freedom fighter more than was good for her? That she wanted her own way too much, as Dan said? Was he right? She saw that in her mother sometimes. Did she suffer from the same trait herself without knowing? Would she ever find in her thoughts a key that would open the door to peace?

Everything around them was slowly revealing its lineaments as the sun rose, but no such emerging light for her. As she sat, watching shadows become shapes, a barrage of rifle fire suddenly sounded from inside the jail. She and Tipsy jumped up together. This fusillade was followed by four single shots at short intervals. The echo of it pounded in their ears and reverberated over the town, on the quiet of early morning.

She ran over to the door and banged on it again, but it was such a weak, ineffectual sound, compared to what had just assaulted their ears. Oh sweet divine Jesus, what was she to do?

She laid her forehead against the door and, from the other side, heard footsteps slowly approaching, then the sound of whistling. Whistling!

She stepped back. There was the sound of a bolt being pulled and the door started to move.

A soldier came out, with a hammer and nails in one hand, a notice in the other.

He was surprised to see herself and Tipsy — to see anyone — standing there. The three of them stared at each other for a long, uncertain minute, then he squinted at Peg.

"Miss Parle, isn't it? The schoolmistress from Mucknamore?"

She nodded. He looked familiar. Was he an O'Donnell? She wasn't sure enough to say. "Is it bad news for us?"

He turned, unable to cope with the question, and pinned the notice he had in his hand onto the door. She and Tipsy went close in, to read:

By order of the Government of the Irish Free State, the following men were executed by firing squad on this day, March 13th, 1923: John Creane of Clonerane, Taghmon; Patrick Hogan of William Street, Wexford; James Parle, of Clover Valley, Taghmon; John White of Mucknamore.

At that very moment, Mrs White came running up. "Did you hear that shooting, Peg? Tipsy! Did you hear it?"

Then she saw the soldier, the notice, the hammer in his hand.

"Oh my God! No. He's not...?" She sounded as shocked as if it was the first she'd heard of the possibility. "He's not, he's not, he's not, he's not."

Peg went to put a hand on her shoulder, but Mrs White shrugged it off as if Peg herself had done the killing, and dropped into the well of pain that was breaking open in her, hands to her face.

The soldier slipped back inside the door as fast as he could, away from the unbearable sound of her wailing, away from the unbearable sight. The latest in Ireland's long line of mothers bereaved.

Dear Dan,

I have been asked to write to you by Mucknamore Company, the organisation that you may recall first fostered your involvement with the Irish Republic.

You must know that the illegal body over which you and your associates now preside has — since the signing of your Treaty with England — declared unholy war on the soldiers of the true Republic.

We, on our side, have at all times adhered to the recognised rules of warfare. In the early days of this conflict, we took hundreds of your forces prisoner, but accorded them all rights of prisoners-of-war and better. We treated them as fellow citizens and former comrades-in-arms. Your soldiers have often been released by us, although captured with arms on each occasion.

But those of the Irish Republican Army (not long ago, your own army) that you have imprisoned, you have treated barbarously. When helpless, you have tortured and wounded them.

We have definite proof that many of your officers have been guilty of the most brutal crimes and have reduced your soldiers to a state of savagery on occasions.

And, now, you have committed murder. Your sham government pretends to try IRA prisoners before make-believe courts. After such mock ceremonials, you have done to death four of your former colleagues. We hereby give you due notice that unless your "Free State" army recognises the rules of warfare in future, we shall have to adopt very drastic measures to protect our Republican forces.

Irish Republican Army,

Mucknamore Company, South Wexford Brigade.

Dear Dan,

I won't send this one, but I need to write it. Did you get my earlier letter? I'm supposing you did, but how will I know, when you made no

answer and we never speak any more? I was told what to write — did
you realise that as you read it?

Dear Dan, my dear Dan, here's what I'd really say to you, if I
could. I know why you took the turn you've taken and I understand. I
do, truly. I know how it felt for you to be the outsider here in
Mucknamore, with the wariness felt towards you and your family
when you arrived here from Cork. You who had always been so liked
and admired. I know it was hard for you. I know how you worried
about what you'd do with yourself since the farm was for Thomas, and
the priesthood definitely not for you.

And I can see how this gives it all to you, all solved. A soldier in
the new army — a lieutenant, no less. A fancy title and uniform and
boots and pay to match: all a young man could ask for.

But Dan, no good can come of it, you must know this. The one true
way is the way of The Republic. Though that way is thorny now,
denying it will do you no good in the end.

Dan, there are so many ways a person can fail to think enough of
himself. The likes of you doesn't need a uniform and a shiny salary,
especially one paid for with English money.

Oh Dan, don't you know that there are good people who see and
know your worth without such trappings?

Oh Dan, won't you come back to us?

Please.

I –

Dear Molly,

Thanks for your letter and your kind words of sympathy. It means
so much to hear from those who knew Barney well and truly mourn his
loss with us.

Thank you too for the compliments about the ballad and Mammy's
pamphlet. It was Mr Connolly, the printer, who said we should put
that it was written "By A Comrade" instead of people knowing it was
by two women (his mother and sister). He said it would sell better that

way, and maybe he was right, because it has sold well – he is going to do a second printing. We just hope we did our boy justice in it.

All the talk here, as you can imagine, has been of the Free State executions. We were so shocked, as I'm sure you were too. The night after it happened, we organised a crowd to gather around the jail to recite the Rosary, and afterwards we marched to St Peter's Square, where we held a protest. The Staters broke us up, of course, firing shots over the head of the crowd. But they won't find it as easy as all that to scatter us.

More and more people are coming onto our side, sickened by their actions. Our main aim now is to make governance of the country impossible by disrupting the railways and destroying public buildings and services. Proper soldiering would, of course, be preferable, but this is all we can do for now, with no money, no arms, no ammunition and no jails.

It's that, or stand idly by while they wreck our Republic, end to end.

We are also to make private "Big Houses" — owned by unionists — a target. The bigger the property, the more likely to receive our attentions. Joe Hickey calls their fine paintings and books and furnishings immoral. "Wealth built on the sweat and starvation of the native Irish," he says. And he's not wrong, but it gives me a queer feeling to think of any private house being burnt out. And to imagine books and paintings that took generations to gather, being destroyed.

What do you think, Molly?

I'm glad to hear conditions are not too bad for you there in Kilmainham. It must be hard to be locked up, even with the company of the other girls. It's very quiet around here without yourself and Norah. I'm in danger of going loo-lah, I sometimes think, from being too much on my own.

Not that I should complain, Molly. I do know, of course, that it's much worse for you, locked away without trial, indefinitely. I'm not really comparing. Don't mind me.

The children in school are a great comfort. When I have doubts, I look to their little faces, and think about their future, and know we work so they may grow up in a new Ireland. An Ireland no longer enslaved.

God bless their innocence. It has saved me more than once in these dark days.

And God bless you, my friend, and may He soon bring about your release.

Yours truly,

Peg

Dear Norah,

This is the letter I wish I was sending, instead of the one I just wrote to Molly that's sitting there on the table before me, all stamped and ready for the post.

I am so tired, Norah, and I'm so lonely.

There. I've said it. I needed to say it. I miss Molly, yes, and all the others imprisoned. And Lama I can't think of without a hole opening in my heart. But it's nothing to how much I miss Barney and you and — yes, let me write this also, for I can, as I'll not be sending this anywhere but the back of my diary — I miss your brother too.

More than anything, how things used to be between us all.

If you were here, Norah, I could talk to you about all this, instead of the half-truths and platitudes I have to feed Molly and Mammy and everyone else. I would tell you how a decade has settled on my father's poor shoulders and bewilderment taken over his eyes.

We could discuss how Mammy squashes any scruples and won't hear of any uncertainty or doubt, and how that can't be good for her, not with her facing her Maker any one of these days.

I'd tell you how each of us in this house lives with the fragility in the other two, making us over-careful of one another — and so separate in our sorrow.

If you were here, Norah, I wouldn't constantly be thrown back on — of all people — Tipsy Delaney, the only one, besides myself, left alive and not imprisoned. He comes down to the shop most evenings now and we always end up talking about the old days, before the split, when we were all together, fighting the English. How simple it seemed then, how happy we were. It was only months ago, yet so far from us, it might as well be decades.

Tipsy and I sound ancient when we get going, harking back, back, back, like exiles in America, lamenting all the fine things we've lost, things we took for granted when we had them.

If you were here, I'd tell you how sometimes I am sickened by our own side's attitudinising. How I'm tormented by all the opposing opinions I carry inside me, fighting against each other.

The latest I heard is that four Stater officers are to be shot dead as a reprisal for the executions in Wexford Jail. Is this right or wrong? Or is there some other category for an event like this?

There was a time you could take a question like that to Mass or to your priest, but the church is a disgrace now, the way it has turned against us to side with the "Free State".

Tipsy says I should stop looking for answers, get used to living inside a question-mark. It was a strange thing to say, but the things he says sometimes make a strange kind of sense. It's funny, we all think Tipsy such a fool, yet he's the only one of us to have come out of this business intact.

He was on the run with the boys in the best days, when the people were still with us and, somehow, without letting anyone down, he seemed to miss out on the most troubling actions, like the Donore raid that still has me waking up in sweats.

Oh, Norah, I'll never forget that bomb dropping in a big, slow arc off Donore Bridge, landing in that lorry and blasting those four soldiers out of this life. Over and again it plays out in my mind, especially when I'm in bed. The sight of it falling from Barney's hands, dropping down and bursting into blast on contact. Then that soldier, who was somehow thrown clear, getting up and trying to run, and Barney and the boys finishing him off from the bridge.

I find myself sometimes with my eyes squeezed closed and my hands over my ears. How stupid, when it's inside myself that the sight and the sounds are sealed.

Tipsy has no such guilt on his conscience. And somehow he's escaped jail too. He just wandered back home when the going got rough and took back up the work on the little farm where he lives with his mother. The soldiers don't ever bother them, while we're persecuted, not able to turn around without them bursting in and pulling the place apart, with no regard for the illness in this house, or our bereavement. Worse than savages, all humanity absent.

Here's something else I'd have to tell you, Norah. Two nights ago, in reprisal for Dan's involvement with the executions, our boys went up to your house, and ordered out your parents and the children, and sprinkled your house with petrol, setting it alight. When I heard of the planned action, I didn't know what side I was on.

Of course, I was right glad when prompt action by a neighbour saved the house, with only slight damage to the front parlour. And nobody was hurt. Nobody was ever going to be hurt; that wasn't the intention. They were ordered out. The intention was to send a message, loud and clear, to your brother.

What side would you have been on, Norah? It was your house, your people, but you'd grown so far from them in the freedom fright, or you'd seemed to. Only Dan said otherwise. Did you really tell him you wanted nothing more to do with our family? I could understand, Norah, given all that happened, if you did — but did you? Did you?

If you were here, I'd get some answers to these questions that plague me night and day. We would sort it, I know, complicated as it is, if we were only one in front of the other. You wouldn't blunder in on top of me, trying to flatten my opinions with yours. We might differ but you'd be reasonable. We'd fathom it out.

I thank you now, as I should have before, for all the times we were able to do that together, Norah. I never knew what a precious thing it was until it was taken from me.

I miss you for it. And I thank you for it. That is what I'd so like to say to you, if I only knew where you were.

1981

I'm told there are those whose lives exceed their expectations. Is this really true? For me, imagining and anticipation are always the high point of any experience. So it was here, now. London life had not turned out as I imagined at the age of eighteen.

In my early days here, I used to wander about the city on my days off, looking at the pigeons strutting about on their wine-coloured legs, wondering where they'd flown in from, admiring their sense of ownership. Two years on I seldom go into the centre where the pigeons gather and, if I do, I almost always find myself staring into the river, twelve times the width of the Liffey, but the same murky colour. The same as all city rivers, carrying so many centuries of human debris that they become unable to reflect the sky.

My home in London is near Brent Cross, in a dark and dank basement flat in a dark, dank and indefinable suburb. Its single opaque window faces the garden above, tinging the light — such as it is — green. Mrs Fairbairn, my landlady, resents her dependence on paying tenants and, aside from visiting us once a week for her money, does her best to pretend we're not here.

I cannot ignore her in return as her dog, Bruno, thumps his tail on my ceiling all through the hours that I am here.

But I am not often here. By day, I work in Montgomery's of Hillingdon, a huge paper products distributor. I am the voice at the end of a phone-line, the person the customers get to shout at when their serviettes, kitchen towels or toilet rolls don't arrive on time, or are the wrong size, or the wrong colour. I take the insults that spill into my ear, the accusations of our company's incompetence, and hand the customers polite apologies in return.

If you cared about the bad and hoped for the best, you couldn't do my job, but it's easy for me. I expect the planning department or distribution to bungle, although I always pretend to be surprised. I despise them for caring so much. It's only toilet rolls, I want to say.

They'll be with you tomorrow, I think, as I'm offering the formulaic words that muffle true thoughts: "I'm so sorry. Yes, I understand. Let me see what I can do for you." Or the next day. Or next week. Who cares?

I'm dead to everything in that office, except the clock circling its hands, slowly, slowly, round the minutes. Morning break, then lunch, then afternoon break and, finally, half-past five when I can cover my typewriter, lock my desk drawer and walk out of the office, out of the building, out though the gate, to a few hours of life.

Evening life. Real life. It usually begins in the Rose and Crown, with some of my new friends, Mark and Sandra or Joe and Frank, Sadie and Melo or Anita, Kim and Natalie, snuggling into soft seats where we'll light up our insides with alcohol, as darkness begins to press in against the windows. All you need to join the group is a willingness to laugh, to tease each other and belittle our bosses.

Or at least that's where we begin. By end of the night, the mood has usually shifted, changed by some secret that's come surfing out on the alcohol. Sandra crying about how she always wanted children and now it's too late. Frank confessing to a bullying father. Natalie talking about the stresses of a Down's syndrome brother.

I share too, but nothing too heavy. When I'm asked why I came here, I talk about unemployment in Ireland, the need for work. I can no more say the A word after doing the deed than I could before. No, I tell them about the convent and the village and other things that are ordinary in Ireland but exotic to them. Nobody realises I'm only handing over the bits that don't matter.

On weekend nights, we follow our drinking bouts with a nightclub, an Eden of wet kisses and grinding hips. I meet men there, lots of them. No one like Rory, but I know now that Rory was not what I thought. He hasn't come, he hasn't even written. And now I know he won't.

So I go with others, expecting nothing of the encounter but desire. Their desire, not mine. Admiration is what I am after, and I collect it from any source, even from those who are too eager. That's the way I prefer to keep them, keen and slightly beneath me, taking what they offer, flitting on to the next.

The key to it all is vodka, clicking me open and surprising me with what pops out. I wait for the moment of intoxication when the sober world gets shrugged off like a dull outfit and resplendent me emerges, arrayed in flashes and sparkles. It usually comes halfway through my fourth drink, sometimes earlier. For a while, then, the whole world seems contained in whatever warm and noisy place we are in and I am suffused with love — there is no other word — for my drinking friends and myself.

It never lasts. Soon it slides into confusion and dejection and sometimes, if I've had too much to drink too many nights in a row, I can miss it altogether, go directly from self-consciousness to self-pity without any exuberance in between. Yet that perfect interval is the promise that alcohol always seems to hold out. That's what I drink for.

That, and the licence it gives me to be bad. Whenever I start to sing or shout or flirt or laugh too loud, Natalie teases me: "So you are Irish, after all." As if they ever thought of me as anything else. One of the guys in the office even calls me that. "Hey Oirish!" he says, by way of hello.

I am the outsider in London, so my ways are not just different, they are wrong. I have never been talkative but now, when sober, I speak only when I must. I slow my sentences, enunciate more clearly, skip around the snare of the English "th", a sound that unsettles the swing of my own words in my own mouth. I swallow Irish jokes, though I know they arise from the very ignorance they mock.

Every immigrant is awkward as they grapple with new ways, but the English don't think of us as immigrants, or Ireland as another country. They label our lack of fluency, our way with their language, as stupidity. Few of them know, or care, about the history that rammed their language into our ancestors, a language so foreign to us that — two whole centuries on — the rhythm of a sentence on an Irish tongue still makes an English "th" impossible.

To them, we're not different enough to be alien; we're just inferior versions of them. And of course there's part of me that agrees.

Most, but not all. Kathleen in marketing, who also happens to be the best looking girl in Montgomery's, chooses to have an Irish passport. Not just because it's cheaper, she tells me. Though born and bred in Bolton, she spent every childhood summer with her grandparents in Donegal. "I feel Irish," she says, her hand to her chest, her eyes shiny, almost damp. And I smile, disarmed.

Sometimes, on the tube or the bus or walking down the street, my ear will pick up on soft, hissy 't's at the end of words, or the thudding 'th's at the start and I'll turn and talk to these strangers, about what part of Ireland each of us is from, and how long we've each been over, and whether we'd like to go back.

There seem to be only two variations — either they yearn to return or, like me, they'd never even consider it.

Exiles or escapees.

Coincidences crop up often with these strangers — shared times or places or acquaintances. I laugh at Londoners who expect me to know everyone from home, but now I find myself doing the same. Ireland seems very small from here.

Dear Jo,

I got your address and telephone number from Deirdre Mernagh. Don't be cross — I bullied it out of her by telling her there was a crisis at home (there isn't). I was going to ring, but I thought it might be better to write first.

I hope you're keeping well. Deirdre tells me things have worked out for you over there. That's good anyway, although it's a pity about your degree. I heard a bit about what went on the night you left, but I don't really understand. Mammy is very upset about it all, but I suppose you know that. Don't worry, I'm not taking sides.

It's just that she'd love to hear from you. We all would. Maybe you might think about coming home at Christmas? Whatever happened, it shouldn't be allowed to drag on.

Granny Peg is not that well. She took a bit of a turn a few weeks ago and has been told she has a heart condition. She's on tablets now and is supposed to give up the fags, but you know yourself.

Mammy is well and Auntie Norah is the same, no change.

I am still working at the school in Terenure where I did my teacher training. I teach fifth class this year, they're a nice bunch so I'm having a fairly easy time of it. Also, I have met a nice fella. He's called Donal and he's an accountant. I've been going with him for six months and I suppose you could say it's getting serious. He goes to England a lot on business so you never know, I might go with him sometime and meet up with you.

Well, that's it for now, Jo. Don't lose touch altogether, you hear?

I'll give you a ring in a while.

Mind yourself.
Love,
Maeve

ONE LATE NOVEMBER EVENING, I return to our table in the Rose
and Crown and know, from the unnatural way my friends are
talking as I sit down, that the subject has been changed. They'd
been discussing me.

Natalie tells me it wasn't me they were talking about but "the
bombs."

The IRA explosions that have been going off all over
England, the most recent — the third this year — killing twenty-
one people and injuring hundreds in Birmingham.

London and Guildford have also suffered. The Guildford
bomb went off in a pub too, and that's what my friends had been
considering while I was in the Ladies. Imagining what it must
have been like for those people. Wondering how we'd react, if
one exploded there and then in our pub.

A conversation they felt they couldn't have in front of me.

Northern Ireland. The residue of England's centuries-old
"Irish problem", the quandary that leaves the everyday English
person squinting, helplessly, into inexplicable darkness. The
Fighting Irish. Irrational, truculent, violent, doomed by fanatical
sectarianism, who could be expected to understand them?

Who can make them see reason?

This is how my English friends play it, but they're not truly
convinced. They know their country is not blameless, but they
feel defensive. What has it to do with them? Ancient history. Can
we please let bygones be and move on?

I don't explain to Natalie how it is not as bygone as we all
wish it was. Instead, I spell out how I'm from Wexford, which is
the other end of the country. How I have no sympathy with the
IRA and no longer care whether Ireland unites or not. How I am

glad to be here in London, even when I feel awkward and different, how it keeps me attentive, stretches me. How I'm not the same as the people of the huddling communities in Kilburn and Cricklewood, who came over in the 1950s and immediately set up their own mini-Irelands over here.

She's not listening. They have put me in the Irish camp. Irish is what I am, whether I claim it or not.

It's been months. Still nothing from Rory. I know now I have to drop the possibility that there ever will be.

I am promoted in work. Customer Service Manager. Mr Green, my boss, tells me my prospects are excellent, if I play my cards right. Work hard, but more important, be seen to be keen. Take a class by night: the subject doesn't matter, the piece of paper is the thing. The higher-ups are on the lookout for career girls. "We have to improve our 'gender quota'," he says, holding the words out and away from him.

My new job often keeps me busy and, often, late in the office. As soon as I can get away, I do, and join my gang down the pub. They thought my new status might affect our drinking dynamic, but I won't let it. I am the last one standing most nights, so they'll know where my allegiance lies.

Between work and socialising, I am rarely at home, except to sleep myself back to recovery. Dirty dishes accumulate in my sink until furred. Magazines, cups, glasses, papers surround my bed, like fallout from a blast. My clothes get picked up from the floor, laundered as I need them, but never find their way back into the wardrobe. Some days I have to turn my knickers inside out because I have none clean and no time to get to a shop before work. Time and money keep calling at me to pay attention, but I am gone, off and away.

Then, suddenly, unexpectedly, I meet Jack. Jack Ward. A teacher. Not just that, a teacher of disabled kids. An unlikely boyfriend for me in every way, so different to any of the others. Jack has none of Rory's flamboyance, but he lets me be and — for the first time in my life — I don't try to impress, don't do what I think will win approval. I carry on drinking as I have always done and in his company I am raucous, shouting and singing and swearing. None of it fazes him. He smiles through it all, goes home when he feels like going, stays and sings along if that's his mood.

Jack takes pleasure in everything – walks in the park, Sunday mornings with the newspapers, nights out to the cinema – but the me he likes best is the one who comes out when we're home, snuggled up, three-quarters way down a bottle of red wine. He is uncomplicated in bed, easy to delight. Kind, gentle, good-looking and more clever than I allow, he sneaks into my life with his openness, his ease with the world.

It seems audacious. Surely it will rebound on him?

Jack rarely meets me straight after work with my friends, though he easily could, his school being just one tube station from The Rose and Crown. He likes to shower his working day away, to change his clothes, to have something to eat before he goes out, instead of making do with crisps and salted nuts until we go to the takeaway after closing time. He rarely comes clubbing with us either, though he loves to dance. He prefers it when it's just the two of us, he says without rancour, without the least pressure on me.

Sometimes it annoys me that he is so agreeable. He has such confidence in himself, in me. He is like me in my old days with Rory, thinking love was enough. Asking for trouble

PART II
REFLUX

1923

North Dublin Union

Dear Peg,

You'll have noticed the change of address above. So much has happened since I last wrote, I hardly know where to start.

I have to say that we felt not altogether unfortunate to be in Kilmainham Jail for Easter weekend. The seventh anniversary of the 1916 Rising felt like a good day to take our Oath of Allegiance again to the Republic and to be one of three hundred Republican girls housed there, where those brave heroes were executed.

Now, a few weeks later, what a contrast!

It began when we were told that we were to be moved from Kilmainham to North Dublin Union, a former workhouse. We were none too keen on this idea, as Kilmainham, with its noble association, suited us far better. Also, Mrs O'Callaghan and Miss MacSwiney were still on their hunger strike (nineteen days by then) and we were very anxious about the effect of such a move on them. So we sent our decision to the governor: no prisoner would consent to leave until the hunger strikers were released.

Our best strategic position seemed to be the top gallery, as it is caged in with iron bars running around the horseshoe-shaped building. So we took up our posts. The place was in darkness, except for one lit window beside a gateway, behind which figures of soldiers and wardresses hurried back and forth. Our officers gave the instructions: we were to resist, but not attack; we were not to come to one another's rescue; no missiles were to be thrown; and, above all, for the sake of the patient in her cell, no one was to cry out. Then we knelt and said the Rosary and, after that, we sang some of Miss MacSwiney's favourite songs.

Suddenly, the gate opened and the men rushed in, across the compound and up the stairs. The attack was violent, but disorganised. Brigid O'Mullane and Rita Farrelly, the first seized, were crushed and bruised between men pressing up the stairs, dragging them down. Our commander, Mrs Gordon, was next. It was hard not to go to her rescue as she clung to the iron bars, the men beating her hands with their clenched fists. When that failed to make her loosen her hold, they struck her twice in the chest, then one took her head and beat it against the iron bars. I think she was unconscious after that. I saw her dragged by the soldiers down the stairs.

The men were determined. Some twisted the girls' arms, some bent back their thumbs. Some were kicked by a particular CID man who was fond of using his feet. One was disabled by a blow on the ankle with a revolver. Annie McKeown, one of the smallest and youngest, was pulled downstairs and kicked in the head. One girl had her finger bitten off, Lena O'Doherty was struck on the mouth, one man thrust a finger down Moira Broderick's throat. Lily Dunn and May O'Toole fainted. They do not know where they were struck.

My own turn came too. After I had been dragged from the railings, a great hand closed on my face, blinding and stifling me, and thrust me back down to the ground, among trampling feet. After that, I remember being carried by two or three men and flung down in the surgery to be searched. Mrs Wilson and Mrs Gordon were there, their faces bleeding. One of the female searchers was screaming at them like a drunkard on a Saturday night; she struck Mrs Gordon in the face. They removed watches, fountain pens and brooches. Our orders not to hite back were well obeyed.

The wardresses were bringing us cups of water and they were crying, and some of the soldiers too looked wretched, but the prison doctor – and a few other soldiers – looked on, smirking, smoking cigarettes. The doctor seemed to have come along for the entertainment; he did nothing to help any of the injured girls.

After another long struggle, we were thrown into the lorries, one by one, and driven away.

Peg, you have to let the world know of this disgrace. I don't know whether word has reached the newspapers or not; we're so much more isolated in this place than we were in Kilmainham. Please also tell the world that Republican women are housed in a place that is filthy and freezing, with no privacy or facilities for washing or bathing. The sentries can, and do, look into our wards on the ground floor. We've asked to have the lower window panes frosted or painted but no, so we have to hang clothes over them to get in or out of bed. We're experiencing every kind of discomfort: hunger, cold and dirt. And, though only a few yards from one of the most populated districts of Dublin, cut off from everything.

We have had no news since of Miss MacSwiney. We hear rumour of peace moves outside, but never see a paper. Please fill me in on everything you know when you write. I haven't heard from Norah this long time: tell her she's not to forget me. The person who gives you this letter will tell you how to get mail through untampered.

Please also tell your mammy and daddy I was asking for them and that I keep Barney in my prayers.

I was thinking of you and the family at Easter time.

You will write soon, won't you, to

Your friend,

Molly

Mucknamore,

26th June, 1923

Dear Molly,

Thank you for your recent letter: what shocking news. Yet nothing should shock us anymore.

What do you think of the ceasefire? I don't know what to make of it. I agree with Mr de Valera that further sacrifice would be in vain but I don't understand what's going to happen next. It can't be over. What was worthy of bloodshed a month ago now can't be unworthy now, surely to God.

And surely to God they're not going to tell us that those who died did so in vain, or that women subjected to the assaults you'd experienced are to pretend it never happened.

Be assured that the few bits of weaponry we have left here in Mucknamore went into a safe dump. I suppose we can add to them as time goes on. We'll be keeping quiet for a while, though. Areas never before visited now swarm with troops and they're bringing in a new Public Order Bill.

So, ceasefire or not, it's clear they don't intend to soften. Flogging as a punishment for arson or robbery — did you ever hear the like?

And I don't think the ceasefire makes it one bit more likely that you, or any of the prisoners, will be let out.

They'd be afraid to have too many of us on the loose, in case we might go to the weapon dumps and start the fight again. Which is exactly what would happen, of course.

Still, it's against any notion of democracy to incarcerate thousands of people without trial or prospect of release. And now we're to have this election. Run by a State we don't believe in, yet we're to field candidates to give the people the opportunity to show they support us. But if we win, they won't take their seats. They can't take part in a government they don't believe in.

It's one of those jokes that makes nobody laugh.

But I'll support the work, of course, and do what is asked of me. Mammy and I have been writing a bulletin to distribute, house to house. See what you think of this:

Dear Voter,

They said this Treaty would fill Irish pockets. It has filled only Irish PRISONS and GRAVES. On behalf of the King and Commons, the Irish "Free State" government has — in fourteen months — murdered, executed, tortured and imprisoned more Irishmen than were killed by the English during six years of terror (1916–1922).

There's more about the SLAVERY and CHAOS created by the Treaty — and then it asks them to come back to us and VOTE AGAINST IT.

Mammy helped me with it. We think it will stir the Irish people in the right direction. What do you think? It would be great to have your opinion.

At least this time we women, and the young men under thirty, will be allowed our vote. Small mercies, but we may as well be thankful for them, because it doesn't look like we'll be having any big ones coming our way anytime soon.

Your friend,

Peg

Oulart, Co. Wexford, 29th September, 1923

Dear Miss Parle,

You don't know me. I am writing on behalf of a friend of yours, Miss Norah O'Donovan. She has asked me to tell you that the reason you haven't heard from her is because she is in the asylum in Enniscorthy. She has been there since May of this year, looked after by the Holy Sisters of Mary where she was held before, but she remains enclosed.

She is in good health and manages all right most of the time, but it can be hard. She is inclined to be a loner and that is not allowed in the asylum, not unless you are sent into confinement.

She also asked me to say that she has written to you many times. It was her firm belief that you never got those letters. We know the asylum holds on to letters if they do not want them sent.

I believe a visit from you would cheer her greatly.

Write to me at the address above if you want more information.

Yours sincerely,

Mary Clooney

*R*ory comes with me to Enniscorthy, takes a day off to drive me to the hospital. He's back again, visiting every night, and I can't help but let him. And when he heard what I was intending to do today, he insisted on coming along, though I could easily have taken a cab. That big building up on the hill always fascinated him, he said, and he'd love to take a look inside.

And after all, Norah was his aunt too.

"It's hard to believe that she used to be good-looking," I say to him, as we set off. "Peg is always talking in her diaries about how beautiful she was."

"I only remember her as an old woman."

"She had deteriorated by then. She had been through so much."

He changes gear, his hand brushing against my thigh. It feels strange to be out with him in the world beyond the two square yards of grass outside my shed. At night, we are careful to keep further apart.

It's so physical, the attraction I feel for Rory: whatever it is that makes one body attract to another, we have it. Always had, since I was ten years old and looking at him across the gap put in place by our relatives.

And I know he feels it too, though he's better than me at hiding all he feels under that jokey façade he's made his.

That part of me, which I thought was numbed forever, is thawing. I know he's not the only reason I feel good these days, but this quivering delight that runs through me all the way down my limbs and into my fingers and toes: that's him.

As we drive through Wexford, he shows me his office, with its view over the harbour: Rory A. O'Donovan, Solicitor. Conveyancing. Family Law. Company & Commercial.

"Rory A.? A.?" I burst out laughing. "Not Aloysius? I had forgotten all about that. Rory Al-oo-ISH-us O'Donovan, Gentleman At Law." I drag out the syllables, as we did when teasing him about that name years ago. "I can't believe you use that."

"I had no choice. They throw you out of legal-land if you don't," he says. "You have to sound important. One name doesn't cut it." He's smiling, but there's an edge under the insouciance. His sense of being in the wrong life.

I feel sorry I brought it up. Then the part of me that wants him to acknowledge its wrongness is glad. He's brought his camera; he will photograph what we find in Enniscorthy. At least I can be glad about that.

Each night now, he fills my sleep. Him and tiny babies, that's all I seem to dream about these days, as if my subconscious mind is funnelling in. Two nights ago, it was that the baby was born and I was running along the beach, with her snug in a sling against my chest. I looked down to smile at her and found the sling was empty. She was gone. Panicked, I retraced my sand footprints, but no matter how hard I looked I couldn't find her.

I have dreamt of breaking her leg while changing her clothes, of dropping her on her head, of her floating out to sea. Once I dreamt she slipped down behind the skirting board in my San Francisco apartment: I was calling everybody in a frenzy, all unknowing that she was there, at my feet, her cries too tiny to be heard. As I shouted down the phone to Maeve, my baby came back, settled into my lap. But another tiny baby was still there, behind the skirting board, crying, crying, crying, while everybody else went around, all unknowing.

It is almost twenty years to the day that I travelled to London with Dee. That's what I'm carrying in me as Rory points through the windscreen at the café where he enjoys his morning latte and Irish Times, and at the pub where he meets his friends after work on a Friday. For the first time since we were students, wrapped around each other, I'm getting a sense of his everyday life.

This carries in it all the longing of the years apart, especially the early years and my time in London. We've never mourned what we made happen back then. I need to mourn it. I need him to mourn it.

Now does not feel like the time to talk about all of that, but if not now, when? We can't go on like this, I say to myself, once again. Yet whatever is next, I'm not urging it on as I would have before. I do know that the time is coming when we must either tilt forward or retreat forever.

For now, I feel safer here on the unknowing edge. And anyway, today is Norah's day.

A mile or so from Enniscorthy town, the building comes into view: a massive, neo-Gothic, red-brick concoction, utterly incongruent with the landscape and other buildings around. In the convent, we used to joke about this place, like we joked about everything we feared. We'd circle our fingers round our temples or turn our eyeballs inwards towards our noses.

The size is staggering and its looming presence at the top of the hill always draws comments from visitors. "What is it?" they ask, awed by its wings and towers and turrets, its two hundred windows glowering down at the road and railway below.

Today, the stigma is supposed to have gone. We've been taught to say "mental illness", not lunacy; "patients", not inmates. Walls have been knocked down, gates opened, people released into the community, but it's still a place apart, moated by green fields and trees, the nearest house a distance away, and the shame that soured the word "asylum" lives on.

Rory's car purrs in through the gates and up the short avenue. The building is tamed as we approach from the side, losing the scale of its vast dimensions. Up close, it's the smaller details that catch your attention: the weeds cracking through the tarmac, the shutters blacking out so many windows, the paint flaking off pillars near the door. Two men sit at the entrance, one beside each pillar, so still they might be statues. One of them is shrivelled with age, perhaps old enough to have been in here with Norah back in the 1920s. Only their eyes move as they watch us park, get out of the car, and approach.

Their staring makes me more conscious of how we must look to them. Like a couple, a man and his pregnant wife. I am acutely aware of my belly, thrust forward, and I want to take Rory's arm and lean against him, to be supported through what is to come. I resist and we walk between the two men with a gap of air between us.

The younger man says, "Good morning," but in a blank way that makes me wonder whether I imagined it.

"Hello," Rory and I say together, our voices too loud.

Inside, we are welcomed by Miss Bell, the administrator, who allocates us one of the many empty rooms with a desk and two chairs and shows us the cupboard where the hospital records are stored. She is sorry about the confused nature of the files. Nobody really knows what is where. A work experience girl tried to get the papers in order two summers ago, but she never finished the task and that was the last time anybody touched them. Miss Bell wishes they were more ordered; she wishes she could be of more help; she wishes us the very best of luck in our search.

The cupboard smells of dust and over-boiled cabbage, stale and unpleasant. We soon find that Miss Bell was wrong, that only the files from the 1960s onwards were poorly kept, sheaves of loose papers escaping their binders. Norah was admitted further back, when records were painstakingly transcribed into big hard-backed registers, gold-embossed with the title: 'Wexford District Lunatic Asylum for the Insane', each person's name and details carefully lined up with those above and below.

It is Rory who, mid-morning, finds the one we want: Casebook 1923. He hands it over to me like a prize. I receive it with solemnity and, blowing dust off its edges, lay it down on the desk.

He moves across and stands beside me — too close — but I let him, liking the nearness of him and that we are doing this together. We each run a finger down the careful column of names, leaning into the words, and we find her easily: May 25th, 1923: Miss Norah O'Donovan, Mucknamore.

He takes out his camera, to photograph the dry, yellowing page with its sloping list of names. I am unprepared for the feelings that rush through me when I see her name: something inside me, in the pit of me, starts to tremble. Each word that describes her shines on the page, clear and cold and distinct as a star, a bright echo of something that once flamed, a long, long time ago.

When he's finished, he takes my hand and I hold his, as we read together.

> *Patient No: 1496.*
>
> > *Name: Norah O'Donovan.*
> > *Address: Mucknamore, Co. Wexford.*
> > *Age: Twenty years.*
> > *Marital Status: Single.*
> > *Religion: Roman Catholic.*
> > *Education: Reads and writes.*
> > *Previous Occupation: Home Duties.*
> > *Category of Insanity: Puerperal Mania.*
> > *Cause of Insanity: Childbirth.*
> > *May 19th, 1923*

Admitted from the Holy Sisters of Mary Convent, New Ross, where she gave birth three weeks ago. She had a troublesome labour, with forceps delivery leading to a severe puerperal rupture. This rupture extends to the rectum and has turned septic.

Patient resisted coming to asylum, having to be dragged up the front steps kicking and struggling wildly. The Convent reported that she seemed all right in mind when she was first admitted there, being quiet and obedient and willing to work in the laundry. Since she gave birth, however, the nuns are unable to control her. Won't sleep or eat, weeps and wails through the night, disturbing others. Threatened to kill one nun; also, to do away with herself.

Patient placed in D Ward and given a bath. Her wound was cleaned and a poultice applied. She submitted quietly to the bath and other attentions and afterwards took some warm milk.

30g Veronal administered.

May 20th, 1923

Patient slept the night and seemed in better spirits this morning. She is a well-spoken and highly-educated young woman, and at first seemed very rational. Says she is not insane, that the convent put her here because they could not cure her birth wound or help her cope with the pain. It was pain that kept her awake at night, crying out loud, and nobody would do anything to help her.

Her family had placed her with the Holy Sisters of Mary when they learned of her condition. When asked if they would be willing to take her back should she be discharged, the patient became agitated. She began to cry and shout: she shouldn't be here at all, she did nothing wrong, we have no right to keep her, she would not stay. She exhausted herself with crying and abusing and I left her to the care of attendants.

She is not so sound in mind as she appears at first.

June 25th, 1923

Patient tried to escape today. Left by front gate somehow unobserved, but was brought back by two local labourers. Very hyped and threatening on her return. Said she had plenty of help outside if she wanted to call on it, that we were as bad as the nuns and we had no authority to keep her here. 30g Veronal administered.

June 26th, 1923

Had long interview with her this morning which started well, but degenerated. Very impudent and resistive still. She refuses to work, saying she doesn't see why she should be expected to provide labour for nothing. Also complains that she never has a minute alone the whole day long, with attendants and patients coming and going. The food is disgusting, she claims. She can't sleep at night with the noise in the dormitory and the heat and the smell. She refused to stay in bed, throwing her arms about, pacing up and down and shouting in a loud voice. 30g Veronal administered.

August 10th, 1923

Patient has built herself a sort of shelter from sticks and old sacking in the field beside the avenue hedge. She sits in this little hut most of the day, talking to herself or feverishly writing, indulging delusions of a persecutory nature. Those who accuse her of wrongdoing are lying: she is a good girl and the bad things that happened to her were not her fault, God sees all and God would forgive all.

She abuses us as she sits there, saying she should never have been brought here.

Attendant Lizzie Cloake gives her paper for her writings and, when it runs out, patient harasses Lizzie and the other attendants, or even doctors — anyone who might be able to procure pen and ink for her. As it is not harmful to herself or others, the behaviour is permitted. She is *less inclined to abuse the attendants or other patients once she has her pen and paper.*

August 24th, 1923

Since last note the patient has conducted herself well, being quieter and generally obedient — though still refusing to work. Spends her days outside in her hut, writing and talking to herself, coming in only to sleep and for meals. While waiting for the meals, she paces up and down the corridor, refusing to talk to anybody.

September 12th, 1923

Attendants today tried to get patient to give up her hut as the weather grows colder, but she resisted.

September 24th, 1923

The patient is now confined to divisions. It is too cold for her to spend all day outdoors. Also, she was becoming very untidy and collecting a large store of rubbish in her hut. She has taken her confinement very badly, becoming troublesome again.

September 25th, 1923

Patient caused a disturbance at breakfast when she accused another patient, Frances Sills, of putting a dead cockroach in her porridge and attendant Lizzie Cloake of laughing and turning a blind eye. Then, at dinnertime, she put an earthworm onto Mrs Sills' dinner plate and a struggle ensued, with them hitting and scratching each other. Patient would not let go of Mrs Sills' hair and had to be forcibly restrained by *attendants and removed from the dining room. The incident led to some patients becoming greatly distressed. It was mid-afternoon before order was restored. Patient placed in seclusion overnight. 30g Veronal administered.*

September 27th, 1923

    Patient out of seclusion today. She emerged quiet and withdrawn. Interview attempted, but now she refuses to speak when spoken to.

October 1st, 1923

    Patient's behaviour has improved, though still not communicating. She is withdrawn and passive, ignoring all around her. Still refusing to speak and to work, but considerably less troublesome than before.

1 9 8 4

When Jack asks me to, I leave Mrs Fairbairn and join him in his two-bed maisonette. We have a "moving-in-together" party and people buy us sauce bowls and matching towels and I buy an apron and a recipe book and spend a few evenings cooking for us, a housewifely turnabout he finds highly amusing. He comes up behind me while I am cooking, puts a glass of wine into my hand, slides his arm around me under my apron. We go to the launderette together and sit watching our underwear and shirts revolving around each other's.

I give my Sundays, Mondays and most Tuesdays to him, but the other nights still belong to the pub. He comes with me less and less often. When I arrive home late, he turns to me in the dark and often we make love, his body hot against my cold skin. I act drunk and outrageous, to make him chuckle into the dark. Next morning when my head is thumping with pain and I am groaning, "Never again," he is still chuckling, still indulgent. He makes me tea and puts his hand on my forehead while I wonder whether I love him or not.

I meet his family, the father and mother and sister who all think he's wonderful. The dad is Jack, with thirty years on; the two women are kind, if puzzled by his choice. I am not what they expected, not — frankly — what they would have hoped for him, but if I make him happy...

When I tell him this, he laughs it off. "They loved you," he says, refusing to see.

And even if they didn't, we do not need their approval. We have our friends, and we have each other.

We spend Christmas away: one year in Scotland, the next in southern Italy. Our Montgomery's group gets smaller as time passes on and individuals break away. The core of us remain: Natalie, Frank, Sally and me. We believe we are connected to each other, but our real bond is to the alcohol and it's tightening all the time.

Sometimes, I have blackouts. I don't tell Jack about this. I don't tell anybody, not even Sal or Natalie, though we love to rehash the shocking or silly things drink makes us do. Everything that happens during an alcohol-induced blackout is irretrievable, I read. It cannot be revived by any of the methods that recover lost memories, like truth drugs or hypnosis. Something about that frightens me. I do magazine quizzes that all tell me what I already know: I should give up, or at least cut down. I resolve to give up drinking doubles, drinking so often, drinking before six, but can never make the resolutions stick.

Ah, what the hell becomes my most used phrase, as I tilt back another glass.

At work, I start to miss targets and deadlines. I gargle with Listerine in the morning, suck peppermints and chew gum all day, spray Gold Spot into my mouth before going out for the evening, but still I stink. People sniff me out and I hate them for it.

I begin to lie, something I have never done. I don't know why. Jack, of all people, can handle the truth, but I never come home late now without a story prepared. He hates lies, but pretends to believe mine. I don't know when it started — maybe at the very beginning — but silence is now piling up around our apartment, masking what we're not saying.

Maeve arrives to London for a weekend to show off Donal, her fiancé. They want to take Jack and me to dinner to celebrate. "Donal's treat. He insists."

She sits enfolded within his arm, sending little glances to her ring. When the waiter arrives, they order each other's food.

"It's more interesting," says Maeve when I ask why they each don't order their own like anyone else. "It's nice to be surprised."

"We know each other's tastes," says Fiancé.

And they shower each other with smiles. I discreetly make a vomiting gesture to Jack. He and Donal talk about work, suss out each other's place on the career pecking order, while Maeve fills me in on the news from "home". All goes fine for a while, where we are almost what we seem to be: two happy couples enjoying each other's company.

During a lull, she leans across her plate of mussels to Jack. "Have you ever been to Ireland before, Jack?"

"No."

"You'll love it. You'll have to get Jo to take you to the West. It's much more scenic over there."

Jack looks at me. "I'm not sure if —"

I cut in: "We've no plans to go to Ireland, Maeve."

"But Jack, you'll surely come to the wedding. We'd love you to come."

"On his own? I don't think he'd fancy that. Would you, Jack?"

"Jo!" Maeve declares, taken aback. "Come on! You didn't really mean what you said about not coming. I didn't think you —"

"Maeve, I told you." I had too, earlier in the evening, when they came to the flat for drinks. I made sure to tell her, in advance of her asking, and had tried to explain why, but of course she hadn't taken me seriously.

"But —"

"I can't, Maeve. Please accept that."

Fiancé says: "Maeve was hoping you'd be her bridesmaid, Jo."

"I'm sorry," I reply. I lift the champagne bottle to pour us all a refill, but find I am the only one whose glass is empty. Replacing the bottle in the ice bucket, I catch a long look sloping between Maeve and Jack and — horrified — I realise my sister has been there already with him. They have discussed me.

Rage makes me tremble. I cannot believe this of Jack.

After that, the night is a disaster. I get drunk while Maeve lectures: why am I being so unwelcoming to Donal? It's so selfish to greet him into our family like this. As for Mammy and Granny Peg, I have broken their hearts. The wedding is the ideal opportunity to put everything behind us. All I can do is throw it back in their faces.

Donal and Jack look at the wreckage. Jack's face is impassive.

"What's it like to be perfect, Maeve?" I ask, at some point. "Does it never get tiring?"

Feeling something on my face, I put up my hand. I stare at my damp fingers in surprise. I am crying. But I never cry any more, not since I left Mucknamore.

"Nobody asked you to come here," I snap at my sister. "Why don't you just go home and leave us alone?"

So it is Maeve's old friend, Anita Shiels, who is her bridesmaid. I receive some photographs in the post: an older Mrs D., heavier but somehow more frail, trying to look composed; Gran and Auntie Norah just the same, Auntie Norah away somewhere in her head, Gran holding her arm.

Jack is withdrawing his love. I can feel it pulling away, like the tide going out, leaving me beached. Nothing is said. I eat breakfast on a stool opposite, The Guardian divided between us. I watch television from a separate armchair, the couch we used to share staring at us from across the room. I lie in bed beside him, not touching, my head blistered with thoughts.

Sometimes, when I am drunk, I insult him, trying to goad him towards a reaction. He looks at me like I'm a crazy intruder and he's wondering how I got in. When I sober up, I get frightened and try to blot out whatever I've done with sex. We do it furiously, long sessions that leave me physically drained but dissatisfied. I am losing the ability to tell pleasure from pain.

Or am I? Do I even care? Jack is not Rory. Rory knew me, every inch: skin and bone and sinew. I would not be able to keep my thoughts sealed off from Rory. He would not be so indulgent, so accepting, so careless. Rory wouldn't hide behind the paper. He would confront the situation. He would make me think, make me laugh, make me change.

Rory O'Donovan. I swore when I was too young to know what it meant that I would love him forever. I said he was the only man for me and that, it seems, is how it turned out.

Or was it the swearing that had made it so?

1923

*V*isitors, Dr Kennedy told Peg, were generally received in the day room by the friend or relative they had come to see, but in this first instance he would wish to be present when Peg and Norah met.

"Her behaviour is unpredictable," he said, index finger prodding the big brown casebook on his desk. "You can never be sure with her."

He began to read to himself again from the heavy book, silently frowning at it as if the words held a personal insult. Peg sat, hands fastened to the handbag on her lap into which she'd packed food and books and a lovely rose-perfumed hand cream for Norah.

At the window, a fly trapped between the blind and the pane was thudding itself wildly off the glass, but the doctor read on, oblivious. His pen-stand held a careful row of identical pens, shiny and sharp. Beside it was a pile of clean sheets of paper, edge to edge, awaiting his words. Peg wished he'd give her a better idea of what to expect. She wished he would tell her what was in that book that made him look so affronted. She wished he had better manners.

"Doctor, are you able to tell me what's wrong with her?"

He answered her without taking his eyes from the book. "Mania. A form of mania."

She tried again. "But can you explain to me what that means, Doctor? In Norah's particular case?"

This time he looked up. "I could only have such a discussion with a member of the inmate's immediate family."

"It's just...It was such a surprise to us, Doctor."

"She showed no signs of her weakness before?"

"No," said Peg, though the memory of a night in the grocery, when she and Norah were working on election leaflets, rose unbidden in her mind. That night, Norah had beaten herself about the head with her hands, decrying her family situation. "Nothing. Not a thing."

He picked up his pen, made a note in the casebook, the scratch of his nib loud in the solemn room.

"So can you?" Peg asked, when it looked like he wasn't going to speak again.

He looked at her over his spectacles.

She began to get frustrated. "Can you tell me what's the matter with her, how she came to be here, whether she's going to be all right?"

"Haven't I just said, Miss Parle, that such a discussion was possible only with family?"

"Norah was my best friend, Doctor. She was engaged to marry my brother, only...only he died. We are very close, closer than many sisters."

"Nonetheless..."

"I want to help her, and so do my parents. We're all so fond of Norah."

"No doubt, Miss Parle. I do not doubt you. But you will appreciate the nature of our work here. It would be most unorthodox to discuss such matters with anybody who turned up wanting to know."

Peg nodded, putting on a reasonable face. She didn't want to get on the wrong side of him. "Do her family know that she's here, Doctor?"

"Most certainly. All the proper parties were informed, by the Holy Sisters as well as ourselves."

"Yet she's had no visitors up until now?"

He hesitated, realising the point to which she'd steered him.

"She hasn't, has she? As soon as I knew where she was, I came, Doctor, but they won't. You see? It's those who care most for Norah who must look out for her now."

"You know them, the O'Donovan family?"

"I do."

"Her father is a farmer, I have been told, of some substance. Is this correct?"

"They have about thirty acres."

"Good land?"

What had that to do with anything? "Yes, good enough. A bit waterlogged b'times maybe."

His lips pursed. He made another note, this time on one of his clean, separate pieces of paper. "Is there insanity elsewhere in the family, do you know? Any other relatives?"

"I don't know, Doctor. The O'Donovans are not from Wexford. They moved here from Cork some years ago."

He took off his spectacles, rubbed the inner corners of his eyes with finger and thumb. Two red pressure marks marked each side of his nose. He asked: "Would your friendship extend towards ensuring that her keep was paid for here?"

So that was it.

Mr O'Donovan mustn't be paying for Norah's upkeep. It was a constant complaint of the asylum, that many of those who could well afford to pay didn't. The governors were always writing in the local paper about it.

"Certainly, Doctor. Of course. That would only be right."

He clasped his hands together on top of the open casebook, white hands with blue veins raised to tracks along the skin, and let another long silence lapse, so long she began to wonder if he would ever speak again. When he did, his tone had changed, become conciliatory. Confiding, nearly.

"What you need to understand, Miss Parle, is that insanity is a dissolution: a regression to a lower nature. In this respect, your friend is a classic case. For years, she goes about her business, a seemingly respectable young girl, until the underlying insanity manifests itself and her true nature is revealed."

He circled one thumb around each other, paused a moment. "You know, I presume, the chain of events that led to her committal here?"

Did he mean what she thought he meant? Peg opened her mouth but shut it again, unsure of what to say. She could feel herself starting to blush. The doctor, also embarrassed, hemmed a small cough. "You will pardon me if I speak frankly. It is essential to your understanding of the case. You are aware of the circumstances that brought her first to the Holy Sisters?"

Peg bowed her head.

"This, as I say, is a classic example of female insanity. In your friend's case, after her gestation and delivery, the balance of her circulation was greatly disturbed."

Peg didn't know where to put her eyes.

"This made her liable to disorder from the application of any exciting cause. Something as simple as a cold affecting the head, a violent noise or the want of sleep distresses a puerperal patient before her milk comes in, and if there is any underlying weakness there, such an impetus is readily converted to the head and may produce either hysteria or insanity."

What was he talking about? He had lost her completely.

She didn't understand the medics, but the whole thing sounded unlikely. Whatever was afflicting Norah, it was nothing to do with head colds or loud noises. The girl had good reason for any mental strain she might be suffering. In the last year, she'd gone against the politics of her family, to the open ire of her father; broken with her closest brother; lost her sweetheart in a shootout; learned that it might have been that same brother who killed him; and found herself in the worst trouble a girl can get into — with the father of the child deceased — and so must have had to ask whether that was the reason her brother might have done it.

Who *wouldn't* be having a breakdown?

"Insanity of lactation is only one such disorder that may affect a woman. We suspect that this is the cause of your friend's condition, but we cannot be sure. Ovarian madness is also a possibility. We have given her the general diagnosis of puerperal mania."

He looked at her as if he expected her to say something.

"Are you saying, Doctor, that women are more inclined to insanity than men?"

"Oh, yes. Yes, indeed. The female reproductive organs are frequently the seat of disease or abnormal function. And men, even when predisposed to insanity through heredity or other factors, have superior powers of resistance that can overcome their latent tendencies."

"But I thought there were more men in the asylum than women."

His eyes opening wide behind his glasses. Oh, why had she gone and said that? Now he thought she was being smart with him. "Maybe there are other reasons for that, Doctor?" she said, in her most compliant voice, the one she kept for Father John and the master at school.

"Indeed. These things are never as simple as they seem."

His eyes still held her, uncertain.

"How is Norah now, Doctor?"

He looked down at the big casebook. "She has improved somewhat. When she was admitted here by the Holy Sisters, she had forsaken all vestiges of self-control and become a prisoner of her passions. Here, she has learned to exercise self-restraint. For some time now, we have witnessed an improvement. However, we would not consider her cured. No. Far from it, indeed. She does no work, for example. She does not mix with the other patients. She is subject to delusions" — here he glanced again at the case notes – "yes, delusions of persecution."

It was all wrong, Peg thought, turning Norah's life into a package to be wrapped up in fancy words that parcelled her off from the rest of us.

"Is she well enough to go home, Doctor?"

"Miss Parle, I do not think you understand what I am explaining to you. At the moment, Miss O'Donovan is moving from acute mania to a more chronic stage that looks like it may settle into one of the many forms of melancholia. I think it unlikely that we shall witness any real improvement for some time. Perhaps never."

"But maybe at home...?"

He shook his head. "I'm sorry, I could not recommend such a course of action."

"I can't believe it, I really can't. Norah was as sane as myself the last time I saw her."

"It may have appeared so to the untrained eye, Miss Parle, but I assure you, insanity does not occur in people who are of sound mental faculties. It does not — like smallpox, for example — attack indifferently the weak and the strong. It will only raise itself in those whose mental constitution was originally defective. Your friend's immorality...and her insanity were both symptoms of an underlying flaw. Now do you —? Oh my..."

The door crashed open, interrupting his flow. Though Norah's arrival was expected, they both jumped off their seats.

"My goodness," Dr Kennedy said, crinkling with disapproval.

Norah was standing in the door frame, breathless, holding on to the handle, her chest rising and falling, looking as if she might fly off again. A sheen of sweat glowed on her forehead. An attendant came running up behind, panting. "I'm sorry, Doctor. I couldn't hold her..."

The doctor waved her away her with the hand of a man who doesn't have time for excuses. "Come in, Miss O'Donovan," he said, curt as he could. "You have a visitor."

It made Peg want to laugh, or it would have, if the sight of Norah clinging to the door handle wasn't so alarming. Lunatics of every order paced this place and the doctor was getting himself in a stitch over how somebody entered a room. Pretending he thought sanity a matter of manners, of keeping your desk tidy and your record book straight.

Norah was transfixed in the doorway. Everything that had happened since she and Peg had last seen each other was flooding the space between them. Awareness of the gap between what she had been and what she had become was leaving her stranded.

Peg took a step towards her, but Dr Kennedy stopped her: "No, Miss Parle, please."

To Norah, he repeated his order: "Come in, I said."

Peg longed to meet her halfway, but under the doctor's eye, she waited. Waited and watched her friend walk towards her, walking as she never walked before, like it hurt her to make contact with the ground. So it was true, she had lost her sanity. Oh God, dear God, would she be able to get it back?

When Norah was almost at the chair, she slumped down. For a moment, Peg thought she had fainted, then realised she was kneeling, and reaching for Peg's hand, and then her other hand.

Peg tried to help her back up onto her feet, but Norah wouldn't let her. Instead, she brought Peg's hands to her lips and kissed them. "Thank you," she said, into Peg's skirts, trying not to let the doctor hear her. "Thank you, thank you..."

"Oh my God," Peg said. "Don't do that, Norah. Please. Don't be doing that."

"No, Peg!" Máire pulled herself up on her pillow. "Holy Mother of God, what are you thinking of? To even ask such a thing!"

Hold on, Peg orders herself in her mind. You knew she wouldn't say yes straight off. Take your time, best words out.

"Mammy, it's not right, is it, that she should be left to rot in that place? That she should have to bear it all alone?"

"I know it's hard on the girl, I'm not saying it isn't. But don't you think we've had enough trouble ourselves?"

This was the first word Peg ever heard her mother say that was anywhere close to self-pity. She was having one of her weak mornings: unable to get out of bed. The good days were becoming fewer, the bad days getting worse. The blood in her sputum had changed in colour from a dark, venous red to bright crimson, and she had passed from the world of the healthy to the separate, shunned world of the tubercular.

Peg sometimes felt she was locked up in that world with her. The house had to be swept and disinfected daily and kept well ventilated. Her eating and drinking vessels and cutlery had to be kept apart; her utensils and bedclothes cleaned separately from everyone else's. They had lost custom in the shop. And nobody ever came all the way into the house to visit any more, except loyal Lil Hayes.

After all Máire had done for the community, and the country, since the first rising in 1916, she was now left alone to her disease.

"You better get started on that porridge before it gets cold," Peg said. "It's made on milk, the way you like it."

Máire picked up her spoon, sliced through the thin skin that coated the surface of the cereal, swirled it round in the milk, releasing steam. Peg could see the effort of will it took for her to lift the spoon, open her mouth, swallow the food. After a couple of spoonfuls, she paused. "Even supposing," she held her spoon aloft. "Even supposing we were to do such a thing —"

"Yes?" Peg felt her head spin.

"Could we not set her up in Dublin or somewhere?"

"That wouldn't work. The asylum would only let her go to us if we were to take charge of her care. Anyway, she wouldn't be able to look after herself in Dublin. She's not what she was."

Máire made a face. "Another person to look after, that's all you need."

"I don't think it would be like that always," said Peg. "I don't believe that old doctor. She'd get better herself if she were out of that place, I'm sure of it. If she were..." Peg paused. This was the tricky bit. Dear Mary, Mother of God. Mother of all that is holy. Help me here now. Give me the strength to say it. "If...if she were to be reunited with her child..."

"Dear God in Heaven! That's not what she wants, is it?"

"It is."

"Are you sure?"

"She's told me. You can talk to her same as ever, you know. She's troubled, but she's no fool."

"You haven't encouraged her in this madness, I hope?"

"Is it madness, Mammy?"

"Pure, utter, complete, unadulterated madness. And there's some excuse for her to talk lunacy, she's in an asylum. But you...You have to help her, Peg, to see the errors of her thinking. To help her reconcile to the inevitable." Máire sighed, put her spoon back in the bowl with the half-eaten porridge. "Will that do for today?"

"Mammy, you haven't even had half."

"I'm sorry, a ghrá. Not this morning. Maybe later on."

She pushed the tray away. Peg took it from her, put it over on the dresser. Guilt pricked her: it was encouraging her mother to eat she should be, not arguing with her and springing surprises that would put anybody off their food.

"Come back over here, Peg, and sit on the bed where I can see your face," Máire said. "Good girl, that's it. That's better."

She took a breath. Peg could see her reaching for the strength to talk through all she wanted to say.

"I don't want to say no to you, Peg. I know you are trying to do right and that's what I've always taught you to do...But think about it. Really think about it."

When Peg said nothing, Máire went on. "Think about the

O'Donovans. They'll be furious, so they will, and they'd be within their rights. We already have Barney and all that business between us. Do we want to further it into an unholy row that will make it irrevocable?" She stopped, reached again for breath, holding up her hand to stop Peg saying anything. "No...wait..."

The rise and fall of her chest hurt Peg to watch, but she knew better than to suggest they might leave it, talk about it later. If Máire had something to say, she would be heard.

"Then...What about Norah herself?' Máire asked, strength marshalled. "Do you think she could settle in here, could be happy in herself, knowing that her mammy and daddy were a small walk away and so upset? Knowing what the whole place would be thinking and saying about her? Is it fair to do that to her after all she's been through?"

Peg let her head fall. Her mother was raising the very questions that had most worried herself when she considered the plan.

"I'm sorry, Peg," Máire said, in a voice that declared the argument over. "I know what good friends you were, but if her family won't help her, we can't. It wouldn't be right to go against her family."

She broke into the coughing fit she'd been staving off and her face took on the unmistakable mask of her disease. On the peak of her cheeks, two bright red spots appeared, as if dabbed on. Her eyes turned glassy and perspiration broke across her forehead. Peg handed her the bowl, stood by while she coughed and spat. Once, not long ago, she used to find this nearly too distressing a job to do; now she was so accustomed to it, she stood holding the bowl while her attention wandered off into the distance. She understood what her mother was saying.

Oh, but the feel of Norah's lips scorching into her hands...

After Máire recovered, Peg covered the bowl with its special clip-on top and put it outside the door. She walked across to the window, where the pale morning sun fell onto her arms.

She asked gently, "Mammy, why should we bother about the O'Donovans? If they object, what do we care?"

It was not something they discussed, Peg and her mother: Dan's part in Barney's death. The subject was too raw. What could be said that wouldn't widen the wound? Each morning still, Peg tumbled out of the comfort of sleep into the heavy weight of consciousness. How could he? was still the question that drove her out of bed as soon as her eyes fell open and that stayed with her all through the business of the day. She no longer had any doubt but that he did it. He'd stood in front of her and lied so completely about Norah that she now knew all he said to be false.

Her mother didn't answer. So Peg said the other thing, the thing she had held back, the thing she'd hoped she wouldn't have to say. "After all, Mammy, it is Barney's baby."

Her mother put her hands over her ears. "Holy God, child! Hush!"

"It's Holy God's own truth I'm saying." She sensed a weakness, and pressed on. "Are we going to let Barney's child be brought up by some strangers from God knows where? Or leave her — yes, her, she is a little girl — leave her to grow up in an orphanage?"

"Stop that talk: we all know what happens. There's no need for that kind of talk."

Peg looked out the window. She was getting to know the view from this room as well as she knew the one from her own on the other side of the house. Everything that made this room Barney's was gone. Since her mother had moved in, that had been swallowed up by the paraphernalia of sickness. Medicines and peppermint drops on the bed table and facecloths and handkerchiefs to cool down or mop up. Bed-bottles and a good fire going all day. The window open for ventilation, no matter how cold. Porridge and soups and beef tea.

"Oh, Peg, I don't know...All my life I've done what I thought was right and I have to say that it hasn't got me very far. And now I'm dying —"

"Ah, Mammy!"

"It's the truth, isn't it, God's own truth, like you said. If that's what we are to have here this morning, then let that be said, along with the rest. I can't say it to your father, you know that, so let me say it to you."

Peg went back over to the bed, sat beside her.

"It's only a matter of time for me," Máire continued. "So here I am. I've lost one child and I'm leaving the other behind with an ageing father and an ailing business. If I thought what you wanted was the best thing for all involved, I'd say go ahead, and the O'Donovans and all the tattlers of the village could go to the devil. But is it, Peg? Is it?"

Peg hung her head. How could she know the answer to that?

"I can't read the future, Mammy. All I know in this moment is that leaving her there might make everyone feel easier — but I can't believe it's right."

Máire lay back. The clock ticked loud in the room, reminding Peg to get up and wind it. When she was finished, she sat back down in the bedside chair. After another silence, Máire spoke. "The child could have been adopted already by somebody else. Have you thought of that?"

"She hasn't been."

"You've checked?"

"I've checked."

Another silence. Then: "But Peg...Tipsy Delaney?"

"Tipsy will do it. I know it's not many men would but —"

"That's not what I meant. I know he'll do it, the poor eejit would jump onto Coolanagh sands if you asked him." She smiled a dead smile. "No, it's you I'm thinking of."

"I'll be all right."

"No." She turned in the bed to take hold of Peg's wrist. "You're not listening to me, girl."

"I am, Mammy, and I understand what you're saying. It's not

like I haven't thought it through. I know what it means and I'm happy to go ahead."

"You can't know what a marriage is like until you're in it. And think of this: supposing Norah doesn't get better? Supposing she's a hopeless case and she ends up back inside? You'll be left tied to..."

She let the sentence trail, worn out maybe, or maybe just afraid to put a word on the man who might become her son-in-law.

"The child has to have a father and a mother," Peg said. "They won't give it to us otherwise. Tipsy is the only man who'd do it."

"Oh, Peg..." Máire lay back, weary.

"Never mind Tipsy. What about Daddy?"

Máire closed her eyes. "You don't need to worry about that," she said, her voice fading into her exhaustion. "You can leave your father to me."

CASEBOOK: *Wexford District Lunatic Asylum for the Insane*
   Patient No: *1496*:
   October 24th, 1923: *Patient Discharged. Not Improved.*

1984

*B*y the time Jack asks me to leave, I expect it, but still, it seems sudden. It doesn't seem right that we can pass through all the stages and arrive at the end without even a decent quarrel. Heaven knows, I've tried to break through with snarls and insults and drunken diatribes. All he ever says is, "I'm happy to talk about it, Jo, when you're calm."

When I'm calmer, though, I'm frightened. Fearful of being alone. So I wheedle or joke or outright humiliate myself, begging him to reconsider, making promises we both know I can't keep, even though I know breaking up is right for me as much as him. Jack always does the right thing.

So we keep going, until the evening he comes home and firmly tells me I have to be gone by the end of the month. The end of the month. His face is set against me, craggy lines around his mouth shutting me out.

"We haven't tried hard enough," I say. "We haven't talked. We should talk."

He shakes his head. "Too late," he says. Two words only, as if they are rationed.

I gabble: "I'll stop drinking, Jack...I know that's the problem. If that's what you want..."

Again, that shake of his head.

I throw myself on his mercy. "I have nowhere to go."

He says nothing, as if he is the one who is helpless.

I am starting to cry. "I gave up everything for you, you bastard. Where the hell am I supposed to go?"

"I'm sorry, Jo."

He doesn't sound it or look it, but underneath my blustering tears, I know he is. His sorrow is an axe, slicing me off.

I move in with Natalie, who owns a flat in Camden Town, and has a box bedroom she never bothered to fill after her last flatmate moved out. The decor is dire and I keep promising myself I will paint the walls and the cheap melamine furniture, but I can't seem to get round to it. I'm too busy — out a lot — home only in time to cry myself to sleep.

Crying is what I do now, especially after a few drinks. I tell everybody who will listen that Jack has broken my heart. This half-truth gives me permission to wallow in sorrow, and to try to drown thoughts I don't want to be having. Natalie and I drink in the pub near the flat now, instead of The Rose and Crown. It's handier. We can just walk home instead of having to negotiate the Tube after closing time. And anyway, the old gang has broken up. People have moved on: to relationships, marriages, mortgages.

Natalie and I have fun in the pub, but at home we bicker, like an old married couple. She is small-minded about money and motives, and not very bright. Often I wonder how I ended up with her. I miss Dee, my old friend from school, and resolve again that I will write to her, a letter that I will finish, all the way to the end of a page, or maybe even two, and put in an envelope, and stamp, and actually send.

Natalie is also a nag. She ticks me off for not keeping to the housework rota she drew up. The effort of housework is beyond me. I always intend to do it, but when we're not drinking, I wind up sitting in a corner of the couch, or on top of my duvet, staring at nothing, locked inside a struggle. Not moving, but with every coil in my brain contorted and all my muscles straining to keep still.

When you're slipping, people think you don't know, but you do. For a long time before anyone raises a whispered note of concern to you, or passes a comment across a sea of laughs from others, you've been telling yourself what's wrong, and how to put it right. Giving yourself sensible advice that you don't know how to follow.

I never drink at home, but I'm not stupid enough to believe that matters. I know what I am. I know I have to stop. And I try, I do try, and sometimes I even succeed. Every day starts with good intentions pressed into place, but many evenings, and sometimes even afternoons, find me again pouring drink down my throat.

I am a limp drunk now, occasionally boisterous, but mostly weepy and full of self-pity. I can't stand her, this interloper who intrudes into my evening, wet-eyed every time, yet still I feed her. Whisky now, Scotch — never Irish — on the rocks. One night, I wake in bed beside a stranger and have no memory of how I got there. The skin on my chest and back stings and, when I investigate, I find I am covered in scratches.

My boss calls me in. I have used up all my leave, paid and unpaid, and my sick days, certified and uncertified. I am late three mornings out of five. If I don't improve my performance, he has no choice but to let me go. So what? I say to myself after this rebuke. It's not like I like this low-grade, beneath-me job, but I have no qualifications and so no hope of a better one. It's a dilemma.

Natalie and I take to the pub to try to solve it.

At some stage in the evening, she goes home, but I go on to a club. Somebody puts me into a taxi at the end of the night. Staggering up the steps to our front door, I trip and burst my lip. Next morning, I arrive late to work again.

I am shuddering a coffee cup to my broken mouth when the

boss calls me to his office, makes me sign a form. My final warning.

"Do yourself a favour," he says. "Get a grip."

He is right, I know he is right.

Get a grip. Stop.

I stop.

I'm in Natalie's kitchen, crouching on the floor, unable to move. Darkness is fondling the windowpane, which means it's late, but I have no idea how long I have sat here like this. In my right hand, I hold a kettle, full of cold water, but I have no memory of filling it. My arm hurts from holding on, but I can't let it go. My hand, my arm, everything is jammed. My body has wound down, like a clockwork toy, while my mind has gone into overspin, spewing up thought after self-lacerating thought.

I am held captive, paralysed by the parade of taunts that come swooping in, cascading one over the other to flay me. Then, somebody speaks to me from behind, over near the door.

Do it, she says.

Fear creeps along my skin. I know that voice and I know she can't be here. She's in Ireland and she wouldn't come here, and if she did she wouldn't speak those words, not out loud. Did I imagine it? It doesn't seem so. It sounds like she is in the room behind me, her voice real and solid as a voice can be. Do it, she says again.

On the table above me is the bread knife, with its row of shiny, sharp-toothed smiles all along the blade. It doesn't hurt: slash, slash the serrated edge once, twice, across the skin, faster than thought. Two burning flashes, then the thoughts fade to silky black whispers...It doesn't even hurt, that's what they say.

Just do it.

My hand jerks and opens. Cold water splashing over my jeans breaks the spell. I can move again, though not quickly, not easily. I leave the kettle on the floor where it has fallen, the lid where it has rolled away, the water gliding along the brown linoleum. On my hands and knees, I crawl away. In the bedroom, I close the door behind me, lean against it. The thudding of my heart echoes throughout my body. Even my toes and fingertips throb. I am so frightened.

I have to go: that is what I realise. If I don't get away, the voice will move in. She will feel entitled, invited by default. I have to go, and I have to go now before Natalie comes back, before I am back into the everyday world where thoughts like these slip down under the surface and pretend they're not there.

I find the backpack I brought from Jack's house and begin to fill it. It takes a huge effort, deciding what to bring. I would prefer to just walk out the door with only the clothes I am wearing, but I cannot afford that. I have very little left and am going to need everything that is mine.

Into the bag they go: clothes, records, books, anything I can fit. When I am packed, I sit down at the kitchen table to write Natalie a note. I'm trying to find words when the key turns in the door. She is home early, but not — I read by the slackness of her jaw — too early to have had a few drinks.

"Whatever are you doing?" Her wide, inebriated eyes take in my rucksack, the other bags, my duvet and pillows rolled into a black sack. "What's going on?"

I put down the pen. "I have to go."

"Go? What are you talking about? Go where?"

"I have to..." My voice has the shakes. "I —"

"What about money for bills, and for rent while I find someone else? Were you going without paying?"

"Natalie —"Aghast, I realise I can't speak. If I do, I'll break.

"Where are you going?"

I shrug. I cannot look at her drunken face, and her swollen, fluid eyes. I crumple up the sheet of paper I have been writing on.

"You're a bit down," she says. "Are you? Is that it?"

I pick up my bags.

"You could have told me, you know. You should have. Sneaking off like this..."

She doesn't get it. She hasn't a clue, about anything. The weakest part of her and the weakest part of me, that's where we connect.

"You should leave here too," I tell her.

"What are you talking about?" Her voice squeaks.

The doorbell rings. "That's my taxi."

"You can cancel it, Jo. We'll call it again in the morning if you still want to go then."

I shift my backpack up onto my shoulder, hug the big plastic bag to my chest so I can barely see over it.

"Jo. Please..."

"I can't stay, Natalie. I don't know how." I turn away and she follows, picking up my other bag and walking behind me to the hall door.

It's raining. I hand one bag to the driver, then the other. Bending my head to the weather, I run down the steps. She follows me out to the gate, insists on hugging me, her skin hot against my cheek. "I don't understand."

Drips slink down the shiny black rump of the cab and the engine grumbles impatiently. I pull out of her grasp.

"Ring me," she says, as I'm getting in. "Ring me soon."

I slump into the seat, dizzy with relief. I'm getting used to leaving, getting to recognise its imperative: shut down; face forward. I'll write to her, I tell myself. As soon as I'm settled, I'll write a long, long, letter, the longest letter ever written, and explain it all. I'll write to Dee as well. And maybe even Maeve.

The driver asks, "Where to, love?"

"Heathrow Airport," I say.

The taxi pulls away from the kerb and I turn to look back, just for a second, but I can't see anything. Already, Natalie and her house have blurred into rain and disappeared.

J let myself in by the side door as instructed by Hilde and find myself stopping in the door frame, transfixed by change. The hinged door swings shut behind me with a slap that nudges me inside. Still I stand, bath towel cradled to my chest, looking at what has happened to our home.

"Well, look at you," I say aloud. The blank, empty rooms echo my voice back to me: "Yoo-oo-oo."

A hallway with a section cornered off by a tall mahogany desk where guests will check in to the new B&B. A row of open doorways, like empty picture frames, stretches away down the corridor.

It seems vast, this premises, as I walk through room after empty room, across floor after bare wooden floor. The square-footage of the house has been doubled, but it feels four times as big: the old strangely-angled walls knocked down and re-erected somewhere more logical, the redundant nooks knocked into place. All the walls are naked, plaster-grey. The entire back wall of the building — along the dining room, bar and lounge — is glass, overlooking the sea. From here, I can see my little shed. Its days are numbered: now that the buildings are almost finished, attention will switch to the terraces and the gardens. Soon it will be time to go.

Which is just as well.

This is my first time inside the house in daylight, since the roof went on. I wait for a new feeling to hit — nostalgia? regret? — but the house is too changed, a blank canvas that has nothing to do with me.

My sandals leave footprints in the dust as I walk up the stairs. Tubings of wire protrude from walls and ceilings, awaiting light fittings. Only the bathrooms are completely finished, tiled and plumbed, and that's where I'm headed for a long soak in piping hot water.

When Hilde came by my shed with lunch today, she found me sitting in my swimsuit at my desk. Yesterday, the small offshore breeze that has been keeping us cool dissolved and the air grew thick and humid. I sat with sweat dribbling from beneath my breasts down my bulging abdomen, hating the heat.

Hilde laughed. "Poor Jo, always the pregnant women find it difficult, the warm weather." It was then she offered me the bath. Usually I say no to Hilde's offers, but after weeks of washing from a red plastic basin I couldn't resist.

I find the bathroom at the top of the stairs where she said. She has left out towels for me, and toiletries: soap and shampoo, conditioner and bath oil, perfume and talcum powder. Kindness in a collection of bottles. The room is stuffy. I open one of the windows a little at the top, but no air comes in. Down on the beach, a mother calls her daughter in out of the sea. "Tríona, come on now," she shrieks. "I won't call you again." But she does: "Tríona! Come in, I said. Trí-í-í-íon-a!"

I turn on the taps and a gush of water drowns her out. Hilde's bath oil smells sweet, like pear juice. Under the torrent from the taps, it bubbles up, a froth of scent. I stand into the water while it's filling and my reflection appears in a big bath-end mirror. It's the first time I've seen myself in two months. I am a new me, brown face and arms and legs, a farmer's tan, and

— in between — the big belly, white and round as a giant mushroom. Underneath is my pubic hair, dark and close.

I face sideways to inspect myself, the miracle of engineering that I now am, front cantilevered out from an improbably flat backside. My breasts, swollen and heavy like overripe fruit, are marbled with veins. With my fingertip, I trace one of the blue coils.

I slide down in the water, supporting my bump as I go. Heat and scent prickle my skin and draw from me a long, slow, sigh. I fill the bath until the water is level with my scalp line then turn off the taps and lie still in the soft water, so different from the salt sea. Lying quiet, enjoying the cosseting, I notice a quivering at the pit of my stomach (me, not you) and realise that it's been there all day, ever since Hilde suggested this bath, lighting up my insides. An old sensation, from long ago: anticipation. I'm not sure whether I want it or not, but there it is, regardless.

I can't lie still under it. I sit up, take the sponge and begin to soap my distended body.

HE COMES UP THE PATH, as always, at dusk. It falls earlier now each evening, making our nights together longer. We sit on the rug outside, watching the light leak from a heavy, purple-clouded sky. Tonight, the sea is grey and flat as a floor. Coolanagh seems much closer than usual.

"A sign of rain," Rory says, when I remark on that.

"I remember," I say, reciting the old weather forecast: "Coolanagh near is rain, Coolanagh far is fine."

"And if you can't see it at all, then it's raining already."

I smile. "It's been so long since we had rain, I find it hard to even imagine."

The word "it" comes out of my mouth long and drawn, with the 't' soft at the end, so it sounds almost like "sh". My accent is slipping back, I hear it myself, the vowels shortening and flattening, returning to what they were.

Rory has brought red wine tonight, instead of the usual beer. He tries to persuade me to join him, stopping in the middle of twisting the corkscrew to curve his eyes up to meet mine. I shake my head to the wine, but smile his long, slow, significant smile back at him.

Yes, we are all significant smiles tonight. Why now? Why "yes" tonight after all the months of "no"? His excitement is mingling with mine, doubling it up, and any feeling I used to have that my "yes" or "no" or "maybe" was the deciding factor has melted away, dissolved by an invisible force older and stronger and far more primeval than either of us.

The cork slides from the bottleneck with a faint, quiet pop. I pour myself a juice and we lift and clink our glasses together. The air is calm, eerily calm, thick and hard to breathe. The low cloud weighs down on my head and, for a moment, I feel something like fear, but I know it's only atmospheric pressure, pressing on my brain.

I tell him, "Your hair is getting long."

"Orla hates it." He imitates her voice: "'Get a haircut, would you?'"

I don't like him mimicking his wife like that. "I always preferred it long," I say.

"I know."

I decide to dispense with the preliminaries and touch his wrist with the flat of my hand. "Do you still want to fuck?"

He flinches. "Jesus, Jo."

"What? Do you?"

"You know I do."

"Why?"

"Jesus, such questions."

"If you can't even say why..."

He spreads his fingers wide, as if he's helpless. "I seem to have made such a mess of my life, Jo. I think it was because we went so wrong, you and me." The pupils in his eyes are welling wide in the dark. The brown irises have almost disappeared. "You were my first love, Jo. Part of me never got over you."

I have stopped breathing.

He goes on: "For so long, I was bitter at you for running away. I used to rehearse in my head the crushing things I'd say when you came back to me. But you never did."

"But Rory, I —"

"I know, I know. I see it differently now. Now I spend my time in my head, wondering which particular thing I said, or did, was the one that failed us."

"It wasn't only your fault," I say after a small silence, able to admit that now he's stopped blaming me.

"I know that. It was both of us and, hey, I absolve us both. We were too young, it was just the way it was. Just life. Well, now life has brought us back together. You're here and I can't pretend you're not. I want back some of what was taken from us. I know I have no right but —"

I interrupt him with a kiss. A long kiss, deep and breathless, and by the end of it his hands are up under my T-shirt, palming across clammy skin. I pull away. I want this to be slow and deliberate, nothing pushy or clumsy. I kneel up and pull my T-shirt over my head and fold it, as if we have all the time in the world. My bra is for pregnancy, more harness than lingerie, but I sit back on my heels all the same so he can get a good look at what thirty-nine-and-pregnant looks like. My eyes hold his, trying to pin him to the moment, to what we are doing. It seems a point of honour to reveal myself and I want the same from him.

He understands. Kneeling up, he unbuttons his shirt, slips it off his shoulders. I stand, take off my shorts and wait. He copies me. So we go, item for item, the garments getting smaller and smaller until we are both naked. Only then do I move back into his arms. His body is changed too, though not as much as mine: his belly is soft from beer and his pecs have drooped. Above his hips swell two handles of flesh. He is softer but his penis, standing to attention in the candlelight, is just the same.

We are naked, here, outside my outhouse, in full view if anyone should decide to climb the small cliff-face, or come in around to the back of the house and shed. But no one will. We kiss on and on. We are quiet, as always: we never spoke during the act. A small spatter of rain drops hits my skin, as Rory traces a tingling line from the hollow at the base of my throat to loop around my right breast, then gives the same attention to the other side, and follows with his hands until both are high points, sending surges of desire in every direction. I hear myself moan, I hear myself say his name, and the scent of him fills my nostrils, unchanged. I would know him by this if we met in total darkness.

He lies down, pulls me on top: the perfect position for a seven-month pregnant woman. He knows more than he used to know. A sudden shiver of wind tears the air but I ignore it, all thought swirling away into overrunning sensation. Large, separate drops of rain start to ping against my bare skin and they feel good, pinpoints of cold caress. I am close, so close. I bear down and squeeze tight and, yes, I am there. Heart, muscle, tissue, blood pounding, pounding, pounding. There, there, there.

I slump against him. It takes a time to come back into myself. He is still with me, still inside me. His turn, his rhythm now. Another gust of rain-logged wind slaps the back of my neck, then it is falling on us. Heavy Irish rain, all over the rug and the wine and our clothes and the sleeping bag, drenching everything, but we don't care. I throw my head back to feel it on my face as we go on and on, believing we'll go on forever. His breath rises and rises and at the top, just before he lets go, catches in the back of his throat. Beloved, long-lost sound.

And then, in a moment, we are back in the world, jumping to our feet to pick up things, pick up everything, quick as we can, and run for shelter from the rain now pelting down, stabbing our bare skins, plastering our hair flat on our crowns. Inside the shed, I turn on the oil lamp to find towels. I am shivering. Water streams in runnels down my neck. Above us, the rain hammers down on corrugated iron, hurting our ears. We look at each other and have to laugh.

"Is this place waterproof?" Rory yells above the din.

"I don't know," I shout back. "It's the first rain this summer. I hope so."

I hold out a towel to him and he catches my hand, pulls me in close. I feel his lips on my wet scalp.

"How are you going to get home in this?" My shed feels like a boat, tipping and rolling on an open ocean.

"Maybe I'll stay," he murmurs into my hair. He looks across in the direction of my small bed. "Would it take two?"

"Two-and-a-half, you mean," I say, rubbing my bump. "I doubt it."

"Let's try."

I get in first and he squeezes in behind me, my back to his front, his hand settled on the base of my big belly, sealed in tight, like two sheets of paper in an envelope. We are damp and our skin is chilled, but beneath is blood, rising warm.

I turn the lantern off and darkness tucks in around us. Above, the rain pounds on the roof, like it wants to be let in. The noise is deafening, but somehow, almost immediately, we plummet into sleep.

A while later, I waken. One part of me feels like I've been asleep a long time, another suspects not. Beside my ear, Rory lets a snore on each out-breath.

We did it. In the end, after all the pushing and parrying, it just happened. And I don't regret it, do I? No, I don't think I do.

His arm lies heavy across me, strangling my waist, and his body is too close, too hot. I slide from beneath its hold. His breathing changes as he feels my absence through his sleep, then he shifts and spreads himself out across the mattress and his slow, noisy inhalation and exhalation intensifies. Only then do I notice the quiet in the shed. The rain has stopped.

I think of his wife, only a short walk away, waking to find he's not there.

And for some reason, my promise to Gran and Richard rises in my mind: I will do this well.

I can't stay there, in bed with it. My shoes are not where I usually leave them. I have to cross the dirty floor in bare feet to the table where I find what I'm looking for: my torch. Putting my hand over the lamp, I turn it on so my fingers glow transparent pink.

I look across. He hasn't budged, so I release the glow and use it to retrieve shoes and clothes. I dress in a dry pair of jeans and a warm jumper, then go to sit at my desk. I have the overwhelming urge to write about what we have done.

I write quickly, lightly, without stopping to think or amend. As I have written, so it was. Physically, more pleasing than before. When we were young together, I used to pretend it was better than it was, so grateful to be with him that I felt no lack. I no longer love like that. How do I love now?

What now?

I imagine myself writing to Sue Denim, as I often do when I find myself lost or confused. Dear Sue, Tonight I slept with my first love for the first time in twenty years. The only real love I ever had, who just so happens to be married and a father of two... How would she answer me?

Granny Peg's stacked diaries tower over my writing hand. On top of them are Auntie Norah's notebooks and all those loose pages of hers that I struggled to organise into chronological order. Rory has been taking pictures of these, and of the other papers, and the letters. He has also taken a series of me, sitting here like this, writing about them, and brought me outside the shed and made me stand just as Gran did in one of the old photographs of her wedding day, the little slit in the wall near the roof showing in the exact same place over my head.

That wedding picture is lying on my desk now. It is old and cracked and somebody has torn a small piece off its bottom right-hand corner. Wedding Day, November 14th, 1923, it says on the back, in Gran's beautiful writing, the kind of handwriting that is both legible and ornate, the kind nobody does any more. She looks out at me from this picture, her eyes unreadable, but as I stare into them by torchlight, I feel something give in my chest.

I put down my pen, go across to the bed and try to shake him awake. "Rory, get up. Rory!" I shake him harder until he feels me, until I cannot be ignored. He groans, tries to roll over. Another shake.

"What?" he grunts. "What is it?"

"You have to get up. You have to go home."

"Don't be silly," he says, eyes shut fast.

I shine the torch full in his face.

"Hey! Stop!" His hand shoots out from under the duvet, pushes the torch aside. "What are you doing?"

"Get up."

He rubs his eyes. "What's happening?" His voice is exasperated. "What's the matter?"

I retrieve his clothes, dump them on top of him in the bed. "Put these on. You need to go."

"I don't understand," he says.

I shake my head, stubborn. "Come on, get up."

I shine the light on him, searching his face. Wrinkles crag his forehead and fan out from round his sleep-starved eyes and I want to smooth them out with my thumbs. He puts his arm up across his face against the light. "Will you put that thing away?"

"Please," I turn to him. "Please, Rory, don't say anything else. Just go."

I cross back to my desk to wait for him to do it, shine the light again on Gran's photo, on the four young people dressed up for the day: bride and groom in front, the groom in military uniform, a rifle resting across his knee, face scrubbed up, looking off to the side.

Rory sighs heavily and my bed creaks under the weight of

him getting out. I hear him search out his clothes, the rustles of him dressing behind me.

The bridesmaid looks in the other direction, locked inside the casing of her thoughts. Both she and the bride wear costumes in the faux-traditional Irish style, fashionable among nationalists of the time: over-the-shoulder capes held in place by Tara brooches. Their heads are bare, their hair tied into chignons at the base of their necks, the bodices of their dresses embroidered with intricate Celtic designs, like those that illuminate the ancient manuscripts held in Trinity College.

Only the bride looks straight at the camera, her gaze serious but steady. The same expression she wears in another picture, of four girls in their early twenties, tweed and gabardine coats over their Cumann na mBan uniforms, pointing their guns at the photographer. "Peg, Molly, Cat, Kathleen. February 1922," that one says on the back. It's a staged picture and it's shocking. And I'm held by this feeling that it — like all the other pictures here, and the diary entries, and the letter — is trying to tell me something.

Rory is behind me now, standing over me. He touches the back of my neck. "It's okay, Jo." His fingers are cold already.

"Is it?" I whisper.

"Yes," Rory says. "Everything is going to be okay now."

"Really?"

He pulls me in close and, for the first time in twenty years, we stand together, leaning into each other.

"Yes, really," he says. "You can stop worrying now. Just leave it all to me."

PART III
SWELL

1986

*G*race Jones purrs her hymn to her Jamaican Guy from two massive wall-mounted speakers, pained vocals underwritten by a pounding bass drum. At the head of the exercise class, an instructor faces the group and leads them through jumps and bends and stretches, shouting her commands to be heard above the music: "...and reach, two, three, four..."

At her bidding, nineteen people arch their arms over their heads and bounce into a waist stretch. She lifts her left knee, they lift theirs; she moves right, they all shift in the same direction, swinging their arms just as she does, half a second behind her in synchronized unison, like one multi-limbed organism.

She is fit, this Lycra-clad instructor: strong, supple and lean. She can run six miles in under forty minutes, bend from her waist to touch her nose to her knee with palms flat on the floor. She can bench-press eighty-eight pounds, leg-press one hundred and ten. While instructing her classes, she stretches further, jumps higher, lasts longer than those following her instructions, though this is the third class she has given in four hours.

Sometimes, the control she has over these people's movements bewilders her. She's tempted to do something silly or lewd — pretending to pick her nose or rub herself between her legs — just to see if they might copy her. She never does, though; she doesn't want to slight what they do together: the giving over of their bodies to the music, letting the beat drive them, push them further and faster, until every muscle is primed. When it goes well, it's a high like no other, and tonight is a good night. This group is one of her most advanced, well trained, responsive: she can push them hard. As the apex of the class approaches, as the faces contort with effort and the smell of sweat rises in the room and the ceiling-to-floor mirrors fog over from breath and perspiration, her shouts grow more excited: "Yes...and just eight more: eight...seven...push harder, that's it...and five...four...three...two...one...And again...ten...nine..."

A good class.

When it is over, after she has cooled them all down with slow stretching and breathing exercises, a short line of people forms, waiting to ask her questions or share their food or fitness dilemmas. Her friend Richard also waits, but over by the window doing extra hamstring stretches, as she works through the line, advising, counselling, consoling or deflecting.

When the last of them has gone, he comes across, pecks her on the mouth. "Terrific, as always." His grey vest is streaked with sweat. "Just what I needed."

"Oh?" She returns the kiss. "Stressed out again?"

He shudders, and she motions for him to turn round. She puts her hands on his shoulders, under the towel, just at the base of his neck. "Let me see." Her fingers slide over his damp skin, her thumbs kneading the bunched muscle underneath. "Work? Or Gary again?"

He lets a long, low groan, physical delight in her ministrations, combined with frustration. "You won't believe what the little B has done to me now."

She nips the flesh of his shoulder. "Ow! That hurt."

"Then don't talk about Gary like that."

"Wait till you hear, though. On Sunday — "

"Tell you what, hon..." She gives him a final manipulation of the trapezius and releases him. "Save it for dinner. Then you can give me the full treatment." Richard's stories are always part performance, and she enjoys the entertainment. "Hit those showers," she says, "and see you down at reception in twenty?"

This engagement for dinner after her Wednesday class has become a fixture for them both. She sees Richard on other nights too, and with other people, but Wednesday's tête-à-tête has become the bedrock of their friendship. There's no one in this city she'd rather spend time with. It was Richard who encouraged her career in fitness. When she started teaching aerobics classes part-time in a local hall she wanted to be more than just another Jane Fonda clone. As she experimented with new moves and methods, Richard urged her on. Whenever she hit on something uniquely her own, he loved it. "Don't be afraid, Squirrel," he used to say. "You're great at this; go for it."

So she did. She shunned the pure dance music used by other instructors in favour of songs by artists like Talking Heads, Marvyn Gaye, Grace Jones, songs with slow beats that allowed muscles and joints to be put through a fuller range of movement. She devised routines that took the body from its highest attainable point — leaping through the air — to lying prone on the floor and back up again, all in a series of controlled moves. To an onlooker, her class might look less strenuous than the more usual fast-stepping, high-impact workouts, but those who did the routine knew just how tough — and effective — it was.

Richard was right. The more experimental she became, the more the punters loved it. She quickly got slots in the top gyms in the city and people began to book for her class in advance, sometimes weeks ahead. Instead of taking one of the full-time jobs she was offered by the gyms, she set up her own company, Rí Rá.

"In Ireland," her publicity material read, "a rí rá is a rollicking and raucous good time. That's just what you're guaranteed with a Rí Rá Workout. A pulse-pounding, dance-based aerobic routine set to an eclectic musical mix — from Classical to Celtic Rock —

that will challenge every muscle in your body. In Ireland, a rí rá sometimes turns into an outright ruaille buaille. What's that? Well, why don't you come along and find out?"

It felt hypocritical to play on her Irishness this way, after years of renouncing the place, but Richard convinced her. "You are Irish," he said, "and if for some misbegotten reason the Irish are suddenly cool, you might as well take advantage."

She knows that other people consider what she does to be superficial, or worse. Another of her good friends, the defiantly large Susan, has put all the arguments to her. Susan is scathing about what she calls "body fascism" and carries every one of her one hundred and eighty pounds with pride, a testament to her resolution to "take up space".

Susan does not approve of exercise classes, and considers exercise instructors to be implicated — "up to their necks" — in a system that uses ideals of beauty as a weapon in the war against women. Susan's arguments sway her, but she knows too, to her core, that exercise saved her.

Often, she sees both sides of an argument; sometimes more than two. This used to worry her, until she read what the American bard of liberation, Walt Whitman, wrote in his 'Song of Myself':

Do I contradict myself?

Very well then I contradict myself

(I am large, I contain multitudes.)

She had the lines written up in large letters and framed, to hang on her wall.

She has men in her life, this woman. Lovers aplenty. Generally she loves them serially, one after another, but sometimes they overlap. Monogamy no longer seems to her like the only way to live. With so many people in her life, she is rarely lonely and if she — just sometimes — finds herself marooned in a moment of yearning, she is able to extricate herself. To catch herself on, as her grandmother used to say. She no longer believes in "The One".

She, of course, is me. I like her, this creation of mine, though I don't quite believe in her. Living in San Francisco has changed me: I am not the person I was when I arrived. If I had stayed where I was, or gone somewhere else, I would be different again. Knowing this makes me feel strange.

Conditional.

Richard and I sit at our table in Mani's, drinking "love bombs": alcohol-free cocktails of passion-fruit juice, wheatgerm and ginseng. We are both dry, one of the many things we have in common. This makes us mildly self-conscious — since its lawless, boomtown beginnings, San Francisco has been a hard-drinking town — but it's just beginning to be cool to be clean. Health is a burgeoning business and sober clubs are opening up.

Over the menus, Richard is making a tale out of his complaints against Gary. On Sunday afternoon, after an argument about Richard's staying out all night after a trip to the Glory Holes, his favourite bathhouse, Gary "flounced" out of their apartment and hasn't been seen since. The word on the gay grapevine is that at least one of those absent nights was spent with Reno Lewis, who just happens to be an old flame of Richard's.

"Reno Lewis," wails Richard, dropping his face into his hands. Under the dramatics, I know his dismay is real.

Real, but misplaced, it seems to me. For weeks — months — I have listened to Richard bemoaning Gary's predilection for monogamy as if it were a vice.

"So what's the problem?" I ask. "I thought this was what you wanted."

"Reno Lewis," he groans. "Reno Lewis."

"I'm confused," I say. "Just who are you jealous of here?"

"I'm not jealous. You know I don't do jealous."

"You're doing a good impression."

"Come on, Squirrel, keep to your script. You're my buddy. You're supposed to pat my hand, tell me I've been wronged."

"I can't, you contrary old queen. For months, Gary has

wanted you to be a couple and you insisted on your inalienable rights to visit the Glory Holes whenever you fancied. Now he's playing things your way and you're outraged."

"Ouch!" he winces.

"Why are you doing this, Richard? You two are so great together."

"And ouch again! Enough, Cruella."

Our waiter comes over, a new guy, dark hair in a pony tail, whiter than white teeth, very young. Richard and I exchange a look that says: nice, very nice. Richard has taught me how to admire men, how to look at them frankly, without fear. It helps when they are younger, as this one is. He takes our order and departs, the strings of his apron tied into a heart shape over his butt.

Richard sees me look and nudges me. "Eyes off, Squirrel, he's mine."

I groan out loud; he can always tell. "Aren't there any straight men left in this town?"

Richard laughs. I'll get no sympathy on that score, I know. And he's right, it is he who is in the minority, even here in San Francisco. I turn back to our conversation about Gary. "You know, Richard, you can't have everything."

"I don't want everything, O Heartless One. I only want..." He stops.

"Go on."

He looks over his shoulder. "Is this an X-rated restaurant?"

I laugh. "Come on, Richard, be serious. What is it that you want?"

"I am being serious. At least half the time —" he lowers his voice — 'I am the horniest man alive and all I want, all I think I'll ever want, is filthy, glorious, anonymous sex."

"And the other half?"

"The other half, I want what Gary and you and the rest of the goddamn world seems to think I should want: side-by-side TV dinners and hand-in-hand trips to the stores. Romance and undying love with one wonderful man."

"So-o-o-o, all you need is to find someone who understands all that and loves you anyway. Somebody who lets you be both."

"That's all, huh?"

"But, Richard, you have that. With Gary. At least, you had, if you haven't blown it. Your problem isn't that you want everything. It's that while you get one thing, you're longing for its opposite."

He picks up his napkin, and mine, stuffs one into each ear.

"I'm right, and you know it. While you're at home with Gary, you're wondering what's going on down the baths. After a few nights in the Glory Holes, you're thinking: what am I doing here when I could be home with that great guy of mine?"

He takes the napkins down. "While I'm at the Glory Holes, honey, thinking is about the only thing I'm not doing."

I giggle. "But I'm not altogether wrong, am I?"

"You're just telling me back what I already told you. I'm a condemned man. This isn't a phase: it's the story of my life."

He looks so miserable that I laugh. "Come on, aren't you the guy who told me that happiness is a decision?"

"Oh, that. I was only trying to cheer you up. You and I know better than that. Come on, could you ever be happy in Mucksville? Could I, in Telport?" Richard comes from a small town in the Midwest. For him, indeed for many of the people we know, home is a four-letter word.

"But we're not in Mucknamore or Telport any more," I say. "We're here, in one of the best towns in the world for people like us." I reach across and touch his hand. "Look, Richard, I just have to say one more thing, so you can't fool yourself that you don't know. If Gary wasn't scared of you leaving him, he would never have gone near this Reno Lewis. Gary is man enough to let you go prowling if that's what you need to do, once he can trust you to come home to him after you're done."

Our waiter friend comes across with our food. Richard

throws him such heavy looks that the poor boy breaks into a blush.

"New to town?" Richard asks.

"Yeah."

"Just arrived from...?"

"Minnesota."

"Well, Minnesota, we'll have to show you around a little. What time do you get off?"

The boy looks uncertain. "Eleven."

"Great."

"Em, I'm not sure..."

"Oh, I'm sorry. Pardon me if you've got better plans."

"No, it's not...It's just..."

"Tell him, Squirrel. Tell him I don't bite."

"He doesn't bite." I say, flatly. The boy looks at me, then at Richard.

"Relax, Minnesota. This is a friendly town. I'll just take you around, introduce you to a few people."

"Okay." He flashes his perfect smile. "Yeah...why not?"

He goes off to attend someone else. Richard is jubilant. "Take that, pal Gary," he says, discreetly punching the air.

Coffee arrives via another waiter and I tell Richard my news. "I got a letter from Ireland today."

"No! Not from the immovable Mom?"

"From her representative, Sister Maeve. She's coming over here for a visit."

"This, I deduce from the droop of your chin, is not a good thing?"

"Oh, Richard, you know what she's like. She only wants to come here so she can have a good snoop around my life and tell me where I'm going wrong."

"That's what big sisters do, I guess."

"She's bringing Donal with her."

His eyebrows lift into a question.

"Her husband. A suit."

"Poor Squirrel. How long will they be here?"

"Two weeks," I wail. "What will I do with them for fourteen whole days and nights?"

"I'll help you."

"Oh...okay. Thanks."

He notices my hesitation. "Unless I'm one of the things in your life that you don't want her snooping around."

"Don't be silly, Richard. It's not you, it's them."

He shakes his head. "She's a big girl."

"Yeah, my big critical sister."

"If she wants to be critical, you can't stop her. Let her be critical."

I make a face. "Come on, what if it was your mother coming to see you?"

He shudders. "That's not too likely, praise be. She can't come because she hasn't told any of her cronies I live here. She's afraid they'll put two and two together and work out why I'm not married." He takes my hand. "Just be yourself, Squirrel. Stand tall."

"I can imagine what she'll say about teaching aerobics." I stick my nose up and imitate my sister's voice at its pickiest: "'I'm sure it's fun, Jo, but it's hardly a proper job, now is it?'"

"Let her come, let her think what she wants, then let her go home again. That's all you have to do."

Richard is the only person who understands why I left Mucknamore and never went back. Why I won't get in touch with my mother or grandmother if they won't contact me. I have told him everything. He lifts my fingers, brushes them with a kiss. "You know you're fabulous, darling. If the Mucksville contingent can't see that, it's their loss."

"Thank you.' I whisper. Then, lighter: "You're right, I am fabulous."

"You are. Too, too fabulous." He looks over my shoulder. "But now," he says, "it would appear that dessert is approaching."

I follow his eyes. Our waiter is crossing to our table, white apron gone. "I got off early," he says, sliding into the chair opposite, his skin glowing with youth and promise.

I get up, leave my half of the check on the table.

"Be nice to him, okay?" I whisper into Richard's ear as I kiss him goodnight. "He's sweet."

He answers me with a horrible leer.

"Night, night," I say, to them both. "Be good."

"Honey, you know I'm the best." His chuckle follows me out into the foggy evening.

San Francisco is my city. I knew that from the moment I arrived, from my very first morning walking through Golden Gate Park, entranced by the smell of eucalyptus and sunny November skies. It was a Sunday, I remember, and the park was full of people, but it was big enough to hold us all. On my way in, I passed a circle of homeless men drinking cider around a set of bongo drums and a guitar. One of them lifted his can to me as I walked past. "You have a good one," he said, smiling, and I found myself smiling back. I couldn't help myself, he seemed so amiable. They all did, though there were eleven of them and only one of me. It was impossible to imagine passing a group of homeless men in London or Dublin and feeling so unthreatened.

I love this place, I found myself saying over and again, as I walked around it. Born out of gold and silver, built on a core of wild spending and carousing, this city that was never a small town but wild and lawless, gaudy and greedy, diverse and world famous, right from the start. In those early days I walked everywhere, getting to know my new city. The first year was difficult, hopping from job to dead-end job, apartment to dreary apartment, trapped inside a void left behind by alcohol's absence. For sanity's sake, I walked and walked — later, jogged — all around the city, up and down the unfeasible hills, through streets where music drummed out from under psychedelic blinds, through parks where grey-haired people went roller skating, through beaches where meditators worshipped the morning sun.

I revelled in the sunshine and also in the fogs that billowed in from the ocean, as if huffed through the Golden Gate by an unseen mouth. I came to love these fogs that shrouded me in a blanket of anonymity as I went, that ensured I never took the sun for granted.

I even came to love the city's faulty underpinnings: San Andreas and Hayward, San Gregorio, Greenville and Calaveras, and the earth shudders they threw up, always hinting towards the long-anticipated "Big One" that might come at any time and topple our town down on top of us, or trigger a tsunami out in the ocean, a tidal wave that would swell and swell as it swept in from the bay, rising taller than the bridges and skyscrapers it broke against, smashing them to smithereens and sweeping away the bits in its flow, like so many pebbles and twigs.

It was frightening to ponder it, especially downtown among the office towers. According to Richard, the risk of earthquake has all San Franciscans permanently on alert. With catastrophe ever imminent, better try whatever you fancy now or else die wondering. I don't fully buy the theory — I can't imagine Richard reining in his excesses, wherever he lived — but he brought me to believe in the value of vulnerability.

I hadn't been here long when I first heard the expression, "only in San Francisco." It came to be widely used afterwards — "only in Hollywood," people would say, or "only in Europe" – and usually used disparagingly, but I first heard it applied to the town I was beginning to own, and I took it as a tribute. So many things could, and did, happen only in San Francisco. This city had given the world beats and hippies, free love and flower power, multiculturalism and gay pride... Only in San Francisco, it seemed to me, was American can-do culture applied so vigorously to realms beyond the commercial.

It was on nights out with Richard that I first cracked open my inhibitions without alcohol. His frankness about matters sexual made me see how I had always stood at the border of my own desires, hesitating, playing safe, nursing my sexual disappointment while berating myself or my lover de jour. By example, Richard taught me to own my full self. By joking, he led me past fear and shame. "Forget what your mother told you about sex," he said. "Apply what she told you about olives instead."

Mrs D. never had anything to say to me about either, but I took the point: sex is an acquired taste and it takes several tries to know which particular flavours you enjoy. There are techniques and responses to learn, social as well as sexual skills to acquire. Richard showed me the way.

But it was the night he turned up at my house with his face disfigured by a gay bashing — for yes, even here in San Francisco there are bigots — that turned our affection for each other into something more. When I found him standing on my doorstep, pretending like he didn't care and brought him in to sit on my sofa and held him hard while he tried to stop his bruised face from creasing into tears, that was when I knew I loved him. With my new, San Franciscan, way of loving.

Susan I met later, and she forced herself on me. I was browsing in a bookshop when she came peering over the top of my book, two enormous brown eyes in a wide black face. "You don't want that," she said.

"Excuse me?"

"That." She pointed at the book I had in my hand: *Woman's Words, Woman's Worlds*. "You don't want it. It's just another whitey whine."

I pulled back from this intrusion, but she didn't seem to notice. "Trust me. This is the one you want." She held out another book to me. *This Bridge Called My Back*, it was called. *Writings By Radical Women of Color*.

I looked up at her. "No," I said. "I don't think so."

"Where are you from?"

"Ireland," I said, instantly regretting that I had answered. I decided to be rude and turned my back.

"I knew it," she said, coming round to my front. "I said so to myself when I saw you. But I'm reckoning on you being the right kind of Irish. That's why I'm saying to you that this here is the one you want." Again, she shoved the book towards me, and resisted as I tried to push it back. When I wouldn't take it from her hands, she carried it across to the checkout. "The lady will take this," she said, pointing across at me.

Now I was annoyed. I worked in a bar back then, a down-at-heel place where the tips were poor and given out once a week with our pay packs. That day I had less than $5 in my purse and, if I bought that book, I wouldn't eat again until payday.

Susan saw my expression and opened her purse. "Here." She handed $20 to the assistant.

"No," I protested "Stop."

"I'm making you do this, honey," Susan said, taking her change. "So don't waste no time feeling bad. But I do have a condition. You've got to call me when you've read it and tell me your opinion." She was writing down her number for me on the paper wrapping. "But you'll like it," she said, handing over the scrap of paper. "Yeah, I'm getting the feeling I know just what you like."

I caught the hint in her voice, enough to make me wonder if she meant what I later learned she did. By the time I knew for sure, I didn't recoil from the notion as I would have on that first day. By then, I knew Susan well enough to be glad that, if she had been mistaken in that, she was right about the book. And about lots of other things too.

It was a great book, just what I needed to read at that time. I had always held that any self-respecting woman had to be a feminist, and living in more than one place had taught me that each culture has its own particular ways of keeping its women under. Just as I was getting used to this idea of a pan-national, trans-historical sisterhood, the essays in this book — by Afro-, Asian-, Latin- and Native-American women — complicated that idea. The essays were eloquent, passionate and thought-provoking, and made me see how I benefited from having white skin. For the first time in my life, I saw myself as a person of relative privilege.

When I telephoned — or called, as I was learning to say — to tell Susan so, she squealed with delight. "I knew it," she cried, her voice an even deeper shade of chocolate over the telephone. "I knew you were the right kinda Irish."

I said, "I don't know what you mean by that."

"Your people come in two types, honey: those who pretend like there never was an attitude that said 'No Blacks, No Irish', the ones like to put as much distance as they can between their black brothers and sisters and their own white, lily-livered asses. Then there's the kind who've learned somethin' more from their own persecution than how to do the same thing to others."

Susan made me quail, still does. I've never had the energy, or maybe the courage, for her kind of stern, one-track anger. All my emotions are mixed. But we talked for a long time on the telephone that first evening and at the end of the call she asked if I would like to come with her on Monday night to Joni's, a woman-only health spa on Polk that hosted CR sessions three times a week.

CR?

What? I had never heard of Consciousness-Raising? I was going to love it. They were a great group of women and they talked about everything, everything, exploring how their personal dilemmas were politically rooted. There used to be hundreds of such spaces all over this town, but in recent years, she didn't know why, they were closing down, little lights going out.

The spa was in what looked like an old factory building. There was no elevator and we walked up three flights of rickety stairs to be met at the top by a dainty Latina woman, about forty years old, wearing a buttonhole that said: Cunt Power! She hugged Susan and then they both turned to me and she said, "Welcome, Jo, I'm Dolores," and kissed my cheek. Her lips were dry, powdery, and she smelled of something herbal. "Susan has been telling me all about you."

The same smell permeated the lemon-and-lavender-striped corridor they steered me through. "Susan tells me you liked Bridge," Dolores said, taking my arm.

"Yes."

"I'm so glad. It's a really seminal book, I think."

"Shouldn't that be 'ovumnal', sweetheart?" Susan called from behind us.

"Hey, that's a great word," smiled Dolores over our shoulders. "Ovumnal. I love that." She turned back to me. "Have you ever done a naked consciousness-raising before, Jo?"

"Naked?"

"Oh, sorry," said Susan, breaking into peals of laughter behind us. "Did I not mention the naked?"

"Please do not mind her, Jo." Dolores's arm locked mine, propelled me onwards. "It is all very non-threatening. Very gentle and supportive. The idea is we present ourselves to each other in all our vulnerability. We take off our inhibitions with our clothes."

In the spa room, three women were already in the jacuzzi pool. "This is Gloria," said Dolores. "And Zoe. And Arlene. Women, this is Jo."

"Hi, Jo," the three responded, together.

Gloria was fortyish and black, Zoe was my age, white with dreadlocked hair, and Arlene, also white, was much older than the rest. That was all I had time to notice as Dolores led us through to the dressing room. In the time it took me to hang my jacket on the hook and unzip my bag, Susan had her clothes off and was parading around the dressing room, her towel trailing from her fingers. The vast expanse of her body drew me out of my own self-consciousness. Furrows of fat cascaded from beneath the bowls of her breasts. Her girth was frightening, each thigh the size of an average waist. She seemed like a parody of a fat woman, the sort you see in cartoon postcards, with feet that looked too small to support her. Gross and magnificent, she postured around the room.

Meanwhile, I slinked out of my clothes and let her lead the way back to the pool. I held my head up and managed not to use my hands to cover myself. I wasn't normally prudish, but the artificiality of the situation, the weighing of our nakedness with meaning, made me want to grab the nearest towel and run.

One after each other, we slid into the pool. Everyone else's breasts were held above the water line so I let mine do the same. The water bubbled and the underlying drone of the pump was soothing, but my thighs clutched the smooth plastic of the seat, unable to relax. Dolores opened the session by introducing and welcoming me, then outlining the rules of the coming conversation. We must suspend judgement. We must listen with respect, seeking to understand rather than persuade. We must speak freely and with sincerity of what has personal heart and meaning. The topic for today would be our experiences with the medical profession.

"Before we get started," said Arlene, "I just thought y'all might like to know that I did it."

"Way hey, girl!" cackled Susan. "And did you find what you went looking for?"

"Tell us everything, Arlene," says Dolores. "Everything. Did you buy the hand mirror?"

"Uh-huh."

"And you took it to your bedroom?"

"Bathroom."

"Ran a bath?"

"Mmm."

"Lit candles?"

"Yes."

"Good," said Dolores. "Candles are good. Low, gentle light."

"Arlene is — or looks like we can finally say was — a masturbation virgin," Susan explained to me.

"Oh," I said.

Arlene reclaimed the conversation, told how she had also bought — she quivered at her daring — some female erotica. And then she...you know...um...down there...

"Not 'down there', Arlene," said Dolores. "Come on now."

'Touched my...vagina," Arlene whispered.

Dolores clapped her hands. "Well done, Arlene." Gloria and Zoe joined in.

Susan was unimpressed. "Can we be a bit more specific?" she asked, melting Arlene's expression of triumph. "It wasn't your 'vagina' you were aiming at, was it?"

Furrows erupted on Arlene's forehead. She began to bite her lower lip.

"Christ, girl! Ain't you ever going to say cunt?" said Susan.

"I don't want to say that word, I've told you."

"Now, Arlene, we've discussed this," said Dolores. "We have to embrace all the words. We have to reclaim our bodies, especially our sexual organs, from patriarchal disfigurement. We have to own ourselves and love ourselves."

"Well, I can't help it," Arlene said. "I just hate that word."

Dolores reached across, put a hand on her shoulder. "You've been conditioned to hate it, remember? Remember last week, when we talked about the word 'country'?"

Arlene nodded.

"You don't hate that word, do you?"

She shook her head.

"It's only a collection of letters, Arlene. If you hate it, what you're feeling is hatred of women. You have to break that in yourself."

"I used to be the same, Arlene," said Zoe. "But now I'm totally able to say any of 'em. Pussy! Vagina!"

"Labia!" said Gloria, cupping handfuls of water and throwing them in the air. "Vulva!"

"Men have plenty of names for their genitalia, Arlene," Dolores said. "And none of them is vague."

"Too right," said Susan. "No fear of them mixing up their

prick and their balls. 'Down there'? I mean, Jesus! It's the 1980s."

"Hold on," said Zoe. "She did say 'vagina'."

"Don't any of you want to hear," Arlene said, pulling herself up into the dignity of her years, "what happened?"

Dolores was contrite. "Of course we do. Come on, everybody, this is Arlene's time to talk."

"But, honey," said Susan, "until she starts naming names, we can't even be sure what she's talking about." She laughed so hard she swallowed some jacuzzi water, while Arlene looked like she might cry.

"It's okay, Arlene," said Gloria. "You take your time. You'll say it in a minute, won't you? When you're ready?"

But she didn't. And afterwards, I found myself beside her in the dressing room while Susan and Dolores were showering. She said to me: "This is your first time here, isn't it?"

I nodded.

"I hope you weren't offended by that talk earlier."

"No." I shook my head. "No, I wasn't offended."

"It's hard at the beginning. After my first time, I was so shocked I stayed away for weeks, but something made me come back."

I dried between my toes.

"I'm still a bit overwhelmed, as you've probably gathered," she went on. "I sometimes have to fight myself not to put my hands over my ears."

"I'm not surprised," I say, with feeling.

"Oh, I'm so glad to hear you say that, I always feel like it's just me."

"Definitely not." I said, smiling back. "Just don't report me to Susan."

"She's formidable, isn't she? But kind too, very kind. I've seen that in her." She zips open her bag, starts to put on her underwear beneath her towel. "But you know, I wish they hadn't gone on about the words again. They didn't give me a chance to tell them how grateful I feel."

"Grateful?"

"To have found it." She beams a smile so beatific you'd think it was God she'd found. "After sixty-three years of being ignored, there it was. And still...still in working order."

We are both smiling now.

"I knew it must be something, from the way you young people are always going on. But, oh my!"

"1923," I find myself saying.

"I beg your pardon?"

"You were born in 1923?"

"Yes, that's right, dear. You must be very good at math."

"No, it's just...You're the same age as my mother."

"Is that so? You must bring her along next time."

"Oh, no," I say and the way she looks at me tells me I've been over-vehement. "I can't. She lives in Ireland."

"That's a pity. But maybe she's more advanced than me?"

"Oh, no," I say again. "She's Irish."

"Then bring her when she comes to visit you. Tell her what happens here. Tell her about me: sixty-three years old and..." She drops her voice to a whisper. "...I can't get enough of myself."

Richard loves this story when I bring it home to him, but he doesn't like much else about the group. Whenever I ever try to get him to acknowledge the links between gays and women, he ostentatiously yawns. "Don't be a bore, Squirrel," he'll say. Or "I've told you before, political is so not your colour."

This is ironic, because in the group I am considered not political enough. Susan, in particular, thinks me hopeless: I wear short skirts, I defuzz my armpits — I teach aerobics, for pity's sake. She wrinkles her nose at all this, and implies that she would probably find it unacceptable in anybody else. Mostly I ignore this unasked-for indulgence — Susan needs her convictions, I am glad to have lost mine.

But I don't like when she starts on Richard. "He's a woman-hater," she says. "Can't you see that?"

"He doesn't hate me. And I am a woman, am I not?"

To him I say, "Susan says I'm a fag hag."

"At least she didn't say fruit fly."

"She says gay men despise women."

"That's her idea of a chat-up line, Squirrel. She thinks you find it seductive."

"No, she doesn't. She knows I'm straight."

Though she thinks I shouldn't be. For Susan, lesbianism is political choice as well as a sexual preference. Men fragment female unity, she says, and heterosex always puts men first. I take her point, but I won't be taking it any further. I shrink from real breasts, smooth faces, soft skin. Men are easily pleased, but don't women always find each other wanting?

So I call my sexual orientation straight and refuse to choose between Susan and Richard. In my new, busy life, I want them both and all the people they bring with them and the other friends I am making in work and other places and the dear companionship of the city itself, its parks full of the rolling beat of bongos, its head shops selling drug paraphernalia, its kaleidoscopic street murals, its pride marches and street demos, the blue theatre of its bay. Still now, three years on, walking across Golden Gate Bridge at sundown thrills me: the glowing, pink-white buildings undulating against the hills down to the sea.

I know as I walk that I am on the "Bridge of Sighs", the "Golden Leap", the best-known suicide site in the Western World, where more than a thousand named people have jumped to their deaths, and countless more have jumped unrecorded, at night or through fog, into the strong current that runs oceanward beneath, into the sharks feeding there and beyond.

I know the homeless in the streets and parks are as broken here as anywhere else, but still. Still, for me, the tourist cliché of this city viewed from the bridge, or this bridge viewed from the city, is a wondrous sight.

But now my sister is coming here to see it. Why do I feel that once she does, its light will dim in me?

1995

*I*t is my week for visitors. At four in the afternoon, I look up from my desk and find Rory's wife is standing at the door looking in at me. A thought jumps into my head: You're too late. Too late by one day.

"I'm sorry to be doing this to you," she says.

Then don't, I think. Don't do it.

Her face is impassive, but I can read embarrassment, though she is not blushing. She doesn't have the complexion for blushing.

"Can I...er, come in?"

I want to say no, but I push my chair back instead, bring her through to the back to sit on the grass where Maeve and I went before. She is better looking than I realised: hair highlighted blonde, body exercised and groomed, good clothes. Not unlike my sister, in fact. For the first time this summer, I feel scruffy in my shorts and T-shirt.

I take Hilde's chair. "Pregnancy privilege," I say, waving at the rug.

"Of course," she agrees, awkwardly folding herself down. "How are you feeling?" A polite enquiry, woman to woman.

"Fine, never better actually. Just tired of looking like a baby elephant."

"What stage are you at?"

"Six months."

"You don't look it at all. That's probably from the jogging, is it?"

"I've no idea."

The conversation dries. After the interval grows too, too awkward, I say: "You better tell me why you're here."

She opens her mouth, falters, takes a deep breath, tries again. When she still can't find the right words, she shakes her head. "I'm beginning to think I shouldn't have come."

You shouldn't, I say in my head. You really shouldn't. What a thing to do to us all.

Eventually she says, "I've come because I want to know the answer to two questions and it seems like you're the only one who can give them to me." But she stops again, trying not to cry.

Well, I'm not going to be the one to speak. I don't have to. I plead fifth amendment.

The silence stretches and stretches until it feels like it's going to snap, then she says in a rush: "What I want to ask you is...Is your baby Rory's?"

"No!" Whatever I'd expected, it wasn't that. "How could it be?"

Her shoulders slump and I see how tension has been holding her rigid.

"I'm almost seven months pregnant. You must know I've only been here since May."

"He was away for a few days in February, on a golf trip. I thought maybe...?"

"The day we met at my mother's funeral was the first time I saw Rory in twenty years."

Things must be bad between them if that's what she thought. And things must have been bad before I came along. A golf trip:

I try not to shudder. She is making me part of something detestable.

"Your other question?" Let's get this over with, let's get her gone.

This one takes even longer to dredge up and out. "Do you want him?"

"Want him?" I echo, foolishly.

"Yes. I need to know. How serious is it? How far has it gone?"

I look at her, aghast. Oh no, my dear, that is a question for your husband, not me. She looks back at me, and whatever she sees makes her face fall into her hands.

"Oh God!" she says through splayed fingers. "It's true."

"Listen, this isn't fair —"

"Are you serious about him?" she asks, in a small and broken voice. "Or is this just a fling for you?"

"Now see here —"

"Please, you must tell me. I need to know. Do you want him for good or do you intend to move on?"

I don't like her categories. To listen to her, you wouldn't know that we existed before she ever came along.

"Rory and I have a history," I say, in a voice that surprises me with its calm.

"I know all about that."

"No," I say, stung by her tone, "What you know is Rory's version of our history. Just like I know his version of your marriage."

She winces and the sick look on her face dissolves my scorn. "I'm sorry, I shouldn't have said that," I say. "He hardly talks about you, to tell the truth."

I am trying to make amends but that doesn't sound much better. I love him, is what I want to scream. I love him. He was mine first. Go away.

"I don't suppose he does." She looks at me and a lighter look, not quite a smile, comes swimming into her misery. "He talks about himself, right?"

That surprises me. I look fully at her for the first time and, in our exchanged expressions, Rory shrinks a little. Suddenly, her questions seem to be for me, as well as her. We both sit quiet, thinking our thoughts, until she says: "I do want him."

"You've got to tell him that, not me. I just —"

She frowns. "I know, I know that. But before talking to him, it would help if I knew your plans. Are you going to stay here?"

"No."

"I don't mean here," she says, indicating the shed. "Obviously you can't go on living here."

"I knew what you meant."

"So you're leaving Ireland?"

"I think so. Probably. Yes."

"When?"

"Soon."

"Before the baby?"

I resent her questions, questions I wouldn't answer from anybody else. So what bond between us makes me answer her?

"No, not until afterwards. It costs a fortune to have a child in the States."

She hangs her head. "If you want him, he'll go with you."

"I wouldn't be so sure."

She nods, her face miserably certain. "I'm too available. I should go off and have an affair myself, shake him up."

That is how she persists in seeing me: the affair. And I suppose that is what I am. She and the children are his base. Having them allows him the luxury of thinking he wants more.

I look away from her resentful face, out to sea. The sun shines and the cloud clusters are light and fleecy, but yesterday's rainstorm changed the weather. It's a few degrees lower today and something in the light says that the best is over for this year. Tonight, it will get dark earlier than last night, and tomorrow earlier again. I gaze, trying to imprint the sea's serenity on my brain, trying to calm the emotions this woman is stirring with her audacity.

"It's nice here," she says, following my eyes. "Sitting here, I can see what attracted you."

"It was what I needed at this time."

"Are you over the worst?"

I look at her, puzzled.

"Your mother's death," she says.

"Yes, I'm over the worst of that," I say.

"It's a pity you didn't get to see her, before she died."

In other circumstances, we might have been able to have a real talk. She has listener's eyes and I'm beginning to see that she is not as insipid as she looks, as she has trained herself to be. But I cannot let us connect. Already we have gone too far.

"I'd better go," she says, realising it too. She stands, pulls her jeans straight. "Look, I'm sorry for coming here...for doing this." She's not able to look at me. "You must think I'm like that desperate woman in that country-and-western song: 'I'm beggin' of you, pleeeez don't take my man.'"

"I don't think that."

"I am that pathetic, I know I am. But —" She breaks off, looks wretched. "He won't talk to me any more. This seemed to be the only way I could find out...anything." Tears rise. "Oh, God, no, I'm sorry." She fumbles in her bag. "I should never have done this. I'm sorry." By the time she's found a tissue, she has got control and no longer needs it. She holds it helplessly, reluctant to leave. "I feel like such a fool."

The sea turns over, wave after wave. Go, I think. Please. Just go.

"We were happy...If we don't...It's the children, more than anything..."

I say, "Talk to him."

She nods into her tissue, blows her nose, then brings her eyes up to mine. "How did you get to be so strong?" she asks.

"Me? Strong?"

"I thought at the beginning, when you came first, that you must be half crazy to be holing yourself up here, like this. But you're not, you..." She lets the words trail off. "Once upon a time I was strong," she says. "It was a word my mother always used to use to describe me."

I look at her jagged face, the fingers grasping at frayed tissue. Maybe, I think, but you are also fragile. As am I. And Rory too.

We are all, all of us, so fragile.

1986

*I*t's September when Maeve comes to stay. The wind blows from the north and the light of the city is so clear that she says she feels her eyes ping whenever she looks out at the shimmery bay. Both she and Donal love San Francisco and are awed by my loft apartment with its grey industrial carpet, its steel racks and track lighting. Relying on Richard, I decide my tactic will be to play up my difference. So I put them sleeping on a futon, feed them sushi and noodles, make little jokes about the Irish way of doing things.

It's petty — and I hate myself while I'm doing it — but I can't help it. I want Maeve to be impressed. I want her to see that there is more than one way to be.

I take them to do all the touristy things I never do: ferries to Alcatraz and Sausalito, sunbathing on China Beach, over-eating in Fisherman's Wharf, snapping Golden Gate Bridge from Marian Green. Richard brings us on a voyeuristic tour of Folsom Street and the Castro. And, at Donal's request, after a book-buying session in City Lights, we go on to an Irish bar so he can have "a decent pint of Guinness."

Another night, I take them to Ice, one of the new café-bars in the Castro. While Donal is ordering drinks, a leering queen gives him the eye. "Don't look now," I smirk, "but I think you've made a conquest." He turns and rebounds in horror off the dissolute, painted face that blows him a kiss.

"Jaysus," he says. "That isn't a woman, is it?"

"Loosen up, darling," Maeve says, delighted to be the cooler one for once.

Maeve decides she'd like to do one of my classes. She has been doing aerobics herself, she says, twice a week in her local hall in Rathfarnam. I bring her to Blues, the premier gym, confident that the best Dublin has to offer will not compete. In our leotards, I see my body is better than hers now, firmer. She still has bigger breasts, and face-wise there's no contest, but the comparison doesn't sting in the old way. She's wrong here. It's not just her clothes and hair, but something in her: the difference between somebody who has lived away from home and somebody who hasn't.

All the way through the class she beams at me, and when we're finished I don't have to ask if she enjoyed it. "It's really different," she says, her face flushed. "Fantastic."

Fantastic is her word for everything San Franciscan, though she's surprised I don't know more Irish people. The 1980s have been tough in Ireland and the Irish are pouring into the States again. There are fifty thousand Irish-Americans in San Francisco, Maeve tells me, and on our trips around the city, she always finds one to talk to. She and Donal get excited when they see the Irish flag hanging from St Patrick's. They buy copies of The Irish Herald. They ask me about the St Patrick's Day parade.

I move away from her chats with these strangers. I don't feel kinship with these immigrants clustering in their pubs or parishes here, any more than I did in London. I don't like that the Irish contribution to American culture is green beer and bigoted parades. I don't like how, since ten IRA prisoners starved themselves to death in Northern Ireland to win political status, an Irish political lobby is growing more vocal in the Bay Area, popping up in bars all over, singing rebel songs and thinking themselves on the cutting edge of The Cause as money for guns and bombs gets dropped in a fund-raising box. And I don't like when another Irish person hears my accent and tries to claim me.

My community is those who think like me, not those who happen to have been born on the same small island. Or in the same small house. I have found people who love me, really love me, not like Maeve — in spite of what I am — but because of it. As I put it recently in a magazine article I wrote, friends are the new family.

But how can I say such a thing to my sister?

To my surprise, Maeve and Richard get on well. He and Gary take us to Troopers, a bisexual club with an indulgent attitude to extra-dancing activities. The four of us spend the night on the dance floor while Donal minds the drinks. As we walk home afterwards, fog swirling white around the streetlights, I link Richard and Gary, and let Maeve and Donal walk on ahead.

"She's fab," Richard says.

"Mutual admiration all round," I say. "She thinks you two are great too."

"You gave her a lousy billing," Gary says.

"She seems different here."

Richard looks at me and I squeeze his arm. "Okay, okay, maybe I see her different here."

"And Hubby coped with Troopers."

"I'd say Maeve spoke to him before we went out."

"I'll never forget his face when Mona gave him the treatment," says Gary. Mona is a butch friend of Gary's who likes to shock: tonight she was wearing nothing but straps around bare breasts under her leather jacket, so she could show off a nipple-ring. She honed in on Donal for the night, as arranged by the guys.

Richard says: "I reckon Hubby would be quite a goer if you could crack the frozen exterior."

"Yeah. Anyone that hung up has got to be repressing like mad," smiles Gary, the psychologist.

Richard nudges him. "Hey, maybe we should see if we can unleash his inner slut."

"Richard!" I warn. "Don't even think about it."

They come back to my apartment for coffee. Donal goes to bed but Maeve stays up, sitting on the chair opposite Richard and Gary, talking about San Francisco's gay culture. I keep the kitchen hatch open, half-listening as I fix coffee. Maeve's feet are curled under her in the chair and her opinions are coming out harder now she's relaxing. As I listen, I decide I prefer her ill at ease. It keeps that damned certainty of hers at bay.

As I put the coffee down in front of them, Gary is telling her that for the past years, five thousand gays a week have been moving to the Bay Area, the greatest influx of immigrants since the gold rush.

"Freedom," he says. "A bigger prize than any precious metal."

"Tell me," Maeve says, with the air of someone breaking a taboo, "why do gays all dress the same and act the same?"

"Do they?" I try to catch her eye as I hand her coffee, stop her in the track I can see she's about to lay.

"It seems that way to me, like there's a uniform of clothes and —"

"Biker gear for the leather-men," I say, trying to head her off. "And crotch-clutching Levi's, flannel shirts and work boots for the rest."

We all laugh because that is what both Richard and Gary are wearing. "The same thing happens in my women's group."

Richard groans. "Oh, no, not the politico-dykes, Squirrel. Not at this hour of the night."

"It does seem to go that way, though," I say, thinking of Susan. "One minute a woman starts making connections between male power and the events of her own life: next thing, she's getting her hair chopped and buying dungarees."

Maeve nods, sagely, and though I don't believe we're on the same side, I go on. "I have wondered about that sometimes, why so many people swap one set of codes and rules for another. Especially people who've been so bruised by rules."

Gary smiles at me. "Not everyone is brave enough to go it alone, hon."

"It's not just clothes, though, is it?" Maeve says. "It's the way they go on."

Richard's eyes narrow. "And how do 'they' go on?"

"Sorry, you know what I mean. I'm not being bad, I just don't understand the obsession with sex all the time. Like that girl, Mona, tonight. It seems so out of proportion."

"Whoa there, Maeve," Gary says, gently. "Don't you think you're generalising a little?"

"What about the keys and hankies and all of that?"

Gay cruising gear. I told her about this the other day, when she asked me about the bandanas she noticed hanging from rear pockets.

When nobody says anything, she goes on. "And the thoughts of those places where you don't even see the person you're having sex with." She shivers. "I'm sorry, it gives me the creeps. I can't help it."

"It's the Roman Catholic in you," Richard says. "You need deprogramming."

Maeve shakes her head, her mouth tightening over her coffee cup. "Personally, I think it's a male thing. Men are afraid of intimacy."

How can she say that, having met Mona? I wish she could have been here for the last Freedom Day Parade and seen the Dykes on Bykes or the Ladies Against Women, carrying their signs — "Recriminalize Hanky Panky" and "Suffering not Suffrage" — or the leather-women strapped and handcuffed to each other in all kinds of bizarre positions, showing the world something that seems to me to be truer and braver than Susan's brand of one-fits-all, earnest lesbianism. Or Maeve's one-fits-all, earnest hetero-ism.

Like so many straights, Maeve thinks she has nothing to

learn from the lessons gay people are bringing back from the sexual front line.

I yearn for her to shut up before she says something even worse. The other night she was quizzing me about "the gay cancer" and looked completely dubious when I argued that there wasn't any such thing, that AIDS also afflicted drug addicts and blood-transfusion recipients and Haitian refugees and others. I feel tainted by her ignorance. But I shouldn't. She is not me.

"Are you sure it's not you who's afraid?" Richard asks her.

"Of course I'm not. I'm —"

"Afraid of sex, I mean. Proper sex: the low-down, dirty variety." He runs a look down the length of her body and back up. "Have you ever had it really good, honey? I mean really good?"

My sister blushes and I feel sorry for her, but she asked for it.

"Richard is right, Maeve," I say. "Sex is sex, intimacy is intimacy. It's perfectly possible to have one without the other."

Richard and I have shared a bed, spent nights together on my couch wrapped around each other while we watch TV. I've told him things I haven't told some beloved lovers.

"But the two together," insists my sister. "That's best of all."

"Best for what?" pounces Richard. "Best for who?"

She shrugs, her face red and set, defeated by our unity but unconvinced. Gary, kind Gary, tries to ease the tension. "You know, Maeve, I don't think you're acknowledging the reality of being gay. After years of trying to conform, don't you think it's natural that some of us act like kids let loose in a candy store when we're allowed to be truly ourselves for the first time?"

"Maybe," Maeve says, doubtfully.

"All that guilt and self-alienation has to find an outlet," Gary says.

"Oh, puh-leaze," says Richard. "Spare us the psycho-babble. Sex rocks, is all."

· · ·

WHEN SHE'S LEAVING, Maeve packs copies of the Chronicle, Fitness World and Zoe that have articles of mine. "They'll want to see them at home," she says. "Mammy will be delighted. They all will."

Ah, here it comes. I was wondering if we were actually going to get to the end of her visit without it. I'm leaning on her suitcase, while she tries to fasten the clasps. When I make no response, she says, without looking at me: "Have you any message you want me to pass on?"

"Did she send one to me?"

She sighs, shakes her head. "God, but there's a pair of you in it." I make a face at that.

"Look, Jo, I know she wasn't the easiest of mothers, but I find it hard to imagine what she could possibly have said or done to you that you could cut her off completely like this."

"Maeve, don't —"

"To just walk away like that, and never come back...Not even to write..."

I'm not going to have this conversation, because she doesn't really want it; she only thinks she does. Nobody in Ireland wants to look too closely at why so many leave and whether it's really about jobs. Those who can bear living there don't want to know the truth about those who can't. At Christmas, I'm told, they make a great show of welcoming the emigrants "home", Dublin Airport doing itself up with Céad Mile Fáilte signs. "A Hundred Thousand Welcomes." So long as you're gone again in the new year.

Maeve would like me to be one of those, but she asks too much. It's too lop-sided.

If Gran had written...I'd have done it for Gran. But she made her choice all those years ago and I don't blame her. Mrs D. made it impossible for her to do otherwise.

Perhaps I should tell my sister the truth: I left to have an abortion, Maeve. And I never went back because, well, I couldn't, could I? I couldn't pretend to you and Mrs D. and everyone else that the biggest thing in my life had never happened. And I couldn't tell you the truth, you all made sure of that. So I — like hundreds of thousands of others — came away and stayed away.

"Was it that she broke up your relationship with Rory O'Donovan?" Maeve asks. "Was that it?"

I make my face blank.

She tries again. "I don't know what went on that night you left, Jo, and maybe Mammy did say or do something so terrible that you just can't forgive her. But what I can't understand...what I really can't understand...is why do you never write to Gran? Why do you never ring me back? I often feel if I didn't contact you, I'd never hear from you again."

"Maeve, leave it. Please. Let's not ruin everything on your last day. We've had such a good time."

She sighs again, folds the magazines away in her suitcase. "We have had a good time, haven't we?"

"We have," I say, meaning it. "We really have."

1923

PEG'S DIARY 12TH NOVEMBER: We were hardly out of the beds this morning when Mrs O'Donovan called, sand all over her boots. She'd come the back way up the strand like Norah used to when sneaking down to us. Wariness had her hunched, her black shawl was drawn in around her. The look on her face said she'd rather be anywhere else in the world than at our back door.

"How is she?" the old woman asked, not saying her daughter's name, and I invited her in to see for herself. Both of us were full of the memory of the last time we faced each other like this, when the boot was on the other foot. I was determined to treat her better than she had treated me and felt a need to warn her before she opened the kitchen door. "You'll find her quiet in herself."

"She was always a quiet girl."

"Not like this."

Norah was in the fireside chair that used to be mine, before all the changes to our household. The chair was in the middle of the floor, looking like a raft in the middle of a pale linoleum sea. She had a blanket across her knees and beside her, on a small table, were a blank copybook and a pen. I had provided this:

after talking to the doctor about the way she liked to scribble, I thought it might be some comfort to her. So far, however, she hasn't picked up the pen.

Since she arrived, she's done nothing but sit silent in this armchair, either turned towards the fire to look into the flames, or in the opposite direction to look out the window towards the sea. She will come to the table when bidden or do any small chore she is asked to do. Otherwise she sits, still and silent.

She didn't get up, or even turn her head, as we entered.

"Your mother has come to see you, Norah," I said, while Mrs O'Donovan squeezed herself into the chair opposite.

Silence.

"You're looking well," Mrs O'Donovan was half-shouting for some reason, as if it was Norah's ears that were affected.

Silence.

"Looks like they fed you enough anyway."

I marvelled at how still Norah could hold herself, not even the movement of her breath in her chest to be seen. After receiving neither gesture nor reply, Mrs O'Donovan looked across to me.

I knelt in front of Norah, trying to look her in the eye. "Norah, are you not going to talk to your mammy?"

Nothing. Just pale, set eyes in a pale, set face.

Mrs O'Donovan frowned. "Maybe, if you were to leave us on our own?"

I wasn't a bit keen on this idea, but how could I refuse to leave her with her own mother? I looked to Norah. If she objected, wild horses wouldn't drag me from that room, but she gave me nothing to go on. Not a flicker.

So, reluctantly, I moved towards the door. Go easy on her, I wanted to say, but of course I couldn't.

"I'll be outside if you want me," I said instead.

I stood right outside the door, leaning my forehead against it, but I could hear nothing. I knew how Mrs O'Donovan was feeling. It's hard to see the girl so. My hope is that once the baby comes, things will improve.

The sound of a voice raised came through the door, breaking my thoughts. "Answer me, won't you?"

I went back in. Mrs O'Donovan was standing over Norah like she was a badly behaved child. "Surely to God you'll not let me go without a word? After I coming down here to see you?"

Underneath Norah's bright hair, her face was as washed out as a bleached rag. I knew what a mine of stubbornness lay under that weary surface, so I drew Mrs O'Donovan away, towards the door. "It's not meant personal. She talks to no one at the moment. It's part of her trouble."

She looked at me, like a bewildered animal. "What should I do?"

"Give her time."

"I can't come again."

So we were still forbidden territory. "Let's see how we get on," I said. "Everything should get easier with time."

She drew her shawl tighter in around herself.

"I'm sure Norah is grateful you came. Aren't you, Norah?" I didn't really expect an answer and I didn't get one.

"Grateful, is it?" said Mrs O'Donovan. "Grateful, by God."

She turned to go and noticed for the first time the big black perambulator that I had brought down from the attic the day before. This is the pram that wheeled me about, as a child. And Barney too. It's old-fashioned and a bit battered, but clean and well-polished after the work I put into it, and it's well up to the job. Mrs O'Donovan looked at it like it was a weapon and, without warning, her head dropped into her shawl and she started to cry. I didn't know where to look.

"May God forgive her is all I can say." The shoulders under the shawl were shaking. "May God forgive you, Norah."

Later.

Since her mother left, Norah has been non-stop writing in the copybook I bought her. The doctor in the asylum had told me about her doing this. "It's pure gibberish she writes," he'd said. This was my first time to see her in action. The concentration she brings to the task is ferocious, her whole self gathered up in the physical act of writing. Her face looked clearer as she wrote, more like herself.

All through the day she kept this up in fits and starts. While we were having our meals, she kept the notebook on her lap the whole time and, afterwards, when we were sitting round the fire with Mammy and Daddy, she sat on top of it. Later when Mammy and Daddy had gone off — one to bed, the other to work — I spoke to her about the way she keeps hiding the book.

"You don't have to worry that anybody will read what you write, Norah," I said. "Nobody in this house would go near it." She didn't reply and didn't change her behaviour either, keeping the book close, bringing it with her whenever she went out of the room and upstairs with her at bedtime, no doubt to sleep with it under the pillow.

It does no harm, but I wish she had more trust in me. I, of all people, would never read somebody else's private writing. I know how I'd feel if somebody read mine.

DIARY, 13TH NOVEMBER: Sunday Mass this morning. Norah didn't want to go, and who could blame her? I had explained all to her last night, that we have to face them down from the first — that if we stayed away today, it would be even harder next week and then we'd never be able to go at all, but when I went in to call her, she made as if she didn't know I was there.

I had a jug of hot water with me and I poured it into the basin and then spoke firmly to her, so there could be no mistake.

"Norah," I said, "I'm only going to say this once and after that you can make up your own mind. I think you should go to Mass and not be hiding up here like a criminal. We need God on our side, Norah. If we can't even face a trip to Mass, what will He think of us? I'm going to leave you now. If you come down dressed, I'll know you're coming, and if you stay up here, that's grand. Nobody will say a cross word to you, I promise. I'll just go ahead with Mammy and we'll see you when we get back."

I went down, praying she'd find it in herself to do the right thing. And she did. I was finishing off the drying when she came in, hat and coat on, ready to go. It was hard for her walking down that road, hard for myself too, but she just closed herself off the way she does and greeted nobody. Mammy and I did as we'd planned, smiled and said hello to the staring face of whoever we met along the way, the same smile and hello we'd give if Norah was not with us, then moved on quickly before they had time to act on their curiosity. It was easier than it would have been one time. Between those who won't talk to us because of the war just gone, and those who are afraid to approach us because of Mammy's illness, we don't have so many wanting to chat.

We made it into the chapel without any scene arising and took our seats in the usual place. The O'Donovans were not yet there and we were waiting for them, knowing well that everybody else around us was doing the same. With only a minute to go, they came. I knew without turning round in the pew that they'd arrived by the change of atmosphere in the crowd. The attention of everybody in that chapel was flying between us to them and back again. Mrs O'Donovan and the family sat into the same spot as usual, three seats behind us. The father stayed at the back, with the old boys, the way he always does.

Then Father John came out onto the altar, eyes flickering about the place, on the hunt. When they alighted on Norah, he gave her —and me and Mammy as well — such a look. He held it on us for ages and I have to say I didn't think it was very Christian behaviour, standing up there like that with his eyes going through us like two bullets for all to see.

Somehow we got through it and, after it was over, we got out as fast as we could without seeming to rush. In the yard, we were headed off by Lil Hayes who came over, and in front of everyone stopped us. "I'm glad to see you back home among friends, Norah," she said, in a big, loud voice.

I was so embarrassed, though of course it was a generous gesture. Lil walked back home with us, giving everybody we passed a look of defiance as if daring them to say a word. The walk from the chapel never felt as long and once we got back inside our front door, we all fell apart.

Lil started us off, doing an imitation of Mrs Sinnott's face. "What's this I see before me, a piece of dirt?" she said, wrinkling up her nose. "My old fella has an eye for every woman, young or old, this side of Waterford, so it's grand for me to have someone else to criticise."

She made us laugh and we all relaxed and started saying, "Did you see the face of this one," or "What about the go-on of that one," and nothing seemed so bad any more.

Norah didn't join in, just sat quiet among us, but her forehead was clear and though I can't say I saw her smile, it felt to me like she felt a bit better too.

Diary 14th November.

I got up early so I could tend to Norah before setting out for school. When I went into her room I found her awake, sitting up in bed with her coat around her shoulders, writing in the notebook again. She looked up as I came in, closed the book over.

"I've told you, Norah," I said. "Nobody will read what you write. You don't have to worry about that."

She held the pen in her hand like an arrow, so tight that the skin of her knuckles stretched white.

"Did you sleep all right?"

No answer.

"Norah, I have to go to school this morning. You'll have to mind yourself until I get home. Mammy's not getting up today, but Tess will be here in a while. She'll get you anything you need."

She lowered her pen onto the cover of her book, drew a small open circle that spiralled into another slightly bigger. Round and round her pen went until the ink ran dry and the nib was scraping the paper.

I said, "Come down for your breakfast whenever you want. There will be tea on the brew. Tess will get the dinner around one. I'll see if I can get a chance to run up during the day but I might not. I take the Feis singers for a practice on a Monday."

The scratching of the pen was annoying me. I took it out of her hand, put it down on the bedside table beside the candle. Her finger and thumb stayed open around the air where it had been.

"You'll be all right, Norah, won't you?"

"I was always a respectable girl,' she said, out of nowhere, and I nearly fell out of my stand to hear her speak. Her eyes were properly on me for the first time since she came home, open wide, the same look in them as I once saw in a little tinker child who plucked hold of my sleeve one day in town outside the Mechanics' Institute and pleaded with me. "Please, miss," he'd said, over and over. "Please." I gave him a copper.

What Norah wanted from me now was not so easy to work out.

"We know that, Norah. Don't be troubling yourself about things like that."

"A sin is a sin, says the Lord."

"Don't be torturing yourself about what's done and gone."

"The sin was not mine alone but I was left alone to face it."

I felt hot and ashamed when she said that, I who had encouraged Barney to keep on fighting when he'd wanted to stop and get married and settle down with her. How had I never thought of that from Nora's point of view before? Of course that's how it must feel to her.

"Oh, Norah, that wasn't his intention, I promise. He was going to give up the fight, so he could go and find you and set up with you. I have a letter, sent to me the day before he died.

I'll find it for you when I come home from school, show you what he said."

She was blanking off her face again.

"I'd find it for you now only I have to go," I said. "There'll be a roomful of children wild as chimpanzees in a garden if I don't get into school quick. First thing this evening, all right?"

She was pulling back, way back.

"All right then, I'll see if I can put off the singers and try and get home at lunchtime. Would that be better?"

Her fists were clenched and on her face, a film of sweat had appeared. For the first time, I saw what an effort it costs her to keep her shell of stillness intact. I couldn't go and leave her like that, I just couldn't.

"All right so, Norah, I'll get it for you now. You're right, it's more important than anything else. Just wait till you see what he said. He was going to give it all up for you, Norah. To get married to you was all he wanted, all he cared about. Wait a second till I get it from my room."

I found the letter and gave it to her and stayed with her another half hour, making me twenty minutes late leaving the house. As I raced down the road, planning my excuses, I met Jem Fortune, who said the priest was looking for me.

"What do you mean?" I asked.

"What I'm saying. Father John is standing at the school gate, asking everyone if they've seen you."

That put the heart crossways in me and, as I rounded the turn in the road, I could see him, his face as black as his clerical robes.

"This is a grand time to be strolling into school, Miss Parle."

"I'm sorry, Father. We had a bit of situation at home this morning..."

"Did you indeed? And did your 'situation' have anything to do with Norah O'Donovan by any chance?"

I just nodded.

"I thought as much. I would have been up to your house on

this matter yesterday," he said, "only I had to talk to the O'Donovan family. They are broken-hearted, as you can imagine, by what you have done to them." He left a gap for me to answer but I gave it the Norah treatment.

"I'm beginning to believe you're a bit unhinged yourself. Is it trying to punish them you are? The O'Donovans?"

I couldn't hold my tongue on that one. "Of course not, Father. I..."

"She has to go back, Peg. The asylum is the place for such cases."

"It may be the right place for some, Father, but it wasn't for her. I saw how it was. No one was caring for her."

He softened a bit then, told me that he understood my intentions were charitable, but that I was misguided. Then he asked me about the baby, said outright that Mrs O'Donovan had told him we intended to bring it to the village and asked if that was so.

I nearly died of embarrassment to hear a priest talk of such things, but I had to get on with it and tell him he was right, which made him shake his head so hard I thought it was going to come off its neck.

"Don't do this, Peg," he said.

"It's done, Father. We've been told we can have her."

"I never heard the like of this in all my born days. I'm very sorry to see you behaving so out of character. All I can think is that the upheavals of the country over the past years have turned your head."

He had to get that dig in, of course.

"What I have to tell you now, young lady, is that if you insist on doing this, we won't be able to keep you at the school."

It was stupid of me but I hadn't expected that.

"We'll have to look for a new mistress."

"If that's how you feel, Father."

He let a small laugh out of him.

"Don't give me that tone, miss. You couldn't seriously think that you could stay on after bringing the evidence of immorality to grow up in your house? You are the mistress in a Catholic school, in case you have forgotten."

I bowed my head. "When do you want me to leave?"

"We might as well make it now."

No chance even to say goodbye to the children.

"Very well." I turned to go.

"Stop," he said. "I have another question for you. Is there a pair of you in it?"

"I don't know what you mean, Father."

"I'm referring to your wedding."

I looked at him, still not understanding.

"The unseemly haste of it."

My face started to flame when I realised what he was insinuating. Even the roots of my hair were blushing.

"No, Father," I said, meek as anything, running off before it was out of my mouth what I thought of him and his small and nasty mind.

As soon as I was out of his sight, I diverted down the strand, while I turned over in my head what I should say to them at home. The thoughts of telling Mammy especially...It had been her own dream as a girl to teach, only her father had matched her in marriage instead. The day I got my teaching certificate was nearly as proud a day for her as the day Barney joined the IRA Volunteers.

Now she has no Barney and I'm no longer a teacher. No other school will hire me after being let go like this. As it all goes from bad to worse then even worse again, it's hard not to feel that we are being punished by God. If we are, whatever it's for, it's not for having brought Norah back. That much I'm sure of, if nothing else.

"So I like fucking strangers. Call me old-fashioned."

I've heard Richard use this quip before. He still wants to be Mr Entertainment, but he hasn't the energy to think up new lines. He hasn't the energy to do anything much, which is why he is lying here in a hospital bed. George, one of his nurses, is holding his wrist and Frank, another patient, sits on the bed beside his. It's for them that he has delivered his line, though it's addressed to me, and they respond with the requisite laughter. In the AIDS ward, good humour is an imperative.

I put his GQ and Esquire onto his bedside locker and lean low to kiss his forehead. His rash is inflamed, red blazing up his neck and face from beneath his white linen pyjama top.

"You're wearing that look again, Squirrel," he says. "You really must try to be more tactful."

George releases his wrist, makes a mark on his chart and hangs it back on the bed. "Make him rest," he says to me, on his way out.

The nurses know me well. I spend long hours here: because of my schedule I can visit at odd times, when Gary and other friends are at work. I bring in soups and salads, the ones I know he likes. I coax him to sleep, chide him out of self-pity, ensure he takes his medication. Often, I sit silently beside him while he sleeps: more like a mother than a friend.

Today he doesn't want to rest: he has something to tell me. "Marcus was in yesterday after you left."

Marcus is a friend and another PWA, as they are coming to be called. Person. With. AIDS. "How's he doing?" I ask.

"He brought me a present. I kept it to show you. It's in the top drawer."

I open the bedside locker, take it out. It's a book. A Bible.

"Oh-oh," I say.

"I know."

"He meant well, I suppose."

"Meant well, shit."

"Come on, Richard, it's not like you to be so tetchy."

"Tetchy." He giggles. "Tetchy." It's been a long while since my vocabulary tickled him. "I'm tetchy, my dear, because I was looking forward to a real conversation with somebody who knows what this damn thing feels like. Instead, he brings me this born-again booby present and an evening of sermons."

He's not joking, he's offended. Deeply.

"What did you say to him?"

"I sent him packing."

"Poor Marcus."

"He deserved it."

"But, Richard, if it gives him comfort..."

"Comfort? Hasn't he registered that the Bible-brigade has us all down as damned, whether we believe their hooey or not?"

I don't respond.

"Do me a favour," he says, with fury. "Put it in the bin."

I'm surprised at his vehemence. Marcus isn't even that close a friend. "Don't be silly," I say.

"I mean it."

I put it in my backpack, go across to sit beside him.

"He actually asked me to repent. Can you believe it? This guy used to be queen of the pleasure dome and now he's turned into one of those freaks who hawk God from door to door, trying to sell Him." He shudders. "I mean, how insulting is that? Do they really think they're going to curry favour with a God who created this foul and fabulous world by marketing him like a household gizmo?"

"Come on, cut the guy a break. Whatever gets him through the night, and all that?"

He lies back, feeling better for his outburst, closes his eyes. Under the rash, his skin is colourless as water. We've seen two close friends go already, Joe and Lucien, and others we loved a little less. Richard knows what this disease's cocktail of assaults can do.

Will do.

He has faced what's ahead and has no patience with those who console themselves with what he believes to be fantasies.

"The Afterlife..." He shudders. "Ugh."

"Come on, I don't believe in it either, but I can see the attraction."

He opens one eye. "Honey, you'd be miserable there. We both would. With the God Squad in charge of the guest list? And the entertainment? Can you imagine? We'd hate every minute of it, believe me."

Thanks to a US visa amnesty for the Irish, I am no longer an "alien". Instead of teaching aerobics to the public for cash, I now franchise my routines to teams of instructors. Thousands of people now do a Rí Rá workout each week, in gyms and halls and studios across the Bay Area and beyond. I even have a small slice of fame through my exercise video and the fitness features I contribute to newspapers and magazines. The Chronicle has approached me about doing a regular column.

I make a good living now: I have an agent and an assistant, a bank account and health insurance, a down-payment on a two-bedroom apartment in the Haight. I eat at Mani's, buy my clothes at Mary Coles, drive a European car, a Saab. All things that might catch me occasionally with pride if I were free to think, if my friend did not have this disease that is going to kill him. Instead, I find I'm going about like an aged English lady who lost her beau in the Great War, or an American who was a flapper in the 1920s and hungered in the Depression, forever looking back in awe. Oh, that younger me! The way I went about my youthful business, all unknowing! The way I had nothing to worry me but my mind's mindless worries!

It was two years now since the night I called to his apartment to hear the results of his test. As soon as he opened the door, there was my answer, in his eyes, in his face, in the stoop of his shoulders: positive. It was what we had been waiting for; we did not expect good news — how could we, with his night sweats and his weight loss and his history? — but still I looked at him and said those stupid words we always seem to say at moments of crisis: "No. I don't believe it."

As if he were not a promiscuous gay man.

As if we knew nothing about AIDS and its predilections.

I held him hard there in the doorway, held him for far too long, like I'd never be able to let him go. Then we went inside and waited together for Gary, who came home steely, well prepared. I made dinner in the little white kitchen while they had their words and, when the meal was prepared, they made me stay and eat with them. Over the food, we talked ourselves out of disbelief so that by the time coffee came round, Richard was able to look at the man he loved — for once not joking — and say with true, discerning knowledge: "We're all going to die."

AIDS punched a hole in our liberation theories. No wonder some thought initially it was a CIA conspiracy to obliterate the community. Who could believe in a disease that targeted only gay men? Those were the days before we realised it was practices, not populations, that nurtured the virus. Now we knew, and now the front rank of our sexual avant-garde was floundering around the Castro, open-eyed with horror. You bump into somebody you haven't seen for a while and feel a flood of relief that he is still alive, followed by a wave of dread that he might tell you he has it. So many are afflicted that those still testing negative are beginning to suffer survivor's guilt.

The Castro men have become like women, Susan says, now their pleasure comes edged with danger too. Women have always known what it is like to live with worms in the sexual bud: unwanted pregnancy, sexual violence, fatal childbirth... That, she says, is why women are responding so generously to their brothers' cause, though the same brothers were so dismissive or even hostile to them in the Castro's heyday.

Susan daily applies her formidable energies to the crisis, organising fundraisers and aggressively lobbying for political and medical attention. Her indignation is voluble: men like Richard are dying not just because they have a medical condition, but because Ronald Reagan's administration doesn't give a two penny god-damn about a disease that, in the main, kills gays. This homophobia that keeps the government from investing in medical research, that keeps our President from being able even to say the word AIDS: that is what is killing people, every bit as surely as the virus.

And it isn't just AIDS, she storms. You can see the work of the Republican vandals everywhere: in her project for recovering drug addicts, now failing her clients because of axed funds. In the growing herds of homeless people on the streets, shouting half-crazed at phantom enemies, hustling for money, or food, or some other, nameless need that isn't so easily granted.

Through all this activism, she and Richard have reached a tentative liking. At a time when he felt he was losing everything — his job, his insurance, his good-time friends — Susan turned up to visit, and to help, and wouldn't be jibed away. Richard accepts services from her, as from me, that he won't take from Gary: grumbling at our "fussing", but acquiescent. Something in him makes him recoil from such solicitude in his lover. We all know that nicety will have to go with time, that he will have to learn to accept his dependence, but for now we are delighted to indulge him.

The other night, the three of us sat around him, Susan sprawled across the end of his hospital bed, while Gary spoke of how lesbians were so ahead of gay men in so many ways, especially in their sense of cooperation and interdependence. Lots of men are now getting this message, he believed, beginning to look anew at ideas of love and intimacy, beginning to make different choices.

"The party is over," he said. "The 'Me generation' must be replaced by the 'We generation'."

Susan was visibly delighted with this, keen to believe that AIDS might have some redemptive meaning beyond the horrors.

But Richard would have none of it. "Oh, my," he protested, "It'll be the 1950s again. Except now it's going to be gays peddling myths, and getting married for all the wrong reasons."

The Faggot Mystique, he called it, and even Susan had to laugh.

He is out, taking pleasure from things that he wouldn't have noticed before, making me stop to look at a garden crowded with primroses and orange California poppies, or a baby crawling across the grass. Everything is dear because soon he won't be able to see them; the virus is chomping at his retinas. Already the light in his left eye is dimming. He leans on me, so frail I feel no burden.

Back in again, another pneumonia. This afternoon, he is sleeping, or perhaps lying still with his eyes closed. His breaths are short and shallow little sniffs. Beads of sweat crawl like insects down his forehead until I wipe them away. I sit in the chair near the window, reading. Everybody is quiet today. Bill and George are talking to Patrick in the corner bed, acting out for him some bureaucratic drama with hospital administration, trying to cheer him up: he got his results yesterday and the news is the worst.

Steps approaching from the hall make us all look up:

something new has arrived. Steps in an AIDS ward are usually tentative, not this stamping tread. Richard opens one eye when he hears the footfalls.

"She's here," he says and he begins to haul himself up his pillow. The doorway of the ward fills with a large middle-aged woman in a red pant-suit. Only North America could have produced her.

Richard's mother. He finally got round to telling her two months ago; now she has finally got round to coming to see him.

Mothers are moving in their droves to San Francisco, to care for dying sons. Our friend Lucien's mother left a disapproving husband and a job in some upstate New York town to move west. She lived in Lucien's apartment until he died, both of them broke, managing to survive only through the kindnesses of friends who kept them supplied with gifts of food outside the door and money through the mailbox.

Richard's is a different type of mother. If I had never heard a word about her, I would see this in the way she holds herself in the threshold of the door, taking in the scene. Her umbrage comes to rest on George and Bill, two nurses, engaged in their camp pantomime with Patrick.

Hurling her eyes heavenwards, she alights on her son's bed. "This is unbelievable, Richard. Beyond belief."

"Hello, Mother."

"Who is responsible? That's what I'd like to know."

"Mother dearest, what are you talking about?"

She puts her handbag down on the bed. Distress contorts her face. "Can we close this curtain?" she says.

"Sure. But first let me introduce you to Jo, one of my very best friends."

I get up from my chair near the window, hold out my hand. She barely takes it, then lets it drop.

"Is she one too?" she asks Richard.

"Excuse me?"

"I think you know what I mean."

"Jesus, Mom!"

"Well, Richard, you're the one who said it's no big deal. If it's no big deal, then what's the problem with asking?" Her double chin is half the size of her face, a cushion on which the rest of her face — her pursed mouth, the hard line of her jaw — reclines.

"Shall I close the curtain for you, Mrs Burke?" I enquire, pulling it across before she has time to answer. I toss Richard a sympathetic face, but he doesn't see me. He is terrified, like an animal on its way to the abattoir. I take my seat a discreet distance away and sit, in case he needs me.

Inside the cubicle, Mrs Burke whispers loudly. "What are those people doing here?"

"Who?"

"I must say, they are the last people I expected to see here."

"Who, Mom? Who?" Richard's voice is lined with pain. I don't know if he is playing dumb or whether she genuinely has him confused. I know that it's George she objects to and Bill: the two nurses who are so obviously gay. "It's a disgrace. They're the last people who should be here. They did this to you."

Light dawns for Richard. He raises his voice, addresses us outside the curtain. "Ladies and gentlemen," he says. "My mother."

"There's no need to get fresh, young man." She scrapes the curtain open again and steps out. "I don't want you here," she says to George. "Or you," to Bill.

Their faces freeze.

"You needn't stand there smirking. I'm going to see what can be done. I am his mother, you know."

She walks out.

"Oh, God," Richard groans. "Why did I ring her? Squirrel, get in here."

I go into the cubicle, try not to laugh at his crumpled expression. "Poor Richard."

"What did I tell you? See, mine wins."

He means our mother competition. I try to imagine Mrs D. here and find I can't. I don't know how she'd be: lost, I think.

I take a tissue and wipe his forehead.

"I can't do this, Squirrel," he says. "She didn't even say hello."

"She's upset. She'll come round."

"What's she trying to do down there?"

"Shhh, Richard, it's okay. Nobody's going to pay her much attention. They're going to realise she's upset."

He groans. "You have the right idea, Squirrel. Cut off. Don't look back. I should never have rung her. Why did I? Why?"

Dear Jo,

Surprise! I hope you haven't fainted away with amazement to see this letter arrive on your mat. I ran into your sister in Dublin last week and she wrote down your address for me. I'd often wondered where you got to, but didn't know how to go about tracking you down — there wasn't much point in ringing your mother, I knew that much. So it was great to meet Maeve. She had the little one with her, she's lovely. I'm an auntie myself, four times over.

Anyway, what's the crickety crack? Maeve says you have it made out there. Things are the same as ever here i.e. boring as hell. I finally finished my PhD and I've got a job offer from an agricultural research centre. It's a good job, and good jobs are pretty scarce in Ireland these days, as you may or may not know, but the way I feel is that I've had enough of microscopes and white coats and root nodules for a while. I want to take a year off and see a bit of the world before I sign my life away.

My mother is having kittens — after all those years of impoverished studenthood to turn down a good permanent and pensionable job! Her plan after I finished my BSc was that I should do a teaching Dip. Mine was a Master's and a PhD. I won, but not without major ructions. Now I've gone and done this to her. I'll never earn a crust, she says, after all her investment.

I have to say I do feel a bit guilty. As you know, it wasn't easy for

her to scrape the money together to send me to college in the first place,
not with what Daddy left in the pot after he'd finished in the pub. But
(BIG BUT...) it's my life — and the way I see it is, once I start
working, that's going to be it until retirement (or maybe maternity
leave, but the way the love life is going, retirement looks closer).
Mammy doesn't understand where I'm coming from at all, so I've
given up trying to explain.

All this is, of course, a roundabout way of inviting myself over to
you for a visit. I'd love to see you and "Sin City" too. Is it true they
have orgies in the streets over there? If so, I might stay on for a bit.

Anyway, one way or the other, write to me, Jo. I'm dying to hear
what you're up to. I've enclosed a couple of pictures so that if I do
come, you'll recognise me when I get off the plane!

Love,

Your old pal,

Dee

SHE STAYS in my spare room for two months, until she gets a job in the Silver Tassie, and a place of her own in The Mission. Before long, she has amassed a crowd of party-loving people and is always asking me out. Sometimes I go along, but they're a hard-drinking crowd and my orange juice or mineral water keeps me separate. It amazes Dee that I don't drink any more.

"What made you quit?" she wanted to know.

"Aerobics. Alcohol really interferes with your fitness level. I gave up smoking back then too."

"Not even take a glass of wine with a meal?"

"No."

She turned a wide-eyed look on me.

"Really, I can't be bothered any more," I shrugged. "It just doesn't interest me."

She doesn't buy this and I tease her, tell her not to be so Irish. I can't tell her the truth. "Alcoholic" is a word I have never spoken aloud and I certainly can't say it to Dee. To her, it spells her father, her nemesis, who still makes her spit hate when she's had too much to drink herself. It is not a word for people like me.

Or her.

She shies away too from Richard and Gary and their world of other unspeakable words: lymphadenopathy, mycobacterium, pneumocystis, Kaposi's sarcoma. I don't blame her, I'm tired of it all myself.

In a dark corner of my mind I often find myself wishing it were already over for Richard. Because I want to spare him what's ahead? Oh yes, yes I do. But I also want to spare myself.

1923

ipsy couldn't take his eyes off the child. Typical of him, he had given no thought to the reality of her at all, not until she was wriggling and squirming in his arms. After they had done all the paperwork and the nun brought her in and placed her in Peg's lap, he looked set to fall off the chair. Pure astounded. But then she was astounding, the dote, with her dark tight cap of hair and her straight little back and her two big eyes, like blobs of dark ink, staring them out of it. Wondering who they were, probably.

Her nose was full of snuffles and tiny flakes of dried mucus powdered her nostrils. She had a bit of a head cold, Sister Margaret said, but nothing serious. Nothing to worry about.

Peg squirmed at Tipsy's stare, nervous that he was about to say or do something he shouldn't. Any thought that came into his head registered across his face and, as often as not, came hopping out of his mouth. At home, he was easy enough to manage — the poor chap was as aware as anybody else of his shortcomings and her pity usually outweighed her irritation — but it was a mite more embarrassing being out and about with him. Especially in Dublin. Especially here.

You couldn't dislike Tipsy. There was not one ounce of

badness in him, but...she felt as if she were a twig caught at water's edge, pulled and pushed and turned over by the waves. The only way for her to keep bobbing back up to the surface was not to look at any of it too close, to stay in the minute and not fret over how she got herself here or what was yet to come. Amends. Amends. This was how she would make amends for the wrong she and Barney had done in the war times.

The baby smiled a gummy smile. "Ah, look," said Peg.

"She's very good," Sister Margaret said, with no trace of anything like a smile cracking her own face. She was a formidable woman, in her black wimple. "Sleeps from seven to seven, or later sometimes. And a good eater. You won't have too much bother from her."

Peg took the baby up in her arms. The little head smelled like something between vanilla and honey.

"It's good you'll have her for the Christmas, anyway," Sister Margaret said, walking them out to the big front door, clearly happy to see another assignment brought to its conclusion. She handed over a bag of baby paraphernalia and waved them off.

"Fierce businesslike, wasn't she?" Peg said to Tipsy, once they were out of hearing range.

"Only short of spitting in her hand."

Christmas again, thought Peg, settling the child over her shoulder for the walk down to the omnibus that would bring them back to the railway station. When Sister Margaret had said that about Christmas, Peg had been shocked. Nearly a year already since they lost Barney. If anyone had told her this time last year that by now she'd be a married woman with a child...well! It was true what people said, you really never do know.

The baby was heavier than you'd think to look at her. Not a peep out of her as they walked along. No sign that she was disturbed by being carried so by a stranger.

How would Norah be, this evening, when they got her home?

She was fierce agitated this morning when they'd been setting off. Not that it showed. She'd held herself so quiet on the front step, watching them set off, but the turmoil was written on her, if you knew how to read it. Peg would have to make a special effort when she got back, to make her realise it didn't matter who got the title of mother. They would mother the child between them and then, later on, when Norah was a bit better in herself, she could take over completely if that was what she wanted.

And later again — they'd know when the time was right — the little girl would be told the truth.

The bus took a half-hour to get to the station, and when they arrived the Wexford train was already in place, huffing on its tracks. They settled themselves in, hoping nobody else would join them. The baby's cold made her sleep noisy, punctured it with snuffly snores, but otherwise didn't seem to bother her. She lay in Peg's arms, her little lashes closed, tiny blue veins marbling the skin of her eyelids. The train pulled away. People rocking down the corridor smiled in at them through the window, and Tipsy preened under their attention, delighted with himself.

"Is she all right, d'you think?" he asked. "She's due that feed an hour past."

Peg smiled. "If she was hungry, she'd wake for it, wouldn't she?"

"I suppose."

As if on cue, she began to stir.

"Now look what you've done," Peg chided, but to tell the truth, pleased as well.

Tipsy reached down to the bag at their feet, took out the bottle, held it ready for when it was needed. Sister Margaret had put everything together for them nicely; they wouldn't have thought of half the things themselves. The baby gave a small cry and when Peg handed her the bottle, she latched onto the teat with a strength that would frighten the life out of you. Because of her blocked nose, she had to stop every so often to take a deep breath between sucking.

"Isn't it a grand life you have at that age, all the same?" said Tipsy. "Nothing to do except eat and sleep and be ferried about the place. Isn't it a pity you don't remember it?"

Peg rubbed the baby's head gently. "She's very good, isn't she?"

After the milk disappeared from the bottle, Peg sat her up on her knee. The child looked swollen, stupidly full. Her eyes were enormous, like two planets in her head, as she looked around her, taking it all in. Tipsy offered her his finger and her little hand curled around it. Peg saw a frightened look in him. She could see why: something in the child's look made it seem like she knew everything and they knew nothing. Then she let a big belch and they both laughed.

"She's wet," Peg said. "But I think I'll wait until we're home to change her. I don't fancy doing it here, with the rocking."

"Do you want me to hold her for a while?"

She was surprised by the request, but handed her across. He rested her into the crook of his arm. Already her little eyes were heavy again with sleep. She was calm, happily sated. He put his hand on top of Peg's and when she didn't move it away, he lifted it, took it in his hold. She let him. Then she was sorry because she could see him wishing that somebody else would come along the corridor and take a look in at them. She shifted away from him in the seat, stretched out her legs.

"I'll be glad when we're home," she said, with a small yawn. "D'you know, I never want to see the inside of another institution. Since this thing started, it's been nothing but big houses."

"That's over now, anyway."

"We've a bit to face yet before we can relax."

He turned a puzzled face to her.

"The reaction of the village, I mean."

"I'd say we're over the worst," he said.

"Don't talk soft, it's only starting. And it will be no frolic."

He shrugged, which was irritating. But then maybe it was different for him. He was used to people not thinking a whole lot of him. That could be a strength in this situation. For herself, she was finding it hard. Bringing Norah back was bad, marrying him was worse, but now, adding this child to the mix. They would be full out for her now.

In Mucknamore it didn't matter too much what you did, so long as you managed to keep it hidden. It was going open that got you punished.

And she would have nobody to share the trouble of that. She had to keep a good show up in front of her parents and Norah, and not let poor Tipsy down either. He was the one she failed on most often.

Peg held out her arms for him to give her back the child. As she looked into the little sleeping face, she immediately felt better. The purity of a child's repose would calm any demon. "We'd better put a name on her," she said. "We can't keep calling her 'she'."

"The nun called her Mary, didn't she?"

Peg snorted. "The nuns call them all Mary."

"Not Mary, then?"

"Norah and I were thinking of Maureen?"

"Heh?"

"'Little Máire'. Maureen."

"After your mother, is it?"

"Norah likes the idea. She thinks the world of Mammy. What do you think?"

"Maureen?" He put his head to one side, considering it. "I'd better prefer Josephine."

Josephine? Did he not realise she was only doing him the courtesy of asking? "Where did you get that?"

"It's my own mother's name."

"Is it? I never knew that."

"Do you like it?"

"Em...I think it would be hard on the child. She's already used to Mary, Josephine might be a bit different for her to get used to. Whereas Maureen is like enough."

"Ye have it stitched up between ye, so." He turned back to the window. Outside, it was pure black and he couldn't be looking at anything except raindrops trailing across the window. After a time, he turned back to her. "We'll have to think how we can keep the child away from your mammy." The words tumbled out of him in a rush, giving the impression that he had been waiting to say this to her and had decided he might as well say it now, while she was cross with him anyway.

"What do you mean?"

"She can't be brought too near."

So it had not been her imagination, the way she thought she'd seen him avoiding Máire. How to explain to him that you couldn't let the illness her mother had rule your own life? How to make him understand that there was no accounting for who got struck down? Look at herself, healthy as a sand-boy, after living with it for years. The disease picked its own. And all the precautions were taken, the house kept ventilated and disinfected daily. "She'll be well minded," she said, pulling the blanket tighter round the baby. "You needn't worry yourself about that."

He turned away again. Was she being fair? A child was different, he was right there — a child was more open to every class of sickness. And she didn't like the sharpness she could hear in her own tone.

Amends.

"Would you like to hold her again for a while?" she asked, in a different voice.

He turned back with a smile. The poor chap, it was too easy to be offhand. She'd have to watch herself or she'd end up walking all over him. Considering that none of this was his idea, that just wouldn't be fair. She'd have to pray for God's help on it.

"You don't mind the name, do you?" she said.

He couldn't resist her, of course. "I think it's a grand name," he smiled. "Fine by me."

The train trundled onwards towards Mucknamore.

Back at the house, Máire got up from her place by the fire as they came in, but Norah, who had been sitting opposite, stayed put. Peg could see the questions glowing in her eyes, though she could see too that another person who didn't know her so well would probably notice nothing.

"She's here, Norah," Peg said, looking down at the bundle in her arms. "She's here and she's lovely."

"Come, Norah," said Máire. "Come look."

Norah stood up, but made no move to come forward, so Peg crossed the room to her instead. As she took the blanket from the baby's face, the little girl's eyes opened to her new surroundings.

"Ah, look at her," said Mrs Parle, from a distance. "The little dote."

Norah looked like someone who'd been struck. She took a step backwards and Peg followed her, holding out the child to her. When Norah made no attempt to take her, she plonked her down into her arms.

"We've fixed on Maureen," she said, with a smile for her mother. "Tipsy liked it too."

Norah was holding the child like you'd hold a dead animal: with straight arms, out from her body. The child, feeling the strangeness of the position, or maybe of the person holding her, was beginning to wriggle.

"Pull her in close, Norah, and give her a little rock," Peg sad. "She loved the rocking of the train and of the trap on the way home."

But Norah didn't do anything. She made no soft words or sounds, gave her no hugs or little strokes. The child started to whimper, low first, then gathering air and noise.

"Norah! Hold her closer to you." Peg folded her arms, mimed a rocking motion to show what she meant. "She feels like she is going to fall, I think."

The baby started to scream, her face growing red, her forehead wrinkling up.

"Do you want me to take her from you, Norah? Just hand her over if that's what you want. No? Then pull her into you, give her a hug. Do it now, Norah, because she's getting very upset. You want me to take her? That's all right, that's fine, just put her in my arms. Good girl. That's it. You've plenty of time to get to know each other, don't you? Of course you do. There, there little one. No need to cry. That's your Auntie Norah. Yes, it is. Let's get you out of that wet nappy and then you'll be in a better mood for your auntie. We gave you a fright, didn't we? Silly us. No need to cry, though. No need to cry."

The child's sobbing began to subside. When the storm had eased, Peg laid her down on the small rug in front of the fire where she could watch the flickering of the flames. Her mother heated a small bowl of water with a drop from the kettle, took the new bar of soap and new cloth that was all ready and waiting, and laid them on the floor beside Peg.

The baby was cleaned and changed and bundled into a nightsuit. She opened her jaws into a little yawn, stuck her fists into her eyes.

From the far side of the room, Peg's mother was entranced. "Ah, would you look, she's tired out, the creature."

Peg asked Norah if she wanted to try again. She got no answer.

"I think I'll take her on up to bed," Peg said.

"You're right," Máire agreed. "A good night's sleep is what you all need."

"Do you want to come up with me, Norah?"

Norah was at the window now, looking out at the night. Peg exchanged a look with her mother, then went and took her by the arm. "Come on, Norah. It's time to go up." With her hand on Nora's elbow and the baby up on her shoulder, she led the way to the stairs.

It was only later, after she had the two of them in bed, that she remembered Tipsy and wondered whether he was all right, left downstairs with her mother.

PEG'S DIARY 10TH DECEMBER: I'm so agitated I can hardly write, but I have to. I'll try to tell it all, just as it happened. The afternoon started well enough with me managing to escape for a walk on the strand. The weather is so strange these past days, like a thick cloud has sunk to earth. I could hardly see two feet in front of me, the fog was that bad, but it felt good to be out of the house, to be on my own, to breathe. I felt like the fog had been created just for me, to cut me off and aid me in my longing for a bit of time alone.

To find the sea, I had to go right down to the edge of the water. It looked like a frill of lace on a roll of grey. Walking along, I was struck by the impulse to paddle in the water. It was late in the year for such a thing but unseasonably, strangely warm, so I decided to risk it and hitched up my skirt to unfasten my stockings. The fog gave me protection, knowing nobody could see me in my pocket of mist.

It was lovely, but I couldn't stay long. I'd left Norah in charge of Maureen with instructions to Tess and Daddy to keep an eye on both of them. I had a string of jobs waiting for me once I got back: the evening meal to prepare for them all, reading to do for Mammy and two sheets to be repaired as well as whatever else might present itself. Little Maureen is always at her crankiest in the evenings and Norah would be put out if I stayed away too long. I had my shoes back on and was beginning to walk back across the sand when I heard my father calling me.

This put the heart crossways in me.

"What's wrong? What's wrong?" I shouted back.

"Come quick."

I hurried towards his voice. When we found each other, we were that close that we nearly collided. "What is it?"

"Dan O'Donovan is here."

"Dan?"

"Talking to his sister. I thought I better come get you. I think he's upsetting her."

I ran as best I could through the mist. When I got to the kitchen nobody was there, except the baby all alone, sitting on the floor having pulled anything loose down onto the floor beside her. She looked up at me all guilty as I came crashing in, one of the antimacassars stuffed in her mouth.

"You little divil," I said, bending and scooping her up into my arms, and going through into the bar. Tess was behind the counter. Pat Duggan and a few others were in. I just gave them a nod and retreated; it was obvious that neither Norah nor Dan had been there, they were all too calm.

Back in the kitchen, Daddy was coming in. "They're not here, either of them," I said. "What was going on between them, Daddy? How did he get in?"

"He must have come round by the back. When I came in to check on Norah and the baby, like you asked, I found him here. I asked him what he was doing and he said, 'I've come to see my sister and I want to speak to her in private.' That's when I thought I'd better get you. I'd have called your mother but —" He ran a crabbed hand across his scalp.

My mind was racing, wondering where they might have got to. Could Norah have agreed to go home with him? Would she just up and off like that? I didn't think so, but if Dan wasn't taking no for an answer...

Daddy said: "The girl was trembling, whatever he was saying to her. He's a right bully, that fellow."

That made up my mind. I planted Maureen into Daddy's arms and told him to mind her until I got back.

"Where are you going?" he asked me.

"I'm going to O'Donovan's to see if he's brought her up there."

"Peg!"

"If he can come down to our place, I can go up to his."

"But —"

"Daddy, I'm not leaving her alone with them. She's not strong enough. Look after Maureen and I'll be back as quick as I can."

The fog that was a comfort to me a short time before now felt like something teasing, on the side of the enemy. I was breathing water instead of air, like I was drowning in my own breath. As I rounded the corner by the side of the house, a shape materialised like a ghost. My hand flew up to my heart.

"You!" I said.

He was startled too, but he composed himself quicker. "Yes, me. I've come to see my sister. That's not a crime, is it?"

"I don't know," I replied. "Has the Free State made it one yet?" I was pretty pleased with that reply and didn't give him a chance to frame an answer. "Where is she?" I demanded. "What have you done to her?"

"She's gone running off. I tried to stop her but I couldn't see a blasted thing in this fog."

"Running off? Where?"

"Not too far, I'd say." Then he spoke in a squeaky voice, imitating what Norah must have said to him: "'This is my home now.'"

"And so it is."

He throws up his eyes. "You're not doing her any favours, Peg, if you think you are."

I snorted. "And you are, I suppose? Why don't you just go on home, Dan, and leave us alone?"

"Ooooh, listen to that! We weren't always so unwelcoming, were we?"

That is what he said to me, I swear it, and he meant it as bad as it sounded. I wanted to dig my nails into his face until they drew blood. I wanted to catch his hair between my fingers and tear it out off his scalp. But I turned on my heel. Norah was the important thing. There was nothing left between me and him anyway.

"Wait a minute!" he called after me. "You might as well know, my family want my sister placed where she can be properly looked after."

I walked back to him. "Return her to the asylum?"

"It's the best place for her."

"You can't do that to her."

"We most certainly can. It's her family's decision, as you well know."

"And what about Norah? Is she to have no say?"

"She's not fit to decide."

"That's not true."

"But it is true, isn't it, Peg? She hasn't been right since she came home, has she? And it's not any better she's getting, is it, but worse?"

"You're only thinking of yourselves, not her —"

"And what sort of concern have you shown her, bringing her into a house with consumption? I suppose you forgot that little detail when you were talking to the asylum bosses. That mother of yours should have been sent to a sanatorium long ago. It's not right that she should be kept here, in a public house. It's not safe."

Even after all he's done to us, I couldn't believe he was being so cruel.

"Oh, yes," I cried, "You'd have her sent away too. You'd like to send all your problems off like they don't exist."

"It's common sense, woman. It's —"

"Get out of here now, Dan. I'm not letting you stay here one moment longer. Go back to your traitor's barracks and let us be."

"I'm not the one going anywhere, Peg."

Something in his voice alerted me. What did he mean?

"No, it's home to Mucknamore I'm coming. I'm getting a transfer to the Civic Guards and, as I'm also getting married, my father has kindly donated a bit of his land to put up a house. It's not me who'll be going anywhere."

So he was to marry Agnes Whitty, the Cumann na Saoirse girl, one of those girls who stood for nothing except her own advancement, and bring her to live in Mucknamore. "Live where you like, with whoever you like," I said. "It's nothing to us so long as you leave us in peace."

"But it's hardly that simple, is it? I can tell you that it is only with the greatest effort that I have kept my father from coming down to this house. He's not happy to let this lie and neither am I. I have no intention of living up the road from it."

I looked at him, the man who killed my brother, the man who was once our friend, and I wondered how he had managed to tuck the knowledge of all he had done away, where it cost him no trouble.

"Look at you," I said, nearly more to myself than him. "Look at what your foul little war has done to you."

"Jesus," he said, bursting into one of his crowing, jeering laughs. "That's a good one. Have you taken a look in the mirror lately?"

We faced each other down, the fog greying the air between us, stared each other out of it for so long that, to our own surprise, our hostility waned. We couldn't hold it up: the understanding we had once shared could not be reduced to single-minded dissension.

I was first to weaken, to take a chance and appeal to the better nature I felt must be there still, somewhere, within him. "Dan, please...Stop this persecution of Norah. Have some feeling..."

"No, you stop, Peg," he said, but more gentle. "Stop fooling yourself that your actions are for my sister when really it's revenge you're after, revenge against me and my family. Revenge for something I never even did."

"I wish I could believe that," I whispered.

"It's the truth, Peg. I've told you. If Barney had come out when called, he'd be alive today. And whoever fired the bullet that killed him, it wasn't me."

I wanted to cry then. I wanted to tell him that I had forgotten nothing, not a single blessed thing that had passed between us.

"The problem with you die-hards is you think people who aren't going round ranting and raving have no feelings at all."

"But Norah..."

"Ah yes, Norah." With that, our moment passed. He changed back to the soldier-in-charge. "I have to tell you, Peg, that Norah is not going to be a pawn in this any longer. The asylum is the proper place for her and the asylum is where she's going."

"Dan..."

He held up his hand. "No more about it. As she won't talk to her own family, you can pass her on a message." Here he paused for effect. "You can tell her that I'll be back to get this sorted and soon. And this time she'd better cooperate."

And with that he took his leave.

It took me a while after he left to get moving, and then I spent nearly half an hour looking for Norah before I found her in the bottling store, hiding among the stacked cases. She wouldn't come out when I called her so I had to get in beside her to coax. No matter what I said, or how I tried, she was dumb. I could get no good out of her until in the end I lost my patience. "Please, Norah," I snapped, "How can anyone help you if you won't let them? Don't be so selfish."

She cried then, the first time I'd seen her cry since she came to us from the asylum, and really and truly, they were tears I was glad to see. They felt more natural than that desperate silence of hers. After a time, as if a blockage flowed away with the weeping, she spoke. "I'll have to go away again."

"No, you won't. Why should you?"

"He'll make me."

"He can't make you. How can he? You have us to protect you now. Come on back to the house and try to forget about it. Everything will turn out all right, you'll see."

So I said, though I couldn't see how myself.

"Things are never as bad as they seem," I said, and it wasn't just her I was trying to convince.

"I can't be here if he's here, Peg."

"I know it's hard, and to tell you the truth, I don't much fancy the thoughts of it myself, but —"

"No, you don't understand. I can't stay if Dan is here." She gripped me by the wrist and turned two wet eyes on me. Something in her words knocked me back.

"What do you mean, Norah?" I asked. "What are you saying to me?"

"I'll have to go away," she said, her fingers so tight on my wrist they were near denting my bones. "He makes everyone do what he wants."

Again I felt it, that there was more in the words than they were able to hold. Something cold and dead slithered across the pit of me. I looked hard at her and she held me in a horrible stare that made me want to look away, but I didn't. I let what I was seeing pierce me. I kept my eyes up and open to her. I let her truth come crawling out, over and under my skin, and realised that one tiny, secret, buried part of me had half-known all along.

When she saw for sure that the knowledge had reached me, she let go of my arm. "You see, Peg, I can't stay in Mucknamore if my brother is living here. I just can't."

1995

*A*fter Rory's wife has left, I feel raw, like a scab that's been picked too soon. All the anger that eluded me while she was there, in front of me, thrashes through me now. But I have learned, this summer, that I don't have to stay within such feelings, allowing them to throw me about. I can write, or run, or swim, or walk: any of those will change the balance, make me bigger than the emotion, shrink it back to its proper place inside me. Not me inside it.

I check my watch — five hours to sunset — and decide to walk.

I move awkwardly down the small climb onto the beach, the weight of my bump pulling against me. It is one of the things I most look forward to regaining after the baby is born: my own way of walking. Off I set, doing my best to stride. Onlookers glancing as I pass see only a generic pregnant woman, but inside, I am Fury unbound. How dare she! How dare she! And as for him... If I think of him, lying off in my bed after sex, snoring, I want to kill him.

I stamp towards The Causeway, ranting and storming, knowing all the while that really it's my own self making me so angry. I am in a mess of my own making. Why didn't I hold to what I said? "I want us to think about what we expect from each other," I had told him, that day we came out here to Coolanagh for the picnic. "I want us to think about where it might take us."

That was the right tack and I should have stuck with it instead of letting myself be swept along, with nothing clear. After all I'd learned and said and written, there I was, still an absolute fool for him.

Snarled in thought but mindful of my balance, I negotiate my way out The Causeway, up and down the rise and fall of the dunes. Ahead lies Coolanagh, fern-green against the summer-blue sea. I am going to walk all the way to the far side, which I've only done twice in my life before. The night before I left here twenty years ago, when I first realised it was going to be me in my life, alone. And the night I thought I was leaving again.

It takes me thirty minutes to get to the Neck, where causeway and island meet. From there I turn right, awkwardly negotiating the shelf that I must climb to get up onto the outer ring path. I find the pathway, bracken-strewn, rising steeply to top the tall cliffs that buttress the southerly side of the island. On this side, Coolanagh is a slow eroder, even to the lash of Atlantic waves. Crags and cliffs, deep caves and extravagant rock formations hold out against the onslaught. A steady climb brings me to the plateau of the southern summit, a high rocky outcrop overlooking a gannet colony. I tiptoe forward, nervously, to the edge. Below me, majestic gannets sweep in and out of home and below them, two hundred feet below, thundering Atlantic waves roar against the base of the cliff. You'd think it a different sea to the one that politely spreads itself across Mucknamore beach.

To the east, arcs of high cliffs curve away, each covered with thousands of birds: guillemots, razorbills, kittiwakes and others I don't know. My attention is drawn by an unusual bird above, soaring on an updraft of air. Black as a raven, but with a longer neck and shorter beak, gliding high and elegant. It is so completely itself, so joyous in its swoops and loops through the air, that my vexing thoughts fall from me to wonder at it.

It's a trigger, taking me out of my head into the moment I am in. I feel the thousands of birds nesting and preening along the cliff face, each one calling its call and feeding its young, is a tiny herald of peace. Deep down, under the tumult of my thoughts, beneath the fury of my feelings, I know what they know.

After a time, I get up and begin to make my way back the way I came. When I come to a turnoff that cuts down the side of the cliffside, I take it, remembering that it leads to a small cove, the only safe place to swim off this side of the island. Somebody — I wonder who? Nobody has lived on this island for a century and a half? — has cut back the ferns and brambles and nettles, making it passable. The evening sun feels warmer down here: the height of the cliff behind me cuts off the breeze.

About now, he is due home from work and she will surely tell him that she has been to see me. What will he do?

"If you want him, he'll go with you," she said. Oh, but I do want him, I might as well admit it, I do. I have only been holding back to protect myself. But is he really prepared to leave her and his two children? Do I really want a man who could do that? If he did, where would we — how would we — live? I couldn't live in Mucknamore and presumably he wouldn't want to be too far away from his two children. I have treaded through these questions many times without ever reaching the finishing line of an answer.

I picture him arriving home today. Parking the car beside hers, putting down his briefcase in the hall, loosening his tie as he walks into the kitchen to find her waiting for him, her eyes swimming with significance. I see her sitting him down, telling him they must talk. And she's right: they must. Didn't I say so myself?

No. Stop. Stop all this thinking, I order myself. Like you did up on the cliff. Feel the fading sun on your eyes and the breeze on your skin. Pull yourself out of your head down into your body, the body that can't be in tomorrow or yesterday but only here, where it is.

This is what I've learned, from reading Gran's diary and Norah's scribblings: that there will always be something to think about, to feel bad about. If it wasn't Rory today, it would be something else. I can let the waves of feeling be, without letting them sweep me away. Underneath the feeling is another part of me, a depth that is tranquil. I can rest back into it.

And I do. In the middle of my trouble, I let it go and experience again that shift in perception that makes the scene before me seem to recompose itself. Everything in my sights — the black juts of rock fingering the waves, the grains of sand being flattened by my feet, the fading light glancing off the water, the gentle evening air stroking my hot cheeks, everything — seems more completely itself than usual, full of its own living presence. And somehow, simultaneously, more connected to everything else.

I kick off my shoes, slip out of my clothes, walk into the sea. My skin is porous, no longer a boundary: I am melting into the water and all the world. Joy surges: the same molecules dance in me and in everything.

By the time I'm back up on the path, the light is being sucked away over the horizon, taking the warmth of the day with it. The breeze sharpens with the advance of darkness, rippling the surface of the sea water and making goose bumps stand to attention all along my arms. Further in, towards the village, the tide has retreated, leaving behind hundreds of tiny sand-pools reflecting the sun, like a scattering of giant, golden coins.

He was due at my shed over an hour ago. Will he come tonight? Maybe she didn't tell him what she did, maybe she will bide her time instead, watch him leave to go to me as he has every other night this summer. Or maybe they talked and he came anyway. Maybe he is still waiting there right now, wondering where I am. Maybe.

About halfway back, I stop near the warning signs, slide down the small dunes to the fencing where I prise apart the two strips of wire and twist myself through, evading the wire barbs that want to claw at my clothes. A further slide down the rest of the slope brings my feet onto flat sand. Coolanagh sand. I am not frightened: here, at the edge, I am safe. The danger is further out and it stays out there; you have to walk out to meet it.

I sit, waiting, watching darkness deepen from blue to indigo to black. No trace of mist or fog on this dry, moonless night, but still I can see almost nothing. I turn on the pocket torch I've brought with me. Beyond its puny shaft of light darkness swells, immense. It would have been the same with an oil lamp, worse in the thick fog that was down that night in 1923.

Walking forward, just a little, I stretch for answers to a different set of questions to the ones that have poked at me all evening. How far out did Dan walk on that fateful night? What if he had refused, overcome her, taken the gun, turned it back on her? He was so much stronger; it could easily have gone that way instead. What if he had decided to make a run for it? Would she really have shot him?

I picture him quick-trudging his way out The Causeway to meet her. In his pocket is the typewritten note that enticed him into the wet night: I need to talk to you, it says, or some such words. Meet me you know where, out The Causeway. Seven o'clock... He walks as smartly as the fog permits, his head down, his shoulders staunch. He can hardly see five steps ahead but he has walked this strip a thousand times. He keeps to the centre and makes steady progress, right-left, right-left, right-left, lieutenant soldier boy to the last.

I see him slow his pace as the light below The Causeway catches his attention. Not in Lover's Hollow, where he expected, but a little further on. He steps down towards it — no barbed wire then to slow his progress — skids down the side through the top, damp layer of sand, not thinking to be fearful. As he comes close to the light, she says his name, hesitantly — "Dan?" — and when he confirms it, she tells him to stop where he is. He does what he is told, halted by surprise. Underneath the glow of the lamp is the barrel of a gun — Barney's gun — pointing his way.

Poor Dan. He thought he was on his way to a tryst with a woman who once loved him: who had, he reckoned, a soft spot for him still. He went to meet her, expecting...what? Not to find a rifle, this rifle, pointing at him, intent on revenge.

Arrogant man.

She blocks his way back to The Causeway and gives him a choice: a close-range shot in the chest or a walk across Coolanagh sands. He picks the chance of unsafe sands over the certainty of a bullet, just as she knew he would. The gun points him in the direction she wants him to go and he goes, walking upright, disdaining to pick his steps. He has taken only a few strides when he feels the ground shift and then collapse.

He is down, sucked by quicksand.

Then he knows fear, oh yes. Freezing, wet, chest-clutching, fear. "Help me," he calls out to her, the lady of the lamp. "Help me...Please."

Oh, sunken, shrunken man: did you really think she would?

Back at my shed I find nothing, no sign of whether he came or not.

I think not. I shine my torch around the door, along my table-desk where I left pen and paper handy if he should want to write. I turn on the lamp to have a closer look, but there is no sign of any visit.

I'm calm, I know what I must do.

Taking my torch, I cross the field, picking my way through builder's mud, to the back door of the house. It's late but there's a light glowing in the kitchen window. Even if they are asleep, I intend to wake them. I need Hilde to make the arrangements tonight.

She will think this odd, but I will insist — it must be tomorrow morning, no later — and odd or not, she will comply, not only because she is so obliging, but because it will suit her and Stefan to get it done, to see me gone. They have been holding off for me.

NEXT MORNING, I am up at first light, heading eastwards towards Rathmeelin, stopping only to pick wild daisies to place on the grave.

As I approach it, up the cemetery path, I see it is a mess, covered in rotting bunches of flowers, plastic wrappings still swathing some of the decayed clumps. I can smell them, fetid in the morning air. Among the wilted stalks, a single carnation clings to a faded shade of its former colour, pink. The whole thing looks terrible, like nobody cares. But who is there to tend things like the family graves now Mrs D. is gone?

I check the inscription on the headstone. Maeve wants to know it is precisely right before she pays the stonecutter. It seems to be just as she ordered: Maureen Devereux, née Delaney. Born 25.5.1923. Died 12.5.1995, aged 71. Go nDéanfaidh Dia Trócaire ar a hAnam. The new-chiselled letters, black on the old grey stone, stand out strong and bold, as if Mrs D's death is the one that really matters.

Some of her rotting flowers have slid across onto Auntie Norah's patch. I pick up the rotting stems and they shrink in my hands, oozing slime. Holding the mess away from my body, I carry it down the slope and over the wall, onto the soft sand of the beach. I dump it there, then go back up for another handful. And again until I have cleared it all away. On the beach then, I kneel and dig a hole with my hands, scrabbling like a dog at sand that is soft on top, like pale brown sugar, but darker and damper underneath.

When the hole is big enough, I transfer in the stinking vegetation and cover it over, pat it down. I stand to finish the job, dragging soft sand across with one foot, stamping it flat.

Then I lay the new flowers I've brought.

Back in the shed, it's still only seven a.m. I haul the two

suitcases I packed the night before up to Hilde's house. One is light, with the clothes I brought from San Francisco; the other heavy, packed with papers. I sit on the heavy one, beneath her new kitchen window, to wait, emptying my head of thought, knowing I am doing right.

Regiments of cloud are mustering on the horizon, the morning air has an autumnal tang and the sea dances friskily under an offshore breeze. After a time, the hum of a car approaches and slows to a stop out on the road. A door bangs, the engine revs away and one of the workmen comes through the passage at the side of the house. The one with the mermaid tattoos. In his hand, he carries foil-wrapped sandwiches and a flask; under his arm is a tabloid newspaper. He doesn't see me.

A demolition machine sits with its steel ball expectant. He climbs into it, ignites the motor. It coughs into a roar and lumbers across the field like a tank, pulling up beside my shed. He turns off the engine then, evacuating the air of noise. Across the dunes, the sea surf sounds again. Opening his flask, he spreads a newspaper across the steering wheel and takes a sandwich from his pack. He eats and reads. In the distance, a dog barks.

Soon the others are arriving, taking out their tools: sledgehammers and mallets and picks. One of them notices me and nudges another, who says something, then they all turn their heads for a look. I stare back at them, protected by distance. The man in the machine switches the ignition again, diverting their attention. With another spluttering cough, it is primed, ready for action.

The time has come. He hoists the jib on high, tugging the chains and yanking the steel ball from its mooring, so the heavy globe plunges towards the ground. It is stopped, mid-drop, by its chain, and it reels and jerks like a fish at the end of a line, but the chain holds strong and it settles, a solid black orb, level with my shed's windows. The other men stand back and I rise to my feet. We all watch as the steel ball swings clumsily and strikes.

One whack is enough: down she goes, my little shed, my childhood refuge, my summer sanctuary, gusting up puffs of dust. At the centre of the collapsed brick and corrugated iron is the bed I slept in, still creased with the imprint of my body. The second machine closes in, bucket tilted to scoop it, and all the rubble, away.

Two other outhouses are also to be knocked, but I can't watch any more. I pick up my bags and go round the front to rouse Hilde who has made me promise that I won't leave without saying goodbye.

1923

The Wexford Weekly
12th December, 1923

"FREE STATE OFFICER FOUND DEAD AT MUCKNAMORE!"

On Wednesday morning last, fisherman John Colfer of Mucknamore was taking to the sea in commencement of his day's work when his attention was caught by a body trapped on Coolanagh strand. The sands at Coolanagh are deceptive, appearing firm, but in fact being subject to a "quick" condition, and this person appeared to have got into trouble there overnight.

As the deceased was dressed in a Free State Army uniform, Mr Colfer returned to land and proceeded with haste to inform the military barracks at Wexford. The military arrived and, with the aid of planks and ropes attached to the military lorry, proceeded to try to extract the body from the sand, a scene which attracted a great number of people from Mucknamore to observe proceedings. The operation took upwards of two hours and engendered great excitement among a growing crowd.

The deceased was identified as Lieutenant Dan O'Donovan of Mucknamore, a National Army officer, and the death has caused a sensation in Mucknamore and surrounds.

It is presumed that he inadvertently wandered off the Point out onto Coolanagh sands in the dark. On the night in question, this area was submerged in fog, and there is much speculation as to what would have taken him out on the Point at Mucknamore in such dangerous conditions. While not a native of these parts, Lieutenant O'Donovan had lived here for some years and it is thought unlikely that he would not have known of the dangers associated with Coolanagh strand, notorious as it is throughout south Wexford.

The remains have been transferred to the morgue, awaiting inquest. Pending investigation, further details will be provided.

PART IV
SURGE

1923

The two brown doors of the public house were closed, which was strange, because it was almost twelve o'clock, well beyond opening time. Brigade Police Officer Patrick-Joe Brosnan turned up the collar of his military coat against the rain and banged on the door again with his fist, one last time — thump-thump-thump — no longer expecting an answer. The motor engine was growling behind him and he turned and shrugged his shoulders at Private O'Dwyer, sitting dry at the wheel of the army lorry, enjoying a cigarette. O'Dwyer made a gesture back at him, but the downpour was so thick he couldn't properly see.

He went across and stuck his head in under the car canopy, a small respite. "What are you saying to me?"

"The door of the house, down the far end," he said, pointing. "You might have better luck down there."

It was what Brosnan had intended to do, the obvious thing to try once he'd got no reply in the shop, but he didn't trouble to say so.

He ran back through the rain. Since the fog lifted yesterday, these bitter, gusty squalls had assailed them. Filthy weather. He put out his hand to bang the brass knocker but, as soon as he touched it, the door nudged ajar. From within, he could hear a strange noise, a child's voice it sounded like, and it seemed to be grunting, querulously: eh – eh – eh. He gave a small cough and knocked politely, at which the door swung inwards and two frightened eyes stared back at him from the end of the stairs. They belonged to a young woman, a fine-looking girl in her early twenties, sitting on the bottom step.

She didn't get up, or change her expression, or in any way acknowledge that he was there. Beside her was a baby sitting up in a pram and it was from this small person that the grunts were emanating. Eh – eh – eh: reaching towards her toy that had fallen to the floor, one of those woollen sacks that makes a noise upon shaking.

"I'm sorry to disturb you, Miss." Raindrops falling from the peak of his cap so he took it off. She didn't answer, just stared at him as if his face was a mirror.

"I'm making a visit to all the houses in the area on behalf of the National Army."

Again she made no reply. Then the penny dropped with him. She must be the loony, the dead man's sister. Gallagher had filled him in on the queer set-up in this house. What a tragedy, a looker like her. That pale skin under the red hair was a striking combination.

"May I?" When she made no indication, he stepped in. He felt his best ploy would be to play innocent. "I'm making enquiries about one of our officers, lost to us here yesterday. A local man, Lieutenant Dan O'Donovan. Was he known to you?"

Her stare was unnerving.

"Eh – eh – eh..." continued the child. He'd have thought no woman could ignore those sounds. He felt like going over himself — him, a man, and a stranger to the child — and picking up the thing and handing it to her. He would have, only it didn't seem right. An internal door opened and another young woman came through, about the same age. Dark to the other girl's red, not as pretty in the face. Not today, anyway: her eyes were swollen and her face blotchy, either she had a bad cold or she'd been crying. She stopped dead when she saw him in the hall and affectedly eyed his uniform, up and down, the familiar sneer of the die-hard distorting her face. "What do you think you're doing in here?"

"Sorry to disturb you, miss," he said. "This lady let me in."

"Did you, Norah?"

No answer for her either. The child raised its voice, turning its grunts to a cry. The second girl saw the problem instantly, retrieved the toy from the floor, beamed back at the wet, pink-gummed smile that rewarded her and turned a frown on him, all in one fluid move. To him she said, "I didn't hear the knocker."

"I'm here about the dead officer found in this vicinity yesterday."

"Well, you should never have been let in here so I'll thank you now to leave the way you came."

"I'm afraid I can't do that, miss. I've questions to put to you both, and to the rest of the household too, if I may."

"You may not."

"Look," he said, trying for patience, "a man is —"

She held up her hand. "Save your talk."

"I have to insist —"

"No, I insist. I insist on your respect. My mother died in the room above us one hour ago."

Jesus, what rotten blasted timing. Was he mistaken or was that a smile from the lunatic girl?

"Oh!" he said. "I'm sorry. I didn't know, I..."

"We haven't had time yet to put up the card on the door."

He found his equilibrium. "I'm sorry for your trouble," he said. "May she rest in peace."

"So we won't be receiving any Free State detectives or whatever you are." She ran that disdainful look up and down his uniform again. "Or answering any Stater questions either. Not today."

She was enjoying this. She was upset of course — her mother

was dead — but a part of her was enjoying his discomfort. The lunatic girl's face looked impassive but somehow managed to register hostility too.

"I'm sorry for your trouble," he said. "Sincerely."

"You shouldn't have let yourself in without a by-your-leave."

"The door was open...I wasn't to know..." He found himself, somehow, walking backwards, towards the door. "I'll have to come back soon. You do understand that?"

She looked at him like he was a person without morals.

"We have enquiries that won't wait," he said. "When is your funeral?"

"We've hardly had time to think of that."

"I'll see if I can leave it until the day after. As a favour, like."

Instead of being grateful, she looked at him like he was pure poison to her. "Suit yourself," she said. "You will anyway."

She turned to the other girl, put out a hand. "Come on, Norah, let's get you two inside." Her voice for the girl was so different, drenched with kindness. She helped her off the stairs, tucked the blanket in around the baby's legs.

"You can close the door behind you," she said in the tone she had for him, "on your way out."

And with an arm around her unfortunate friend, she steered the perambulator towards the door at the end of the hall.

Outside, O'Dwyer had the engine turned off and was smoking again, warm and dry in his vehicle, unscathed by female hostility. "How did it go?"

"Terrible," he said, climbing in beside him. "They've had a bereavement. The mother of the house has died."

"Ah, Mrs Parle, has she gone? Lord have mercy on her, she's been sick this long time. And she was only a young woman, forty-five at most."

"They were in no mood to answer questions. I said we'd come back."

"Fair enough."

"So where to now?"

"Have you any recommendations?"

"You could try Mrs Mythen in the post office. She's usually good for what's going on."

"All right," Brosnan said. He didn't hold out much hopes of it, but it would give him time to unravel his twisted-up thoughts. How had that interview gone so awry? He shouldn't have let himself be put on the back foot like that, as if he had done something bad to her on purpose. If only he'd known, he'd have done them first, yesterday, instead of spending the day on the men in the barracks and that girl from the pub. Kavanagh, his superior officer, wouldn't be too pleased: the Parles were central witnesses.

"What do you think, O'Dwyer? Do you believe they —" he nodded towards the house — "had anything to do with it?"

"Hmmm. I'd be inclined to say no, but with the state of the country, it's hard to tell which end is up these days."

"They had a motive."

"They wouldn't be alone in that."

"Really? Was O'Donovan not liked? Kavanagh seemed to think he was."

"Not by die-hards, he wasn't."

A pause. Then: "Do you know her, the daughter of the house?"

"Not well. She'd know my sister."

"She's quite a fury."

"Really? I never heard that of her. She was the schoolteacher here for a time. Well respected."

Yes. Kavanagh had filled him in on all that, how she'd lost her job for taking in the lunatic girl and the baby. A rare sort, to do a thing like that. And she was also Cumann na mBan. The country was learning only too well what vixens they could be when roused.

Brosnan sighed again: to think that when he applied to join the Guards, it was to get away from killing. When he was offered this job in Wexford, he'd jumped at it, thinking policing milder than soldiering, and the divide less bitter here than in County Kerry.

After the Ballyseedy affair, he'd have jumped at any offer that took him away from his own county. That whole business sickened and shamed him. Some nights when falling to sleep, he'd find himself trapped in a nightmare watching his colleagues tie those Irregular boys together around a ticking bomb, and seeing it explode them into smithereens. In his dream, he looked through the eyes of the one who had, miraculously, survived intact, who hid watching the body parts of the other eight being divided into nine coffins by the Free State. He didn't want to be part of an army that did such deeds — and then denied them.

But he needed an income. He had a wife, two children, a third on the way.

The Civic Guards had offered him a way out. Some said the Guards were only a tame branch of the army, others that this was not the time for their introduction, but Brosnan believed in the idea of an unarmed force and thought Ireland could not have it soon enough. That was what he wanted to be part of: the force of law, not the law of force.

Yet here he was, somehow, still in the middle of the worst of it. Wexford turned out every bit as embittered as Kerry and he found himself floundering around like a blind man who'd stumbled into the wrong house.

"You have some chance of getting somewhere with them," Kavanagh had said, when he was explaining the job to him. "A local man would be devoured."

It was a strange, closed village, its people full of a strange, closed pride. Most of them wouldn't talk to him at all and those who did had a drawly, dawdly way with their words so that he had to stretch his ears to make sense of what they were saying. Even his army colleagues seemed to be wary of him. A foreigner, he'd heard himself called.

And now this. Brosnan took off his cap, smoothed back his

hair, wished himself far from Mucknamore, far from Kerry, far from Ireland altogether.

They'd try this post-office woman, but he hadn't any great hopes of her. People who knew the dead man well were his best hope.

"A good soldier," Kavanagh had said, describing O'Donovan. "Nothing showy, but brave as he was needed to be. Good leadership ability. All qualities that would have stood to him in the Guards. I'd say he'd have made Inspector."

"Could it have been an accident, Sir?"

"It could, I suppose, but I don't believe so. Why would he go out that way by night unless he was forced? Especially the night that was in it. Can you think of any good reason?"

"It's hard to, all right."

"You know the danger good men have been living with. He was shot at before, you know, and his house set fire to this autumn gone out. Mind you, this has a different feel to an Irregular shooting, more underhand."

He had handed him over the file. "Whatever the motive and whoever the cause, we can't have the likes of this going on, Sergeant, or we'll have the English looking to come back, claiming we can't keep control. Over to you. Don't let us down, like a good man."

O'Dwyer looked askance at him. "Are you all right, Sergeant?"

"Have you a spare cig?"

He took it and bent to the light that O'Dwyer struck for him, inhaled the smoke deep. What next? He hadn't the faintest idea. "Right, let's go to the post office, see can we get any good out of them there."

1995

$\mathcal{N}$o silence is ever total. Here in this hotel room, the quiet is thicker and the underlying noises more muted than the swoosh of the sea and the whine and whack of building work that was my soundtrack for the summer. Here it's corridor voices, wheels whirring over carpet, tea trays tinkling and, outside the window, the rattle and drone of Dublin traffic, muffled by double glazing. Beneath it all, the subterranean creaks and gurgles of a huge central-heating system. The air here is thicker too than the open air of my shed, lined with lemon polish and carpet dust and a trace, despite the cleaners' best efforts, of other people.

I wonder about them, all the others who have slept in here, the business travellers and holidaymakers, as I lie between my laundered linen sheets, trying to persuade myself to get up. It's four in the afternoon and I've been asleep since two, would be asleep yet, had I not been kicked into waking by you. But it's good that you've roused me; I should already be up.

In less than an hour, Maeve will be sitting in Bewley's Café, a fifteen-minute walk away, waiting for me. I need to shower and dress and turn myself out. I need to plan what I am going to say when she asks me again why I want to "waste good money" on this hotel room. It is expensive, this square beige space with its peach-and-cream curtains, its pallid furnishings, its innocuous matching paintings of flowers from four different angles in their identical wooden frames.

So why, my sister wonders, am I staying here instead of at her house, where she has not one but two spare rooms? Neither she nor anybody else would bother me, if that's what I'm afraid of. I could come and go as I pleased. All this she has already said on the telephone, and I know she will say it again today. She will do her best to persuade me. I will not let myself be persuaded.

She'll also want to know how the writing is progressing and all about hospitals and birthing arrangements and the question of afterwards. The prospect exhausts me, and has me clinging to the mattress. I would ring and cancel our meeting — as I have once already — were it not for her saying at the end of her call yesterday that she had "something" to tell me. Though it seems unlikely, I cannot rid myself of the idea that this something might be to do with Rory.

I seem doomed to repeat every action of my life. Here I am, pregnant again, having made an abrupt exit again, and here he is, again failing to follow me. It wouldn't be difficult for him to track me down; Maeve's name is listed in the telephone book and though it might be mildly awkward for him to have to telephone her and ask if she knows my whereabouts, it's a small test. Tiny.

Is he really going to flunk it? After all that he said, surely he cannot leave it like this?

I throw aside the covers but I can't propel myself out. What I'd like to do is escape into another nap. Since coming to Dublin, that's all I seem to do: drift in and out of sleep between bouts of writing. I no longer run, have to force myself even to walk. Breakfast and dinner come to me via room service because going downstairs to negotiate waiters and other diners feels like too much bother. I'm growing heavier and slower. My face and arms and wrists are swollen now, as well as my belly, and I get short of breath just taking a shower.

It's all your fault, especially the tiredness, not helped by your inability to tell night from day. Whenever the mood takes you, off you go on the move, kicking and nudging and poking me from inside. I have surrendered to your rhythm and spend some of most days asleep and some of most nights awake (last night I worked from two to five a.m., transcribing some of Norah's notes onto my new computer).

So here I am. This is as far as I've got: lying in an anonymous hotel room, teetering on the edge of sleep, feeling what I think is your heel against my rib, convulsed inside my own longing. Longing, longing, longing like a lovesick teenager, pinning my hopes on this meeting with my sister, shrinking from what I suspect will be their disappointment.

I walk in sunshine through the regimented flower-beds of St Stephen's Green to meet Maeve, past ducks that look just like the ones Rory and I used to feed when we were students. People sit on benches and stroll or stride along the paths, but Dublin's short lolling-on-the-grass season is over until next year. The park is busy, though it's mid-afternoon and the after-work crowd has not yet started to pour through. Despite the crowds, I can never believe in Dublin as a real city. It's about the same size as San Francisco, but feels much smaller, and its loudly touted, new-found cosmopolitanism always seems to me unconvincing, like a child rigged out in its mother's high heels. The biggest village in the world, Oscar Wilde called it, and the description still fits.

I negotiate my bulk through the throngs, down Grafton Street and into Bewley's, past the pile-up of pastries at the take-away counter, into the bowels of the cafe. It takes my eyes a time to adjust to the dim light. Maeve is sitting in one of the low red booths at the back, waving at me. She looks haggard, forcing her mouth into a crooked smile. I bend to kiss her cheek and up close I can almost smell the misery from her. I want to turn and run out the door.

Her skin, despite its pallor, is hot under my lips. "You okay?" I ask.

"Sure. Fine. You?"

"Fine."

Our eyes meet and we hover inside a moment of possibility. Disconcerted, I point at her cup. "Would you like another one of those?" There's a ring of cold coffee lining the inside of the half-empty cup in front of her. She must be here a while.

She nods. "Please."

"Black?"

"Lovely. Thanks."

This is ridiculous, I think as I shuffle along the line-up at the counter, waiting to order. She is not fine. I am not fine. So after I return to the table, and hand out the coffee and the spoons, and put away the tray, I ask her straight: "Maeve, what's wrong?"

She shakes her head, takes a slim tin of artificial sweetener from her bag, tips two small, white pills into her coffee. Shrugs. Sighs. Shakes her head again. I wait. Eventually it comes. "Donal's gone."

"Donal?" This is so far from what I expected that I sound like I've never heard of anyone called Donal. "Gone?"

"Yes, Jo." She wipes a hand across her forehead, irritated. "Donal, as in my husband. Gone, as in left me."

So there is nothing of Rory here, thinks selfish, selfish me. "Maeve, that's terrible."

Her mouth wobbles, goes misshapen. "I know. Of all the times...Now...Mother —"

She breaks off. I know what she means, and yet I can see how this, and her way of saying it, even her way of feeling it, could infuriate.

"But is it permanent? What's going on?"

She reaches into her bag again, this time for paper tissues, crinkly in their plastic handipack. "He blames Mother," she says, snapping the pack back into the bag. "While she was sick I had to go down to Mucknamore, a lot. Naturally. But he resented it. And I resented him not supporting me through it." She shrugs. "According to him, in that time we grew too far apart."

"And is he right?"

"If we did, there was no need for it. He always griped about Mother, you've no idea. He could be completely ridiculous about it. It was pathetic: a grown man jealous of an old woman and her needs."

I recall Donal's sarcasm at the funeral and realise as she is talking that I don't know the guy at all, that he has never seemed quite real to me, just Maeve's husband, slotting into his allotted place in her ordered life.

"He never made it easy for me, if I wanted her to come on holiday with us or to go down to Mucknamore for Christmas."

"You went down every year, didn't you?"

"We could hardly have left her on her own for it."

Why not? I ask myself and she catches my face. "You think he was right!" she accuses.

"I haven't a clue, Maeve. It doesn't matter, does it, what I think? I'm hardly an expert on marriage."

"You know more than you pretend to know," she says, blowing her nose. "Well, you and Donal might be happy to pretend you never had a mother, but most people appreciate their parents and look after them when they get on a bit. I was happy to do it; it was the right thing to do." Red-faced, she shrugs. "It's not like we had her with us day and night. She would have liked a lot more attention than she got."

"You were pulled between the two of them."

"I could never see why he had to make such a big deal about it. We always had at least one other family holiday, without her, each year. And as for Christmas...well, it's what you do, isn't it, at Christmas? The family thing."

I grimace, recognising my part in this. "It all fell on you," I say.

"Well, yes. We were the only family she had left after Auntie Norah and Gran were gone. She used to say that, often."

I bet she did. I take a sip of coffee to stop my retort.

"And it's not like I didn't put her off. I did, many times. For him. And felt awful about it. None of that ever counted for anything with him."

"But, Maeve, I don't understand. If Mrs D. was the problem between you, then surely things should be better now that she's...gone?"

Her face closes over like a fist. "This is why I went down to Mucknamore, to you, that day two weeks ago...to tell you...And I should have, I know I should, I felt so wretched driving away. But I was so overcome by your news...Are you really okay, by the way? Have you seen a doctor yet?"

"Maeve, never mind all that. We can discuss that later."

She nods. "You're right, I should have talked that day. Having gone all the way down, to drive back up without...But, Jo, I'm finding it very hard to talk about this. None of my friends know, not one. I can't seem to get it out."

I know that feeling.

"And...our friends...I don't know how I've done it but...none of them...I don't seem to have anybody I can confide in." She screws the rumpled tissue into her eye sockets. "Also, saying it somehow makes it more real, less likely to..." She lets her hopes trail away into silence.

"Where's he staying?" I ask.

"He's rented an apartment. And..." She falters.

"And there's somebody else?"

Two wide eyes expand wider. "How did you know?"

"I was just asking," I say gently.

"She's only twenty-five."

Is she indeed? I didn't think Donal had it in him.

She starts to cry then, weakly, like she's cried so much that she's tired of it, but it's all she knows how to do. With a grimace she says, "Jo, I want to ask you something."

I nod.

"I wanted to ask if you..."

I wait.

"If you would come...and stay with us for a while?"

I turn from her wet eyes, their entreating heat. The stained glass here in Bewley's turns the light blue, making its close, shabby warmth seem cooler, airier than it would otherwise. Above us, four wooden gargoyles, magnificently ugly, jut out from the wall, and all around, at other tables, Irish and continental and American voices talk and laugh and cups clink against their saucers.

"I wouldn't ask, only...Having you there would be a distraction for Ria...She's such a good kid and I...at the moment, I'm...I can't seem to..." She takes a steadying breath, starts again in a stronger voice. "Jo, it's for Ria, really, that I'm asking. It's so awful...She and I...each trying not to crack..."

At the word, tears break in her again. "Ria's heartbroken, you see...She doesn't understand. How can she? I don't understand myself..."

I think lovingly of my beige hotel room, my solitude. Inside me, I am constricting, like somebody is shrink-wrapping my neck in cling film, working their way up towards my face.

"I'm sorry, Jo," she says into her tissue. "I don't know what your plans are. I shouldn't...I don't want to be a..." The bag clicks open again. She takes out a fresh tissue. I find I'm putting my hand on hers. She cries a little longer, sniffles to recovery.

"It's okay," she says then. "I can see you'd rather not."

"No," I say. "It's not that. I —"

"It's okay, Jo, I understand. I know how you value your privacy."

"Maeve, I'm —"

"You don't have to explain, honestly. Really...I shouldn't have asked..."

"Christ, Maeve! Will you stop for a second?"

She stops, looks at me through the dampness of long lashes that I have always envied. I squeeze the hand that is under mine and it feels like I'm squeezing my own heart.

"Of course I'll come," I say. "Of course I will. Of course."

*R*ichard dies on the evening of October 17th, 1989, a date known to every San Franciscan. And when he dies, though I have been told in time to know, I'm not there. Gary has called me. Susan has called me and for days I've known his time is getting close. But that last afternoon, after hanging up the phone on Gary, instead of making my way there immediately, I sit back down to finish the article I was writing when he called.

An article entitled, somewhat ironically, 'Urgency Addiction: Why You're Not As Busy As You Think'.

It is a perfect October afternoon, blue and balmy. I have an orange juice — freshly squeezed — before me. I am wearing my favourite, most comfortable T-shirt, my fastest pen is between my finger and thumb, filling my page with the words and phrases that will keep my editor happy. All is as it should be, except for the awareness of my failure underlying every thought and act.

I haven't been to the hospital for weeks. Weeks. In August, the disease started in on his brain. For the longest time before that, he had seemed to us too fragile to last. Just skin on a shrunken skeleton, everything that made him Richard, including his sense of humour, gone. Just a sick man, full of sickness's self-pity. And after that came the dementia.

I push on with my work. "The stress addict has the same troublesome dependence as any other addict," I write. "Just because your mood-altering drug of choice is the physiological responses of your own body doesn't mean you are safe. Surging epinephrine or glucocorticoids won't get you in trouble with the law or leave you bankrupt, but like any addictive substances they trigger side effects that can wreak havoc with your health and happiness..."

Though I am getting proficient at this writing, learning just the right tone of certitude, part of me despises it, especially magazine-land's breezy conviction that life is eminently fixable, just a matter of tweaking the right buttons. I won't be able to do this forever, I say to myself, not for the first time. As I write, the table begins to vibrate beneath my notebook and I feel — or is it hear? — a subterranean growl, like a deeply buried tummy rumble. The windows rattle, making me look up. Quake?

I set to sit the tremor out, as I always do, but then the earth growls and everything is wobbling, violently. The floor jerks and screams rise from the street outside, flying in through my open window. Could this be the long awaited "Big One"?

So, I think, it may not just be Richard. We may all go together.

The thought leaves me strangely comforted. At the same time, all the facts I have heard about old concrete, new concrete, stress levels, earthquake procedures are flashing through me. There is a low-roaring snarl underfoot, then the world bucks. Books come crashing down off my shelves. A second newsflash from my mind asserts that I don't, in fact, want to die and for the first time since I came to San Francisco, I go to stand in the doorway. The steel L-shape shelving unit that lines one corner of my living room is flapping back and forth violently, trying to tear apart. Crockery is falling, smashing against tiles and more books are tumbling down in heaps. Oddly, my television, atop another shelving unit, doesn't budge.

It goes on for what seems like a long time, though it can only really be seconds, then the world slowly settles to stillness. I wait. Yes, it is still.

It seems to be over.

It seems I am to live.

Now I have a good excuse for not being at the hospital. Crossing the city becomes an impossibility, I give up even pretending that I might go. I stay home, listening to the news reports coming in on my battery-operated radio. A building has collapsed here, a gas-main has flared into fire there. The upper deck of Bay Bridge has collapsed onto the lower, squashing hundreds of cars. Of the inhabited areas, the reclaimed land in the Marina district and parts of the inner Mission are worst hit. Liquification, they call it, when earthquake dissolves reclaimed soil, so that it temporarily acts like quicksand. Those with power still up get to see it all on TV — history's first real-time disaster movie — available on three major networks, thanks to the World Series football game that was in progress when it struck.

Sixty-seven San Franciscans died that day from being in the wrong place, at the flash-points of the quake. In the weeks that follow, the whole city is in mourning, which feels fitting for Richard. But I am not good at grief. I cannot cry and I don't want to. I go about my days, aghast. Stunned by what it is to know that he is dead. His mouth was covered in ulcers and his body, inside and out, in excruciating KS lesions. He was blind in one eye, only barely sighted in the other. He couldn't hold his own coffee cup, his own medicine, his own shit. A time ago, I heard him writhing through the night, pleading with no one: "Please...please..." And it got worse after that. That last day I arrived to the hospital and he screamed at me from the bed about stealing his food, I looked at his face disfigured by KS and rage and thought: you are not Richard.

But who, then, was he, this crazed stranger in Richard's bed and body?

I couldn't bear it. By the end, Susan was going into the hospital more often than me. There: that is how loathsome I am.

Death was a release. That's what I tell others, at the funeral. Not at his family's Episcopalian cremation, but at the memorial held by our friends. Mozart's Requiem. Judy singing 'Somewhere Over the Rainbow'. Gary reading Thom Gunn and Oscar Wilde. Me reading my own poem: "...We thought the laughter would roll on and on / But we were young and we were wrong."

The horror of scanning the room, seeing those who were going to die next and all the other missing faces, those gone already. And afterwards, everybody talking about Richard's enthusiasm for life, his humour, his irrepressibility.

He would have had none of this, I found myself thinking, even as I clung to the compliments. He would have taken pleasure in bursting our burbles of comfort, with his particular brand of starkly honest humour. He would never have let me get away with it the sentence I dole out to all — that his death was a release. It's true, but also so completely insufficient to the truth of his final macabre months and minutes, that it's no consolation at all.

His dying and his death were an offence to nature. An insult to all that is most human. An affront to everything I had come to hold dear. I am outraged, outraged, outraged, by his loss.

Sometimes I dream about him, dreams where he is fleshed out again, his old self. These dreams are usually silent, but once I dreamed that I answered my buzzer and his voice said, "Hello."

When I opened the door, there he was, standing on my step, looking sheepish. "Hi! I'm back!"

"But you're dead," I said to him. He turned his eyes away from me, evasive. "Richard, you're supposed to be dead."

"I went to Ireland."

"No, you didn't. You died. I was at your funeral. You were cremated."

"Hmmm," he said, ambivalently, smiling a maddening, unanswerable smile.

Everyone tries to be kind. Susan goes into motherly mode and I have to pull out of her grasp. Maeve sends a surprisingly thoughtful letter. Dee, too, tries to help, but she's at a loss; Richard was sick before she arrived out here and she never knew him in his heyday. She is getting impatient with me, can't understand why I'm taking it so hard.

I don't fully understand myself. He was my friend. I loved him and I miss him, but why do I feel like it is my own life that has ended?

What Gary finds hardest is that he wasn't there for the end. He rang Richard's mother in Telport to let her know and she thanked him by making him leave when she arrived so that it was she, not Gary, who saw Richard out of this world. The hospital let that happen because she was next of kin. This rule has since been changed, permitting the patient to nominate their own person.

Richard would have wanted the man who had loved him most from the moment they met. Gary wanted — needed — to be there. But, instead, his last sighting of his beloved boy was his face muzzled by the ventilator, and Mrs Burke standing guard over him, arms folded across her chest, an empty fortress of righteousness.

Gary can't shake that image — of Richard's eyes rotating wildly over the plastic cup, unable to see, unable to speak — out of his head.

The two of us spend a lot of time together, sitting in slumped silence or in front of the TV. Is it worse for him? Everybody says it is, and I suppose it must be, but I cannot imagine how.

I am offered a new job, as an agony aunt. A "sexpert", as Lauren, my new editor likes to call it. She knows just how she wants it to be: my name will be Sue Denim and I'll do four letters per page, one Problem of the Month and three others. The advice will be responsible but worldly, the approach caring but daring.

"Women love the truth," she says. "It's men who are the prudes."

Lauren is evangelical about women's magazines. It incenses her that they are disparaged, not taken seriously by the world. "It's because they're for women," she says. "Baseball and automobiles are important, you know, but what we wear and eat and who and how we love — that's trivial girl's stuff? Yeah, right."

She offers me a sum of money that sounds ludicrous and when, unsure whether I want the job or not, I seem hesitant, she offers me half as much again. I take this offer; I can't afford not to. The aerobics boom is dying off and numbers in the Rí Rá classes are beginning to drop. Aerobics is now an activity like any other, with its own adherents, rather than a craze igniting everyone.

Hearing word of my new job, Dee turns up at my door with a bottle of champagne. "I know you're Miss Healthy America and never let alcohol cross your lips any more, but this is a celebration."

She takes down two champagne glasses from a high cupboard, places them side by side on the table, holds the bottle at arms' length, pops the cork. As the fizzy liquid flows up and out of the glasses, spilling out over the table, she laughs. I take the glass she hands me: it's wet on the outside from the overflow. I put damp fingers to my mouth and lick. The alcohol tastes sharp, but sweet too.

Dee is lifting her glass, smiling across at me. "Sláinte," she says, the Irish salutation.

"Chin-chin," I reply.

We both tilt our heads back and drink.

The column is a success. It's because it's so different, Lauren says. So refreshing. I don't know why it works or what happens when I "become" Sue. That is how I think of it. I even have a ritual for the transformation: I dress in an old loose trousers and smock top, no bra and bare feet; I burn joss sticks and put Mozart on the stereo. That way, it is her perspective, not mine, that pops onto the page. This sounds silly, but left to me, as me, I'd never come up with any answers. Sue believes in sexual liberation, that the heart of freedom lies there, in what we are prepared to do and think and be, sexually. And in part, I agree with her.

In part.

But...

Who is this "I"? What is this "but..."?

Dear Sue,

For most of my life I've lived monogamously with one man after another. At the same time, I've always been bothered by the world's obsession with couples and longed for love of a different kind. I dreamed of a sexual energy that could flow free between me and a variety of people at once, without guilt or shame, games or betrayal, free of the insecurity that demands ownership.

I turned thirty this year and realized that it wasn't going to happen if I didn't make it happen. So I decided to launch an experiment. I had been living with a man for almost a year as part of a two-couple household. One night, after the four of us had consumed a lot of alcohol, I made the suggestion that we should extend our sexual intimacy beyond our two complacent couples. Everybody was willing and excited by the prospect, so I got together with the other guy and agreed to share "my" man with the other woman (none of us was interested in a same-sex encounter).

All seemed to go well for a while. I thought the four of us were growing, setting ourselves free of societal constraints, having the courage of our desires. But now I've found out that while the other man and I were just expanding our relationship, breaking out of nuclear bondage, etc., our respective mates were falling seriously in love with each other.

He told me last week. He loves her and wants to live with her exclusively. Sue, it hurts so much. I have never in my life been so full of rage and jealousy: I fantasize about killing them both in their sleep. The other man is devastated and spends his time either crying on my shoulder or berating me for starting the whole thing. What should I do?

Chastened

Dear Sexual Adventurer,

What should you do, you ask? What can you do, except carry on living through the fruits of your experiment?

Freedom is not safe. But you already know that.

You cannot control how other people will respond. But you already know that.

Emotions pass. In time, when the rage and hurt have subsided, you may recognise your urge to push out your boundaries as something bigger than the transient pain it caused. Or you may come to think of it as a lesson you needed to learn about faith and faithfulness.

Whichever, don't be "chastened." Look deeply at what's happening and accept it, without letting it quash the spirit that makes you so venturesome.

You are a big person, riding the big waves of a big life.

Live on.

My postbag swells and Lauren is delighted. The publishers take note and, before long, the column is being syndicated to magazines in South Africa and Australia as well as the States, and in Britain, which also means Ireland. I even get occasional letters from there; their problems seem no different to anybody else's. Things are changing in Ireland, Maeve tells me over the phone, but when I ask how, she talks about jobs and money, bars and coffee-houses. Racing to jump aboard the globalisation express doesn't sound like much of a change to me — still acquisitive, still conservative, still aping other, more "advanced" places — but if life is easier for more people, I guess that's progress.

A politician in Idaho denounces my column as filth. I wish Richard were here to help me enjoy the accolade.

Then comes the day I'm standing in my hallway with the telephone in my hand, listening to Maeve tell me that Gran is dead. I stood at the end of the phone, the radio from the kitchen blaring through the open door into the hall, and asked all the right questions in a voice that didn't sound like mine. Maeve wanted me to go back for the funeral, tried hard to persuade me and a part of me very much wanted to be there, releasing the tides of my tears. But if I was going to go back for Gran, it would have been while she was still alive. We both would have preferred that.

With her gone, I wasn't about to deliver myself up to Mrs D. — who hadn't even asked.

Thirteen weeks later, another phone call. Auntie Norah this time. She couldn't live without Gran, Maeve says during this call. She willed herself to die.

I hate, hate, hate the tone of Maeve's voice as she tells it. This time, I don't even think about going back.

Sue Denim has all the answers, but she's no help to me. I don't even know what my question is.

Richard would know how to make me believe in what I'm doing. I miss the way things were when he was here, when life was exuberant and I had flings and relationships and experiences that gave me pleasure. Pleasure.

It doesn't sound like much — and I do remember sometimes feeling that I wanted more — but it seems like all a person needs, now it's gone.

I used to have lovers; now I have pick-ups. I used to have fun; now I have alcohol. Everything I'm doing is bad for me, I know it. I've done it all before and I know where it leads, to where I swore I'd never go again, but I can't stop myself. I'm a vessel unmoored, with somebody else at the helm. The old me, perhaps? Or maybe somebody from further back, somebody who could have taught me how to navigate, but never did.

"*D*onal drove me mad the whole time," says Maeve, recalling her visit to San Francisco. "I spent nearly every night after we'd gone to bed calming him down."

"I knew he was a bit fazed by the scene, but I'd no idea he took it so bad."

"Dreadful. He was even afraid to drink out of cups that Richard or Gary had used."

I feel the skin on my face blaze up. I was right to never like him, I think.

"I know, I know," she says. "But you have to remember the times. Afterwards, people came to understand a lot more about AIDS, but then...Well, he was hardly the only one, was he?"

It is Richard's anniversary: six years ago today since he died. Six years. Where did they go? It's so hard not to think of them as wasted. All day, as I went about my business in Dublin, I've been dispirited, struggling against the suck of misery. None of the things that make this year different — writing, pregnancy, being in Ireland — were able to keep me buoyant today. The writing I have been so wedded to seems hollow and useless, a concoction of nothings. I'm getting fearful about the baby and about afterwards, of how we will be together. Together, alone.

Rory still has not come or sent any word, and is unlikely to now.

As for Ireland, the faction fighting goes on, the antagonism that seems more virulent here than anywhere else. Each day, the radio brings belligerent adversaries into Maeve's kitchen and, over breakfast, we listen to them slinging their tirades at each other over Northern Ireland. The IRA has declared a ceasefire, but the gesture is insufficient for the British government and Unionists. They are calling for all Republican guns and bombs to be destroyed before peace talks can begin.

The IRA refuses. Irish Republicans have never handed over their armoury. Not in 1921, during The Truce with Britain. Not in 1923 after the Civil War, when weapons were dumped, not surrendered. And not now.

The second talking point is the scandal of what has come to be called abuse, the slime under the rug of power. Beatings, humiliation, molestation and rape were, and are, endemic in Irish schools, seminaries and institutions — and in that other great Irish institution, the family, too. Every time I hear a priest or politician pontificating on the radio, I am reminded of why I fled this country. It is not that such things don't happen in other places, but the Irish version is too virulent for me.

I have to tell Maeve so repeatedly. She keeps making suggestions about how good it would be for the baby to grow up with an aunt and cousin nearby; how raising a baby all alone is hard work; how, in a few years, Ria will be old enough to baby-sit...Tonight, such is my sense of frailty, that I almost feel I could be persuaded. Almost.

It's her thoughts on Richard that have made me warm to her. I didn't realise until this evening how much she really liked him; she has so many memories of him from her visit to San Francisco, memories we never discussed before. Through dinner, we regaled Ria with some of the more repeatable stories and, since Ria went upstairs to bed, the two of us have been sitting together in front of the sitting-room fire, turning over memories.

Maeve occupies the armchair, a whiskey and water in front of her; I recline on the sofa opposite, in the only position that is comfortable for me these days: half lying on a nestle of cushions, my belly protruding upwards like a hill.

"You and Richard never had a thing?" she asks. "Or did you?"

"God, no. You met him, didn't you?" Five minutes with Richard should be enough to locate him at the furthest, gayest end of the sexuality spectrum.

"Mmmmm."

"And what is that sceptical sound supposed to convey?"

"I just find it hard to understand why his death flattened you so."

"He was my friend, Maeve. Simple as that."

"I mean, more than your own mother's! It's unusual, you have to admit."

Oh, no...So long, soft, sisterly feelings. She shrugs her puzzlement and the gesture makes her neck and shoulder bones protrude. Her neck could be held in the grasp of one hand. I have pity for that neck. I also have the urge to choke it.

So far, we have avoided conflict. In the morning, after she and Ria leave for school, I get up and go into the centre to write. I go to the Winding Stair, a rickety old bookshop café on the north bank of The Liffey. Each of its wide windows has its window box of valiant flowers fighting the traffic fumes gasped up from below. There I write, looking down at the floods of shoppers rising and falling over The Liffey's Ha'penny Bridge, under high, complicated Irish skies.

It's a good view of Dublin — almost soothing. I write well there, which is why I take the trouble to travel in each morning, even though this house of Maeve's lies empty all day. I tried writing here, just once, up in the bedroom, but Maeve's years with Donal were in the air, and all those years when I was out of the country clustered in the silence.

Sometimes I return to my hotel room. I like knowing it is there, available to me. I've managed to spend the occasional night there by inventing a friend, somebody I knew in college that I "meet" every so often and, when I do, I call Maeve to say that I am spending the night at her apartment. Then I go to my beige bolthole and breathe free for eight or ten or twelve hours, refreshed enough to return. Maeve suspects the truth, I think, but appreciates the lie.

"Don't take this wrong," she says now, "but it strikes me that being so fixated on Richard allowed you to avoid something else."

"Something else?"

"A relationship of your own."

"You've been seeing too much of that shrink of yours," I say, lightly.

Maeve is attending a counsellor, to try to understand where she and Donal went wrong. Can she hear the menace under my airy tone? If she's not more careful, she will break our truce.

I would like to say it straight to her, tell her that Richard gave me what I should have got from her and Mrs D.: unconditional love, as her therapist would no doubt call it.

Richard's simple acceptance of me won him my undying devotion. Literally undying, staying with me even though he has gone. Maeve, who I suspect has never had a real friendship, still thinks romantic love is the best. That it has recently — and presumably for some years now — let her down, in no way diminishes her belief in it. Though Donal is now refusing to see her at all, asking her to drop Ria outside his apartment block for her custody visits without meeting him. Still, she nurtures hope that he will come back.

And how can I despise this hope when I live with my own version of the same affliction? I want to be gentle with her, I really do, but she makes it so hard. If I can be careful of her, why can't she extend me the same favour? Why always this need of hers to make me face the hard questions? (Like: how small a thing was my devotion to Richard if I couldn't even be with him at his end?)

I want to get up off the sofa and pace the room, but it would take a crane to lift me, so I confine myself to stretching out my swollen legs. The ankles are so puffy, an older, fatter woman's ankles, pooled with blood. New veins, like blue in a Stilton, have surfaced all over my legs. The skin of my abdomen is stretched to transparency: I never imagined skin could stretch so far.

You are so big now that the discomfort is constant: heartburn arrives at regular intervals to sting my oesophagus. You ripple my belly with each movement you make. You too are cramped and uncomfortable. We both want out.

But I am also dreading the labour. After years of suffering no worse physical pain than a small cut or bruise, I am scared.

"It's time to get closure on it, I would have thought," Maeve says, still harping on Richard.

When she starts on like this, I think that maybe I shouldn't be here, that we are not helping each other at all. We disagree on almost everything. Yesterday it was the North. All her patriotism is affixed to the Republic of Ireland. It stops at a border created by the British and she sees no irony in that.

I take up that topic again because, though we differ on it, it will distract her from Richard. "I've been thinking about what you said yesterday, Maeve, about the North, and I wanted to ask you: do you not see what's going on in the North today as a continuation of Granny Peg's 'War of Independence'?"

"Things were different then," she says. "The old IRA were men of honour."

"All of them?" Has she not been reading the manuscript pages I've given her?

"They killed and died for an ideal."

"The ideal hasn't changed, has it? Isn't it the same struggle, the same methods? Just that a bomb kills more people than a gun?"

"But..."

"Don't get me wrong, it's not that I agree with that struggle. I personally think we'd have been better off growing up in an Ireland that had remained part of the UK."

This statement swings things round. Maeve stops in the act of twisting her hair up into a clip, and stares at me with green eyes aghast, wearing the exact expression that Rory wore when I said the same to him. "You can't mean that?" she gasps.

"Why not?"

"You're being provocative. You don't mean it."

"But I do. All the damage done by English colonisation was well done by the time of the so-called War of Independence. What the Irish did to themselves afterwards only made a bad thing worse."

"I completely disagree with you. And why do you say 'so-called' War of Independence? That war did get us our independence."

"Did it?" I ask, thinking of Granny Peg and Mrs D. And me and Rory. And think about those moments that I have felt more frequently this summer, when I found within myself a tranquillity below thought. When I realised that I am something more than a bundle of nationality, or gender, or sexuality, or any other kind of identity I want to throw into the basket called "me". Down in those depths, I am suddenly sure, is where true freedom resides.

I am trying to formulate this insight into words that I can pass to my sister when the doorbell interrupts: Ding-dong, ding-dong.

"Good God," Maeve says. "Who's that? At this hour of the night?"

Ten fifteen. My stomach takes a small flip. The kind of time you'd arrive if you left Wexford at around seven thirty or eight o'clock. After coming home from work at six and having a conversation and packing a hasty suitcase...

"Maybe I won't answer it," Maeve says. "You can't see the lights in here from the front."

"I think you'd better," I say. "You never know."

"I suppose." She gets slowly out of the big armchair, uncurling her legs from under her, giving a small grouchy stretch as she goes, leaving the door ajar. I hear her open the front door and the surprise in her greeting. She says a name, but I cannot catch it. I cannot hear her words, but her tone makes something in my stomach start to ferment.

Then the other voice speaks, muffled, but a male voice. Definitely male.

You give a strong kick. What do you know or sense?

There's the door closing. More suppressed talk. A silence. Footsteps approaching across the tiled hallway. Two sets of footsteps. The door opening. I'm afraid to look up.

"Jo?" Maeve's voice is tentative, a whisper.

Her head is peeping round the door, her face flushed. "He's here, Jo."

"He is?" I get up out of the chair. Blood swishes into my head, probably from standing up so fast. I forgive him, I realise as I wait for the black amoebas before my eyes to vanish. Whatever may lie ahead, I forgive him all. But why is Maeve keeping him out there? Is she afraid that I don't want to see him?

"We'll be in the kitchen," she says.

"Kitchen?"

"Yeah. We need to talk. Obviously."

I give my head a waggle. When I see her again I know what I should have known from the start. A memory rises: Mrs D. and Daddy, the day he came back home to us after leaving us for four years. Maeve is wearing the exact same expression on her face as our mother did back then. Hence, perhaps, the anger I feel, white and hard as bone.

"Well, well," I say. "The prodigal returns." His words to me at Mrs D's funeral. "Why don't you bring him in here?" I manage to say, in a steady voice. "I was ready for bed anyway."

She opens the door wider, flourishing him in.

Ashamed of my pettiness, I jump on top of my anger, wrestle

it down, and change the tone of my voice: "Welcome home, Donal."

DONAL'S RETURN CHANGES EVERYTHING. Now, I am in the way. Maeve says this is nonsense, but I am. Neither of them want me here, knowing what I know, and I don't want to be here either, witnessing their travails. Things she has told me about him rankle.

Also, I don't want to lose what she and I have so recently gained. Living together is straining our newly-won, tenuous bond.

But she won't let me go. I was good enough to come when she needed me, now I must stay until the baby comes. It wouldn't be right for me to have to go into labour alone, in a hotel room. What about those pains I am having in the night?

It is true that you have started to bear down inside me, that I am assailed by stabbing pains in strange new places, pains that sometimes stop me in my tracks. It is true that I am afraid to face into labour alone. It is close now, very close: a week to the due day. Even if I go over my time, it can be no further away than a fortnight.

Can Maeve and I live in the same house for that long without a breach?

Fingers crossed, I stay.

1923

*S*ergeant Brosnan gave Private O'Dwyer the nod to start the car. A day and a half now they'd spent, questioning witnesses, and the only useful one so far was the bar girl from Ryan's of Rathmeelin, who, as far as he could make out, was the last person to see O'Donovan alive. He had taken a drink there around teatime and left, telling her that he had an appointment in Mucknamore at seven o'clock. At 7.14pm his watch stopped, presumably in the wet sands.

Stuck in sinking sands waiting for the returning tide to take you: what a death. If he was lured, Kavanagh was right in saying it was one evil act.

The car spluttered and coughed into its workaday rumble and they were pulling out onto the road when a man came lumbering up to them and started to wave his two arms like a windmill. He was poorly dressed, two strings of twine where the belt of his coat should be.

"Stop the car!" he shouted and O'Dwyer did.

"Yes?" Brosnan snapped.

"I'm hearing that yez are investigating what went on here the night before last. Would that be so?"

"If you mean the death of Lieutenant O'Donovan, then yes, that is so."

"In that case, I've something of interest to yez."

"Have you indeed?"

"I have."

He stood there, like a child waiting for a pat on the head.

"Well? Go on."

He looked around, over each shoulder. "I'm thinking it would be better if we went somewhere more private. I don't want to be handing it over in front of the entire village."

"Handing what over?"

The fellow tapped a finger to the side of his nose, looked about him again. The street was empty, the little windows appraising.

"Sit into the car," Brosnan said. "If you must."

"I don't know, sir. I don't think that would go down too well with some, to see me voluntarily climbing into this particular vehicle."

Brosnan looked at O'Dwyer, who slid his eyes upwards. "Go on, so, be off with you."

"Don't misunderstand me, sir. Myself, I'd be entirely happy to get in. But these are dangerous times we're living in."

"For Christ's sake, man. What is it you want?"

"It's not so much what I want." He gave a slow, stupid grin. "Sir," he added, belatedly.

"Is this a game?"

"I'm quite disposed to satisfy you. But in order to do so, I have to ask yez to make it look as if I'm being forced."

Forced? The devil. And he probably had nothing at all. But what if he had? So far, not one single lead...

He nodded at O'Dwyer to do it. The blackguard made a convincing — O'Dwyer would probably no doubt say too convincing — attempt at resistance, until the private's hat was knocked askew on his head and Brosnan said, "We've had enough of your nonsense. Get in now or we're going."

The fellow let himself be taken by the scruff of his collar and shoved into the back of the car. "Drive down to...the...back strand," he said, breathless.

O'Dwyer ignored that and took them out the Wexford road. Once outside the village, he pulled to a stop by the ditch.

"Right," Brosnan said, turning round. "Let's be having it, whatever it is."

A sly look. "I don't know how to put this, sir. Is it a Sergeant you are?"

Brosnan nodded, peremptorily.

"Well, Sergeant, I'm supposing that the army would be grateful for information about why Dan O'Donovan went walking The Causeway in the dark that night?"

The fellow still had his teeth, but every one of them was black-rotten in his head. The car was filling up with an unpleasant pong.

"And if so, how would such gratitude be demonstrated?"

So that was it. He should have known from the first. "That would depend."

"On?"

"On the quality of the information," Brosnan said, not looking at him.

"But there would be a...token of your appreciation?"

"Bear in mind, man, that it is your civic duty to help in a...in such an enquiry." He nearly said "murder enquiry", but that wouldn't be right. Despite what was being said abroad, they had no proof of foul play. And he wasn't going to promise this repulsive creature anything. Let's see what the fellow had first.

"I'd need to be sure, Sergeant."

Brosnan could see the future of this village written on this blackguard's face. From here on out, it would become ever more closed and insular. Fright at what they'd shown themselves capable of doing to each other had thinned their souls, souls that were already reduced from hundreds of years under the British yoke. None of them — maybe himself included? — was able to face the true shame of this dirty little war, the wicked whys and wherefores of it. Some would react by making too much of small differences, because otherwise they'd have to admit they'd been killing and dying for nothing. Others would try to pretend the horrors never happened at all. Least said, soonest mended. Whatever you say, say nothing.

Well, he might not think their cause worth killing or dying for, but he wasn't afraid of the truth. He said, "You won't be let down, man. Not if you have something worthwhile to pass on."

Satisfied, the creature reached inside his coat and made a great commotion of taking something from his inside pocket and presenting it with hands aloft. A gun. A Webley rifle. He held the booty under Brosnan's nose. "I found it this morning," he said.

Brosnan nodded. "Go on."

"There I was, after bringing out the cows, walking back up the road towards my house..."

"Which is where?"

"Down by the Tench, Sergeant."

Brosnan shook his head.

"Don't you know the Tench?" He made a show of surprise. "On the other side of the village, down towards what we call the Hole in the Wall." There was that knowingness again, that simple-minded delight at knowing something that Brosnan, an outsider, a stranger — a foreigner! — did not. "The strand exit nearest The Causeway, Sergeant. Which is the way out to Coolanagh, if you get my drift. There I was, strolling along behind the cattle, minding my own, when next thing I spied it, out of the side of my eye. Lying there, half in and half out of the ditch."

"And you think it significant?"

He looked at them with feigned surprise. "You don't? Don't you know what this is? Ser—geant?" He drawled the title with sneering affectation, as if Brosnan was the greatest dunce that ever walked.

"Just keep to the facts, please."

"There was only one rifle of this sort owned around here."

"Go on, man."

"It belonged to Parle." He flashed his sly, conniving grin again. "Yes, Sergeant. Barney Parle. I presume you've heard of him?"

1995

*W*hen the fight comes, it's about Mrs D. We're sitting over the remains of dinner, darkness bulked against the glass walls of Maeve's dining room. Donal has gone to the gym, Ria is in bed, Maeve is finishing a bottle of wine and, since the others left, we have been fixed on the topic of our mother.

"How much of her pain was in her situation," I ask, "and how much in her person? That's what I could never work out. If she didn't have Daddy and all-that-had-been-done-to-her to complain about, I still don't think she'd have been happy."

"She was happy after Daddy died. You didn't know her then."

"I did. Daddy was dead a year, I seem to recall, when she kicked me out of the house."

"She did not kick you out, you walked. And in that first year, she wasn't herself...Naturally. Afterwards, she was very happy. She loved her bowls and her golf and her bridge. She liked her life then."

"The merry widow, eh?"

She shakes her head at me. "You're so hard sometimes, Jo. You know how unhappy he made her."

"What about him? What about his unhappiness?" I appear to be shouting, though nothing in the conversation calls for it.

"Yes, he was unhappy too. And he, too, behaved badly. You never blamed him, though, did you?"

I look down at the debris on the dinner table.

"She was your mother, Jo. Does that count for nothing with you? Now that you're about to be a mother yourself?"

She begins to clear away the plates, scrape off the food. "And look what she gave you — all the family papers, the opportunity to put this book together," she says, in the voice of somebody trying hard to be patient. "Anyone can see what that means to you. Can't you be grateful to her for that?"

"She wanted me to do a glorious history of our glorious family. It was for her, not for me."

"Or maybe she knew exactly what you'd do..."

"Come on, Maeve. Mrs D. wouldn't have passed these papers on if she knew the full story. She said in her letter that she never read Norah's notebooks. And you have to read Norah's stuff, as well as Gran's, to get it. No, she thought the extent of the secret was that she was 'illegitimate'." I put two fingers around the word my mother would have used. "Not that Norah was her mother, rather than her aunt."

"My God, Jo, don't you realise what a big thing it was for Mammy to share that."

"I do. But she did it because she wanted a glorified —"

Maeve cuts me off. "She did it because she wanted to draw you back into the family. And, what's more, she succeeded."

"You know, you don't have to defend her every move, Maeve. She was shitty to you too."

She shakes her head.

"Maeve! Don't pretend she wasn't." I have to stop shouting. How can I break through her denial? "She was. I remember. And I remember the way you'd always go crawling back for more."

"She wasn't easy, Jo, I never claimed she was easy." Her

moderate tones are a deliberate contrast to mine. "And yes, I had my difficulties with...Let's just say that since she died, I...Well, she wasn't easy. I can agree with that. But don't you see, Jo? Nothing that she did or failed to do can alter the plain fact that she was our mother. Denying that hurts you as much as it ever hurt her."

"No, sorry. Mothering is something you do, not just something you are. You do it, with Ria." She does. No matter how tired Maeve is from work and running the house and now all the stress of Donal, she still does the mothering thing. Sometimes I feel jealous of Ria, and sometimes impatient at how she is so careless of that.

"I get it wrong, often," she says. "And I hate when I do. Mammy's failures hurt her. Just as yours hurt you, and mine hurt me."

I want to go on arguing, but I can't think of any words.

"Sometimes, now," Maeve says. "I wonder whether it was because you reminded her of Auntie Norah."

"What?"

"There is a physical resemblance, you know. Your hair: she was a redhead too. And around the eyes..."

"Gee, thanks."

"Come on, Jo, just in certain ways."

Could that be right? At least it gives her a reason. Can Maeve stretch herself to imagine how it might feel to be on the receiving end of that? Can I dare to ask her?

My knees are clenching each other, alarmed at what I am about to say. My voice slides down the decibels, so that this time when I speak it's only a whisper. But I speak: "She couldn't stand me, Maeve."

There: it's out. The shameful truth. The truth I have only ever told Richard before. My own mother didn't love me. She didn't even like me.

"Oh, come on..."

"Please, Maeve. Don't pretend. I know you knew it too."

At last I have silenced her. Will she admit it? She never has before, it makes her — the favourite — feel too guilty. For a long moment, we hover; it feels to me like forever. Then she stands up with the plates, looks down at me.

"Jesus, Jo, for once, just for once, could we drop the self-pity?"

I am on my feet, moving too fast, storming past the corners of the table, the kitchen units, my arms around my belly for protection. Mine or the baby's? I don't know. I can't see. My head is drowning in darkness and I am shouting again. "Fuck off, Maeve. Just fuck off. Just fuck off." Like a child, throwing the words back over my shoulder as I hurtle away, down the hall, up the stairs.

The fight has taken us over, the way it used to when we were children. It's quivering in my arms and legs and making her run after me, shouting: "If you'd come out of that self-obsessed haze of yours for five minutes, you'd know that it isn't even Mammy you're mad at, but Gran."

All those years — tiptoeing phone calls, awkward visits, careful conversations — are ripped away in an instant and here we are, hatred wrenching our faces out of shape, its breath panting in its eagerness to strike, to dive, hard and deep into each other's weakest places.

"Isn't that true, Jo? It was Gran not going to you, Gran 'choosing' Mammy instead of you" — now it's her turn to use two fingers to put quote marks round the word — "in some mad competition that existed only in your head. That's who you're sore at, really. That's what you can't bear to admit."

It's true, it's true, it's true. Why, Gran? Why did you never ring, or write? Why? Maeve had Mrs D. I had no-one but you. You knew that.

I hurry on, away from them all, into the spare room that has been mine while I stayed here, locking the door behind me. I expect Maeve to come bounding up the stairs after me, banging on the door, but she doesn't. I tear clothes from their hangers, stuff anything I can see into my bag, brush everything that's on the dressing table in with one sweep of my arm. I'll sort it out later, in the hotel. My hands are shaking so hard I can't get my toothpaste and toothbrush into the wash bag.

Never trust them, never. I knew, but still I came here, left myself open to this. Never again. Never. Never.

A last glance round the room to make sure that I haven't forgotten anything vital. Out in the hall, I see Ria's door ajar. What did she hear? "Goodbye, Ria," I say, but I get no reply.

Maeve is at the end of the stairs, waiting for me. "Oh, what a surprise," she says. "Jo's packed her bag, Jo's decided to leave. Where to this time, Jo? Aren't you running out of places to go?"

I have to take each stair carefully, my balance unsteady. One – step – at – a – time – then – the – next. There: I've reached the bottom. Maeve is standing off to my left. Ahead is the hall door, waiting for me to open it. All I have to do is cross the hallway.

Cross the hallway.

Open the door.

"Don't stop now, Jo. What are you waiting for?"

You.

You are what is stopping me. As I take the final step of the stair, you go whompf within me, and a stabbing pain shoots through my lower belly. Now I have crumpled.

Now I am folded into sitting on the step and I am crying, my face in my hands.

Now I am saying I am sorry, I don't know why, but that is what I am saying, over and over again: "I'm sorry, Maeve. I'm sorry. I'm sorry."

I say it to her, but really I'm addressing everyone: Richard. Granny Peg and Auntie Norah. Maeve, Ria and Rory. Even Orla, Rory's wife. Oh God, yes, even Mrs D.

Now Maeve has her arms around me, telling me that it's all right, that she is sorry too. I burrow my face into her shoulder, trying to explain that's not what I mean, that I am drowning in a remorse so deep and sore that I think it's going to kill me. "I had to get rid of...It would have been..."

I want to tell her more, tell her properly, but I can't snatch enough breath. The skull of my forehead is grinding against her shoulder bones.

"I know," she says. She begins to stroke my head, my shoulder, my back. "I know."

"No, you don't."

"I do, Jo."

This time, the words reach me. I look up and see in her glistening eyes that she does.

She touches my face, nodding gently, gently.

"It's not that I think..." My sobs won't let me form the words right, my tears are wetting the skin of her neck. "If I had to do it again, I'd do the same...I had to...But..."

"I know, Jo," she says, her voice so soft, so soothing. A voice I've heard her use with Ria sometimes. "It's okay. You did what you had to do." She's stroking my hair. "It's okay now. Let it be. Let it go."

"It's just..."

"I know, I know."

Something about the way she keeps saying that... "How do you know?"

Her eyes pierce into mine. "I know because you weren't the only one."

Can she mean...? Surely, surely not? Not Maeve?

"Yes," she nods. "Different reasons, but yes."

I am without words.

"Why so shocked, Jo? Ten thousand of us take that trip to England, every year."

"But I can't...It's just...Did Mrs D. know?"

"Are you mad? Of course not."

She looks so indignant that I start to laugh. Then she joins in, and we find we can't seem to stop. We sit there, at the end of the stairs, waves of hysterical laughter breaking over us, while all the time I'm looking at her, at her head thrown back, and her wide open mouth, and her shoulders shaking and I'm telling myself, over and over in my head, as if somebody is listening in: this is Maeve. This is my sister, Maeve.

DEAD MUCKNAMORE OFFICER'S INQUEST!
Gun Belonging to Dead Irregular Found!

Mother of Deceased Calls for Murder Trial!

An inquest into the death of Lieutenant Dan O'Donovan, National Army, was arranged by the military and held in the courthouse, Wexford, on Friday evening last. Lieutenant O'Donovan was found dead at Coolanagh, Mucknamore, on the morning of Wednesday December 10th. Brigade Police Officer Jas Brosnan conducted the enquiry.

Evidence of identification was given by Dan O'Donovan Snr, father of the deceased. It appears that Lieutenant O'Donovan was granted a few days' leave by the army and that it was on the first evening of this break that the tragedy occurred.

John Colfer, fisherman, deposed as to how he found the body and immediately notified the military authorities. Next witness, Doctor Matthew Morris, testified to having examined the body. There were no marks of violence, the doctor said, and he was of the opinion that death was due to asphyxia. At this point, the mother of the deceased interrupted proceedings, saying her son had been murdered whichever way you looked at it.

Police Officer Brosnan responded by saying to the jury: "I understand the deceased man's father is here. It is open to him to cross-examine the witness if he wishes, but he has not done so." Mr O'Donovan, the father, rose to his feet and heatedly replied, "This inquest is nothing but a farce to my mind." The Chair informed Mr and Mrs O'Donovan that they would have to behave themselves. If they wanted to cross-examine a witness, they could do so in the ordinary way.

Miss Anne Comerford, employed at Ryan's public house, Rathmeelin, three miles from Mucknamore, testified that the deceased had called in there the night he died, between the hours of half-past five and six o'clock. He was wearing a National Army uniform, a cape and a civilian cap. He only remained in the shop long enough to drink one bottle of stout, saying he had an appointment in Mucknamore at seven.

PO Brosnan: Did he describe the nature of this appointment?

Miss Comerford: What he said to me was he had to see a man about a dog.

The night was dark and very foggy, according to witness, and the road was in a bad state, but he went off in good health, sober and cheerful.

Staff Captain Sean Kavanagh, National Army, stated that he was one of the party that proceeded to Mucknamore on the morning the body was discovered, on receipt of the report from Mr Colfer. With some difficulty, they had extracted the body from the sand with the aid of ropes and an army truck. It was he who identified it as that of Dan O'Donovan. There was nothing to indicate foul play. The hands had not been tied.

They took the body to the morgue. On his person, they found a typewritten letter rendered unreadable by the wet sands in which he had met his end. Also a tobacco pouch with tobacco, a pipe, a book and a photograph. There was a watch also, stopped at 7.14. "The time of the murder," cried Mrs O'Donovan, again interrupting proceedings.

Captain Kavanagh continued, testifying that when O'Donovan left the barracks that evening, that was the last any army personnel had seen of him until they received the emergency call the next morning. The army authorities had recently agreed to transfer O'Donovan to the new police force, the Civic Guards. He was a man with further promotion before him, most reliable, and his death a loss to the army and the country.

Final witness was Miss Margaret (Peg) Parle of Mucknamore. As this witness took the stand, commotion broke out, with much talk among the audience and again, cries of protest from the family of the deceased. After order had been restored, the police officer appealed to the jury to decide if the inquest was being properly conducted. The jury pronounced themselves perfectly satisfied that the case was being conducted in a most excellent manner by Mr Brosnan.

Testimony continued. Miss Parle said she was speaking on behalf of her family, as her father was too unwell following a recent bereavement. She was then questioned about a gun that was found in a ditch between her house and The Point the morning after the night in question. A witness had identified this gun as belonging to her brother, an Irregular killed in action some months ago. Miss Parle said she had no idea how it had turned up where it did.

PO Brosnan: When did you last see it?

Miss Parle: Before my brother was shot, I think. I can't really remember.

PO Brosnan: We've witnesses who say it was seen at your house recently.

Miss Parle: I'd say any such witnesses were only trying to bring us trouble.

PO Brosnan: We also have witnesses who say you blamed the deceased for the death of your brother.

Miss Parle: There's those who say so, I know that.

PO Brosnan: And what do you say?

Miss Parle: I say leave us alone. I say, stop trying to make something out of nothing.

PO Brosnan then asked Miss Parle about her movements and the movements of her family on the night in question and witness gave answers that showed all had alibis for the entire evening.

Therein the evidence ended. Mr O'Donovan rose to his feet again. He wanted to know why others had not been called on to testify. He became very excitable and made a number of allegations and was again ordered to be quiet or to leave the court.

Police Officer Brosnan said that he was as aware as the next man of the horrors dividing the country in two and so he had done everything to procure all the evidence possible. If anything in the nature of foul play had occurred, he had no evidence of it. All the evidence that had been unearthed he had placed before the jury to whom he now left the case.

The jury retired and returned with the verdict that the deceased had died from asphyxiation in sinking sands. There was no evidence to show how he came to be walking in such a treacherous area so late at night. Their verdict was "Death by Misadventure". They extended their sympathy to his relatives.

PART V
CREST

*L*et go, my sister suggested, that night after we calmed down. Let go, the sea waves whispered throughout my summer in Mucknamore. Let go, my own musings on freedom had urged. Then along you come and do it for me.

Nine months you spent dissolving my self from within and then at last you are here, out in the world. At last, I am holding you and knowing that your need, your ferocious, helpless human baby need, will reconstitute a whole new self around you.

From now on, I'll still be me, but I will also be all yours.

What an entrance you make! It begins with small contractions, well spaced, and for hours I cope well, but then I end up on a hospital bed the height and width of an ironing board, under orders not to move. All I want to do is get down on all fours. Maeve is there beside my bed, her cheerleader's face making me snap, pain growling through me. It was a mistake to bring her: I'm not going to be able to do this, I am going to fail at what she did effortlessly.

They put me on an oxytocin drip to speed the labour along: it is now four p.m. and I have been having contractions for fourteen hours. When I came into hospital, after holding out at home with Maeve as long as I dared, I was only two centimetres dilated. I later learn that it is normal for first labours to be lengthy, but my midwife tells me it's a problem. I hold out against her first offer of the oxytocin "to help me along", and her second. But when she tells me if the labour goes on "too" long you may become distressed, I capitulate.

As soon as the drip goes in, the pain becomes intolerable. I feel that the God I have always doubted has my belly in His fist and is intent on proving His power. Before long, I have a drip in my right arm, a blood-pressure monitor on the left, an epidural anaesthetic in my lower spine, a catheter bag to my bladder, a foetal monitor through my cervix onto the baby's head. My limbs tremble.

Every so often a falsely cheerful midwife comes in, snapping on a plastic glove to do another "internal". I hate her, I hate them all, and their steel instruments and unfeeling machines, but it is a machine, the foetal monitor spinning slow scrolls of paper etched with stalagmites and stalactites, your heartbeat, that keeps me from wanting to die.

"Phhhhh."

"And again, push," says Midwife One, looking at the monitor screen. She stands to the left of my bed with one of my legs in her arms, her colleague on my right has the other, and between them is a baby who's refusing to arrive. The epidural means I can't feel my contractions and I only know to push when they check the monitor and tell me.

"Push," says Midwife Two.

"Ph-ph-phhhhhhhhhhhh."

I feel no active pain, nothing except a growing nausea in my stomach and a ferocious, dead trembling in my numbed, spreadeagled legs that extends up into my trunk. But Maeve, who's down at the other end, watching, is excited.

"Oh, Jo, there's the head," she says. "Black hair! Black! Thick as a brush. Go again."

"Push," says Midwife One.

"Good girl, push," says Midwife Two.

"Yes, push," says the obstetrician, two of the ten words he has so far exchanged with me in the fifty minutes he's spent fiddling with, and staring into, my nether regions. The others were, "Hello, Mum. How are we doing? Good, good."

Phphhh. Phphhh. Phphhh. Phphhhhhhhhhhhh. Oh God, I'm going to vomit. "I feel sick, I'm going to be —"

I gawk and Midwife One whips a silver-tin bowl from somewhere and sticks it under my chin. My insides contract, hurtling vomit out at one end and at the other squeezing you, like I'm a tube and you are a squidge of paste. You spurt out and the obstetrician and the two midwives all pitch forward to catch you. It is he who succeeds, grasping you with two firm hands, and for the first time I feel gratitude towards him.

"Oh, Jo," Maeve says. "Just look! Oh, the little darling!"

At last you are here. You are pink and purple. Your eyes are open. Your forehead is furrowed under a thatch of black hair and your hands are under your chin as if you're praying. Two fists like unbloomed buds. Four limbs curving close to the trunk, fat knees and elbows bent. A blue-and-cream woven cord attached to the stomach. A pair of distended, swollen testicles.

Testicles?

"You're a BOY?" I shout it out loud, my surprise filling the whole room and flowing out into the corridor.

Maeve laughs. "He's gorgeous, Jo! Oh, he's beautiful. A real beauty."

I want to hold you, but my stomach is taking another heave.

"She's going again," says Midwife Two, putting the tin bowl, still full of vomit, back under my chin. I spew again, trying to look at you at the same time. A second, deeper heave and I gawk – auggghhhh! – and something else spurts out of me. The placenta. It too flies through the air, as you did, but this time the medics fail to catch and, splat, it hits the obstetrician's face like a slap of liver.

"Oh dear," I say. Blood is dripping from his jaw. "I'm sorry."

"It's not your fault," says Midwife One.

I know it isn't. Really, I'm not sorry at all. Their whole way of doing this was so awful, so heedless of my needs, so careless of my hopes. It is their fault, not mine, that I am stirred and shaken to vomiting.

Though later I'll resent them and their hospital procedures for utterly failing to give this holy moment its due, right now it doesn't seem to matter, because they are handing you over. Here you are, in my arms at last. Your skin is smooth, silky new. You give your arms and legs an awkward jerk, astonished, it seems to me, to find space where the womb wall used to be. You are wrapped in an aura of serenity, still attuned to that other place, wherever it is you came from. I pull you in close. Your first holding in this new world.

Babies are our chance, I understand, our best stab at heaven. Life is always offering us the opportunity to give, to help, to serve, to take the path of the good, the path of the happy, but most of us only manage it for our children.

And some fail even in that.

What about me? Your new blue eyes are looking up at me like I'm all you'll ever want and I make a vow into them, to strive to be enough.

"Do you want to try to feed him?" Maeve suggests.

I look at her and see that her eyes are glittering with standing tears reflecting the light now coming in the window, as dawn breaks on what appears to be another shell-grey, Irish day.

Maeve has brought me in Ria's old swimming ring: without it, I could not sit. Once the epidural wore off, I felt how I'd torn. Sixteen stitches in three layers. I walk like a cowboy on hot coals, but it doesn't matter. Nothing matters, everything zings. I'm still euphoric, higher than an acrobat, higher than an aerobat.

Hormones, Maeve says. She may be right, but that's not how I want to think about it.

She and I can't stop talking, talking, talking, like we've only just met. Last night she stayed late, laid across the end of my bed like I used to lie across Richard's. I'm giving her tips on how to handle Donal, Sue Denim style. She manages to implement about a tenth of the advice, but it's keeping them from settling back into the habits that ran them into trouble. In return, she gives me tips about baby care and mothering, which I intend to implement completely. If I can.

She's practicing freeing up, while I look forward to pinning part of myself — the part that spun loose when Richard died — right back down.

You start to cry and Maeve picks you up and hands you over. I am struck again by how beautiful you are, much, much more beautiful than any of the other babies in the ward. Maeve has told me that when researchers gave new mothers T-shirts worn by their own and other babies, all the women were able to smell out the one their own baby had had on. It's the kind of thing I wouldn't have believed before, but that now makes perfect sense. Now touch and smell and taste have the solidity of sight. I run my nose along the sweetness of your skin between earlobe and chin, then follow the trail with a line of kisses, while Maeve watches, smiling bounteously on us both.

The door opens. A massive bunch of flowers comes in, and behind it is Rory. He looks around the bouquet, hesitating in the doorway. Nervous. As well he might be.

Maeve gets up. "I think it's time I was off," she says, awkwardly. "Ria will be home from piano practice."

She bends to kiss my cheek, while squeezing my biceps tight enough to bruise, and whispering in my ear: "Treat 'em mean to keep 'em keen."

What I said to her earlier about Donal. I manage to keep a deadpan face as I wave her away with a "See you tomorrow."

"I'm sorry," Rory says, once she's gone. "I know it shouldn't have taken me so long to get here."

"Damn right it shouldn't."

His hair has got longer; he has it tucked behind his ears. "I couldn't come until I was certain, Jo."

His eyes are close to mine, shining bright. And though I'd prefer if I could be angry with him, I know that if I were to look in a mirror, I'd see mine are their twin reflection.

RORY PUTS the flowers on the table under the window, the briefcase he's carrying on the floor beside the bed, and sits down beside me. "Congratulations," he says, easing back the blanket that wraps the bundle in my arms. He smiles at the sight. "Did everything go okay?"

His voice quavers. He is nervous, but I am calm. Already blooded.

"Fine," I smile, lying the mother's lie, discounting the barbarity of the process, the three layers of stitches, the nipple that's beginning to crack.

"Do you have a name?"

"Richard," I say, smiling.

"It's not —"

"A boy? Yes."

He laughs.

"I know," I say. "So sure and so wrong."

"You don't mind, do you?"

"Mind? No, not at all. It wasn't that I particularly wanted a girl."

He looks back in at the little sleeping face. "Richard, eh?" He tries it out. "Richard."

He takes a chair and we relax a little and I tell him about the birth, the drip and the vomit and the hurtling afterbirth. I make a good story out of it and when I reach the part about the placenta going all over the obstetrician's face, he throws back his head in a laugh, the way he does.

"And then," I continue, keeping up the entertainment, 'when it was all over, they handed him to me and I was brought face to face with these two enormous purple balls."

Why didn't somebody tell me about that in advance? I

thought there was something wrong with you: such an angry colour and so huge, like an accusation.

"It was the same with Daragh," he says. 'Orla and I were shocked."

Daragh? Orla? Is this how it is to be?

"But they're shrinking now, right?" he says to you, putting out a gentle hand, stoking your black hair flat across your head. Watching his palm passing over that dip in your scalp makes my insides clench. "Get used to it, son," he says. "It'll be the story of your life."

You stir at the touch, then settle back down.

"How's the writing going?" Rory asks. "I suppose it's on hold now?"

"No, I'm still managing to take some time with it. It won't let me go."

"You're nearly finished, then?"

"Near enough."

He reaches down to the floor for his briefcase, clicks it open. "In that case, I've something for you."

"What? You're not serious? More from Mrs D.?"

"Your final delivery. You were only to get this if you fulfilled the request made in the first one and produced a family history. I reckon you've done that." He hands me a mail-bag envelope, padded and very full.

"What's in here?"

"More letters, I believe."

"Really? Whose? Why were they kept separate from the rest?"

"I don't know. I was just..."

"...Following orders."

"Yes."

Yes. Mrs D.'s yes man, keeping this from me all summer. Is this why he is here? Nothing to do with us at all?

He hands me a white envelope, just as he did back in May, after her funeral. This time I open it immediately and read it in front of him.

The same salutation: Dear Siobhán.

Dear Siobhán,

Mistakes! My life, like everyone else's, is full of them. As I draw
near to meeting my Maker, I am trying to put mine right.

Because you have appreciated the other papers and photographs I
left you, I now give you these letters too. They will come as a bit of a
surprise, I don't doubt — then again, you're surely getting used to the
surprises by now.

You'll see there's a lot of letters, going back a long way, to just after
the time when Maeve first got your address in England. From that day
forward, your Gran wrote you a letter on the last day of each month
and give it to me to stamp and send with the rest of the post. Only I
never did. Each month, I'd put the letter in the secret drawer at the
back of the bureau instead.

Now I know you'll think the worst of me for this, so let me say a
few words in my defence. Your grandmother blamed herself for your
leaving and staying away, a version of events which was all wrong —
I'm sure you'll agree with that much. That woman was forever putting
herself in the wrong and the older she got, the worse she became on that
front. It was my strong belief that she should have some sign of interest
from you before running after you with letters and attention.

I also thought, for a long time, that in giving them over to me, she
was leaving the decision in my hands. That although we pretended the
letters were sent, she was content that they wouldn't be, unless I was
happy to send them. We had those kinds of understandings around a
lot of things, no need for words.

By the time I realised that wasn't how it was in this case, that she
only gave them to me because it was me who handled all the post for
the house and the shop, it was too late. I couldn't start sending them
off to you suddenly, out of the blue. You'd surely have told her. So I had
no choice but to continue doing what I'd always done.

And so it went on to a few weeks before she died. Around that
time, she spoke of you, said that if I ever saw you again, I was to

*tell you she was sorry. I told her I wouldn't, that she of all people
had nothing to be sorry for, she was entirely misguided, etc. etc., but
she became quite fixed and agitated on the matter and made me
promise.*

*Now, by your actions, you have shown you care enough to know, so
now I can tell you that.*

*And allow you the letters of that good woman. And as I do I think
that perhaps it all turned out for the best, for I believe you will be a lot
more open to them at this point than you would have been back when
they were sent.*

*This is the last of it, Siobhán. No more communications from me,
no more surprises. And I do hope that you will see my gesture for what
it is.*

*I'm not one for the words, as you know — and those who don't
write themselves get forgotten. I've accepted that. The only other thing
I have to say is that your grandmother was the best person I ever met.
None of us measured up to her. We can but try.*

*Which is why, as I go towards God, I want you to know that I, too,
forgive all.*

Your loving Mammy.

I TAKE a quick look at the letters, conscious of Rory's eyes on me.
Enough to see that they are lovely, simple and straightforward,
each one passing on the doings of the days that had passed since
the last.

Auntie Nora's health and Mrs D.'s golf scores and Maeve's
teaching triumphs. News from the village and stories from the
pub. Her work for Fianna Fáil. Helping to set up a credit union
and a running-water scheme. And, at the end of each one, the
same two sentences: "Know that we think of you and pray for
you every single day, Jo. God bless you and keep you safe, Your
loving Gran."

So of course I begin to cry, with Rory watching, unable to

help myself. I look for the anger with Mrs D. that I expect to be there and find only confusion.

I'm saved by you, starting to stir, and I realise, from the snuffling you begin, that you are due a feed. Rory sits on, looking, as I lay down the letter and open my nightdress and nursing bra and distract myself from tears by fastening you on. We both watch your ears, moving as you suck.

Rory says, "Hungry little beggar, isn't he?"

I smile, stroke the little head that he stroked a few moments ago, feel the throb of the pulse beneath the membrane and the answering thud in myself.

"Motherhood suits you," Rory says after a long silence.

"Don't sound so surprised," I say, though I'm surprised myself.

"Where did you stay before you came in?"

"Maeve's."

"How was that?"

"Yeah. Fine. She's been very good to me."

You have fallen asleep now, mid-sip. Blissed out. Your lips — lined with milk — lie open round my nipple.

"So," Rory says. "What are the plans now?"

I look up at him, suddenly afraid, and begin to fix up my clothing to get a moment of time. I need to be in order for this.

"I'm going home." I use the word consciously.

"Home?"

"Back to San Francisco."

"I see. You've booked a flight?"

"Not yet. But I expect to leave in a week or ten days. As soon as we get the all clear from the doctors."

"So...?"

So...? Is that all he has to say? What does "So...?" mean? So...can I come with you? So...don't go? So...I've left my wife? So...what, Rory? What?

He drops his eyes. "I'm sorry about Orla coming to see you that day in Mucknamore," he says. "I had no idea."

"It's all right. We got on quite well, actually."

"That's what she said." And he frowns, as if that idea doesn't quite appeal to him.

"Are you two going to be okay?"

He narrows his eyes, as if refocusing. "Is that what you want? Me and Orla to be okay?"

"What do you want, Rory? Isn't that what we need to know?"

He moves his head in something between a nod and a shake. "I'm still so confused...I wish I could be sure of the right thing to do," he says.

And, in that moment, I find that it's okay. He doesn't need to be sure, because, finally, I am. I sit perfectly still then, letting him bring it up, all he has to say that I somehow know before him.

"I feel I need to go away from here," he says. "And I want it to be with you. I like myself so much more when I'm with you. I feel young again, and free, when I'm with you."

He's just the same, he'll always be the same. The younger me was right. She did what she had to do. But I can't resent him. I know how he feels, like he is splitting in two...

"But that's not how it's going to be," I whisper. "Is it?"

"Oh, God, Jo. I really do want to be with you."

"I know you do, Rory. I know."

"Then let's."

"But it's not just you and me, is it?"

"You mean the baby?"

"And your kids. And Orla."

"But people do it, people get over all that."

I shake my head.

"You don't want to," he says, stunned. Part of him thought all he had to do was ask. Neither of us has forgotten just how fiercely I once loved him.

I reach for his hand, hold it. His fingers curl up inside mine.

"Loving you ruined me for love," I say, wanting to give him something. "I never loved properly again."

"But now you will," he says, miserably.

"I don't think that's what I'm looking for at the moment."

"You will."

He sounds so glum that I laugh, and he frowns at me, offended. He wants to keep us in love-story land, but that's not how it is for me, not any more.

I look down at your sleeping eyes. "Loving this little fellow properly will be quite enough for me for now.'"

He opens his mouth to say something, closes it again. We sit for a long time, the three of us, in the quiet of the room, hospital noises outside.

After a long time, he says: "You never told me the end of the story."

"I'll send you a copy of the manuscript," I say.

"Jo, you promised..."

In the middle of our loss, he is still avid for narrative resolution, his questing eyes full of its hold. What happened? Who did it? Was it really Peg? Tell me, tell. Of course, it's not just a story to him, any more than it was to me. He wants the ending that was our beginning.

"I'm almost finished," I say. "And the book will tell it better than I can."

He shakes his head at me, resigned.

I slip from the bed to lay the baby down in his cot beneath the window and Rory comes to stand beside me, looking in as I wrap the blanket tight around him. The little hands are curled into fists, one on either side of his closed eyes. We stand looking at him for a long time. Then Rory says, "So this is goodbye?"

I'm afraid to look up at him while the feelings that goodbye always bring on are welling into my throat. I think of the aeroplane I will take next week, that will wing me and my son — my son! — westwards, towards yesterday.

"You'll come back again to Mucknamore, won't you?" Rory says. "For a visit?"

"Sure," I say, what I said to Hilde. But then I remember it's him. "Actually, I don't think so, Rory. Not soon, anyway. You come and see me instead."

"I will. I definitely will." He is fervent, like it's a vow.

"I'd like that," I say.

"And you'll send me that manuscript?"

"I promise."

He reaches for me then and we turn to hold each other. With my bump gone I feel, for the first time this summer, the full length of him, with nothing between us. We hold each other, hard. Then our lips search the other's out and we kiss. One kiss, firm and long and deep, with eyes clenched tight. One kiss with everything in it.

Then we let each other go.

PART VI
BREAK: NORAH

1932

*C*hild made her Confirmation yesterday, all glowing in white. Like a shiny little angel, but with the devil's eyes when she looks at Norah. Norah would have liked to go to the Confirmation, to see the bishop on his throne, his hat half the height of himself, and the white flowers and the prayers, but the devil eyes that didn't want her made her stay at home.

Peg thinks Child is so good and Child wants to keep it that way. "Isn't little Maureen such a good girl?" says Peg, never knowing it's only like that while she's around, that behind her back it's the nasty looks and faces, and the cold hard words for Norah.

Yesterday, when the two of us were on our own in the kitchen, Child told me I was to stop looking at her. I have the eye of a jackdaw, she said, always following her around, gawping at her, whatever she's doing. Like the eye of a dirty old crow.

"Is Mrs Duggan against Fianna Fáil?" Child asked Peg.

Fianna Fáil is Mr de Valera's latest big idea, the new political party that got him back the power.

"No, Mrs Duggan is not against Fianna Fáil," said Peg. "She's got her eye too much on the next world to care what goes on in this one. Why do you ask?"

Child told her what wee Willie said, that his mother, the praying *woman, told him to keep away. From her, from us, from all Parles. Why? Child wanted to know, and out it all came, pouring, all the people who say all the bad things.*

Miss O'Neill who is always looking at her with a frown on, as if she has done something wrong, when she's doing nothing at all.

Young Cissie Cummins who said she was surprised that Child was allowed to do a Confirmation at all. Surprised she was even let go to Mass. And Rita Breen, trying to be kind, saying: You shut up, Cissie Cummins, hasn't she as much right as anyone else?

And Mr White, who the other day was going to pat her on the head, but pulled himself back at the last minute.

And most especially Father John, who's always picking her out on his visits to the school, saying to Miss O'Neill that there was more joy in Heaven over one lost lamb than all the rest, looking at her when he said it.

Why is she a lost lamb? Child wants know of Peg. Why is he always telling her to keep up with her prayers? Why doesn't he say that to the others? Why is it only to her?

And Cissie Cummins again, when they were talking in the schoolyard about the plaque going up to her Uncle Barney, said: Uncle, how are you!

What did she mean by that, Mammy?

Poor Peg, her face pulled tight, didn't know what to be saying. The Child was close to crying with all her questions and Peg gathered her in so tight it must have hurt her back.

"You're not to mind that Cummins one," Peg said into Child's hair, her voice all cracked. "Do you hear me? Pay no attention whatever to the likes of her."

"But what did she mean, Mammy?"

"Lord above knows, child. How could anyone know what's going on in a head like that? You're not to mind her, d'you hear me? You're not to mind any of them."

Child came out of her hug and saw Peg's face and put one hand up to touch it.

"It's all right, Mammy," she said. "I won't mind any more."

. . .

Now Child goes sneaking round the house, her ear pressed to doors to see what she can hear. Or through the shivery darkness after everyone's in bed, to read the diaries that Peg thinks she's kept under lock and key. Oh, Child, Child, you'd want to watch out. You're going to find more than you want to find...

Coolanagh. The word hurts me too.

Write it down, Peg says. Don't try to forget.

Don't shy away, is what she means, don't be afraid.

Never wondering if maybe she's too brave for her own good.

What I want to write is the real wrong of it, which was mostly in what came after. The way he would look at me, eyes twisted up whenever they had to turn my way, as if he believed his own made-up story.

That was the worst wrong of all. What is that made him do that? That's the only question I'm left with, and all the answer I'll ever have.

We went together, Peg and I, the two of us peering into the fog. Double-blindfolded, once by dark and twice by fuddling mist. Six days we'd had of it by then and the feeling that it would never again move off. Small and careful our steps, because under our feet was a road of slush, and ahead of us who knew what?

It's hopeless, Peg said. We can't see a thing.

But we couldn't go back to the house to sit by the fire, nerves scraping, so we kept on going and we were glad we did. For it wasn't hopeless. We found what we went looking for.

They all think it was Peg who did the deed and they all go shrinking silent round.

As if. Our kindly Peg? The country might have turned itself upside down, but some things are set. The sun comes up of a morning. The sea *pulls in and out with the tides. Peg Parle could not kill my brother; she had too much love for him.*

And anyway, what she did to unknown Free State solders was a matter of enough remorse to her. The desire to atone for that drives her goodness to all — and always will, for all her living days

No, it wasn't Peg who killed Dan, only Peg's old talk. Too much talking, she did, up there in the sickroom with the door well closed. I didn't know she was doing that: saying those things to her mammy. Things I never said to her. Things I never thought anyone would say.

Mrs Parle did it for me, Peg says, but I was never asked. If I was, I'd have told her...

But Mrs Parle wasn't a woman for asking.

IT WAS *I who saw her first, through the fog. Like a pile of rags she looked, all in a heap by the ditch. I nudged Peg and pulled her over.*

"Mammy!" Peg cried, a muffled cry, for who knew what might be beyond the next layer of mist. "Mammy, is it you?"

Mrs Parle was lying still, a lump of black in the dimness. Peg went over to her, tried to lift her, and her mother roused. "Peg?"

"Oh, Mammy, yes. Yes, I'm here."

"I...fell..."

But was it on the way to do the deed, the thing she had said to Peg she would do, if she only had the strength? Like a woman possessed she had been above in her room, Peg said. Her eyes glittering and her mouth saying all sorts of unspeakables. Was she on her way there, or on the way back?

"Didn't..."

"It's all right, Mammy. Don't talk. We're going to get you home."

"Didn't..." She was bad for breath, very bad. "Not shot..."

"Oh, thank God, Mammy. Thank God."

"Yes, God. I let...God...decide..." She dribbled a bit and flopped on us, seemed to go.

"Merciful Jesus," Peg said. "Is she . . . ?"

But she wasn't, only passed out.

We took her up between us, our shoulders under her arms. She was heavy, though dwindled with her sickness, and her bones felt thin, like they were almost about to snap.

"What did she mean?" Peg asked me. "What did she mean, 'I let God decide'?"

Between us, we hauled her home, careful at first, but after a while too muscle-sore and frightened of being found out to be gentle. In the end, we were pulling her along between us, her boots dragging behind. In the house, the light felt bright. Child was still asleep in her pram where we left her.

Now Peg could see the state of what we had brought in: her mother, so reduced you'd want to howl, but we had no time for tears.

"Lie her down," Peg said. "We'll have to take her up the stairs on the flat. Hurry, before Daddy comes in."

Peg took the weight of her shoulders and chest, and I took the legs. It wasn't easy getting her round the twist in the stairs. In the bedroom, we took off the nightdress Mrs Parle had on under her coat, all mudded up and sandy at the bottom, to make her clean and dry. In the middle of it, Peg's father called up the stairs and I was left alone with the mother and the two pinpoints of red on her chalky face, like a bee stung her — once, twice — on the bones of her cheeks.

She let God decide, she said. Decide what? The question was a scourge to us. We never thought of Coolanagh, not then, not until next morning when John Colfer came back in his boat.

"She could do with Dr Lavin," Peg said, coming back into the room. "But I'm afraid to call him. What if he notices her wet hair?"

She took a towel and lifted her mother's insensible head off the pillow to slip it under, and then she broke. With the worst danger past, the full knowledge of what her mother had set out to do flooded through her, and she dropped her head into her hands. I thought she was going to cry, but it was more of a wail that she let out.

And then a vow. "I swear this, Norah. Whatever's been done this night, that child below won't suffer. No more tit-for-tat. Whatever happened dies in this room."

Dear Peg. As if she had the giving of what flows and what will be stopped. A strange notion, inherited from her mother.

Her mother — who did what she did for me, according to Peg — trying to pull something sweet-smelling from the mire. But I never asked for that. My brother did me wrong, the way he put it all over onto me, but I never would have wanted that.

For what Peg and Mrs Parle and Dan himself could overlook, I never could: he was my brother. He did me wrong, but he was my brother.

THE END

ACKNOWLEDGMENTS

My thanks to Jane Dixon Smith for cover design, to Margaret Hunter of Daisy Editorial for editing and proofreading and to Sarah Begley and the Book Whisperer team, especially Emily Volpe, for assistance with editorial and formatting.

County Wexford is blessed with an abundance of talented, devoted local historians, and I am greatly indebted to their work, particularly that which acknowledges the lives of women.

PUBLICATION NOTE

The early parts of this work were first published in 2006 by Penguin Ireland as part of *Lovers' Hollow,* subsequently republished in two volumes *After the Rising* and *Before the Fall* by the author in 2011. In 2020 the release of a centenary edition as part of Ireland's Decade of Centenaries: DecadeofCentenaries.com led to its further development of the trilogy.

IN THE HOUR

THE IRISH TRILOGY: BOOK III

Click here for the sequel to Before The Fall, the third book in the Irish Trilogy, In The Hour

In the final book of the trilogy *In The Hour*, again set in San Francisco, California and Wexford, Ireland, it is now 2010 and Jo

Devereux is a single mother, living with her son Richard, the baby who was born at the end of *Before The Fall*.

Richard ("Don't call me Ritchie!") has a secret, which Jo knows about but they never discuss, but that—and Jo's enduring loneliness—aside, they have been as happy as a mother and son can be. But now, as Richard enters his teens, life is growing fraught.

As he sets about breaking free and becoming his own person, Jo begins to question her long-held narrative about her own coming of age. When he starts his own investigation into his father and his grandparents, new secrets come tumbling out. Jo realizes that there were questions she never even thought to ask.

In the Hour finds that scouring through family history is a process greatly helped by the Internet. Richard has no need to travel to Ireland as Jo did back in 1995 and when he finds Rory online, and now a widower, Jo's carefully constructed life begins to fall apart again.

You can find In the Hour here.

The first two chapters now follow.

READ NOW

IN THE HOUR: CHAPTER ONE & TWO

2010

*O*kay, that's it. I've done it. No more drafts. It's done. It's simple. It's to the point. It works. Just press Send.

From: jodevereux@aol.com

To: roryodonovan1995@eircom.net

Dear Rory,

Hello, surprise, a blast from your past! I read about your wife's passing in RIP.ie. She seems to have been a wonderful woman, so popular. I hope you were happy together after… well, you know, after…

It was Richard who found you online. He's a terrific kid. If you ever feel it would do you good to get away for a while, you should come over and meet him. Bring your kids too, if it suits. I'd love to meet them.

Your old friend (and more!)

Jo

To leave in that "and more!" or take it out, that is the question. No it actually isn't. It's not that important. It really doesn't matter, I'm just using it to hold back, because I'm nervous to send. I've been fiddling with it for days. Putting words in. Taking words out. It's too short. But anything else I put in sounded wrong. It doesn't matter what it says. The significance is in the sending. Click send. Now. Send it. I'm clicking Send. I am clicking Send. I *am* clicking Send. There. Done. Sent it. *Sent.*

1976

IF YOU EVER VISIT WEXFORD TOWN AND travel along the quays from the south end, where the Talbot Hotel is now, towards the north railway station, the sight of the sea emerging on your right-hand side will surely charm you.

That wide expanse of water where the Irish sea and Slaney river meet in Wexford Harbor has been rightly renowned, across centuries. You'll see the bridge, the longest in Ireland, and across the mudflats or the sea–depending on the height of the tideline– you'll see the stranded remains of Begerin island, an islet of glacial drift, protruding. This is where St Ibar established a monastery long before St Patrick, someone from Wexford might tell you, arguing that he should rightfully be the national saint.

Along the dockside—call it The Quay—you'll see the pleasure crafts and fishing trawlers lined up, and signs everywhere of old maritime ways: coils of rope, and stacks of nets, and stained brown sails, and mooring posts, and bollards. Old men sit, staring out beyond the estuarine water at ships that sailed into the distance, long ago, as young families pass. On the landward side, rows of little alley streets lead down to The Quays, passageways created by Vikings, who arrived here a millennium and a half ago, from the land now call Denmark. The streets have hardly changed their shape since they went in, except to get more solid, brick and concrete replacing wood, and more commercial with the coming of money.

They seem a long way from the water, these little streets, and most of the time they are. Most of the time, the sea and tidal river are contained by The Quay but every once in a while, they rear up. Such a surge happened on a Saturday night in October 1975, when a storm, and a tide swollen by that year's harvest moon, converged. The underground Horse River that runs beneath the little alleyway houses rose and rose until the drains burst, and in a matter of minutes Wexford became a little Venice, a watery town of mists and shadows, with there was a mysterious drowning.

❦

WE SAW the storm's beginnings in Mucknamore. At about four o'clock, the wind whipped up and the sea got choppy, but we never thought for a moment, my father or I, that it should keep us home. It was the highlight of the week for us both, our trip to town, where he'd go boozing with his friends, and I'd go to "drink coffee" with mine.

By the time we were leaving, the rain was tipping down, and it took us nearly twice as long to drive in as usual, with Daddy sitting over the steering-wheel, nose to the windscreen, and the wind rocking the car in gusts. We didn't get out at Brady's little pub on The Faythe, where he hung out with his cronies, as we usually did, leaving me to walk the rest of the way to Main St. He drove on, to drop me down.

As we came to the quays, great waves were riding down the estuary, tossing boats around like shells. "Jesus!" he said. "Maybe we should go home."

Then he looked at me, laughing at my disappointed face. "Alright, but you're to be careful. No gallivanting tonight."

Gallivanting was his word for whatever he suspected I did on these nights out, and for whatever he got up to on his. Secrets we'd never tell each other, but that still were shared in the permission to enjoy ourselves, and in the keeping of it away from Mrs D.

He pulled to a stop outside the Main St entrance to White's Hotel. I pulled my hood up, against the blast of wind and rain that hit the side of my head as I got out, but also to hide. In those years to be seen with a parent was the ultimate in sad shame.

That was the last thought I gave him. "See ya!" were my last words.

My friends and I had a good night, and when it was time for us to go home, four of us left together. I was with Jewel Rossiter and my best friend Dee, whose parents now lived in town, had gone along with his friend Domo. We did a little kissing in two adjacent doorways, squeezing ourselves into the shadows, out of the wind and the rain, while we waited for my father to drive up, in the usual way, and park at the corner.

He was late, but that wasn't surprising with the weather. I was always happy when he was late, it meant extra time with my friends. There was water flowing down North Main Street, but nothing impassable. I knew nothing (yet) about how quickly water levels can rise when drains flood, or what water does to a car if it rises up to the level of the doors and gets into an engine.

Afterward, everyone puzzled about why my father had turned into King St, when it was so clearly dangerous. By then, we were all scared, as the water moved like a frightened, living creature itself. He turned down towards Distillery Road, towards the worst part, where the river had burst its banks, and was meeting the high tide washing over the quays. He'd had a lot to drink, witnesses from Brady's pub said, afterwards. He was in no fit state to drive.

At the time he was turning into King St, I was running to the phone box, head down, hair plastered to my forehead through my hood, to call home. Jewel squeezed in beside me and as my mother answered the phone–"Hello? Siobhan? Is that you?" he was grabbing me in places he shouldn't.

"Where are ye?"

"Daddy hasn't arrived."

"Oh dear Lord, Siobhán. The sea is like a wild thing. You can't see an inch in front of your nose out there."

"I know," I said, trying to fend Jewel off and placate Mrs D at the same time.

"Honestly, you and your father. Going out on a night like this. Home never good enough for either of you."

"We weren't to know."

"Ye knew well enough. And now… look at it. Mikey Moran said the river's burst its banks. That there's three feet of water on the quays."

"He right. What will I do?"

Jewel put a cold hand up down my jeans and I yelped.

"What? What's wrong?"

"Nothing, sorry." I pushed him away, made furious faces.

"If Mikey's right, your father hasn't a hope of getting to you. Or you to him."

The pips sounded.

"My money's running out, Mammy. If he doesn't come by half-past, I'll go home with Dee."

"But…"

I didn't wait to hear her. I put down the receiver.

Jewel was smiling. "Let's go up to Brick's place, up John's road. It will be better up there, up the hill."

So that's what we did. Went back to Dee and Domo, and pushed our way up, though rain and wind, to where a crowd had gather, with cans of beer and bottles of cider and guitars. If we're all going to be locked in by the water, we might as well make a party of it.

And now what I remember most is what I never saw. The car windows rolled up but the water inside, smelling like salt and fish and fish guts. The engine coughing and sputtering, like it's gasping for air. The floodwater flowing over his legs, up his clothes, across his chest, his neck. At what point did his bony hands leave the wheel? The water, peppered with mud, brackish and raw, flooding his mouth, gurgling into his nostrils, the back of his throat.

After that, all I see is him floating, though I don't suppose he did.

ABOUT THE AUTHOR

Orna Ross is an award-winning and bestselling novelist and poet. She writes historical fiction and inspirational poetry and is a founder-director of the Alliance of Independent Authors (ALLi). Born and raised in Wexford, in the south-east corner of Ireland, she now lives and works in London and St Leonard's-on-Sea, in the south-east corner of England.

Find out more at
OrnaRoss.com

I'D LOVE YOUR FEEDBACK

If you enjoyed this book, would you consider leaving a brief review online on your favorite online bookstore that takes reviews: Amazon, Apple, Barnes and Noble or Goodreads?

A good review is very important to authors these days as it helps other readers know this is a book worth their time.

It doesn't have to be long. Just a sentence saying what you enjoyed and a star-rating is all that's needed. Many thanks.

BECOME A FICTION PATRON

My patrons are first to get all my best stuff and many exclusive books and bonuses too.
Including an exclusive novella, each month

Become A Patron at:
OrnaRoss.com / fiction-patrons

FONT PUBLICATIONS IS THE PUBLISHING IMPRINT
FOR ORNA ROSS'S FICTION AND POETRY AND THE
GO CREATIVE! BOOKS AND PLANNERS AND
ALLIANCE OF INDEPENDENT AUTHORS PUBLISHING
GUIDES BY ORNA A. ROSS.

ALL ENQUIRIES: SARAH@ORNAROSS.COM

After The Rising & Before the Fall

ebook: 978-1-913588-43-4
standard paperback: 978-1-913588-44-1
large paperback: 978-1-913588-45-8
hardback: 978-1-913588-46-5
Audiobook: 978-1-913588-47-2

❀ Created with Vellum

Made in the USA
Monee, IL
23 September 2022

14528320R10361